CHRONICLES OF THE LESCARI REVOLUTION

BANNERS IN THE WIND

ALSO BY JULIET E. MCKENNA

CHRONICLES OF THE LESCARI REVOLUTION

Irons in the Fire

Blood in the Water

THE ALDABRESHIN COMPASS

Southern Fire

Northern Storm

Western Shore

Eastern Tide

THE TALES OF EINARINN

The Thief's Gamble

The Swordsman's Oath

The Gambler's Fortune

The Warrior's Bond

The Assassin's Edge

CHRONICLES OF THE LESCARI REVOLUTION

BANNERS IN THE WIND

JULIET E. McKENNA

SOLARIS

First published 2010 by Solaris
an imprint of Rebellion Publishing Ltd.
Riverside House, Osney Mead,
Oxford, OX2 0ES, UK

www.solarisbooks.com

ISBN: 978-1-906735-74-6

Cover illustration: David Palumbo

10 9 8 7 6 5 4 3 2 1

A CIP catalogue record for this book is available from the British Library.

Designed & typeset by Rebellion Publishing

Printed in the UK by CPI Mackays, Chatham ME5 8TD

For Lisa

ACKNOWLEDGEMENTS

This is my twelfth novel and Lisa has been involved in all of them; first introducing me to the mysteries of book production as The Thief's Gamble moved from draft to print. Ever since, she's kept a keen eye on my work, to catch those slips and idiocies that every writer is prey to. I have learned an incalculable amount as her input has invariably improved my writing.

So, Lisa, my heartfelt thanks for your generous friendship and professionalism, including but not limited to your saving one hero from grabbing a sword and heading out to battle without first putting on any clothes…

Closer to home, the regular support network continues to do sterling service. Steve, all my love and thanks. I could not do this without you, for so many reasons.

Mike and Sue, Rachel, Gill; having you all to share the myriad ups and downs of work and family life lightens the load beyond measure. Thanks once again.

Sam, thanks for everything thus far and here's looking onwards and upwards. Jon and the team at Osney Mead; I look forward with keen interest to working together on new projects.

Among so many writerly friends and allies, my thanks to Chaz, Sarah, Jess, Deb, Kari, Ian, Stan and Anne, Mark, Kate, Catie, Charlie, Paul, Guy, and Sarah P.

Last but in no sense least, my sincere thanks to all of you who read these books and enjoy them and take the time to let me know. Never doubt how much that inspires me.

More than that, you share your enthusiasm; on the Net through 'zines and fansites, by telling your friends, family, and even chance acquaintances on trains and buses and those hotel receptionists you notice with a book to hand. (I shan't name names, to protect the guilty and the innocent, but you know who you are…)

In these days of so much uncertainty and change in the book trade, word-of-mouth recommendation remains the writer's truest friend. Fans like you are invaluable.

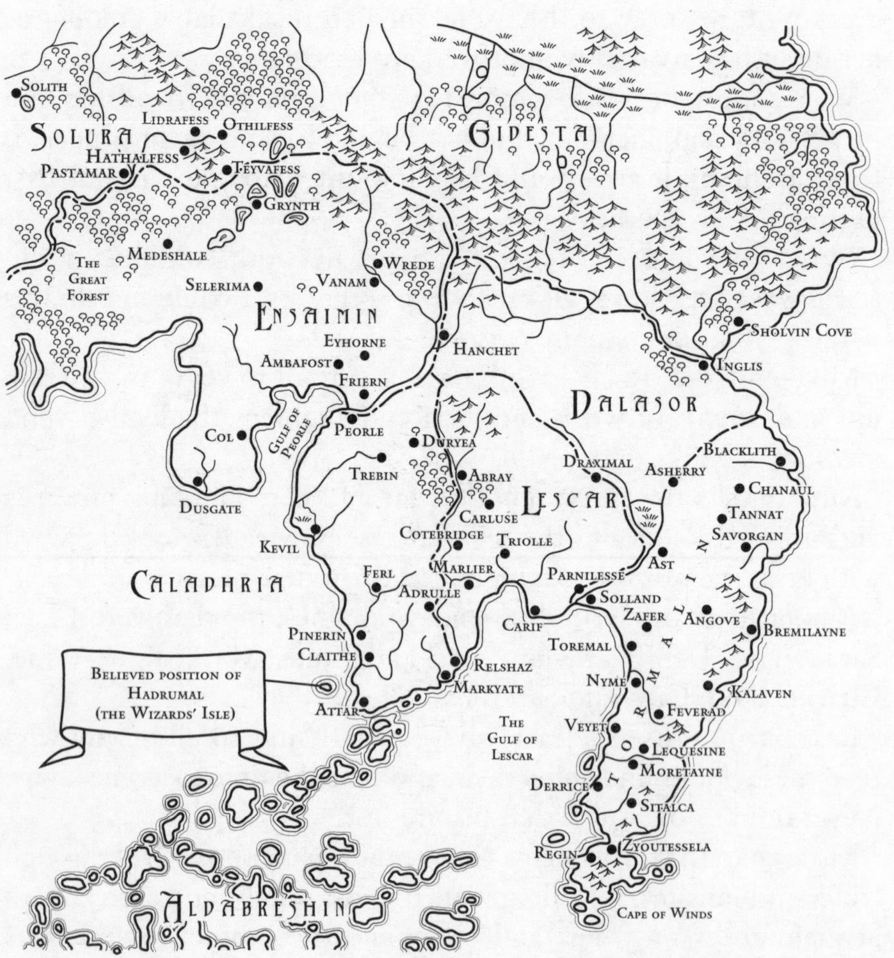
Solith
Solura
Lidrafess
Othilfess
Hathalfess
Pastamar
Teyvafess
Grynth
Medeshale
The Great Forest
Selerima
Wrede
Vanam
Gidesta
Ensaimin
Eyhorne
Ambafost
Hanchet
Friern
Sholvin Cove
Inglis
Dalasor
Col
Gulf of Peorle
Peorle
Duryea
Trebin
Abray
Draximal
Asherry
Blacklith
Chanaul
Tannat
Savorgan
Dusgate
Carluse
Lescar
Kevil
Cotebridge
Triolle
Ast
Caladhria
Ferl
Marlier
Adrulle
Parnilesse
Solland
Carif
Zafer
Angove
Bremilayne
Toremal
Pinerin
Claithe
Relshaz
Markyate
Believed position of Hadrumal (the Wizards' Isle)
Nyme
Kalaven
Attar
The Gulf of Lescar
Veyet
Feverad
Lequesine
Moretayne
Tormalin
Derrice
Sitalca
Regin
Zyoutessela
Aldabreshin
Cape of Winds

Dalasor
Fawril
Maerden
River Asilor
Ashery
River Palat
Sharlac
Wellan
Draximal
The Great West Road
River Drax
River Rel
Losand
Bekkin
Viscot
Ashgil
Wyril
Chinel
Thymir
Deflin
Abray
Dromin
Emirle bridge
Quirton
Carluse
Tewhay
Tyrle
River Anock
Hardrew
Skebban
Triolle
Adel
Inchra
Hengere
River Dyal
Pannal
Brynock
Tormalin
Cotebridge
Parnilesse
Solland
River Oisin
Capast
Toremal
Marlier
Caladhria
Carif
Adrulle
Saltebre
Gulf of Lescar
Lescar
Relshaz

Chapter One
Thathrin

Triolle Castle, in the Kingdom of Lescar,
10th of For-Winter

THEY'D COME SO far together. Now they were leaving. His comrades-in-arms, his allies. All gone, as soon as they were paid the gold they had been promised. Tents were being struck, the picket lines for horses unstrung. Soil was being shovelled back into latrine pits.

His father always said it was much easier to tear something down than it was to rebuild it. Who was going to rebuild Lescar?

Looking down from the battlements of the castle's gatehouse, Tathrin shivered. The sun might be shining but ten days into For-Winter was a far cry from that scorched summer in the northern hills, where he had helped gather this army. Now both halves of autumn were done and so was their campaign.

The Summer Solstice felt like a lifetime ago. No, more than that. It could have been some memory of a different life in the Otherworld. But every priest swore those passing through Saedrin's door to rebirth in this world remembered nothing of any earlier lives. Tathrin recalled every step of the way that had brought him here, from the quiet life of a merchant's apprentice in distant Vanam to cutting men down as a . . .

What was he? He had marched with this mercenary army but he was no sword for hire. He had served as the captain-general's clerk through this swift and brutal conquest of Lescar but Evord had briskly replaced him once his command post was established here in Triolle.

Well, Tathrin was a man of Lescar, if nothing else. Captain-General Evord had reminded him of it that very morning. The time had come for the ordinary folk of Lescar to determine their country's future, the Soluran soldier had said. It was no longer the business of Dalasorians, of mercenaries like Evord himself or of the stocky blond men from the remote Mountains who had been hired to fight these perpetually warring dukes to a standstill.

His army could deny rule to the dukes, Evord had said, but they could not hand it to Tathrin or anyone else, not unless he wanted to pay their wages to keep their boots on the populace's neck, just like every other tyrant who had gone before.

So, like every other Lescari man or woman, Tathrin must look to himself to surmount this winter's challenges. Could they possibly celebrate the Winter Solstice Festival in peace a mere thirty-seven days hence? How would they maintain any such peace after that?

Where would he be celebrating? Tathrin wondered glumly. Not with his family, that much was certain. He'd made the mistake of hastening home just before the Autumn Equinox, only to find his parents aghast to learn of his part in bringing this war to Lescar. He had fled their condemnation, all the more wounding in the light of his own misgivings once first blood had been shed. But that blood, and all that had followed, could no more be unshed than the smoke escaping a chimney could be recalled.

He looked up at the creamy banner that had been devised in Vanam, when they first swore to end Lescar's strife. Hands made a golden circle, each one grasping a symbol of the peace they sought: the farmer's hayfork, a sheaf of wheat, the goodwife's broom; a scholar's quill. The priest's handbell proclaimed the rule of law rather than ducal caprice, and the foot soldier's halberd asserted every common man's right to defend his hearth and household.

If they could build a lasting peace for Lescar, would that allay his guilt for bringing so much death and destruction to his countrymen?

Tathrin ran a hand through his unkempt dark hair and winced as his fingers caught in a tangle.

He was so bone-achingly weary. When had he last had a night's sleep untroubled by dreams of mayhem?

Could he possibly persuade these people of Triolle that their lives had truly changed for the better, now that this army of foreigners and mercenaries had won the autumn's bloody battles? Why should they trust Tathrin? He might be Lescari but he was a Carluse man. Even in the best of times, the dukedom of his birth and this domain of Triolle had eyed each other uneasily over their common border.

This was very far from the best of times. Beyond the stream dammed to create the mere defending the castle's flank, Tathrin saw the shuttered windows and barred gates of Triolle Town. Evord's swift campaign had spared Lescar the devastation left by rampaging armies but the meagre trade that the townsfolk counted on to save their families from winter starvation had been thrown into utter confusion.

'They say lowlanders haven't got the sense to come in out of the rain.' A mail-clad man opened the door from the bastion's stair. 'I don't know about a gale.'

'It's barely a breeze.' The banners snapping on the topmost coign gave the lie to his companion's words. His close-cropped hair gleamed golden in the sunshine.

'Gren. Sorgrad.' Tathrin greeted them curtly.

'Some girl undressing with her shutters open, long lad?' Gren leaned on the battlement. He was a little younger and shorter than his brother, though neither man topped Tathrin's shoulder. Neither spoke with the accents of the Mountains they had left nearly two decades since, when they were both younger than Tathrin was now.

'The Dalasorians are leaving.' Tathrin nodded towards the camp whose sprawl rivalled the walled girth of Triolle Town.

Men and women in the dark garb of the northern grasslands were roping long lines of horses; their own dead comrades' steeds and those animals, panicked and riderless, that they had captured in the aftermath of the battles. Whatever animals they caught, they kept. That had been written into the clan lords' terms of service with Captain-General Evord, when they had agreed to risk their necks in this Lescari war. Horses were wealth in their homeland, hundreds of leagues away.

'They're carrying a goodly amount of booty.' Gren's pale-blue eyes fixed on the laden packhorses.

Tathrin could only hope it was mostly plundered from the dukes' mercenaries, who'd stolen it in the first place, leaving their victims with no chance of redress.

'No more than their fair share,' Sorgrad assured his brother.

'It's a difficult time of year on the roads.' The wind tugged strands of Gren's unruly blond hair loose from the leather thong that bound it. 'Why don't the Dalasorians winter here and go home in the spring?'

'So you can win some of their loot for yourself?' Tathrin had seen Gren's talent for throwing a winning hand of runes rather more often than mere chance would predict.

Sorgrad was watching the dancing pennants that indicated the clan lords' personal troops. 'The sooner they leave the better, now that their job is done.'

Was it? Truly? Doubts plagued Tathrin. But they couldn't ask any more of the Dalasorians. One in three of Sia Kersain's regiment had died or been wounded in the sixty days since they had marched on Carluse, on the first day of the Autumn Equinox. Rega Taszar's men hadn't faced such fierce fighting, or such ill-luck, but his force had still lost one in ten of their number.

Every total, every amendment that he had made to the captain-general's ledgers was engraved on Tathrin's memory. His facility with numbers, that blessing which had led him from life as a humble tavern-keeper's son to all the opportunities in the city of Vanam, was now an unforeseen curse.

'They'll be carrying your name far and wide, long lad.' Gren glanced at him, eyes bright with mischief. 'There'll be songs sung in every tavern along the highway praising the Liberator of Lescar.'

'You think so?' Sorgrad looked sceptical. 'Their job's done, my friend, but yours is barely half-finished. Duke Secaris might have lost his heir but he's still safe in Draximal, while Duke Ferdain of Marlier is sitting as pretty as he ever did. Then there's this chaos Reniack and his cronies have cast Parnilesse into.'

'Why is everything my responsibility?' As his protest sounded petulant and foolish, Tathrin could have bitten his tongue. But the words couldn't be recalled any more than shed blood.

'You started this,' Sorgrad reminded him. 'You and Aremil and Master Gruit. There's no going back now. So you'll have to see it all through to the end, whatever that might be.'

Tathrin gritted his teeth to stop another unwise response.

'You'll be heroes, the three of you,' Gren said comfortably, 'in the songs and the broadsheets and whenever the scholars write up their annals in Col and especially Vanam. You're one of their own.'

Tathrin wished he shared the Mountain Man's certainty. But he knew he was nothing like those mighty shapers of history celebrated in tavern tales and learned discourse. How could he possibly see peace truly restored to Lescar when allies like Evord and Dagaran, whose skills and experience had brought him this far, were leaving him bereft?

Looking down at his hands, now tanned and scarred, Tathrin contemplated the silver seal ring that marked him as a scholar of Vanam's famed university. He feared those mentors in their faraway hilltop halls would be far more inclined to condemn him for trying to solve problems with blood and steel rather than words and reason. Their disgust would be all the greater if they suspected any desire for fame and fortune had spurred him on.

He glanced at Sorgrad. 'Do you have any news of Triolle's duke or duchess?'

He knew Sorgrad had been scrying for her, using the arcane skills bestowed by his magebirth.

Sorgrad shook his head, apparently sincere. 'I'm abiding by the Archmage's edict.'

Tathrin found that very hard to believe. On the other side of the coin, he'd be relieved if it was true. Their task of rebuilding trust across Lescar would be a hundred times harder if the guildsmen and yeoman learned they had flagrantly defied the age-old ban on wizardry in Lescar.

So perhaps the brothers had just come up here to tease him, with nothing better to do. Sorgrad knew boredom and Gren was a dangerous combination. The younger Mountain Man relished the chaos of warfare more than any other mercenary Tathrin had encountered this past half-year.

Gren's eyes brightened. 'Dagaran's brought news from the camp.'

Dagaran Esk Breven, summoned from their revolt's headquarters at Carluse Castle to replace Tathrin as the captain-general's clerk. He had long been Evord's most trusted lieutenant, both men born and bred in the ancient kingdom of Solura, a thousand leagues to the west. They had learned the fiercest arts of war against the savages and wild beasts who menaced King Solquen's wilderness border. Lescar's petulant dukes hadn't known what hit them.

'Let's hear it.' Tathrin turned to the narrow spiral staircase descending from the battlements.

Even now, he was glad to have Sorgrad and Gren behind him. Everywhere in this castle, Tathrin listened for following footsteps. Triolle's late and unlamented spymaster Hamare had been admired from easternmost Tormalin to the most westerly cities of Ensaimin, by anyone whose business was trading information. A few of Master Hamare's eyes and ears must still be lurking, in hopes of learning something of use to their absent duke. Iruvain of Triolle was fled, not dead.

Tathrin fervently hoped none of the sullen-eyed Triollese, who'd chosen grudging submission over the perils of resistance, learned it was Sorgrad who'd stabbed Hamare to death, to stop the spymaster strangling their Vanam-hatched rebellion at birth. That knowledge would surely spark smouldering resentment into blazing defiance.

As they emerged into the castle's broad bailey, Arest, mercenary captain of the Wyvern Hunters company, waved a hand broad as an axe-head. Since they'd captured Triolle Castle, the massive warrior had commanded its guard. The scaly black predator that was their emblem flapped its wings on the banner beside the cream and gold Lescari standard.

'Dagaran's in the Chatelaine's Tower.' Arest's forbidding face creased with a slow smile. 'Shall we serve wine and cakes? Though I don't know if we can find any fresh flowers.'

'Wine and cakes will suffice.' Tathrin wasn't about to give Gren the satisfaction of betraying his irritation.

'As you command.' Chuckling, Arest swept a florid bow, incongruous given his chain-mail hauberk, travel-stained breeches and iron-studded boots.

All the mercenaries were still geared for war, even inside the castle. Before the town gates had been barred to them three days ago, there had been some nasty incidents in the taverns.

How by all that was holy was he supposed to convince the Triollese to trust these battle-hardened men who had swept in to drive out their duke and seize his domains? Tathrin supposed he should be honoured that Captain-General Evord had delegated that task to him, but thus far his efforts had been met with non-committal words and icy stares. Common folk had scant reason to think these mercenaries would prove any different from the scavenging dogs who'd harried their wretched lives for generations.

He turned for the Chatelaine's Tower, one of two flanking the bastion. Sorgrad and Gren sauntered alongside him. Tathrin knew better than to try and shake them off.

Triolle Castle was notable among Lescar's fortresses for its lack of a central keep. Instead, the massive curtain wall was interrupted by lofty towers, looming over the mere on one side and a deep rock-cut ditch on the other. Arrow slits squinted suspiciously outwards. Triolle was a low-lying dukedom, bracketed by rivers and sodden throughout the winter. Its dukes had no advantageous high ground to claim for their fortifications.

So even if the mighty gatehouse was stormed, each of Triolle Castle's towers was defensible in its own right, linked only by the high wall-walk running around the lofty battlements. None of which had saved it when the Duke of Triolle had taken to his heels, leaving the gates wide open.

Tathrin ran up the steps to the Chatelaine's Tower, traditionally housing the castle's foremost noble lady short of the duchess. Some trusted confidante and holder of the keys would have relieved her from the cares of running the household, most particularly when her liege lady was doing her foremost duty in filling the ducal nursery. But Duchess Litasse had fled along with her husband and they'd not even been wed two years, so there were no infants to slow them down.

Where had Triolle's duke and his duchess ended up in the chaos after the Battle of Pannal? Were their nameless corpses rotting in some ditch, murdered by faithless mercenaries who'd fled that slaughter? Had they fallen victim to the Parnilesse mob, who had risen up to massacre their own duke and his family? Or were Iruvain and Litasse safely holed up with some unforeseen allies, intent on retaliation once winter was past? How could a decisive battle leave so much unresolved?

Salo, a mercenary whose bandy legs hinted at childhood starvation, was guarding the heavy oak door. 'My lady.'

'Good day to you too.' Tathrin knew any retort would only amuse the mercenaries still teasing him about playing chatelaine to Captain-General Evord's stewardship. Besides, it was a mild enough jest compared to the savage humour the fighting men could delight in.

Dagaran, the Soluran lieutenant, was waiting in the hallway, studying a portrait of some former duchess. A narrow smile relieved his saturnine face. 'I haven't called at an inconvenient time?'

'Not in the least.' Tathrin unlocked the reception room door.

All within was as pristine as any duchess could have demanded, thanks to Tathrin wielding broom and feather duster. He wasn't inclined to trust those castle servants who'd remained and he'd done enough cleaning back in his father's inn, even if being found with a mop had first prompted the mercenaries' mockery.

He swiftly assured himself that no one had touched the coffers on the polished table holding so many confidential letters and lists. Tathrin had the only keys to those locks. But some key to this elegant room might have escaped Arest's vigilance.

Triolle's successive duchesses had increased the castle's comforts, dividing each tower's interior into richly furnished apartments and insisting on broad windows to admit more light. There was a pleasure garden on the far side of the bailey, though the arbours were drab and forlorn, summer's roses long since fallen. Apparently it had been the particular delight of the late Duchess Casatia.

What would Iruvain's mother have thought of his headlong flight? Tathrin grimaced. Every coin has two faces. The disgraced duke might be bereft of father and mother but at least he need never face them to explain his actions.

'There's news from Carluse.' Dagaran crossed the room to look out into the vast courtyard.

'Word of Iruvain?' Sorgrad asked quickly.

'Or his duchess?' Gren shot a sly glance at his brother.

'We've still no notion where Their Graces might be.' The mercenary handed a sealed scrap of parchment to Tathrin. 'The captain-general's compliments and he'd value a prompt response.'

The note was short and to the point, in Evord's elegant penmanship.

My scouts report that the renegade mercenaries who seized and sacked Wyril are now advancing on Ashgil. Please advise how you intend to stop them. Naturally I am happy to offer my advice on your first campaign as captain-general of the Lescari militias.

'Why must I—?' He crushed the parchment in his hand, knuckles whitening.

'Lescar's future is now in Lescari hands.' Dagaran looked steadily at him. 'It's time for you to prove that to anyone who might doubt it.'

'I see.' Reluctant, Tathrin understood nonetheless. Of all who'd plotted to overthrow the dukes back in Vanam, he was the only one who had served Captain-General Evord throughout the autumn's campaign. But could his limited knowledge of warfare possibly meet this challenge?

Sorgrad tugged at the crumpled note still in his hand. 'You can let me have this or I can break your fingers,' he offered.

Tathrin didn't doubt it, so loosened his hold.

'A fight for Ashgil?' As Gren peered over Sorgrad's shoulder, the prospect clearly delighted him. 'That'll shake the stiffness out.'

'As long as the renegades hold Wyril, they cut the highway to Dalasor. If they can take Ashgil, they're masters of the most direct route to the Great West Road. They're looking to rob our northerly friends as they head for home.' Sorgrad glanced at Tathrin, sapphire eyes penetrating. 'Failla's in Ashgil, isn't she?'

Tathrin cleared his throat. 'She went to speak to the guildsmen there, on her uncle's behalf.'

Master Ernout would have gone himself but the priest was still suffering the after-effects of the vicious beatings he'd endured. Duke Garnot's henchmen hadn't spared fists or boots on the old man.

Which simplified things for Tathrin. The woman he loved faced mortal peril. He would have to prove himself a worthy commander. Those renegades had murdered countless innocents since slipping their leashes after Lord Cassat, Draximal's heir, had died in a vain attempt to retake the vital border town of Tyrle, seized from the dukes of Carluse and Triolle by Evord's army.

'The captain-general's already begun paying off his mercenaries.' A frown creased Sorgrad's brow. 'You'll have to pay twice the coin to rehire them.'

Tathrin shook his head. 'Those who've been paid off can keep on walking.' He knew Evord had begun by ridding Lescar of those fighting companies whose rank and file hadn't impressed him in battle, and those whose captains had proved lackadaisical in following orders or imposing discipline.

'The captain-general will not release any of the mercenary companies still on his muster roll,' Dagaran interjected, apologetic. 'He insists you Lescari must raise your own militia to meet this threat. Now that the rule of the dukes is done, the sooner you show you're fit to defend yourselves, the fewer scavengers will be sniffing around.'

Tathrin opened his mouth to protest, then closed it. If that was Evord's decision, there would be no changing it. His throat tightened.

'We'll start by raising a militia in Triolle Town.' Gren cracked his knuckles in happy anticipation.

Sorgrad frowned. 'The Guild Council will want to keep every able-bodied man here, in case these mercenaries head this way next.'

Relieved to see this pair had no intention of deserting him, Tathrin nodded reluctantly. 'The Triolle Guilds will say Wyril is Draximal's concern and Ashgil is in Carluse territory. They'll say this is none of their affair.'

'If Draximal could raise half a company, they'd be whiskerless boys and greybeards,' Gren scoffed. 'Duke Secaris's militias were cut to pieces in the battle for Tyrle and these thrice-cursed mercenaries have hunted down those few that escaped.'

Sorgrad was already thinking beyond their immediate task. 'Once these vermin are beaten back from Ashgil they must be driven out of Wyril, otherwise they'll just lick their wounds there and attack again.'

'The captain-general thinks much the same.' Dagaran looked steadily at Tathrin.

He knew they were right. He chewed his lip dubiously all the same. Could he possibly convince the resentful Triollese to take up arms on another dukedom's behalf? When their sons had so often been forcibly recruited into the militias, to bleed and die in their liege lord's endless futile quarrels. He knew the tavern chimney-corner sages were saying the dukes of Carluse and Draximal had merely reaped what they had sown.

In all honesty, Tathrin struggled to care as much for those slain in the atrocious sack of Wyril as he now feared for Ashgil. Even if Failla had not been there, Ashgil's inhabitants were Carlusian. They were his kith and kin in a way the Draximal folk of Wyril simply were not.

But they had come to bring peace for all Lescari. He had to do this. There was no other option. Tathrin resolutely thrust aside all the doubts and preoccupations hanging around him, as dispiriting as the chill mists rising from Triolle's sodden turf. In some perverse fashion, having a clearly defined task came as a relief. Anything was better than contemplating the looming, elusive ordeal of bringing a lasting peace out of all this uncertainty.

He turned to Dagaran. 'If the captain-general won't release his mercenary companies to us, I hope he won't object to us recruiting some sergeants to stiffen our militiamen's backbones?'

The Soluran smiled. 'I'm sure he won't.'

'We can tell you who to tap on the shoulder.' Gren was honing a dagger with his whetstone.

'They'll want paying,' Sorgrad reminded Tathrin.

He nodded. 'So we must ask Aremil what's left in the war chest.'

And surely Aremil would have more success raising a militia inside Carluse, to defend their own people in Ashgil?

Chapter Two
Aremil

**Carluse Castle,
10th of For-Winter**

He contemplated the final reports from the mercenary captains in charge of Sharlac and Losand, the first two towns they had captured. Now he needed to decide who to promote in their place, from the militia companies each town had raised against the possibility of the dukes attacking. Given a taste of freedom, none of the guildsmen and merchants was willing to resubmit to their authority.

Which was all well and good, Aremil reflected. But would those same guildmasters begin quarrelling with their rivals in other towns and dukedoms or would they see the benefits of cooperation? If so, who among them would expect to be in charge? Who would make most trouble if they felt overlooked?

Then there were the heaped letters from Lescari nobles, more arriving every day. Captain-General Evord had made it plain that answering those was Aremil's responsibility.

What should he say to those gently born folk who'd swiftly thought better of riding to assist their liege lords, once they'd realised the Soluran was intent on carrying his shocking campaign to a decisive conclusion? A good number wanted recognition and, yes, reward for their forbearance, some share of the plunder they imagined the mercenaries now hoarded.

What of the tear-stained appeals from the families of those who had dutifully answered their dukes' call and paid a brutal price? They begged for news of their loved ones, asking what ransom might buy their freedom. Everyone knew that mercenaries bought and sold their captives as readily as they traded their booty.

Before he could answer those, Aremil must consult Dagaran's ledgers, to discover which fathers, sons or brothers had died, to be burned on some battlefield pyre. Then he must discover where those who still lived were being held – not for ransom, but until they gave their oath not to raise a hand in any duke's cause. Was he now responsible for imprisoning those proving obdurate?

Aremil's head ached at the thought of trying to decipher any more scrawl. His eyesight had always been weak, but lately even the clearest writing blurred in all but the strongest light. The grimy windows of this cramped room were already dim as the afternoon slipped into evening.

Letters from the Guild Councils of Lescar's market towns made another pile. Some were defiant, others abusive. All demanded what was to be done regarding highway dues and town gate tolls and rents and levies due at midwinter.

Aremil gazed at the flames dancing in the hearth. How quickly might those letters burn? Especially that one double-sealed with the fire-basket emblem of Draximal pressed deep into the wax? But that would be no answer.

Only he had so little to say to all these people. Yes, their rebellion had overthrown the dukes and taken possession of their castles in Carluse, Sharlac and Triolle. No, they would not stand for the return of the old tyrannical order. But what did they propose in its place?

Why had all this responsibility landed on his twisted shoulders? He contemplated his crutches, propped against the desk. Because he couldn't ride into battle like Tathrin or undertake the vital journeys their fellow conspirators were currently making.

He contemplated the inkwell and the sticky quill. His fingers and cuff were stained and his page was blotted to illegibility. He must find someone reliably discreet to do his scribing since haste made his shaky handwriting even worse.

Some keeper of his secrets could also run up and down Carluse Castle's stairs, even ride a horse when speed was of the essence. Someone hale and strong, unlike Aremil, crippled by his mother's ordeal in her first childbed. Crippled, yet generously provided for. Sent into anonymous exile, but sent to Vanam and its unrivalled scholars once it was apparent his intellect was undimmed, even if his legs were weak and twisted, however much his hands shook and his voice faltered.

He contemplated the Draximal-sealed letter, still unopened. At least Tathrin had faced his father's wrath. Aremil still had to endure his parents' condemnation, their grief over his unknown brother's death. As word of his true parentage spread, how many would whisper behind their hands, wondering how long it would be before this supposed Master Aremil of Vanam claimed his rightful place as Lord Aremil, heir to Draximal, since he was indeed Duke Secaris's first-born son?

Aremil's heart was hollow with a different loss. Branca knew he had no desire to claim any such rank but she was travelling to Tormalin on Lescar's eastern border, carrying their carefully crafted response to Tormalin Imperial outrage at the autumn's slaughters.

With such chaos raging just across the River Asilor, within bowshot of his nobles' holdings, Emperor Tadriol was surely already mustering Tormalin's legions to defend those border domains. Placating him was one of their most urgent and difficult tasks.

Aremil glanced at the modest timepiece over the mantel. How soon would Branca use her enchantments to speak to him, reaching through the unseen aether that offered a conduit between minds to those who had mastered the mysteries of Artifice?

Until then, should he use his own apprentice skills to contact Tathrin? Unlike the elemental magic of wizards, who could only speak to each other through their spells, Artifice offered a skilled adept the enchantments to contact folk with no knowledge or understanding of their craft.

Aremil sighed. It had seemed so simple. Sending information hither and yonder as swiftly as one adept could talk to another would give their rebellion a decisive advantage over enemies still limited to letters carried by horse or courier dove. They could recruit some of Lescari blood from among those scholars studying this ancient, largely forgotten magic.

It was little more than a curiosity after all, offering none of the lethal potential of magecraft. Such ferocious sorcery was expressly forbidden to Lescar's armies. Any duke enlisting a wizard to cast spears of lightning across a battlefield or to summon up elemental floods to drown his foes would face the Archmage's extreme displeasure. No one knew quite what that might be, because no one in recorded memory had dared risk it. But no Archmage had ever claimed suzerainty over Artifice, and as Aremil had predicted, it had proved central to their victory.

Only they hadn't quite understood what they were dealing with. Talking to Tathrin face to face was one thing. Reading his thoughts, Aremil found himself increasingly weighed down by his friend's doubts, with fears that Tathrin surely had no intention of sharing. He saw glimpses of the men Tathrin had killed, and felt echoes of his uneasy dreams, caught between the torments of guilt and defiance, knowing his only choice had been to kill or be killed. He knew how much Tathrin feared falling short of the myriad challenges before him.

He had done his best to reassure his friend, and not with empty platitudes. Aremil had faith in Tathrin's mettle, and besides, he gave far less credence to tales of great men alone determining the destiny of thousands. Cities and dominions rose and fell according to the ebb and flow of circumstance. Their whole conspiracy could never have succeeded thus far without riding the tides of resentment already rippling across Lescar.

That didn't mean he was confident of ultimate success, any more than Tathrin was. Unforeseen events were sweeping them all in different directions. With this daily flood of letters and demands, Aremil felt like some miller desperately trying to manage his sluices while winter rain swelled an uncaring river, threatening to smash all he had worked for into ruins.

He could only hope his own uncertainties weren't adding to Tathrin's burdens. Aremil knew he was by far the least proficient of the adepts. Branca and her fellow scholar Kerith had studied Artifice in Vanam's peaceful halls long enough to be skilled at veiling their innermost selves from such unwanted intimacies.

As had Jettin. Aremil looked at another pile of letters. Those all demanded to know what was happening in Parnilesse. Had those leading this rebellion planned the brutal execution of Duke Orlin all along? What crimes had his family, his children, committed that warranted their unsanctioned murder?

Aremil, along with Branca and Kerith, burned to ask Jettin those exact same questions. Their most youthful adept, born in Vanam of exiled Lescari parents, had been sent to Parnilesse with Reniack after their decisive victory in battle at Pannal. The rabble-rouser had promised that the common folk of Parnilesse would follow the rebellion's banner. They had not doubted him.

After all, his skills had been worth another regiment of mercenaries in their campaign. He had written scurrilous pamphlets to entertain gutter riff-raff. His soberly argued broadsheets persuaded those who fancied themselves loftier thinkers. As thatchers and sweeps, stockmen and peddlers wore out their shoes on the byways criss-crossing Lescar, they carried Reniack's writings. They hummed the engagingly seditious songs that he composed for rough-hewn musicians rolling from tavern to tavern.

Only Reniack had gone his own way now, intent on bloody revenge for all he and his long-time confederates had suffered through their years of defying their duke and his tyranny. Somehow Reniack had convinced Jettin to rebuff any approach through the aether. Now none of them had any idea what might be happening in Parnilesse.

A knock rattled the door. Before Aremil could answer, the unheralded caller entered.

'Master Gruit?' Astonished, Aremil looked at the sleepy little girl in the burly merchant's arms, cloaked and creased from travelling. 'Anilt?'

They should be safe in Abray, in Caladhria, along with Kerith. Master Gruit's task was keeping Caladhria's nobles from interfering in Lescari affairs. Who was doing that now?

'Good day, Master Aremil.' Master Gruit smiled wearily. 'Where's the little one's mother?'

'Mama?' The child twisted in his arms, looking around.

Was she looking for Failla, who had borne her in such secrecy? Or for Lathi, the cousin who had fostered her since birth?

'Failla has gone to Ashgil,' Aremil replied. 'She will be surprised to learn you're both here.'

Surprised and displeased. Had Gruit no notion of his folly in bringing the child to Carluse?

'Delighted too, I'll warrant.' The snowy-haired wine merchant sat on a chair, settling the curly-headed child on his knee.

'Mama coming?' The little girl's brown eyes were huge with uncertainty.

'Soon, chick,' he promised.

'Where is Lathi?' demanded Aremil.

'She had a letter from her husband,' Gruit said tartly, 'insisting that she return to their farm now the battles are done.' His arms closed around the child, a steely glint in his eye. 'Halcarion help the pair of them if they choose to run the gauntlet of beggars and bandits on the road with their own children, but I won't risk Anilt.'

'You think she'll be safe here?' Aremil retorted, taut with anger. 'If she's known to be Failla's child, everyone will guess who her father must be!'

Gruit scowled and the little girl began to grizzle, burying her round face in his cloak's fur collar.

'She needs supper, a bath and a bed.' The merchant's expression brooked no argument.

'Tegel!' Aremil rang the little brass bell beside his inkwell. The youthful lackey came quickly from the outer room.

'He said he was a friend of yours.' He shot an accusing look at Gruit.

'He is,' Aremil assured the youth. 'Please, can you find Serafia?'

The youth nodded. 'Of course.'

'She's another of Failla's cousins,' Aremil explained, low-voiced, as the boy departed. 'She's been nursing the wounded here. She can take Anilt outside the castle, well away from the gossips.'

Serafia's son Kip was another fatherless child, both of them bereft when her beloved Elpin had died in Duke Garnot's militia. Aremil stifled a qualm. Surely she wouldn't refuse to shelter Anilt, just because the child was Duke Garnot's daughter?

'Very well.' Gruit's jowled face sagged.

Aremil tried to recall the portrait of Lord Ricart that had once hung in this chamberlain's office, before the acknowledged heir to the dukedom had died, along with his formidable mother. What about Anilt's legitimate half-sisters? He tried to recall their faces, before they were sent away to be securely housed with Duke Moncan of Sharlac's widow and orphaned daughters. Overthrowing the dukes was all very well but their relicts were proving yet another unforeseen complication.

Did Anilt bear any striking resemblance to her father? Aremil couldn't decide. It hardly mattered. Everyone in Carluse knew Failla had been Duke Garnot's mistress these past four years. Any child she had borne could only be the duke's bastard. No man would dare trespass in his bed.

Failla had gone to such desperate lengths to protect her child; otherwise Anilt's life would have been spent as a plaything in the dead duchess's diplomacy. When chance had offered the hope of concealing her unwanted pregnancy, Failla had seized it. After giving birth, she had lived for the day when the duke would discard her, to reclaim her child from Lathi and travel far enough away to live in anonymity. That was why she had joined their conspiracy: to see Duke Garnot thrown down, never again to cast a shadow over their lives.

Aremil wondered if Failla had even shed a tear when she learned Garnot had died. He glanced at the letters demanding to know exactly how the Carluse duke had been killed. That was another question he had no answer for. But one thing at a time.

'Why not keep Anilt safe in Abray?' He looked searchingly at Gruit.

The old man forced himself to his feet, walking around and patting the child's back to soothe her. 'Caladhria's barons are still muttering into their soup, complaining about these feckless Lescari and their squabbles, wondering how best to profit by selling winter fodder and blankets to both sides. It's business as usual for them.'

'There's no word of them summoning their parliament before Solstice?' Tension knotted Aremil's shoulders.

'They won't tear up their customary calendar on our account.' Cradling the child as he resumed his seat, Gruit's tone was certain. 'But we had better have some path to peace pegged out before the barons gather in Ferl. Otherwise this Winter Parliament could be the first in living memory where enough Caladhrian barons agree on the same thing to take some decisive action. Duke Ferdain of Marlier is writing to all his allies on the far banks of the Rel. No end of Carluse and Triolle nobles have washed up in Relshaz and the riverside towns. They're calling in debts and favours and promising both moons and the stars in between to whoever helps them reclaim their own.'

'Then why aren't you in Abray to hobble such talk?' Aremil demanded. 'Why risk yourself and Anilt on the road? What does Kerith have to say about this?'

Why hadn't Kerith warned him? The scholar could have reached through the aether before Gruit's coach had rattled through Abray's town gates.

'Kerith thinks I'm visiting Baron Dacren's country estate, with the chick and her nurse.' Gruit held Anilt close now the little girl was asleep. 'Please offer my sincerest apologies.' He contemplated Anilt's tear-stained face. 'Warn him to quit the house in Abray. There's Tormalin coin in a bag under my bedroom floorboards, enough to pay the servants what they're owed until Solstice. I settled all the tradesmen's accounts to the end of Aft-Autumn but there's no coin to clear For-Winter's debts. Though Kerith's name is on nothing. He cannot be held liable at law for anything I have done.'

'I don't understand.' A tremor shook Aremil.

'There's no money left.' A mischievous smile lightened Gruit's lined face.

'But . . . the captain-general's disbursements?' Tathrin had assured Aremil that the chests of gold coin had arrived, discreetly conveyed to Evord's camp by the Soluran's most trusted men. 'The funds from Lescari exiles?'

There were enough such outcasts, in every town along the great highways running east and west. Over the generations, those who could scrape together enough coin to flee had settled in Tormalin, in Caladhria, among the independent cities and fiefdoms that made up Ensaimin beyond. Those who prospered had long offered shelter to unfortunates cast onto the high roads with what little they could carry when they had failed to pay their duke's levy at Equinox or Solstice. Other years saw the utterly bereft stumbling along the verges, lucky to salvage the clothes on their backs as their homes and livelihoods burned because smouldering noble hatreds had flared into open warfare.

Such exiles sent gold and silver to their beleaguered families left behind, so their kinsfolk could pay the levies or bribe mercenaries to leave them alone; purchase food and goods, so often in short supply; even buy passage away from their wretched existence for their sons and daughters.

But Aremil had realised that flow of coin merely perpetuated the endless round of blood and pain. That's why he had approached Gruit. Was there any way to deprive the dukes of their gold and silver without starving the commonalty to death? It had been the first step on the road that had brought them both here.

The lengthening silence finally forced Gruit to speak.

'That well of goodwill ran dry by the close of For-Autumn. I still had to buy arrows by the barrel-load, and grain for bread and beer, and meat on the hoof, and pay for everything the captain-general's commissary sergeants have commandeered while he's been campaigning.'

Now the old man's grin was boyishly wicked. 'So I secured more coin with false promises and outright lies. I've sold property I don't own and guaranteed delivery of goods that don't exist and faked letters of credit from Selerima to Toremal. Come settling-up at Winter Solstice, there'll be a hue and cry for my blood in Abray, so I intend to be long gone well before then.'

'So every Caladhrian or Tormalin who's ever abused the Lescari as fools and thieves, as less than the scum in a pisspot, will feel vindicated.' Only choking on his outrage silenced Aremil.

'The men I've defrauded are frauds themselves,' Gruit retorted. 'I've only robbed those who've grown fat from Lescari misery.

Who've sold mouldy rye for the cost of the finest wheat. Who've bought Lescari flax and hides for a pittance and sold back the cloth and leather for twice the prices paid in Caladhria. Who've sold silks and furs and brassware to our dukes and their duchesses, never caring that Their Graces beggared honest men and women to scavenge the coin for such finery.'

Aremil simply stared at Gruit. Whatever the merchant's justifications, how were they to rebuild Lescar if there was no more money to be had?

A knock interrupted his desperation. 'Enter!'

It was Serafia, slender and wary, drying her chapped hands on the apron protecting her faded green gown. 'Tegel said you wanted me?'

'Please, shut the door.' Aremil waited until she'd done so before continuing. 'This child—'

'I can guess who she is.' Serafia looked apprehensively at Anilt. 'Very well. I'll take her.'

Gruit made no move to surrender the little girl. 'How will you explain her arrival?'

'Half the town's households are sheltering infants and their mothers who fled the burning of Tyrle.' Serafia's expression hardened. 'No one will question one more orphan in my Aunt Derou's kitchen.'

Aremil saw Gruit was still reluctant. 'Who better to care for her than her own family?'

Gruit grunted. 'I can call to see her tomorrow?'

'Aunt Derou will be pleased to see you,' Serafia promised with deceptive mildness.

Aremil had no doubt that formidable matron would rebuke Gruit with scalding words, for his folly and selfishness in subjecting the child to such a journey in winter weather, all to put her in still greater danger. Which would serve Gruit right.

As the merchant rose to hand her over, the little girl woke with a protesting whimper.

Serafia set her down on her feet and stooped to look her in the eye. 'Anilt, would you like some bread and milk? And a cosy bed?'

The little girl nodded, her rosebud mouth quivering.

'Very well.' Raising Anilt's hood to hide her face, Serafia led her to the door. She glanced at Aremil. 'I'll call on you later.'

Gruit smoothed the rumpled front of his tunic, his aged face momentarily forlorn. Then he turned to Aremil, still defiant. 'Bread and milk's hardly to my taste. Where might I find meat and ale?'

'Try the kitchens.' Aremil fixed him with a hard stare. 'Come back as soon as you've eaten. I need to know every last detail of your dealings.'

In the meantime, he would use his skills with Artifice to warn Kerith of the strife about to entangle him. But first, he must tell Tathrin what had happened.

As the door slammed behind Gruit, Aremil closed his eyes. The ancient enchantments of Artifice came more readily now. He need only think the words as he focused his thoughts on his tall, long-limbed friend.

Al daera sa Tathrin ne fol. Sast elarmin ash feorin el sur.

There he was, so muscular now, far more soldier than the scholar he had been when they had first met. He was standing in that elegant reception room in Triolle Castle. If Aremil didn't begrudge Tathrin those light and spacious quarters, he certainly envied them.

'*Aremil?*'

Despite all the times they had done this these past seasons, Tathrin still looked startled to hear Aremil's voice in his head.

'I've troubling news, I'm afraid.'

Aremil could feel Duchess Litasse's rich carpet under his feet, and smell the beeswax that polished the table. If he turned, he would be able to see out into the dusky courtyard. It was as if he were there in person. Better than that, he could walk as swiftly as he chose, unhampered by his crutches.

But Tathrin couldn't even see him. Whatever great deeds Tathrin had done, however expert he had become with that sword he wore, Artifice was one skill he didn't have. Though Aremil took care to veil his satisfaction. He didn't want Tathrin to think he was so mean-spirited.

'*Ashgil? What's happened?*'

'Ashgil?' Aremil was confused.

Then he saw all Tathrin's thoughts laid open. Ashgil was menaced by the renegade mercenaries? Appalled, he couldn't shield his dismay from his friend.

'*You can't warn Failla?*'

'I still haven't mastered that skill.'

Though he hated to admit it, Aremil could still only reach through the aether to other adepts and those closest to his affections like Tathrin.

Could they possibly warn Failla in time? Before those bloodthirsty renegades slaughtered everyone in Ashgil?

Tathrin's stinging rebuke made his head spin.

'*Get Kerith to warn her! He can reach her even if you can't!*'

CHAPTER THREE
Branca

The Hall,
Betwixt and Between,
10th of For-Winter

'WHY ARE WE meeting here?' she demanded.

Jettin shrugged. 'It's as good a place as any.'

'This is Aremil's place.' Kerith appeared between two of the stone pillars supporting the lofty fan-vaulted roof.

Jettin turned to him. 'Have you fathomed this particular mystery yet? Why does our crippled friend fashion all this out of his imagination, whenever he reaches through the aether to us?' An unkind smile tugged at the corner of his mouth. 'Do you suppose it's some kind of crutch?'

'I think you imagine this will stop us discovering where you are,' retorted Branca.

Ordinarily she would easily have caught some glimpse of wherever Jettin was finding the peace and calm necessary to work his enchantments. Just as Kerith should know she was in the library of this modest manor just within Carluse's borders, she would have seen the honeysuckle panelling of Master Gruit's house in Abray. Instead her mind's eye was filled with this single vision.

The older adept shot her a stern look before addressing Jettin. 'If this is where you feel most comfortable talking to us, so be it.'

'Indeed.' Branca forced an acquiescent nod.

They had been trying to draw the younger man into conversation for days now. She must not drive him away.

To her surprise, Jettin chose to answer her challenge. 'We're in Brynock, if you must know; me and Reniack and a double handful of our friends.'

Branca recalled the town, just on the Parnilesse side of the River Anock that separated it from the dukedom of Triolle. Was it still as cowed and fearful as it had been when she was last there, risking her neck along with her companions, to tally up the forces Lord Geferin was leading to battle in Duke Orlin's name? Was the river still spewing up the corpses of all those who had died under his banner so soon after?

'We have many friends here,' Jettin was assuring Kerith, sauntering down the wide central expanse of the flagstoned hall. The torches bracketed on the pillars flared as he passed. The light flattered his handsome features and olive skin, complemented by his curly black hair and lithe build. 'Plenty of folk are glad to see Orlin and his brothers repaid in full for all their abuses.'

Branca didn't doubt it, though she longed to ask Jettin how answering one wrong with another could conceivably be called justice. But Kerith was standing silent, dour faced, so she did the same, while the youth reiterated all those arguments that Reniack's writings had spread so effectively, even before the first mercenary in their rebellion's service had drawn a blade.

The dukes owed a duty to their vassal lords and to the commoners who in turn owed those vassals their fealty. That was what balanced Raeponin's scales. The dukes should defend the low-born, not abuse them. They should ensure all folk had shelter and food, not merely indulge their own appetites. In Raeponin's name, they should uphold justice for all, from highest to lowest, not grind the populace beneath their noble heels, leaving them no hope of redress.

The dukes owed the folk of Parnilesse all this and more in return for the loyalty they demanded. But they had broken that compact, for generations now. Duke Orlin, Lord Geferin and their kind had merely answered for their crimes and those of their forefathers. No god would deny it, not Raeponin or even Saedrin himself.

Branca could barely restrain herself. Didn't Jettin see the gulf between these weasel words and Reniack's self-indulgent revenge? Why was he mouthing this corrupt piety, when Reniack was just as ready to quote the arguments of the Rationalists when it suited him, denying the existence of any gods?

The boy had been a scholar. Logic was one of the most rigorous disciplines taught at Vanam's university, where Jettin's father had so proudly sent him. The spice merchant was one exile who had prospered splendidly, thanks to hard work and his determination to ignore the unthinking disdain that even the most well-disposed Vanamese reserved for Lescari blood.

If only he had taught his son such restraint. Branca had seen Jettin seethe, overhearing some contemptuous remark in a Vanam tavern. As often than not, he would challenge the thoughtless speaker to justify their words. He'd been caught up in more than one brawl as a consequence.

She and Kerith had thought nothing of it, simply glad to enlist Jettin's passion in the service of their unknown homeland. They were paying for that lack of insight now.

Harsh questions were on the tip of her tongue when she saw movement in the gloom at the end of the hall. Branca stiffened. Aremil? The shadowy figure was striding confidently forward but that meant nothing. Here in this imagined refuge, she had become used to seeing him freed from all the infirmities inflicted by his disastrous birth.

No. As the figure moved closer, she recognised that stocky build, the short beard jutting belligerently. Though it seemed Reniack had cropped his hair. Before, he had worn it long to cover his ragged ears, nailed to the pillory when Duke Orlin's men had finally caught him.

His writings, smuggled around markets and taverns, had long accused Orlin of poisoning his own father. According to Reniack, Lord Geferin had also been complicit in that murder, along with their sister Tadira, duchess to Duke Garnot, whose blood now stained Carluse Castle's cobbles.

Orlin's men had planned a lingering, painful death for Reniack, only for the rabble-rouser to rip himself free before fleeing into exile.

The simulacrum walked through a pillar as though it were not there. Branca saw no awareness in its eyes and guessed this was merely some reflection of Jettin's newfound devotion to Reniack's cause. She shivered uneasily and stole a glance at Kerith.

He stood, implacable, eyes hooded, beard and hair trimmed close as befitted a scholar, just like his long black tunic. There was no hint that he saw the phantasm, any more than he ever saw those reflections of Aremil's unconscious longing for the health and strength denied him. Branca had concluded she only saw such things thanks to the strengthening affection linking her to Aremil. But she shared no such fondness with Jettin, which made this somewhat unnerving.

'So the common folk of Parnilesse will see justice done for themselves,' the youthful adept concluded. 'You should make sure the other dukedoms soon enjoy the same liberties, most particularly Draximal and Marlier,' he added ominously. 'Prove you are dealing in good faith with all Lescari.'

'Is that a threat?' queried Kerith. 'If we don't murder Duke Secaris, Duke Ferdain and all their innocent children, you and Reniack's ruffians will do it for us?'

Jettin simply smiled. 'Then there's the settlement in Sharlac to be considered. Reniack asks that you present his compliments to Lady Derenna and suggests she curb her husband's ambitions.'

That was a perverse roll of the runes, Branca reflected. Lady Derenna had first met Reniack when they were both exiles in Vanam. Her noble husband, Lord Rousharn, had been unjustly imprisoned by the late and previously unlamented Duke Moncan of Sharlac. Derenna had travelled the length and breadth of that dukedom and beyond, making sure other nobles knew of Moncan's infamous conduct. Reniack had been only too glad to use his eloquence to help her.

When she had joined their conspiracy, Branca had served as Derenna's maid and her link to the others through Artifice. She knew Derenna's scholarly arguments had persuaded decisive numbers of landed lords to keep their swords sheathed and their horses stabled when the rebels sought to chastise their despotic overlords.

But with three of the six dukes now dead and anarchy threatening, Derenna had yielded to her husband's arguments. He insisted the old order be renewed. All that was necessary was a balance of rights and responsibilities as advocated by Rationalist philosophies.

Rationalism be cursed, Branca thought briefly. Had Derenna ever thanked them for restoring her overbearing pedant of a husband to her meagre bosom?

Kerith didn't respond to Jettin's barely veiled threat. 'What of Triolle? Can Reniack shed any light on what's become of Duke Iruvain and his wife?'

Lord Rousharn had persuaded Duchess Aphanie, widow of the unlamented Moncan, to appeal to Emperor Tadriol of Tormalin for protection. His irate Imperial Majesty had also demanded the surrender of Aphanie's daughter, Litasse, along with her husband Iruvain.

Jettin shrugged. 'We've no news of them.'

Was that true? Try as she might, Branca couldn't read Jettin's thoughts. If it was, then no one knew where the duke and duchess of Triolle might be.

That didn't stop Rousharn insisting that Aremil and Tathrin's denials were a lie, and it seemed he had the Emperor's ear. Unless they could discover Litasse and Iruvain's fate, Branca wasn't at all sure the letter she carried would placate Tadriol, even though Charoleia, the rebellion's unrivalled mistress of intelligence, had risen from her sickbed to compose it.

'Are you sure?' Kerith persisted. 'We know they fled eastwards towards Parnilesse after the battle at Pannal—'

Jettin cut him off with an arrogant gesture. 'I told you I've no news, and I have better things to do than bandy words with you.'

With that he simply vanished. Kerith choked back an obscenity.

'I thought we didn't want to drive him away,' observed Branca.

'I think we have better things to do than bandy words with him.' Kerith scowled. 'Did you feel any hint of his deeper thoughts?'

Branca shook her head. 'Nor any clue as to how he's hiding himself so thoroughly.'

That was another savage irony. Confident in their knowledge, she and Kerith had agreed to use their Artifice in the rebels' service, keen to develop their understanding of these enchantments outside the sedate confines of Vanam's libraries and their cautious mentors. Now it seemed Jettin had outstripped them both, garnering knowledge he had no intention of sharing.

She braced herself. 'We should ask Mentor Tonin—'

'No.' Kerith's refusal was absolute. 'Not until we know more.'

'Mentor Tonin might know how we could learn more,' she retorted.

'By forcing Jettin to yield to us?' Kerith's face twisted with revulsion.

'That's not what I meant.' Branca knew better than to suggest that.

She had seen the guilt that gnawed at the scholar after his violent invasion of Failla's thoughts when they suspected the Carlusian girl had betrayed their conspiracy. None of them had imagined that cruelty would rebound so comprehensively on Kerith. He had endured every pain Failla had felt threefold.

Branca persisted. 'Mentor Tonin might have learned something new that could be of use.'

They knew their understanding of Artifice was incomplete. So much lore had been lost in the collapse of the Old Tormalin Empire. Scholars were only now piecing it back together, from fragments in dusty archives and, according to Mentor Tonin, with the testimony of some survivors from the Old Empire, rescued from enchanted, aetheric sleep.

Branca wasn't at all sure she believed any such thing but since encountering Sorgrad and Gren, she'd learned of the Mountain practitioners of Artifice, the mysterious *sheltya*. If Sorgrad and Gren's stories were to be believed, the scholars of the lowlands barely understood the most basic enchantments.

Most unnerving of all, even Gren, who feared nothing and no one as far as Branca could see, referred to the *sheltya* with cautious respect. Sorgrad had his own reasons for fleeing them. Apparently they decreed the few mageborn among their people be driven out into the uncaring wilds, to live or die as fate might decree. None escaped. *Sheltya* always knew if they were being lied to.

That was an enchantment Branca would dearly love to master.

'I think,' Kerith began slowly, 'that Jettin has succumbed to the force of Reniack's personality all unawares. If only we can devise some way to shield him from that influence across the aether, perhaps he'll regain his senses.'

'Could we do that?' Branca had honed her skills at hiding her innermost thoughts this past half-year. Learning how hard that could be, in the throes of fear or emotion, had been shockingly unexpected. Using Artifice amid the challenges encircling them was so very different from calm academic studies in Vanam.

Perhaps Kerith was right. But she couldn't begin to imagine how they might wrap such a veil around Jettin without his consent.

Kerith turned away. 'How is Mistress Charoleia?'

Branca yielded to his determination to change the subject. 'Well enough, considering.'

Considering that Master Welgren, their apothecary in Carluse Castle, had shouted himself hoarse when she insisted on travelling with Branca. He had ruthlessly laid out all the consequences that might still arise from the tortures that Charoleia had endured.

'We're resting at the manor of a lordling who's long been a friend of hers.'

Even on her sickbed, the subtle enquiry agent's web of friends and debtors was proving of use, as it had done since the earliest days of their conspiracy.

Kerith frowned. 'You didn't make for Triolle?'

'She needs quiet and calm, and it's not as if we had any news for Tathrin.' Branca hoped Kerith didn't see her reluctance to visit the castle, to face all Tathrin's questions, his anxiety on Aremil's behalf. His friend must surely have let slip how she had withdrawn from him. 'We take passage on a sailing barge down the Dyal tomorrow,' she continued briskly. 'Then a seagoing ship will take us to Solland.'

Despite her injuries, Charoleia was insistent that only her charm and eloquence could rebuff those Tormalin princes intent on interfering in Lescari affairs. No one was prepared to argue that point.

But her suffering was something else none of them had foreseen. Neither Branca nor Charoleia should ever have come within any duke's henchman's brutal grasp. Her maid, loyal, gentle Trissa, shouldn't have been tortured to death. In her frantic efforts to save them, Branca should never have been forced to—

'Aremil?' Kerith turned.

Branca saw a high-backed chair had appeared in the midst of the hall. For the moment, it was empty.

'I must go.' She looked down at her skirt, to reassure herself it was still the demure brown of her travelling gown. Aremil's imagination was wont to clothe her in brocades and silks if she let him.

Not any more. She couldn't bear to share more than the remotest connection with him. He knew what she had done. She couldn't bear to feel the horror shading the pity in his thoughts. She certainly wouldn't stand for Kerith knowing her appalling secret, and she wasn't at all sure she could summon up the resolve to hide those dreadful memories from him. Not when her ties to Aremil left her so horribly vulnerable.

Summoning all her resolve, she thrust the enchantment away, fleeing to the sanctuary of the Carlusian manor's silent library.

She barely managed it in time. As she felt the firm leather chair beneath her and focused on the lamp she had lit against the afternoon's gloom, Aremil's hesitant voice echoed in her ears.

'*Kerith, forgive me, but I need you to send urgent word to Failla.*'

Chapter Four
Failla

Ashgil Market Hall,
in the Lescari Dukedom of Carluse,
10th of For-Winter

As she passed from the fading sunlight into the shadowed arcades of the market hall, dizziness overwhelmed her. She hastily sat on the broad base of a stone pillar.

'*Failla, it's Kerith.*'

Why was he assailing her with his foul enchantments? Her heart skipped a terrified beat. Had something happened to Anilt?

As he explained, her breathing barely slowed. Finally his loathsome voice concluded.

'*So you must leave, at first light, before the renegades come anywhere close.*'

'Once I've warned the guildmasters.' She knotted her hands in her lap, knuckles white, as his abrupt departure from her thoughts left her trembling.

Then she squared her shoulders and rose, walking quickly through the stalls where Ashgil's traders sold their goods in the market hall's open lower storey. Whatever the current uncertainties, people must keep themselves clothed and fed.

Halfway along, a broad stone stair filled the space between two pillars, rising to the long upper room. In more normal times, local merchants would gather there to make deals and share news while their apprentices and journeymen conducted more mundane commerce below.

This market day, the guildsmen had been discussing the town's uncertain future, after the withdrawal of the Dalasorians under Pata Mezian. His lancers had first captured then defended Ashgil in Captain-General Evord's name. It had been one of Duke Garnot's most loyal towns, but Pata Mezian's lightning assault had drawn his startled watchdogs' teeth before they had even been able to bark.

Word of the Dalasorians' recent departure must have reached Wyril, Failla reflected, to prompt this new boldness from the renegades.

She knew the Ashgil guildsmen were wracked with apprehension and uncertainty. She'd seen the strain in their faces when she had delivered her uncle's letters. Would they accept his reassurances, sealed with his authority as Carluse Town's most revered priest, sworn to Saedrin's shrine?

She'd also noted which guildsmen had most shamelessly tried to see down the neck of her gown as she curtseyed. Master Satril, for one. The master butcher had eyed her like a wolf coveting a suckling lamb. Did he fancy his chances with the dead duke's whore? Did he think she was so unprotected?

Little did he know. As she had delivered Uncle Ernout's letters Failla had been careful not to catch Master Odlan's eye.

Though of all the influential men of this district, the miller had been the only one to join her uncle and his allies in helping those suffering under Garnot's rule. Odlan had discreetly set aside a hundredth share of flour ground from ducal grain, its loss attributed to rats. Ernout's men would leave it on the windowsills of the hungry, or stow it inside looted doorways. They'd had a visit from the Woodsmen, grateful recipients whispered to trusted friends. Naturally the priests and guildsmen all professed themselves astonished that anyone still believed those old wives' tales of hidden benefactors living unseen in the forests.

Failla was waiting for the miller's clandestine reply to the private letter she'd brought him from her uncle. Back in Carluse, Aremil and Ernout needed to know every detail of the Ashgil Guilds' discussions in this upper hall.

Grey skirts flowing gracefully, Failla walked to the foot of the stair. The watchman drowsing in his cubbyhole was too slow to stop her. But as she reached the upper landing, she saw a burly sergeant-at-arms standing before the council room's closed door. He looked at her unsmiling, leaning on his halberd. The infinitesimal shake of his head told her all she needed to know.

Failla favoured him with her sweetest smile as she swiftly considered her options. Barely slowing, she turned to the smaller room opposite that claimed barely a quarter of this upper floor. As she knocked on the door, low conversation inside stopped dead.

'Come in,' a surprised voice said.

Faces hardened as Failla entered. They knew who she was. Of all the town's sewing circles, this would be the most well informed, the most influential, dominated by guildsmen's wives and mothers, with their daughters by birth and marriage invited to listen and learn the more subtle governance of the town.

'May I ask what you want?' A grave-faced woman set the linen cap she was embroidering down in her lap.

'We've nothing to say to the likes of you.' A stout woman in a sprigged pink gown snapped her scissors viciously.

'I have urgent news which you must share with your husbands.' Failla met the grave-faced woman's gaze. Whoever she was, it was a safe bet the sergeant-at-arms wouldn't deny her.

Through her lashes, she saw the younger women were agog, questions burning their throats. What had her life as Duke Garnot's mistress truly entailed? Were the jewels, the gowns, the delicacies served at his table sufficient recompense for her duties in his bedchamber? And those duties . . . ?

'We don't consort with whores.' A dark-haired woman threw a hunk of wood into the fire with venomous precision.

'No?' Failla stood her ground. 'So Ashgil's shrines provide for every woman left destitute? No mother who's lost her husband to Duke Garnot's militias need ever choose between selling her body and feeding her children? Any girl abused by some passing mercenary can hope for an honourable man's love, not to be cast out as ruined goods?'

'Is that—' A fresh-faced young woman broke off and shook chestnut ringlets forward, to hide her blush of mortification at speaking out of turn.

Failla answered her regardless. 'I made my own choice. There was only my mother and myself. My father abandoned us long since and he'd no trade, so there was no Guild for us to call on. There was rent to pay and the quarterly levy, even when we had no coin to put bread on our table.'

Though they would never have entirely starved, thanks to relatives sharing what little they could spare from the little they had. Naturally Failla was expected to be properly grateful, fetching and carrying and minding babies and cleaning floors and running countless errands, endlessly told to be glad of such charity. Eventually she preferred to go hungry rather than choke on such barbed generosity.

Folding her hands at her waist, she looked around the room. 'Those who prosper in Carluse Town are generous to Saedrin's shrine. My mother and I could take our place with the paupers, for our share of leftovers and remnants cleared from the back shelves of pantries. I could unpick cast-off gowns in hopes of enough good fabric to make up a dress. Or I could sell the one thing I had that men value. So I sold it for the best possible price. I was young and I was foolish but I believed that was the least of the evils besetting me.'

If these women expected shame-faced tears of remorse, they were mistaken.

'You're not the first to make such a bargain.' The grave-faced woman contemplated the yellow silk flower she had completed.

'I'm guessing you were Duke Garnot's last.' A broad-hipped matron on the far side of the hearth nodded with a glint in her hazel eyes. 'Shut the door, girl. You're letting in a fearsome draught.'

As a goodwife with shadowed eyes nudged her neighbour along their bench, Failla bobbed a curtsey and perched on the end.

She still felt the chill of hostility in the room. If these women were to believe her warning of approaching renegades, if they weren't to let loose their own fears and frustration upon her, like hedge sparrows mobbing a hawk, she must win them over, at least a little. This conversation would have to follow its natural course, until she could turn it to her purposes. As long as the guildsmen knew what threatened them before nightfall.

She contemplated the three goddesses on the mantelshelf. It would be a brave and foolhardy guildsman who challenged the women's tacit claim to this place by removing them.

Maewelin stooped over her stick, swathed in a voluminous shawl. Her sharp eyes were vigilant for any who'd abuse the widows and orphans she cared for. The Winter Hag always had plenty of devotees in Lescar.

Crowned with a circle of braids, Drianon held her besom in one hand, her other arm cradling a sheaf of wheat. Her level gaze reminded Failla of her Aunt Derou. Like Derou, the mother-goddess would curse any who abused her hospitality, driving them from her threshold with a clout from her house-broom if needs be.

Halcarion was more modestly dressed than Failla was used to. Garnot had favoured paintings of the goddess of love and luck clad in gossamer and a winsome smile. He paid artists to model her luscious curves on Failla's naked form. Why shouldn't he strip her for other men's eyes, when he paid for every stitch that clothed her? These Ashgil women doubtless prayed their more decorous goddess would protect their daughters from the perils of catching the wrong man's eye.

'What's this news of yours?' the hazel-eyed matron demanded after a few moments. 'What truly befell Duke Garnot in Tyrle?'

Was her husband currently discussing some fresh rumour with his colleagues across the way? Or had the guildsmen's wish to know been a recent topic within the privacy of her marriage bed's curtains? Either way, Failla had some measure of the truth to share.

'He was found dead in an upper room of the Triolle Gate after Tyrle was taken by the rebellion's army. A Carluse man lay fallen beside him, and another in Triolle livery. There were bloodied blades on the floor. As to who killed who and why?' She shrugged. 'Poldrion only knows.'

'I'll wager the marsh-squatter murdered both Carluse men,' muttered the woman in pink.

'One Triolle man overcame two of our own?' The dark-haired woman who'd called Failla a whore was indignant. 'The duke such a noted swordsman?'

The grave-faced woman raised a work-roughened hand. 'You can tell us how Duchess Tadira died.'

Every linen rustle stilled. Failla was equal to this challenge.

'Tadira ordered my death. I had made my way into Carluse Town and up to the castle while the rebels and their army besieged it. The Soluran had already driven Duke Garnot away. Captain-General Evord didn't want to storm the town and see innocent folk caught between his men and the castle's swords. He wanted the garrison to know the truth, along with the militiamen holding the walls. Duke Garnot was beaten, his hold over Carluse broken. Carluse men had the chance to rule themselves, just as your husbands and brothers have done since the Dalasorians set you free of Garnot's leash.'

Her brief gesture took in the whole town beyond the room.

'When I was discovered, Lord Ricart beat me bloody. Tadira wanted me dead before I could tell anyone the Soluran offered mercy. Before I told her household how her men-at-arms had plundered the town, taking food and fuel from their kin even though they had no hope of finding more. All so Tadira could hold her vanquished husband's castle for half a season longer.

'One sergeant stood between me and Tadira's henchman's sword. He said if I'd committed some crime, I should be fairly accused and tried. Only Tadira had already locked up Saedrin's priest. Her men had hanged one guildmaster and beaten another close to death. She cared nothing for justice.'

Despite her best efforts, Failla's voice shook. 'A groom in the stables was thrown into a dungeon just for trying to leave the castle to visit his mother. The boy was left starving in the darkness shackled to a corpse.'

As the women shuddered, she went on. 'Tadira took up a sword to kill me herself. A crossbow bolt from the battlements stopped her. Another archer brought down Lord Ricart when he tried to cut my throat.'

'Have these men been brought to answer?' the ringletted girl whispered, horrified.

Failla shook her head. 'They haven't come forward and no one has given them up.'

'Raeponin's scales must be balanced.' The dark-haired woman glanced at the other statues above the fireplace, set in formal niches.

Robed in blue and hooded in white, Raeponin, god of justice, stood with his scales and his warning bell. Mightiest of gods, Saedrin brandished his keys to the door leading to the Otherworld. Ominous in black, Poldrion leaned on his oar, ready to ferry the dead to that final threshold.

'You have a great deal of blood on your hands, for people who claim to be seeking peace.' The grave-faced woman looked sternly at Failla. 'Moncan of Sharlac and his heir died first. Our Duke Garnot, his duchess and heir are all slain. Secaris of Draximal has lost both his heir and his army. Orlin of Parnilesse and his family have been murdered to the last infant.'

'If we could have brought peace to Lescar without warfare, we would have,' Failla promised. 'As Saedrin will judge us all at the gate to the Otherworld.'

'You call this peace?' the dark-haired woman demanded. 'With our duke dead, what's to stop Ferdain of Marlier putting his boot on our necks?'

'Duke Ferdain was hamstrung when his mistress the Vixen threw in her lot with the Soluran,' Failla countered, 'rather than see her men killed for no more gain than Parnilesse's advantage. She commands all Marlier's mercenaries and militias and they haven't the strength left to venture beyond their own borders now.'

The hazel-eyed matron ripped the cambric she held, startling them all. 'You have torn Lescar into rags. Who will stitch it back together?'

'You can help,' Failla retorted, 'unless you're willing to leave it to your husbands.'

'Fighting's none of our affair.' The pink-clad woman's needle stabbed the linen in her tambour. 'Men do as they please while we staunch their wounds and sweep up the wreckage.'

'You don't share any blame for Lescar's strife?' Now Failla challenged the whole gathering. 'How many of you have some scrap of a bloodstained shirt, a torn kerchief passed down from mother to daughter? Deny that you've restitched the name of the place where he died, that brother or husband for whose sake some woman first hemmed and embroidered that remembrance, her own urn long since set in a shrine and forgotten.'

'We honour our dead.' The grave-faced woman's eyes were flinty.

'Truly?' Failla threw discretion to Poldrion's demons. If these women cast her out, so be it. She'd kick down the door to the council room if that's what it took to pass on Kerith's news. 'Do you honour them or do you betray every hope of peace they died for? I'll wager each of you can relate every battle, every skirmish, every defeat or victory within twenty leagues of Ashgil these ten generations past. You tell your sons and grandsons how their forefathers died as heroes fighting in their defence. All the while, you sow the seeds of suffering to come. So warfare plagues us year after year like thistles springing up in a cornfield!'

She had to raise her voice above a rising swell of indignation. 'Would your sons be so willing to fight if they didn't learn hatred of other Lescari at your firesides? You mock the marsh-squatters? You tell your children the tale of the Triolle man who put a sign by the river saying "If you can't read this, there's a flood"?'

Now she saw the women caught between instinctive agreement and embarrassment at this echo of their prejudices. Anilt wouldn't be raised with such lies, Failla had sworn it. She wouldn't let Lathi curdle her daughter's innocence with such bile.

'The men of Sharlac are no better than brigands, so my mother told me. They share their beds with their dogs, and catch their fleas. Why else call Duke Moncan the Jackal? Marlier men grow fat as butter on their rich trade with Caladhrians, but no honest Carluse man gets even a stale slice of that loaf. Parnilesse is a byword for treachery. They'd sell their whole dukedom to Tormalin for a half-decent price. Year in, year out, Draximal steals a plough-length of good Carluse land here, a stretch of Parnilesse woodland there, thieves sneaking into the Triolle hills to steal Duke Iruvain's silver. Shake hands with them, my mother said, and you'll lose the rings on your fingers. But in Ensaimin they say the same of all Lescari.'

Her blunt declaration silenced the aggrieved protests rising to the rafters.

'I didn't know it, till I went to Vanam.' Failla shrugged. 'But no one outside Lescar gives a second thought to our rights and wrongs. No one cares a tinker's curse which duke should be High King. They think we're fools, worse than brute beasts. A fox caught in a snare might chew off its own foot but at least it does that to be free. Lescari tear each other to shreds for no one's benefit.'

She swept the room with a searing glance. 'Since we're such fools, why shouldn't they profit by selling us the weapons to kill each other? Any Lescari with wits or skills has long since fled to civilised lands to make a more worthwhile life.'

'That's wicked lies.' The dark-haired woman's voice shook with fury.

'Quite so,' Failla agreed. 'But that's what children in Ensaimin, in Caladhria and in Tormalin all learn at their grandmother's knee. So I'm wondering what lies I've been told all my life. Because I've met men and women from Marlier and Sharlac and know them to be as honest and as good-hearted as any in Carluse. I've heard the tales of suffering and injustice in Triolle and Parnilesse, no different from our own. I've met Lescari in Vanam and in towns all along the highways. They don't care if their neighbour's mother was born in Draximal or their father's of Carluse blood. They scrimp and save and send coin and cloth and pots and pans to their beleaguered kin regardless.'

'What of it?' rasped the pink-clad woman. 'What has that to do with you and your brave friends bringing mercenaries and uplanders and grasslanders to run roughshod over Ashgil?'

'They saved your brothers and sons, your husbands and fathers from being drafted into Garnot's army to die.' Failla didn't yield. 'I've seen plenty of country folk here, seeking the safety of these walls. Ask them what happened, when Garnot's militiamen surrendered as he lost battle after battle. Honest men given no choice but to follow him were set free to go home and defend their families. The exiles' army has no quarrel with them.'

She saw the ringletted girl exchange a glance with her neighbour and knew that shot had struck home.

'The Soluran could have attacked in Aft-Summer and burned the standing crops, to make sure Garnot's army starved and let Saedrin save the innocent. But the captain-general didn't begin his campaign until all your harvests were safely gathered. There's been no looting, not in Carluse or Sharlac or Triolle. The Dalasorians who've defended you, they paid for whatever supplies they asked for, didn't they? Paid with good Tormalin coin, not the duke's lead-weighted silver. You'll pay no levy to Garnot at Solstice to dress Tadira in fine new silks. Your own Guild Council will decide what dues are needed to pave your roads and restore your town's gates.'

Failla could see some of the women still wanted to protest but none could deny those particular truths. They exchanged covert glances in the grudging silence.

'You said you had urgent news,' the grave-faced woman said acidly.

'Ill news, forgive me.' Failla braced herself. 'Not all the mercenaries our noble dukes hired have been driven off. You've heard what befell Wyril?' The women's shocked faces showed her they had. 'Those renegades are now marching this way.'

'Who's to protect us with the Dalasorians gone?' cried the woman in pink.

First she resented the rebels' army. Now she objected to it leaving.

'You will protect yourselves.' Failla nodded towards the Guild Council chamber. 'When your husbands call on every household to send a man to serve in the militia, you can make sure every wife and mother understands her duty to see them answer. You can fetch water and carry messages, when the time comes to hold Ashgil's walls. Until the militiamen of Carluse, and of Triolle and Sharlac, drive off these curs snapping around your gates.'

The hazel-eyed woman was merely the first to exclaim. 'Sharlac is marching on us too?'

'They're marching to your aid,' Failla assured her, 'and the men of Triolle will fight alongside them. The common folk of those dukedoms want to live free from warfare just as fervently as you do. That cause unites you all, now that no dukes can stir up hatred and division. Tell your men to write to the guildmasters in Sharlac Town, and in Fawril and Maerdin. Send word to Triolle Town and Pannal. They all yearn for peace.'

If she could convince these women of that, if such a notion prompted thoughtful conversation with a husband or son beside a glowing hearth late at night, Failla could hope she'd done more than just warn Ashgil of the immediate threat.

'If all this is true, I don't know why we're sitting here clucking like hens.' The grave-faced woman stowed her sewing in her work bag. 'Come and tell my husband your tale.'

Failla rose with her. 'Gladly, Mistress . . . ?'

'Mistress Kinver. My husband's the master mason.'

The grave-faced woman threw open the door and Failla meekly followed.

Then, once she had told the guildsmen what threatened them, she had to find Dinant. The mercenary sergeant had commanded her escort travelling here. Failla was confident he'd agree to offer the Ashgil militia his advice. Hopefully, they'd be glad to have him.

Just as long as Tathrin didn't make a liar of her, by failing to bring Triolle's militia to their rescue. As she smiled at the startled sergeant-at-arms, who stepped back hastily as Mistress Kinver rapped on the council chamber door, Failla stifled her fears. How many more battles could her honest-hearted lover still come through unscathed?

Come the morning, though, if Kerith thought she would be taking to her heels, he was sorely mistaken. She would show him, and anyone else who doubted her, that she was as committed to the cause of freedom in Lescar as any man who could take up a sword. She would show them all she was far more than some discarded whore.

Chapter Five
Tathrin

The Ashgil Road, North of Tyrle,
in the Dukedom of Carluse,
13th of For-Winter

THE COLUMN TRUDGED sombrely along the high road, pursued by the stink of burning. Tathrin could taste wood ash tainted with lime plaster and all the lost possessions that still smouldered amid the ruins of Tyrle's narrow houses.

A more nauseating reek drifted from the pyres along the Carluse Road. The dead were still being found under broken walls, crushed by the rafters that now fuelled their funeral rites. Even with the cold weather, Tathrin hated to think of those corpses. It was thirty days and more since the town had been overrun.

They had passed on the eastern side last night. As they had camped beneath Tyrle's shattered towers, townsfolk had flocked to their fires, begging for food, for news and, most desperately of all, for any scrap of hope that their wretched lot would improve.

The Triollese had shared their bread and bacon, many going hungry themselves. Tathrin had seen two take a barrel of apples from the column's provision carts. He hadn't needed to save them from the quartermaster's wrath. Sorgrad had taken the man aside for a genially menacing word.

Tathrin had been glad to see Triolle men open their hands and hearts to the hollow-eyed Carlusians. But this morning he rode a few horse-lengths ahead of a mounted group of journeymen who didn't hide their disdain for such unfortunates. Their apprenticeships completed, they cherished ambitions of setting up their own workshops. Many of their fathers were eminent among Triolle's guildsmen, providing the coin to buy the horses the youths rode with all the awkwardness of novices.

No Lescari duke wasted his coin training mounted forces. It was quicker and cheaper to thrust a halberd into a reluctant militiaman's hands and to hire mercenary horsemen. Too late, the dukes had learned the error of their ways, as the fearsomely skilled lancers of Dalasor had helped Evord win this war.

But none of these callow youths was prepared to sacrifice his dignity by admitting defeat and dismounting. Or, from what he'd overheard, to give up the chance of fleeing at breakneck speed if danger threatened. Contempt soured Tathrin's stomach.

He gazed northwards but a rise dense with coppices blocked his view. Had Kerith warned Failla? Had she fled Ashgil or would she simply be in more danger on the open road?

Couldn't these Triollese march any faster? The guildmasters had kept him waiting a full day before they agreed to muster a militia. They had complained and protested like their journeymen sons riding behind him. No, Tathrin realised, the youths had moved on to a new topic.

'Those northern barbarians sacked Tyrle? The ones from the Mountains?'

'No doubt about it. The Soluran kept them leashed in Carluse but they slipped their collars here.'

'Did they kill Duke Garnot?'

'I wouldn't be surprised.'

Tathrin took a deep breath. He was loath to rebuke these self-important youths. Too many of the Triollese looked to them in their fathers' stead. If he sent them scurrying back before they even reached Ashgil, this militia column could dissolve into chaos.

'Didn't you see the uplanders in our streets, when the Guilds yielded to the Soluran and opened our gates?'

That peevish voice was Brimel's, journeyman and assiduous toady to Triolle's pre-eminent brewer, a man who owned half the taverns within a day's ride of the town.

'We were overrun before the noon bells,' he sneered.

Overrun by mercenaries who drank in his master's inns and tupped the whores renting the houses he owned in back alleys. Tathrin didn't doubt a share of that coin jingled in Brimel's acquisitive pockets.

'The curs infested the shrine to Maewelin.' Halarey, plump journeyman baker, couldn't have been more disgusted if he had found sewer rats in his bread troughs.

'Were they causing trouble?'

Tathrin was relieved to hear Akaver's mild tones. The lean tailor's shrewdness had impressed him before.

'Not as such,' Halarey admitted grudgingly. 'But they heaped cloth-wrapped bones in front of the goddess's statue.'

'Forbidding anyone to touch the foul things,' added Brimel, indignant. 'At least the Dalasorians burned their dead, like decent men.'

The swarthy horsemen had then raised great earthen mounds over the massed pyres of their fallen comrades and their steeds. Tathrin didn't think such rites had been seen this far south in time out of mind.

Quenel the blacksmith spoke, deceptively kind-faced. 'We went to throw them out—'

Tathrin's horse tossed its head as he gripped his reins. But no, he would have heard about any trouble. Gren and Sorgrad would have been in the thick of it.

'—only Old Mayet had a fit of the vapours at the thought of strife,' Quenel continued contemptuously.

Tathrin breathed a sigh of relief. He must thank the aged stonemason on their return to Triolle.

'You'd think the old fool would show more concern for goodwives and widows making their offerings to the Hag.' Halarey was still aggrieved.

'Especially with their daughters accompanying them,' Brimel agreed.

'Tyrle will see a crop of yellow-headed bastards next summer,' Quenel predicted with malicious satisfaction.

Tathrin turned his horse around and trotted briskly back. Those not too busy controlling their own restive mounts looked at him, startled.

'Captain Sayron?' Akaver dressed more soberly than his companions even though his father's seamstresses clothed them all.

'You need not fear for a woman's virtue around any uplander,' Tathrin said crisply.

Not counting Gren and perhaps Sorgrad, whom he suspected was an accomplished seducer. But they were far from typical Mountain Men.

'They hold all women in the highest regard,' he continued. 'Their sisters and daughters inherit the mines in the upland valleys, and the wealth of timber and furs in their forests. A Mountain Man proves himself worthy to marry by earning gold with the sweat of his brow.'

Which was why near on a thousand uplanders had heeded Captain-General Evord's call, intent on winning the price of a bride. Like the Dalasorians, the survivors were taking their spoils home before the worst of the winter weather.

'Those bones belonged to their fallen comrades,' Tathrin explained curtly. 'They wished to invoke Maewelin's protection, before their journey home. They call her the Mother, and Misaen, the Maker.'

He decided against any further explanation of upland rites. He was also grateful the Mountain Men had boiled down their dead on the battlefield at Pannal, to strip the flesh from the corpses in stinking vats, the easier to return the bones of the fallen to the valley that had borne them.

Halarey coloured as though he'd opened a hot bread oven. 'How were we to know? They barely spoke to us.'

'They barely speak our tongue.' Tathrin forced a smile before returning to the head of the column.

These green youths were barely capable of looking beyond Triolle to consider other Lescari concerns. It was folly to expect them to understand men so different in appearance, their very words incomprehensible.

Letting his horse pick its own way along the muddied road, Tathrin wondered if he would be as fearfully ignorant if his father hadn't sent him to distant Vanam, to escape Carluse's fratricidal follies and see the world beyond Lescar's borders.

His father was much of an age with Brimel's master, and Halarey's father. Those men had doubtless similarly spent their lives striving to protect their kin and property whenever their duke's bickering with his neighbours spawned open warfare, as disagreeable a fact of life as the seasonal pestilences carried up the rivers and along the roads. But Tathrin's home had been an inn on the Great West Road. Jerich Sayron was used to dealing with merchants and traders from Tormalin to Ensaimin and beyond.

Tathrin could only hope these youthful Triolle guildsmen discovered that their contemporaries in Ashgil muttered just as darkly into their ale, as resentful of all they endured for the sake of their own duke's lust for the empty crown of High Kingship. It could make scant difference to the common folk, whichever duke might succeed. In the meantime, they all paid the price.

Then he realised Quenel had a new bone to gnaw on.

'Is there any word from Parnilesse as to who murdered Duke Orlin and his family?'

Tathrin was repelled by the blacksmith's satisfaction at knowing Triolle's ancient enemy was so thoroughly cast down. Though that question needed answering. The sooner they proved Evord's men had nothing to do with the outrage, the better, not least for Charoleia and Branca's quest to placate Tormalin's Emperor.

'Marlier,' Brimel promptly asserted. 'Duke Ferdain hated Duke Orlin as surely as their fathers loathed each other and their grandsires before them.'

'How soon will the Vixen's mercenaries be at our throats?' quavered Halarey.

Irritated, Tathrin did understand the man's fear. Marlier and Parnilesse were larger, richer and stronger than Triolle. Dukes of both had sent armies to trample Triolle militiamen into the mud in generations past. More often than not they were merely taking the shortest route through the lesser dukedom to attack each other.

'Ridianne the Vixen fought alongside the Soluran's army,' Akaver the tailor reminded his companions. 'Duke Ferdain of Marlier cannot threaten us while she remains his captain of mercenaries.'

Brimel was not convinced. 'Until she decides to make a gift of Triolle Castle to one of her clutch of his bastard sons.'

Had that thought crossed Ridianne's mind? Tathrin wanted to trust the redoubtable woman, but he was guiltily relieved that her forces had taken such heavy losses in the battle at Pannal. She'd be hard put to challenge anyone for a few seasons at least. Though the question of just how to unseat Duke Ferdain remained a knotty problem.

'What do you suppose will become of Carluse Castle?' wondered Quenel the smith.

'That depends who the Soluran anoints as duke.' Brimel let slip a sardonic laugh. 'When he claims the High King's crown.'

Tathrin's forbearance snapped and he wrenched his horse's head around.

'Captain-General Evord will leave Lescar before Winter Solstice. He waged this war at the behest of honest Lescari, within these borders and in exile. He undertook to throw down the dukes because they have betrayed every bond of fealty in pursuit of their selfish ambitions. It's for us to determine—'

Before he could continue, horn calls rang across the barren winter fields. Startled, Tathrin saw his sergeants, mounted and on foot, rallying the men who had straggled out wide of the highway to avoid the ruts and puddles. The shouts sent his mount leaping forward, instinct telling it to flee. This was no nimble Dalasorian steed used to the chaos of battle.

Tathrin hauled on his reins. The horse bucked and reared. He saw armed men erupting from the coppices on the ridge line. Quelling his horse with a vicious clout behind its ears, he managed to draw his blade. 'Hold fast!' he snarled at the journeymen.

It was too much to expect them to charge these renegades. The first attackers were soon upon them, leather cuirasses filthy but steel blades bright and sharp.

Tathrin dug a spur in his horse's flank. Panicked, it turned Tathrin's unprotected side to the foe. Only the horse's skittish leap saved him from a slash to his thigh. Managing to wheel the animal around, he swept his blade across, very nearly slicing through the hapless beast's ears.

His attacker was already advancing a second time and Tathrin only just parried the renegade's stroke. At full stretch, his backhanded thrust had no strength. The renegade knocked it aside with a contemptuous hiss. Thankfully he had to dodge the frightened horse's hooves before he could follow up his advantage.

Tathrin gathered his reins and his wits and drew back to lure the renegade closer. Now he threw his weight into a downward stroke, with all the advantage of his mounted height. The renegade raised his sword but couldn't resist the descending blow and Tathrin's blade skidded down to bite deep into his shoulder. The man stumbled backwards, blood pouring down his arm.

Before Tathrin could pursue him, another renegade menaced. He let his horse swing its haunches around to force the man away. As the beast gathered itself to flee, he restrained it with harsh heels and hand and met this new foe's swinging sword with a clash of steel. He felt the blade bite into leather and flesh as he brutally spurred the baulking horse forward. The man disappeared under his terrified mount's hooves.

A body fell from a horse ahead of him. With a shock of horror, Tathrin recognised Brimel. The journeyman brewer clutched at his bloodied chest, his last petulant shriek cut short by death.

Men and horses jostled all around, blades slicing the wintry sunlight. Tathrin saw one panicked steed rear up to attack another with flailing forelegs, not understanding where the true danger lay. The stink of sweating men and beasts, of blood and terror, choked him.

Four men surrounded Akaver. One seized his horse's bridle, while the rest pressed too close for the youthful tailor to use the full length of his blade. He struck down hard with the metal pommel, gashing one man's cheek. Another had a dagger in his hand. He stabbed the tailor in the flank.

Before Tathrin could reach him, Akaver was dragged from his saddle to fall amid the renegades' savage blades and boots. As Tathrin charged, the four men scattered. His satisfaction at landing a blow, shattering the closest man's forearm, was momentary. Akaver lay dead, his bloodied face crushed like a trampled melon.

'Bastards!' Halarey screamed with incoherent fury.

He had either dismounted or fallen able to regain his feet. The baker launched a flurry of two-handed blows at a leather-clad renegade. Terror not skill drove his blade, but that proved enough to knock the man's sword aside and bury itself in his boiled-leather helm.

Ashen-faced, Halarey tried to pull his sword free. It was stuck firm in the dead man's head. Tathrin spurred forward and drove his own blade through the renegade about to attack the baker's unprotected back.

'Where's Quenel?' he yelled at Halarey.

The baker simply looked up, uncomprehending eyes white-rimmed with terror.

'Shearlings!' A tall man with a tawny beard shoved Halarey aside.

'Run or die, you scum-suckers!' A second man followed, wearing the same russet surcoat over his chain mail.

The renegades clearly recognised these newcomers' ram's-head badges, ringed with the rebellion's circle of hands. As more bellowing men surged forwards, the attackers took to their heels, disappearing into the coppices.

The mercenary sergeants would have pursued them but Tathrin saw the Triolle militiamen stumbling to a halt. They stared, appalled, at their butchered friends and comrades. Halarey dropped to his knees beside Akaver and shook the dead tailor's shoulder in a futile bid to rouse him. Tathrin had no comfort to offer.

'Not dead then?' Gren appeared on foot and smiling brightly. He was liberally spattered with blood.

Tathrin knew none of it would be his own. 'Where did they come from?'

Sorgrad rode up on his other side. 'You didn't think to send scouts forward?'

'Didn't the sergeants—' Tathrin broke off, appalled.

'You're in charge of this masquerade.' Sorgrad's merciless eyes narrowed. 'They take their orders from you.'

'Your boys needed blooding sooner or later,' Gren said impatiently. 'You've only lost the weaklings.'

Before Tathrin could answer such callousness, fresh chaos erupted down the road.

'Best assert your authority, Captain,' Sorgrad advised, 'before the Tallymen kill any more of your heroes.'

Tathrin saw the four sergeants he'd enlisted from that particular mercenary company had drawn together across the road. They were trying to stop Triolle militiamen from fleeing back the way they had come. Too many were evading them. Elsewhere, as their fellow militiamen tried to restrain them, individual fist fights were spreading into a widening brawl.

'Do you suppose the rabbits will stop at Tyrle?' Sorgrad mused.

Gren shook his head. 'They'll scurry back to Triolle, shitting their breeches every step of the way.' He took an apple from the bag slung at his hip and bit into it.

Tathrin's mouth was dry as dust. 'Help me rally them before we're attacked again.'

He desperately searched the trees for any signs of lurking foes. What was he going to do with the dead and wounded?

'We won't see those curs again today.' Gren's words were half-consolation, half-reprimand. 'That was a feint to test our strength.'

'They'll be back tomorrow,' Sorgrad warned, 'and the day after that. Now they've got our measure, they'll be snapping at our flanks all the way to Ashgil. Or until we turn tail and leave them an open road. That's what they'll be betting on now.'

Tathrin's fist clenched. He would dearly love to silence the Mountain Man but he had no argument that would do so. Besides, he wouldn't come close to landing a blow. The disaster of this first skirmish would have shredded the column's fragile morale. Seeing their captain knocked on his arse by Sorgrad could only make their dire situation worse.

He stood in his stirrups. 'Rally to your sergeants,' he roared, 'or run back home to hide under your beds. You won't be able to outrun your disgrace though. Every man who stands true will spit in your face for the rest of your lives, along with everyone else who learns of your cowardice!'

Amid the tumult, his shouts didn't carry very far, but at least those close enough to hear were given pause. Scuffles subsided as men looked at each other, shamefaced. Plenty of those further away were still running.

Gren munched a mouthful of apple. 'Let's hope we've got enough men to save Ashgil.'

'Is this how you uphold Triolle's honour? Is this the tale you'll take back to your parents? The legacy you'll leave to your children—' Tathrin broke off, coughing.

He swigged water from the bottle tied to his saddlebow. At least he could see the sergeants regaining some measure of control now that the first searing panic had cooled. More renegades lay dead on the dusty ground than he expected. Perhaps this wasn't quite the calamity he had first feared.

'You'd best have Aremil tell you everything he's learned from Failla, when you report this misadventure,' advised Sorgrad. 'You need to know what you'll likely be facing, so you can start planning ahead. Feel free to ask my advice, or any of the other sergeants.'

Tathrin rode away without answering. Otherwise he felt he truly would try to punch the Mountain Man. That really wouldn't be fair though. This debacle was no one's fault but his own. He turned his lacerating guilt on the wide-eyed Triollese.

'If you're so craven, we don't want you holding us back. Run and see if you can catch up with your gutless duke. Hide down whatever rabbit hole Iruvain's found!'

Chapter Six
Litasse

Adrulle, Caladhria,
16th of For-Winter

Two elegant women and their burly footman approached. She drew in her skirts to move closer to the shopfronts. That was only common courtesy. She also didn't want anyone getting too close. Her blue twill gown was shamefully stained from her recent ordeals by boat and by horse.

Despite sluicing her own underclothes each night, Litasse was horribly aware of her rank odour. All her perfumes and soaps had been lost in their desperate flight along with most of her clothes.

The women made no attempt to accommodate her presence on the flagstones flanking the cobbled street. They barged past, shoving her into the open shutters of a drapery.

As Litasse gasped, the women's escort turned to spit with deliberate malice. She looked down to see phlegm glisten on her skirt.

'What do—' Before Litasse could vent her outrage, the trio were lost in the uncaring crowd.

The draper clapped his hands sharply. 'If you're not buying, madam, make space for those who are.'

She drew herself up to rebuke him. Then she realised he didn't know who she was. Just one more dispossessed Lescari cluttering up their well-to-do town in her dirty gown. Claim to be duchess of Triolle and they would call some constable to detain her till she could be secured in a madhouse.

Her eyes stinging with humiliation, Litasse retraced her steps. If her noble husband wanted to know what was proclaimed in the broadsheets nailed to the hoardings of the Buttermarket, he could cursed well go and look himself.

She turned into a narrow lane, cobblestones uneven on either side of a noisome drain. The inn was halfway along, its woodwork in need of paint and its stonework green with the moss that thrived in this damp, low-lying district. Regardless, the price of a room had been her topaz earrings, last of the gems concealed in her bodice.

At least Iruvain must feel at home. Litasse's mortification was warming to wrath. His erstwhile dukedom was little more than a swamp.

Brushing back a tormenting strand of black hair, she threw open the door. But as she climbed the scuffed and dusty stairs, her anger cooled to leave her despairing. Who could command respect living in such a hovel? Did that sly-faced innkeeper even believe they were who they said they were? Or was he simply content to empty their purse before throwing them out into the gutters?

They had come too late to Adrulle. Sharlac nobles most closely aligned with Duke Moncan had prudently retreated as soon as Sharlac Castle fell. More followed when this Soluran invader didn't claim the dukedom or assert another duke's claims to be crowned High King. Such uncertainty was dangerous. Sharlac's lords agreed there would be time enough to reclaim their domains when all this dust had settled.

Those Carlusian nobles who'd prospered under Duke Garnot had shown scant loyalty after his successive defeats. Once Duchess Tadira had been murdered, when news spread that Ridianne, Duke Ferdain's whore, had saved Marlier by turning on Triolle and Parnilesse, that flight had become a rout.

Those noblemen and women had still found time to pack. They had abundant clothing and servants to care for their comforts. Men-at-arms guarded their coffers of good Tormalin gold and Ensaimin-minted silver. Caladhrian merchants scorned leaden Lescari marks. So even the humblest lordlings fleeing to the Caladhrian bank of the Rel had the money to maintain their derisory titles, leaving no decent accommodations for latecomers who outranked them. Thus she, daughter to Duke Moncan of Sharlac and duchess of Triolle by marriage, was living in a single room in this squalid tavern.

Her knuckles whitened on the newel post as she turned to the final flight of stairs. Because her fool of a husband had fled from his own castle like a housemaid scared by a mouse. After that, he led his troops to disaster at the Battle of Pannal. Then he made their dire situation still worse.

As Iruvain insisted they flee down the River Anock to the coast, their haphazard household and pitiful hoard of coin had been packed into commandeered barges. Litasse didn't believe those other boats had sunk. No wreckage or bodies had followed them downstream. Those scoundrels had stolen such tempting cargo, doubtless abetted by some of their faithless servants. More had slipped away each night.

They would never have suffered such losses if Iruvain had listened to her. If they had gone north or east to make common cause with Lescar's remaining dukes.

Reaching the landing on the topmost floor, her certainty faltered. If they had gone to Parnilesse? That thought made her blood run cold. They would have been slaughtered with Duke Orlin, Duchess Sherista and their children.

But they would have fared better if they had thrown themselves on Duke Secaris's mercy, for her father's sake. Draximal had long been an ally of Sharlac. Litasse's generous lips narrowed as she flung open the door to their garret.

'If you—'

She stopped, dumbfounded, on the threshold.

Iruvain lay sprawled on the bed. He wasn't naked; this unheated room was too chilly for that. But his doublet and shirt were unbuttoned, his breeches and smallclothes shoved down to his knees.

His hardier companion had stripped to her chemise, her blue gown tossed carelessly onto a chair. The fine linen was bunched around her waist, exposing her shapely buttocks as she rode him hard. Lace hung loose about her shoulders, her full breasts exposed for his grasping hands and greedy mouth. Murmuring with pleasure, she threw back her head, chestnut locks tumbling down her back.

'You bring your harlots to my bed?' shrieked Litasse.

The girl gasped, blushing scarlet. One silver-braceleted arm shielding her breasts, she tugged up her slipping shift. She would have risen but Iruvain took hold of her hips, refusing to release her.

He glared at Litasse from his pillows. 'Get out.'

'How dare you?' Her voice rose still more shrill.

'Get out or stay and watch.' Iruvain didn't blink. 'But don't think I'll be servicing you, my lady wife.'

The girl moaned with inarticulate protest, turning away from Litasse. A silver and lapis necklace gleamed through the tangles of her glossy hair.

Iruvain smiled beguilingly up at her. 'No, you're not done yet, sweetheart, and neither am I.' His strong fingers dug into her white thighs, forcibly rocking her back and forth. 'It would be a sin against Halcarion not to finish what we've started.'

He would do it too, while she stood there. Litasse could see the cruel satisfaction in his brown eyes. He'd enjoy it all the more, his blood pumping harder with his pleasure at her embarrassment.

Leaving the door swinging open, she stormed back down the stairs. Let anyone who wanted see her rutting swine of a husband, wallowing with some fool of a girl seduced by his handsome face and honeyed words.

She nearly fell down the last steps to the turn in the stair. Barely managing to keep her feet, she stood for a moment, fighting treacherous hysterics.

Below, the tavern door opened and someone came hurrying upwards. Litasse pressed her hands to her face, trying to quench the blush burning her cheeks. But where could she hide her humiliation?

A lithely muscled man, his light-brown hair shaven close, rounded the first flight. He looked up, startled. 'Your Grace?'

'Karn—'

As Litasse struggled to explain, Iruvain's groans echoed down the shabby stairwell. The girl's gasps rose with ostentatious ecstasy.

'He has some whore—?' Karn took two steps in a single stride, his grip on the banister murderous.

'No—' Litasse choked.

Karn saw something in her face to change his mind. He threw open the door on the landing. 'In here.'

Mute, Litasse acquiesced. Little better than a linen closet, the innkeeper swore this was the only chamber available for their remaining servant. She sat on the narrow bed that took up half the space. She had no choice. Her knees wouldn't support her.

Karn pressed his back to the closed door. Even in the inadequate light filtering through the grimy window, she saw him glowering. At least he wasn't cross with her.

She gathered her wits. 'She's no whore, with a new velvet gown and Inchra lace trimming her linen.'

'She's ruined, whatever her family.' A sneer curled Karn's lip. 'Once word spreads that Iruvain's tupped her.'

Litasse shook her head. 'I can't disgrace her.'

Karn was perplexed. 'No one will trace any whispers to you.'

True enough. He'd learned every dark art of spreading lies from Triolle's much-lamented intelligencer, the cruelly murdered Master Hamare.

Litasse still shook her head. 'Iruvain will know. I was the only one who saw them.'

'Not if I go up now.' Karn wasn't easily dissuaded.

'Iruvain will retaliate.' Litasse picked at the threadbare coverlet with a chipped fingernail. 'He'll tell everyone that I am the whore.'

He had reason. Litasse had been the first to betray the vows they'd exchanged before Drianon's altar. But she had been so lonely, so frustrated. What leisure Iruvain could spare from his ducal duties, after his father's untimely death, he lavished on his hounds and horses. But could she honestly blame him? They had obeyed their parents' dictates in wedding. Iruvain sought a decorative bride while Litasse sought the highest rank. Had either of them ever truly considered the realities of marriage?

Whereas Master Hamare had adored her. Little by little Litasse had realised, as he tutored her in the ciphers and secrets reserved for Triolle's duchess. One tedious day she succumbed to temptation; discreetly flirtatious at first, more openly alluring the next time. Hamare had overcome his scruples to prove himself a skilled and passionate lover.

She blinked away her tears. So Iruvain was finally taking his revenge. Was the girl the first or had there been others?

'I would like to know who the trollop is.' She was pleased to find her voice calmer.

'I'll follow her.' Karn glanced upwards at the cobwebbed rafters. 'What do you suppose she's getting out of this besides sticky linen? What can His Grace offer beyond his skill at stud?'

Master Hamare had taught him always to suspect hidden truths, to be as adept at finding secrets as concealing them.

'Wherever she's come from, her family's wealth is intact, given her clothing and jewels.' A vile suspicion curdled Litasse's stomach. 'Would Iruvain sell the promise of marriage,' she said slowly, 'in return for support in reclaiming his domain? He'll need money if he wants to hire any of the swordsmen sniffing around these alleys.'

Karn's frown darkened. 'You are his wife and his duchess.'

'You don't think he'd set me aside? Who could blame him, after all the rumours?' Litasse ran a hand down her thigh. Yes, the dagger was safely strapped there. The blade that had killed Master Hamare.

According to Iruvain's bold, foolish lie, Litasse had stabbed the intelligencer when Hamare had forced unwanted advances upon her. After all, the two of them were alone, a guard outside the room's closed door. Litasse had screamed and the man rushed in to see Hamare dead at her feet. His blood was wet on her skirts and on the knife in her hand.

Who could possibly believe the truth? That two assassins had appeared in an azure flash of wizardry and murdered Triolle's spymaster? Because he had come so close to uncovering this conspiracy of Vanam's exiles to stir rebellion among Lescar's malcontents.

Hamare had done his utmost to persuade Iruvain of the danger but the young duke had refused to listen. Whatever the wrongs on both sides of their marriage, Litasse would never forgive Iruvain for that. If he had heeded Hamare, her father Duke Moncan would still be alive along with her surviving brother. None of this autumn's catastrophes would have followed if Sharlac hadn't fallen.

'Or he'll just say I am barren. In all honesty, there'll be no offspring from our union.'

Iruvain had sworn he'd never touch her again after she'd ripped that slender blade across his hand. When he'd turned on her, drunk and raging, in that seaside inn back in Triolle. Shedding his blood had been the death of her marriage, as surely as if she'd cut his throat.

'Just as well,' she said bleakly. 'If he's sheathing his sword wherever he fancies, I don't fancy a dose of the itch.'

Karn smiled with charming malice that relieved the severity of his gaunt face. 'At least let me find that young lady's maid, to warn her that His Grace's steel has a few spots of rust.'

Voices above interrupted them. Litasse sat silent while Karn stood motionless. The bedroom door slammed shut and the girl's slippered feet pattered down the stairs. Litasse saw her own conclusion reflected in Karn's hooded eyes. There was no sound of Iruvain following.

Karn slipped through the door like a shadow. Litasse turned the key in the lock. Where else could she go? Upstairs to face Iruvain's brazen satisfaction? Down to the reeking taproom, to excite whispered speculation? She didn't even have enough coin in her purse to buy a glass of wine. All that was left were the halves and quarters that the destitute of Lescar cut their copper pennies into, to buy a heel of bread or the dregs of someone's ale.

Weariness clawed her. Even though Iruvain had forsworn her body, she still woke a handful of times every night. Each time he shifted in that bed they were forced to share, she feared habit would rouse him, half-sleeping, to force her thighs open, to slake his mindless lust. She was terrified of what he might do if she tried to refuse him.

Then there were his nightmares now he couldn't afford the wine to drown them. Whatever memories tormented him, Iruvain moaned and whimpered inarticulate pleas.

She stretched out on the lumpy mattress stuffed with flock. Litasse only hoped it wasn't too verminous. She shifted as the dagger hilt beneath her skirts dug into her leg.

Would she have fared better or worse if she'd killed Iruvain? Or if that wound to his palm had festered? Iruvain would never let a surgeon take his sword hand, not until he was too far gone to be saved.

Then she could have decided where to go next instead of dutifully following Iruvain first to Relshaz and then to this miserable sump of a town. She would still have had Karn to protect her, for the sake of his dead master, Hamare.

A suspicion teased her; one she hesitated to entertain in her innermost thoughts. Would Karn kill Iruvain if she asked?

According to her husband, the enquiry agent had already slain one duke. Garnot of Carluse had fallen victim to Karn's swift knife, in the upper room of Tyrle's southern gatehouse. Contemptuous in his cups, Iruvain had taunted her, when she had insisted Karn was more loyal to her.

What had they been arguing about, when she had spat that pointless insult? She couldn't recall. But she remembered wishing Iruvain and Garnot both had died in that upper room. In the next breath, she'd been glad Karn wasn't there, lest he see that unspoken wish in her eyes and take it as warrant to act.

Litasse still believed she could trust Karn for Master Hamare's sake. But she had been unnerved by the ruthlessness the lean man had betrayed as they had struggled to rise above the chaos sweeping Lescar.

Perhaps she was being unfair. It had been much easier to trust Karn when he had looked less threatening, before the near-fatal wounds he'd suffered in Lescar's service had left him lean and hollow-eyed.

She sighed and returned to contemplating her possible futures.

Would she fare any better as a widow? She would still be as thoroughly adrift. She had no child, no innocent heir to the dukedom, to rally the Triollese. Indeed, till his body was found, it was possible Iruvain's brother, Lord Roreth, had survived the carnage at Pannal. If he had, and Iruvain died, Roreth would be the next duke.

What would her brother by marriage do then? Take her on as his brood mare, for the sake of her claim to Sharlac now that both her own brothers were dead? Or would he see that obligation best avoided and her reputation too tarnished? Litasse judged Lord Roreth's loyalties would be to Triolle first and last. He'd want rid of her as soon as possible.

Would she be married off to some captain of mercenaries? Some hard-faced ruffian who'd overlook her rumoured adultery for some share in the spoils of Triolle or Sharlac's restoration?

Tears trickled down her exhausted face. Should she leave Iruvain and flee to her mother, go back to being a dutiful daughter? She doubted she'd be any safer. This Lord Rousharn, supposed protector of Duchess Aphanie, was hand in glove with these exiles. Karn had established that. Apparently his wife had been part of these Vanam plots from the outset.

Anyway, how could she even get a letter to her mother? She had no courier doves, ready to fly back to the castle lofts where they had hatched. None of Master Hamare's remaining informants knew where the widowed duchess was, to pass discreet letters on.

Was her fate sealed regardless? How long before the Archmage of Hadrumal accused her of defying his ban on wizardry in Lescar's wars? She was as guilty of suborning sorcery as she was of adultery. How could she defend herself? By insisting those exiles had used wizardry of their own, sending those Mountain Men to assassinate Master Hamare?

Even if anyone believed her, how could that justify what she had done? Her crime hadn't been one of impulse. She had sent Karn to search out a renegade mage. She had promised the wizard gold and jewels to use his arcane powers against Triolle's foes.

Litasse pressed her wet face into the stained pillow. She didn't even have the consolation of success. Minelas the mage had proved worthless. Whatever his wizardly talents, Litasse had only seen huckster's tricks and lies. Worse, he had tortured those women, those rebel spies whom Karn had captured. Not to learn what they knew of these exiles and who had encompassed Hamare's death, but just to satisfy his own revolting, perverted lusts. And Karn had thought that a price worth paying.

The Archmage knew every shameful detail. The wizard woman had made that plain, when she appeared in that foul garret, intent on punishing Minelas. Litasse would have been taken captive to the wizard city there and then, if not for those same assassins sent by some magecraft to rescue the captured women. That was the cruellest wound of all; that she owed her escape from such utter folly to the very men who had killed Hamare.

The most quick-witted had challenged the magewoman. Did the Council of Hadrumal want Minelas's crimes shouted from the rooftops? His guilt would stain every wizard, in the eyes of ordinary men and women. He swore he would spread the whole shameful tale from sunrise to sunset if the Archmage pursued Litasse. Leave her penitent and humbled and no one would be the wiser.

Litasse wept in earnest, the pillow stifling her sobs. The assassin had saved her but she owed him no gratitude. He or one of his confederates had killed Pelletria, her faithful maid, longest serving keeper of Hamare's secrets and the one person left to whom Karn deferred. The loyal woman had been brutally thrown down a stairwell to break her aged neck.

When the opening door startled her awake, Litasse realised grief and fatigue had brought blessed oblivion. The dim light through the window was unchanged, so she had no notion how long she'd slept.

Karn tossed silver bracelets and a lapis necklace onto the darned coverlet. 'I'll sell these later so you'll have some coin that Iruvain doesn't know of.'

'What did you do?' Still woolly-headed with sleep, Litasse looked askance at the jewellery.

'Iruvain won't find her so alluring with two black eyes and a broken nose.' Karn smiled with cruel satisfaction. 'And she'll have some task convincing anyone of her virtue when she's found stripped and robbed in a surprisingly well-travelled back alley.'

Litasse contemplated his spoils feeling a little sick. Had the foolish girl really deserved that?

'She's the eldest daughter of Lord Zervan,' Karn continued. 'His estates are near Dromin in Carluse. I don't think he knew she was whoring herself. Perhaps Iruvain was hoping to win some coin from her for his silence.'

'Truly?' However much she despised him, Litasse struggled to believe her husband would stoop to blackmail.

'Better news.' Karn sank onto one knee, confiding. 'I have a letter from Her Grace your mother, passed to one of Master Hamare's friends here. Lord Leysen remains steadfast in his support for you both.'

'Truly?' Litasse's relief drove all other considerations aside. 'Can we get her a message? Can she send me money?'

Karn's smile widened. 'All in good time. Leysen has more news. There's been fresh fighting in Carluse, on the road between Tyrle and Ashgil. These rebels have no secure hold on whatever they think they've gained.'

'Who's fighting who?' Litasse tried to decide what this could mean.

Chapter Seven
Failla

The Tyrle Road Gatehouse,
Ashgil, Carluse,
17th of For-Winter

'DINANT?' SHE SHADED her eyes to study a distant plume of dust. 'Who are those men?'

'I can't see any banners.' The grizzled man held his spyglass firmly against the buffeting breeze. He was an experienced soldier though he no longer wore Carluse's black and white livery along with his buff breeches and metal-studded boots.

Now his dark leather jerkin bore the five-spoked wheel, badge of Losand. That northerly town had suffered long and often in Garnot's quarrels with Jackal Moncan of Sharlac so its inhabitants had readily accepted the new freedoms offered by this rebellion. Dinant was one of four-score who'd volunteered to form the town's new militia and he'd soon been promoted. Now he was serving as a sergeant-at-arms for Ashgil's hastily mustered defenders.

His expression gave Failla a chill despite the sunshine.

'What's wrong?'

'Did you know some merchants' sons decided to try the road south a few days ago?' Dinant chewed on a tuft of his straggling beard. 'They reckoned folk around Tyrle would be desperate for Ashgil goods now they've no market of their own.'

Failla shook her head. 'I'd no idea.'

'The gaggle arrived back at daybreak after whipping their horses bloody.' Dinant's expression was somewhere between contempt and concern. 'They met up with a column of Triolle militia marching under the Soluran's standard. They said the Triollese had already taken a vicious kicking.'

Failla clenched her fists. That was Tathrin's column's second beating at the renegades' hands, according to the little that Kerith had told her. 'But there's still no word where these renegades might be? Or our allies?'

Dinant lowered his spyglass, scowling. 'We have scouts out on all the roads but we've no way of knowing what's befallen them. They might still be hunting for the curs, or they might be lying dead in a ditch.'

'We can't spare any more men to find out?' Failla asked reluctantly.

Dinant slid her a sideways glance. 'Can we spare one to ride for the captain-general?'

'Even the swiftest horse couldn't reach Triolle soon enough for him to send help to us now,' Failla reminded him.

Dinant grunted. 'Well, let's make sure they're not sneaking up from some other direction.'

'How sound are the defences to the east?' Failla asked quietly as they walked around the battlements. She saw their conversation was attracting attention from other men on the gatehouse and those stationed further around the ill-kept walls.

Dinant grunted again. 'The men of Ashgil are stalwart and a goodly number who served in the duke's militia have come forward.'

Failla knew Dinant was a shrewd judge of men but he hadn't answered her question. 'So what's your concern?'

'Those gate timbers are rotten, the hinges rusted. That's why the duke's militia couldn't close them against the Dalasorians. We've got them shut and barred now but how well will they hold?' Dinant shook his head doubtfully. 'Then again, why bother attacking gates when these walls have been left to crumble? A mouse couldn't run all the way around these battlements without risking its neck.' He spat his disgust over the outer face of the masonry.

Beyond the next set of steps leading down inside Ashgil's walls Failla saw the walkway had fallen away entirely for a stretch and a sizeable chunk of masonry had toppled outwards into the ditch. 'You think the renegades will scale the walls?'

'We'll be hard put to stop them, or even to see them before it's too late.' Contemptuous, Dinant gestured at wood-shingled roofs crowded close around the town. 'Every approach is cluttered with these paupers' hovels. Those fools of guildsmen built workshops and warehouses right against the walls. Renegades could sneak up with a siege-tower and no one would notice.' He shook his head again. 'Never mind them creeping close with grapnels and ladders after dark.'

Failla wrapped her cloak close, hoping he would think she shivered from cold. 'Then Saedrin send that Tathrin and his men rout them first.'

Otherwise there was going to be a second battle for Ashgil. This wouldn't be a near-bloodless affair, as when Dalasorian horsemen overwhelmed Duke Garnot's guard. That assault had happened so fast that most Carluse militiamen had just thrown down their weapons and thrown up their hands.

Though if there was a battle, Failla might understand the nightmares that had Tathrin moaning in his fretful sleep, on those few precious nights when he shared her bed.

Blinking away tears prompted by the cold wind, she turned back to look at the road and the rising dust. The marching men approached the shallow ford where a stream cut across the highway. The leaders slowed and the rest bunched haphazard behind.

She saw rags of green and yellow fluttering above the men's heads: Triolle colours tied to their halberds even if they scorned disgraced Duke Iruvain's green grebe.

'It's them.' Failla searched for the rebellion's standard of cream and gold. There it was, towards the front of the column. Surely that would indicate Tathrin and his lieutenants?

Dinant choked on an obscenity before bellowing to the men on the gatehouse. 'Stand-to! Stand-to!'

Motley attackers were swarming out of a hollow between the stream and the town where they'd lain hidden in thick undergrowth. Failla watched, uncomprehending, as they swiftly blocked the high road with bundled brushwood, stacking faggots fore and aft.

As the brass horns screamed their alarm, every archer on the walls made ready. The militiamen whom Dinant had drilled were rushing to the most vulnerable stretches of the wall, bright steel at the ready.

But before the horns could alert the marching men, the chill wind snatched their warning away. It wasn't till the first company crossed the stream to crest the shallow rise beyond that they saw what lay ahead. Halting, those first militiamen sent runners back to the banners still hesitating on either side of the water. The white and gold standard fluttered.

'Ware behind!' Failla screamed pointlessly. She could see more renegades charging up the road to attack the rear of the confused column. Those curs must have been trailing just far enough behind to escape notice.

'Get over the water, you bog-hopping bastards!' Dinant growled.

Failla saw what he meant. The Triolle men needed to use the stream to slow those renegades instead of having it cut their own column in half.

She could only watch, anguished. Too late. Triolle's militiamen were forced to draw up on the southerly bank, the rushing water at their backs.

At least on this closer side of the stream, the Triolle men were now forming tight ranks across the road. She saw mounted men forcing their horses through the hedges into the dull green fields beyond, some clearly mercenaries in the Tallymen's quartered brown and blue.

'Will they outflank that palisade?' she wondered aloud.

But after an initial foray, the horsemen returned to ride along the hedge line, moving little faster than the men on foot.

'Turnip fields,' Dinant said savagely. 'All holes and Drianon knows what else under those toppings.'

Failla saw he was right. Discarded turnip leaves waiting for the plough cloaked the pocked ground, hiding hollows to trap an unwary hoof. Spurring on a horse would be lethal folly.

A rush of arrows hissed from the town's walls. The renegades holding the road were much too far away and every missile fell short, utterly wasted.

'Sheepshit!' Dinant stormed along the battlements back to the gatehouse.

Failla saw the renegades behind their brushwood barricade were using crossbows to harry the advancing Triollese. Men fell writhing in the road as the leading edge of the column hastily withdrew. Scuffles broke out amid those militiamen being driven back towards the stream by their retreating comrades.

Those still penned on the far side were engaged in a vicious struggle. Worse, more renegades were splashing through the shallow water to either side, outflanking the fighting on the road.

Failla breathed a little easier when she saw mounted Triollese cutting across the perilous fields, intent on intercepting them. But there were far more men approaching on foot than barred their way on horseback.

'Do not open that gate!' Dinant bellowed wrathfully. 'Any man tries and I'll cut off his hands!'

Failla spared a glance inside the walls to see a confused gathering in the archway below. Halberds waved frantically above helmeted heads, shouts loud in the confined space. The Ashgil men were desperate to go to the aid of the Triollese despite the breach that would open in their own defences.

Then sentries on top of the gatehouse raised a new cry. 'Fire!' 'Ware fire!'

Failla saw dark smoke billow from the outermost ramshackle huts where the high road met the buildings that ringed the town. She hurried back to the gatehouse in hopes of a clearer view.

Dinant leaned perilously out between the crenellations, trying to see. 'Are there renegades in the alleys?' he roared.

The closest archers shook their heads. Shouts from those further along the walls echoed their apprehension and bemusement.

'What caught fire down there?' Dinant was asking himself more than Failla. 'Didn't we get everyone inside the walls?'

'Maybe someone from a hamlet arrived too late, after the gates were shut last night?' Though that still didn't explain why some cooking fire had rioted out of control at this precise moment.

Frowning, Failla sucked on her forefinger and held it up to the breeze. The wind that had been blowing steadily from the south all morning had dropped. It hadn't ceased entirely – she could still feel its breath on her cheek – but the smoke from those smouldering hovels wasn't following it towards the town walls. Nor was it rising upwards in this unexpected calm. It was drifting back towards the renegades holding the road. Dense smoke rapidly obscured the barricades. Low billows rolled across the fields towards their friends advancing across the stream.

She couldn't see what was going on. She couldn't even see Tathrin's banner. All they could do was wait. One by one all the voices along the walls fell away. The tumult in the arch below stilled. Waiting militiamen looked up, their faces pale and strained.

'Ware!' Some unconscionable time later, Dinant's shout shattered the tense silence. He took a pace back from the battlements. 'Mark your targets carefully!'

Men were stumbling out of the swirling smoke. Coughing, pawing at their eyes, renegades waved unseeing swords at the empty fields ahead of them.

They must have lost their bearings entirely, Failla guessed. Or they were simply heading away from the sounds of the battle still raging on the roadway. Only they didn't realise their wandering had brought them so much closer to the walls.

Now Ashgil's arrows found their marks. Renegades collapsed to their knees, skewered through chest or belly. They sprawled, writhing, mouths agape in unheard agony. Others fell headlong to bury the scarlet wreckage of their faces in the dark earth.

Failla flinched at every death, desperately hoping none of these dead were Triollese, fatally bereft of whatever coloured tokens they had carried.

A swirl of wind snatched the smoke away. For an instant, she saw the road and gasped. Those renegades barring the Triolle column's path had fled to join their comrades in the fields.

No wonder; their bundled brushwood was burning, penning them between two walls of spitting flame. Failla saw Triolle men were already thrusting their halberds into the barricades. Ripping them apart, they tossed the bundles over the hedges to smoulder damply on the wilted turnip tops. More militiamen were breaking through to follow them, kicking aside showers of sparks as they ran to cut down as many choking renegades as their ferocious blades could reach. Those beyond their halberds' murderous reach fled in all directions.

Failla searched desperately for Tathrin's standard. Across the stream, the smoke was still as dense as when it had first arisen. Battling men were indistinguishable shadows. The dead toppling into the stream were impossible to identify.

She caught her breath as figures emerged from that uncanny gloom. She snatched Dinant's spyglass from his startled grasp. Raising it, her hands shook so hard she couldn't bring the distant vista into focus. Failla clenched her jaw and forced herself to stand rigid.

That man in a russet surcoat must be a Shearling. She knew that mercenary company had supplied Tathrin with several experienced sergeants. Those men alongside him must be Triollese. They were all splashing across the ford, barely slowed by the running water. Now they were running headlong towards the town, closing the gap with the militia cohort busily destroying the burning barricade.

Failla saw a mounted contingent had formed a resolute rearguard on the road. Horses jostled but obeyed their masters, slowly backing and sidling through the treacherous stream. In their midst, Failla saw the captain's standard: their rebellion's golden circle of hands. Surely Tathrin must be safe if that banner still waved so boldly?

'Open the postern, not the main gates!' Dinant was bellowing through the trapdoor to the ladder leading down to the watchroom below. 'Send twenty men out to block off all the alleyways, in case any scum are lurking there!'

Straightening up, he assessed the advancing column's ragged progress and yelled along the walls. 'Watch for vermin among the warehouses. We don't want renegades sneaking into cover while we're beating them back from the gate!'

The only thing Failla saw moving amid the ramshackle buildings was the inexorable fire. It was spreading in all directions. Shutters flapped open as roofs sagged, their rafters consumed from within. That was another puzzle. Those mouldering buildings were very far from tinder-dry, after all the autumn's rains. Whenever she'd been up here on the walls, the stink of mould and rot had tainted the breeze.

New cries came up from below. 'Buckets! Buckets!'

'We let everything outside the walls burn!' Dinant shouted down the clamour of protest as he ran to the inner face of the gatehouse to look down into the town. 'That leaves no cover for attackers to get close to the gates. Just get buckets ready to quench any embers blowing over the walls!'

The upturned faces looked horrified at that prospect. Men and women hurried away to the town's wells.

Looking at the burning hovels, Failla didn't think there was too much danger of sparks drifting on the wind. Fierce golden fires swiftly consumed the damp timbers and shingles, leaving only dull black charcoal. Now there was surprisingly little smoke rising. She used Dinant's spyglass to look more closely. Was that a glimpse of flickering crimson at the heart of each conflagration or just her suspicious imagination?

'Here they come!' Dinant was warning those clustered within the gatehouse.

The battered Triolle militiamen staggered into Ashgil. Failla watched sergeants in the quartered brown and blue of the Tallymen and the Shearlings' bold russet surcoats swiftly rally each separate militia company. With shouts and gestures, they directed men to tend to their own casualties as they reckoned up how many had come through unscathed. The Triollese were less hardy, collapsing all along the street. Some men were weeping; others slumped against the buildings to sit dead-eyed with shock.

Failla saw townswomen offering water, bandages and salves to the injured. There was no sign of concern over these men's erstwhile allegiance. They had come to Ashgil's aid and in the current crisis, that was enough.

Looking back to the road, at long last she saw the captain's standard approaching. Kilting up her skirts, she hurried down the ladder to the watchroom and on down the spiral stair to the cobbles smeared with blood and soot.

'Tathrin!'

For a heart-stopping instant he looked blankly at her, as if he had no notion who she was. Then a smile of delight lifted the exhaustion from his face. Only for a moment though.

'Is there some headquarters for the town's militia?'

As Failla nodded, Tathrin leaned forward and stretched out his hand.

'Show me. I must tally our losses and wounded and see the rest billeted and fed.'

'I can help you.' As he clasped her forearm and pulled, Failla set her foot on his stirruped boot. 'We should send for a man called Dinant.'

Springing up, the soldiery doubtless got a splendid glimpse of her garters. But they were too far gone to express admiration and Failla couldn't have cared less.

Tathrin smelled of stale sweat and fresh smoke. As she settled herself sideways in front of his saddle, his arm tightened around her and he pressed his face into her hair. 'Thank Saedrin you're safe,' he murmured.

'And you,' she said with equal fervour.

Gren rode up on the side that Failla was facing. 'Come to ride in triumph with your hero?'

She felt Tathrin stiffen. 'Where's Sorgrad?' he demanded.

'Here.' Loose-reined, the other Mountain Man rode up behind his brother.

Tathrin reined back his horse and looked sternly at Sorgrad. 'Don't you want to keep watch over those fires?'

'Everything's burned out now.' The Mountain Man smiled genially at Failla.

A burly Tallyman ran up, waving a bloodied hand. Thankfully Tathrin's horse was too burdened and weary to shy.

'Sergeant Estrid's compliments,' the crop-headed swordsman said swiftly. 'He wants to know when you propose paying us. Before nightfall, if you please, and you should know a fair few of us will march for the Great West Road come morning.'

The man clearly didn't relish relaying that message, though Failla saw the contempt in his eyes as he glanced at the Triollese militiamen.

'I'll send for Estrid as soon as I have established my headquarters,' Tathrin told him curtly. 'And Correll can come too and whoever else is so eager to run away clutching a purse.'

'Yes, Captain.' Looking rather startled, the surcoated mercenary went to rejoin his comrades.

Gren drew a hissing breath through his teeth. 'You'll have a job and a half to persuade them to stay on after this miserable showing.'

'I know,' snapped Tathrin.

'So don't rebuke me for saving the day out there,' Sorgrad said coldly.

Tathrin's arm tightened around Failla but she could see his thoughts were ranging elsewhere. 'Do we know how many renegades got away? How far do you suppose they've run?'

'As far as the nearest village,' guessed Gren, 'or whatever farms might still be standing hereabouts.'

'Are all the locals inside the town?' Tathrin asked her.

'I think so.' The desperation in his voice pierced Failla. 'Those hamlets that held out when the Dalasorians came mostly changed their minds once they heard what had happened to Wyril.'

Like Tathrin, Sorgrad was assessing their situation. 'We should be able to hold the town now, once all those outer buildings have burned down. But you won't drive those vermin out of whatever lairs they find hereabouts, not without more men. Renegades will be thorns strewn across whatever path you take till then.'

'You've no hope of retaking Wyril, not without ten times this muster,' snorted Gren. 'Not without Lescari who can show some true steel instead of these lead-weighted dullards.'

'Stop telling me things I know full well,' Tathrin snapped bitterly.

Failla gestured ahead, where the road forked to either side of a tavern. 'Go down that lane.'

'The Sundial.' Gren contemplated the tavern, forgetting his disgust with the Triolle militia. 'That looks promising.'

'No.' Sorgrad overrode him.

'Maybe later.' Tathrin kept his tired horse walking on, brooding behind Failla.

Gren continued speculating about the attractions of Ashgil's inns. Which might offer a song or some game of chance?

How many men had he killed today? Failla wondered. It never seemed to bother him. Indeed, he relished the rush and flurry of battle. Its hazards were no more or less than the risks of a game of runes. A wound was a trifling inconvenience.

Because, as he'd told Failla more than once, always with a cheery grin, he wouldn't be killed by a blade. A Mountain soothsayer had foretold he'd been born to be hanged.

That was only one reason why she kept him at arm's length, for all he could be such excellent company; cheerful, amiable and always ready to answer an insult with a jest. Indeed, goading someone bigger than he was only entertained Gren further.

She looked sideways through her eyelashes at Sorgrad. Who might suspect those fires outside the walls were a wizard's work? Could anyone possibly suspect that Sorgrad was the wizard in question?

Few people would believe any Mountain Man could have such an affinity with the elements that wizardly magic drew on. None of the tales of great mages had ever featured an uplander, or even one of the Forest Folk. Failla would never have imagined it, not till she'd encountered Sorgrad and learned of his arcane abilities.

She folded her hands across Tathrin's gloved grip on the reins. Would the Archmage, Planir the Black, know what Sorgrad had done? Tathrin had told her something of his terrifying encounter with the magewoman who had been pursuing that treacherous wizard hired by Litasse of Triolle. The dread in her beloved's voice had deterred her from asking further questions.

Now she wished she had. What had Tathrin said? Evidently this magewoman, Jilseth, had grudgingly forgiven Sorgrad's stealthy use of magic on those few occasions she knew of. He had led her to that traitorous mage and that seemed to balance those scales. But now the vile man was dead. There was no excuse for Sorgrad to break the Archmage's age-old edict against wizardry in Lescar's wars.

Failla knew Aremil dreaded the wizard-council of Hadrumal interfering in Lescari affairs. If the mages asserted their interests here, all because Sorgrad had burned down a few hovels, how could they keep the Caladhrian parliament of barons at bay? Or the Magistracy of Relshaz? Or most daunting of all, His Imperial Majesty, Tadriol the Provident of Tormalin?

Chapter Eight
Branca

The Three Fountains Inn,
Solland, in the Tormalin Empire,
19th of For-Winter

THE FOUNTAIN IN the courtyard below the window was ringed by creamy paving. It was smaller than the other two since it symbolised the Lesser Moon rather than the Greater or, mightiest of all, the Sun.

Symbol of mysteries, yet to be discovered and never to be uncovered. Branca wondered what she and Charoleia would find here in Toremal. How successfully would they hide everything they must conceal?

Blind white marble, Arrimelin, goddess of sleep and dreams, gazed into the blue-tiled basin, empty now to save the spouting spiral seashells from damage by winter's frosts. It seemed she was particularly revered in Solland. That was apt given her associations with rivers and shorelines, in this port city where the River Asilor reached the Gulf of Lescar.

Branca looked up at the mottled clouds, grey as oyster shells. Should she turn to Aldabreshin cosmology? The Archipelagans said the Lesser Moon was a heavenly Opal, offering omens of harmony and truth among the patterns wrought with the other jewels and stars of the night sky. But the Lesser Moon had waned almost to darkness, now outshone by the full circle of her greater sister.

The ancient races of Forest and Mountain had their different foretelling rites. As Branca recalled, the Lesser Moon was a sharp-edged rune. Its closed circle could be a task completed, or one cut short before it was done. It indicated aloofness that could be serenity or madness. It might reflect chastity or virginity; a hopeful state for some, the bitterness of disappointment for others.

There were times when scholarship was no help whatsoever. Knowing so many creeds, she couldn't value one above any other. She could blame neither all-powerful deities nor uncaring cosmic fate, or beg either to pardon what she had done.

Voices sounded in the corridor. Thankful for the interruption, she hastened to the door.

'Thank you.' Charoleia took a silver mark from the mesh reticule hanging from her wrist.

'Thank you, my lady.' The lackey deftly palmed the coin.

Branca noted the pinched pallor around Charoleia's glossed lips and snapped her fingers. 'White brandy, if you please.'

'As you wish.' The obliging man hurried away.

'You're getting used to ordering the domestics.' Charoleia was wanly amused.

'How are you feeling?' Branca escorted her to the cushioned daybed.

Charoleia sat down with a heartfelt sigh. 'Just help me off with this cursed wig.'

'There's no news at the shrine?' Branca began removing enamelled pins securing the elaborate hairpiece

'Just the same fevered gossip as yesterday and the day before that.' Charoleia winced.

Branca carefully lifted the wig away. 'At least you're getting the benefit of salt bathing.'

This prestigious inn was notable for its proximity to the town's shrine to Ostrin. Many of Tormalin's leading princes and their ladies sought a cure under the auspices of the god of healing and hospitality. Though Branca found the nobility curiously reticent about what exactly they sought this renowned cure for.

Then there were the dowagers and decaying princes who preferred the clement winters on the coast, along with all their servants. Aristocratic esquires and demoiselles made dutiful visits to their elders retired from the complexities of managing Tormalin's great houses, their vast estates and tenants and sworn retainers.

Charoleia flinched as the hairpiece's netting foundation stuck to her burned scalp. 'That white gauze scarf, if you please.'

'Air will help the healing.' Branca recalled their invaluable apothecary's advice, before they had left Carluse Castle despite all his admonishments.

She handed over the scarf regardless, guiltily relieved to see the evidence of Charoleia's torments covered. Tied to a chair, starved, tortured with thirst, and beaten, then that vile mage had scorched away her hair, one lock at a time, while Litasse of Triolle's henchman looked on.

'Master Welgren isn't here.' A spark of mischief lit the older woman's amethyst eyes.

Branca was still astonished by her resilience. As soon as she'd come to her senses, Charoleia had ordered Branca to crop her remaining tresses, so wigs would sit more evenly. She even joked it saved the trials of stripping away the dye of her last disguise.

She fanned her scabbed scalp with a hand. 'Our noble callers will expect me to make some effort.'

'Noble callers?' Branca was torn between misgiving and curiosity.

Charoleia smiled pertly. 'Pass me that crackle-glazed jar and some muslin.'

'At once, mistress.' Branca bobbed a curtsey like the dutiful lady's maid she had never been, nor wanted to be, despite her mother's tales of the rich pickings from such work.

Not that Branca had particularly wanted to be a maid of all work in Vanam's university halls, but if that was the price of admittance to their libraries and learning, she wasn't too proud to pay it. Pride was something few Lescari living in Vanam's lower town could afford.

She watched as Charoleia dampened the muslin with perfumed lotion and stripped away her mask of rosy good health. Her face was left pale, her eyelids dark with weariness. Sickly stains still marred her cheekbones and jaw. Branca's own bruises had been much quicker to fade.

Regardless, Charoleia was still beautiful. With her fine features and dazzling smile, an alluring figure and innate elegance, she had turned admiring heads all her life. This naked evidence of violence against such beauty was all the more appalling.

So she had some plan best served by showing these noble visitors the full extent of her injuries

Charoleia closed her eyes for the barest instant before smiling brightly up at Branca. 'Help me into a dressing gown and tell me what you've learned on your morning walk.'

Branca deftly unlaced Charoleia's gown. 'There are liveried swordsmen on every corner,' she commented. Noble houses' well-drilled retainers; chosen men ready to take up arms at their liege lord's command.

'Wearing what badges?' Charoleia demanded.

Branca tried to recall. 'A red flower, a dog-rose I think. A honeysuckle coil. A black goat.'

'Den Breche. Den Dalderin. D'Orsetis.' Charoleia identified the blazons without hesitation.

As Trissa would have already done. Branca swallowed the painful realisation and her still aching grief at Charoleia's faithful maid's death.

Charoleia stepped out of her plum-coloured skirts, donned a yellow dressing gown and sat back on the daybed.

'You look dreadfully sallow in that colour.' Branca couldn't help an appreciative smile.

'Indeed.' Charoleia arranged the lace of her shift to expose the burns on her throat and the swell of her breasts. No one could doubt that more shocking injuries were modestly hidden.

She glanced at Branca, her lavender eyes dark. 'Don't ever doubt my gratitude, for all you did for me and Trissa. I know I owe you my life—'

A knock interrupted her. Relieved, Branca hurried to the door. She might even take a glass of white brandy herself.

But she found no inn servant in the hallway. A plainly dressed man of unremarkable appearance waited with a fresh-faced youth whose slender build belied the promise of his height. Both wore fashionably full-skirted coats over dress swords that looked more ornamental than useful.

'Your . . .' Branca's mind went blank. 'Majesty?'

'For this journey, I'm merely Sieur D'Istanel,' the brown-haired man advised placidly. 'And this is Esquire Yadres Den Dalderin. May we come in?'

'Of course.' Stepping backwards, Branca wondered how many more heavily armed men were escorting the Tormalin Emperor and how far away they might be.

'D'Istanel; a cadet line of your late mother's family, Highness,' observed Charoleia. 'Not the most impenetrable of disguises.'

'It suffices, as long as everyone politely accepts the fiction.' The Emperor, perhaps a handful of years older than Branca, raised his brows. 'What should I call you, madam? Since I refuse to believe in Alaric of Thornlisse, any more than I believe in the Relict Den Sarascol, taking the waters as she recovers from the fire that killed her husband.'

Whoever kept Tadriol informed was very well informed himself, concluded Branca.

'You may call me Charoleia.' She folded her hands demurely in her lap.

'Your home?' Tadriol persisted. 'Your family?'

'My home is wherever I find myself.' Charoleia smiled serenely. 'My family are those tied to me by affection, not by haphazard bonds of blood.'

The Emperor contemplated her for a long moment. 'Sieur Den Dalderin tells me you carry a reply to my letter from this disaffected son of Draximal who's appeared from the shadows now that all Lescar's going up in smoke.'

Branca hid her clenched fists in her skirt. How dare he refer to Aremil with such contempt, even if he was the Tormalin Emperor?

Charoleia sighed. 'Eofin Den Dalderin should know better. Master Aremil is a scholar and while he was indeed Duke Secaris's firstborn, his concerns are with Lescari peace and prosperity, not Draximal's petty anxieties.'

'Petty anxieties?' Tadriol snapped. 'Duke Secaris's acknowledged son and heir is dead! Need I remind you that amiable and virtuous young man made a good many friends on his visits to Toremal? '

'Lord Cassat took up arms against the Soluran,' retorted Charoleia. 'The fortunes of war are notoriously fickle, so don't blame us for his death. Has Draximal been overrun? Has Duke Secaris's castle been sacked? Is His Grace begging for bread by the high road? Hardly,' she answered her own question scornfully. 'No more than Duke Ferdain of Marlier.'

'Duke Moncan is dead, and his son and heir,' Tadriol countered. 'Sharlac Castle is a burned-out shell.'

Charoleia shook her head, unrepentant. 'Had he surrendered, they would be alive today.'

'Duchess Aphanie and her daughters—' Tadriol began wrathfully.

'Branca, please fetch His Imperial Majesty's letter.' As Charoleia brushed the straying edge of the silk swathing her head, her lace cuff fell away to reveal the rope scars on her wrist. 'Forgive me, I am weary. You'll find all your answers in there.'

Conscious of them all watching, Branca unlocked the travelling chest tucked behind the door. She removed the plaited straw baskets fitted into the topmost tray, then flipped the wooden tray over and pressed the dowels that released the bottom panel. Emperor Tadriol's letter was secured inside with a blob of soft wax. She twisted it free and silently handed it over.

He made no move to crack its three solid seals, looking at Charoleia. 'I take it you know what this says?'

Charoleia nodded. 'You demanded that we surrender Duchess Aphanie and her daughters. I'm afraid we have no say in where Her Grace might choose to go. Naturally if she wishes to accept your hospitality, we'll see her on the road with every comfort and protection.'

The Emperor swept back his black coat to stick the unopened letter in the pocket of his breeches. 'You'll be glad to be rid of her so no one can rally to her cause?'

'That's hardly likely.' Charoleia covered a faint laugh with an apologetic hand. 'We'd rather Duchess Aphanie helped us build a peaceful future for Lescar. We sincerely hope Duke Secaris and Duke Ferdain of Marlier will prefer that option to exile.'

'That's the choice you're offering?' Tadriol looked sceptical.

Charoleia shrugged. 'We've received encouraging letters from both dukedoms.'

Branca relocked the travel chest, glad that her back was turned to the Emperor. Though Charoleia wasn't telling outright lies – letters were going back and forth across Draximal and Marlier. Just not to the dukes. Charoleia had persuaded Aremil not to approach either of them until she had done all she could to turn lesser nobles, guildsmen and yeomen against their erstwhile liege lords.

'Duchess Aphanie must do as she thinks best,' Charoleia continued, 'for herself, for her daughters, and for the orphaned daughters of Carluse in her care. We all agreed that was for the best.'

Branca was reluctantly amused. Charoleia made it sound as if Duchess Aphanie had been consulted, rather than simply presented with the distraught children. Soothing their hysterics should keep Her Grace out of mischief, she recalled Charoleia saying at the time.

Making sure her face was expressionless, she went to stand by the window, every measure the dutiful maidservant. The Emperor's man stood just as silent by the door.

Charoleia raised a finger as Tadriol opened his mouth to speak. 'As for Litasse, we have no idea where Her Grace of Triolle might be. We are as anxious as you to know that she's safe.'

'Don't you want Duke Iruvain's head on a gatehouse spike?' Tadriol asked sardonically.

Charoleia met the Emperor's sarcasm with chilly calm. 'You cannot imagine our regret that the Soluran's army didn't reach Parnilesse before Duke Orlin's own people punished his crimes with death.'

Tadriol twisted the heirloom rings that were his only jewellery. 'The Convocation of Princes demands that the leaders of this rebellion answer for the deaths of the dukes of Sharlac, Carluse and Parnilesse and their murdered families.'

'So your letter said.' Charoleia gazed at Tadriol. 'What's the legal basis for that demand? What jurisdiction do Tormalin courts claim over Lescari affairs? What authority does the Convocation assert over mercenary soldiers and citizens of Ensaimin's towns and fiefdoms? And Captain-General Evord Fal Breven? What would King Solquen of Solura say if Tormalin's legions seize him so far outside Tormalin's borders?'

'The Convocation will not stand for a Soluran as the ruler of Lescar,' Tadriol warned. 'Nor can I stand idly by while this chaos in Parnilesse spills across the Asilor.'

Charoleia swept the gauzy scarf from her head, revealing her ugly burns. The youthful Esquire Den Dalderin winced.

'You don't think the people of Parnilesse were justified in removing their overlord? He sanctioned such viciousness and worse, against anyone protesting at his abuses. Lord Geferin was there in Adel Castle while I was being tortured. My maid Trissa was murdered because she knew nothing of sufficient value to save her life.'

While Branca turned away, unable to hide her distress, she still couldn't help admiring Charoleia's carefully chosen words. Lord Geferin had been at Adel Castle but Branca would swear he'd had no notion who was imprisoned in the lake-swept keep's garrets, much less that they were being tortured.

'If Parnilesse's troubles encroach on Tormalin peace—' Charoleia broke off, a wicked smile fleeting across her face like a glimpse of sunshine through cloud. 'Forgive me. If it is in Tormalin's best interest to send your legions across the river, far be it from me to stop you.'

Tadriol raised his eyebrows. 'Because that will serve your purpose?'

Charoleia relaxed against her cushions. 'Few things will prompt Lescari unity faster than a Tormalin incursion.'

'You're as ready with your answers as ever.' Tadriol was torn between admiration and exasperation. His tone hardened. 'Will you threaten me this time as well? Or my betrothed?'

'No, and I should ask your forgiveness for being so ill-mannered at our last meeting.' Pensive, Charoleia twisted the scarf in her hands. 'Let me make amends by offering a warning. The man who murdered my maid, who tormented me, he was a wizard.'

She looked up at Tadriol, her eyes hollow. 'Some Lescari might accept Tormalin legions marching in to force a peace. But I cannot think any would accept you supporting the restoration of Iruvain of Triolle, or establishing any new duke in Parnilesse. They were both guilty of suborning sorcery.'

'A renegade mage? Is this true?' The Emperor startled Branca by turning to the young Den Dalderin.

'I cannot say,' he stammered.

'Contact the Sieur D'Alsennin,' Charoleia advised the youth. 'I know your father relies on his discretion when he wishes to contact the Archmage. Planir has an inquiry agent of his own, a magewoman called Jilseth, who will swear to that renegade's crimes. His name was Minelas and he was already pursued for murders committed in Caladhria.' For the first time, her voice trembled. 'Believe me, your Imperial Highness – you don't want to come within a hundred leagues of being associated with that monster.'

Branca couldn't help it. Sinking onto a chair, she buried her face in her hands. She heard the Emperor and his escort stride across the room.

'Forgive me. You're tired and unwell. I will read your letter and consider my response.'

The door hastily opened and closed.

Branca rubbed her throbbing temples, not sure if she was going to faint or vomit on the expensive carpet.

'Well done.' Charoleia was amused. 'Few men can cope with a weeping girl.'

Anger flared amid Branca's turmoil. 'You think this is some pretence—?'

'No,' Charoleia said swiftly. 'You suffered terribly too, only no one can see your scars. But you must stop tormenting yourself because you couldn't save Trissa.'

'Because—' No. Branca couldn't admit her far graver offence.

'Because that old woman died, after you pushed her away on the stair?'

Branca stared at Charoleia, aghast. 'How—?'

Charoleia's own eyes sparkled with tears. 'When I was lying in Carluse Castle, under Master Welgren's care, I realised I hadn't been dreaming. I remembered Sorgrad and Gren's tales of the *sheltya* in the Mountains. So I wasn't dreaming of walking in Vanam's Physic Garden with you and Trissa. You were wrapping us in an illusion, to protect us from that bastard wizard. If you couldn't save our bodies, you could at least save our sanity.'

Though tears spilled down her bruised cheeks, Charoleia's voice remained firm. 'It seems Artifice cuts both ways. I saw the duchess's maid die and I know you didn't mean to kill her, just to push her away. You simply wanted her to forget that she had seen you.'

'Truly, I didn't mean—' Branca didn't know who she wept for – Trissa or the dead old woman.

'You're no murderer, but don't expect me to grieve for her death. If she had lived, you'd have been captured and then we'd all have died. Now, where's that white brandy?' Charoleia wiped her face with the creased scarf. 'We have letters to write if we're to enlist advocates in Toremal's law courts.'

'What?' Branca struggled to follow her.

'Tadriol is sincerely concerned with the fates of Lescar's ducal families. He doesn't want to see more deaths.' Charoleia tugged on the silken bell-pull to summon an inn servant. 'But sure as the shine on Tormalin gold, he doesn't agree with the Princes' Convocation. He won't want Tormalin's legions imposing peace on Lescar.'

'How do you know?' Branca wondered.

Charoleia smiled thinly. 'Because he came to see us here in private. If we had travelled all the way to Toremal to deliver that letter as planned, this whole matter of Lescar would be the talk of the capital. Every noble household advising the Imperial Court would voice their opinion and His Imperial Highness's choices would be so much more constrained.'

'So what do we do now?' At least this new puzzle was a distraction from everything else besetting Branca.

'For a start, let's be glad we're spared the journey to Toremal.' Charoleia tossed aside the soiled scarf. 'Let's consider where we shift our own pieces next. Tadriol had no answer when I challenged him on the legality of a Tormalin incursion. So we want bold and eloquent advocates schooled in the Empire's own jurisprudence arguing for Lescar's independence before the first legionary straps on his armour.'

She paused for a moment's thought. 'In the first instance, we'll write to Advocate Mistal Tathel. He has an impressive tally of successes to balance his inclination to controversy and his loyalty to the Emperor cannot be doubted.

She might have been playing a game of white raven; the board set with carved wooden trees and bushes and painted bird figurines, to see if the fabled bird of prophecy could outwit its humbler forest brethren or be forced to flee their pecking beaks.

'A judgement in their law courts will stop Tormalin's princes marching?' Branca found that hard to believe.

'Not if enough noble sieurs see some advantage in going to war,' Charoleia admitted, 'but it may win enough time to agree a peace of sorts in Lescar, to cut the warmongers off at the knees.' She fixed Branca with a penetrating gaze. 'So tell Aremil we need a settlement with the remaining dukes. By all that's sacred and profane, tell him that no more disasters can befall Duchess Aphanie, her daughters or any of the rest of the ducal families. Otherwise Emperor Tadriol will surely send in his legions.'

Branca nodded and steeled herself to summon up the aetheric enchantments. After all, as long as she and Aremil had such complex and weighty matters to discuss there should be no danger of straying into more dangerous territory. He knew she had killed the old woman. There was nothing she could do about that. But she could not bear to see whatever condemnation lurked in his innermost thoughts.

Chapter Nine
Aremil

Satheron Manor, near Wellan,
in the Dukedom of Sharlac,
27th of For-Winter

'CHAROLEIA SAYS WE *should receive an opinion from Advocate Tathel today or tomorrow at the latest.*'

Branca's voice rang around the lofty vaulting of the pillared hall.

'The Imperial Dispatch is admirably swift,' he commented. Those riders would have covered nearly twice the distance he had in these past eight days.

'*Thankfully it's not limited to His Imperial Highness's business.*' Amusement coloured Branca's tone. '*As long as one has the coin to buy the right seals.*'

Aremil allowed himself a twisted smile. 'What would we do without Charoleia?'

Sunlight momentarily strengthened the colours on the flagstone floor; distorted reflections of the patterns in the stained-glass windows.

Aremil was glad to see it. Whatever burdens Branca refused to share, they seemed to be lifting a little. For the moment, though, he was relieved she still kept her distance. That made it easier to conceal the cramps and nausea that assailed him.

Imperial Dispatch riders had the benefit of Tormalin's enviable roads and the finest horses. They didn't bump along rutted forest tracks from Carluse to Losand, because the highway running through Ashgil and then north to the Great West Road was still beset by renegade stragglers.

When they had finally reached this discreet manor inside Sharlac's borders, Aremil had been carried to his bed, wracked with pain. A cripple for all to gawp at.

'*Are you all right?*' Branca's concern darkened the windows.

'I'm tired.' Aremil forced his thoughts from that shameful arrival. 'Failla makes sure all my needs are met. It stops her fretting about Anilt and Tathrin.'

She was as ruthless as necessary with the hot compresses that went some way to relieving his aches. Gritting his teeth, Aremil made sure to thank her, and for making sure his bed was thoroughly warmed, and what little food he could stomach was easy to manage with his uncertain hands.

'*Have you heard from Lord Rousharn?*'

'He and Lady Derenna should arrive around noon.' Aremil glanced towards the wall where a brass arrow slid down the long scale of a timepiece. Not long now.

'*You can tell me what they have to say for themselves when I let you know what Charoleia's advocate advises.*'

Without so much as goodbye, Branca was gone; her voice and her intangible presence.

Aremil looked sadly around the high-roofed hall. Would she ever join him here again to discuss books and plays and songs and all the interests they had found they shared, when she had undertaken to teach him Artifice? Would they enjoy those debates prompted by some clash between his sheltered life and the hard truths of her upbringing?

Would they ever solve the puzzle of this place? Neither Branca nor the other adepts focused their Artifice through such an illusion. But from the outset Aremil had found himself in this hall. He knew Kerith disapproved of what he saw as frivolity. He knew Jettin merely mocked. But Branca had been intrigued, even allowing Aremil's fond imagination to dress her in brocaded silk. She had so wanted to know what aspects of Artifice this place might reveal.

No longer, it would appear. Shadows gathered in the aisles as the windows turned to night. Torches appeared in brackets on the pillars. Aremil sighed and closed his eyes.

He opened them to see the modest dining hall of Satheron Manor. Plain glass windows admitted wintry light to illuminate the whitewashed walls. Dark above, a hammer-beam oak roof was decorated with carved leaves. He sat on the shallow dais by the wide fireplace at one end. Massive logs smouldered, doing little to soften the chill. His head ached.

'Well?' Failla waited expectantly beyond the little table by his elbow.

'Nothing of significance from Kerith,' he said briefly.

The scholar had retreated to Carluse now that Master Gruit's crimes had destroyed his standing in Abray.

'And Tathrin?' Failla twisted a plaited gold bracelet around her wrist. 'Does his errand prosper?'

'He says it's too early too tell.' Aremil saw his own exasperation reflected in Failla's eyes. 'But the captain-general said he thought this was a sound stratagem,' he added, as much for his own reassurance as hers, 'when they discussed it in Triolle.'

Tathrin had been lucky to catch Evord there. The Soluran was all set to march north to the Great West Road with his remaining force and renegades could take their chances attacking him if they wished.

'No bad news at least.' Failla glanced over her shoulder, smoothing her demure grey gown. 'If you're ready, they're here.'

'They're early.' Aremil tried to sit straighter in his chair. 'Can you fetch wine and cakes after you help me to the parlour?'

After the trials of the journey, he was still too weak, too subject to unexpected cramps, to manage his crutches.

'Duchess Aphanie wishes to see you in here.' From Failla's tone that was no request. 'With her retainers at the far end of the hall, so they can bear witness even if they cannot hear what's said.'

'What does she think I'll do behind closed doors?' Exasperated, Aremil leaned forwards as Failla tidied his cushions. 'Are her daughters with her, and Carluse's girls?'

Failla nodded. 'With Lord Rousharn and Lady Derenna.'

Aremil sighed. 'Let's see what they've cooked up between them.'

It had seemed so simple back in Vanam. They all wanted to end the dukes' tyranny. Whatever their differences, they agreed on that. But even before the fighting was done, those different reasons had begun driving wedges between them. Now their earlier accord with these noble allies was split as surely as a log riven with hammer and iron spikes.

The hall door edged open and Lord Cullough entered as Failla carried chairs from the dais's long table to the fireside.

Aremil watched Duchess Aphanie leaning on Lord Cullough's sturdy arm. She was solidly built, her dark hair copiously threaded with silver. She wore a high-necked gown of unrelieved black and her jewellery was mourning jet. Her eyes were as hard and dark as the stones, with no hint of weeping.

Lord Rousharn strode confidently at her side; as tall as Tathrin, broad-shouldered and straight-limbed. Though his sons and daughters were of marriageable age, his full head of dark hair was barely brushed with grey. Soberly gowned in the same green broadcloth as her husband's well-tailored doublet, Lady Derenna escorted the four fatherless girls of Carluse and Sharlac.

As Duchess Aphanie stepped onto the dais, she turned to nod to the small knot of leather-armoured men who had followed her into the hall. Still vigilant, they sat on the benches beside the door and grudgingly accepted tankards of ale from a manservant.

Aphanie glanced contemptuously at Failla. 'Get rid of her. My daughters will not breathe the same air as this whore.'

Before Aremil could answer, Failla's curtsey conveyed utter disdain for the noblewoman. 'Your Grace.' She smiled kindly at Garnot's daughters before she stepped down to the floor of the hall and departed through a side door.

'Please, be seated.' Aremil took refuge in convention. 'I trust your journey wasn't too tiring?'

'Don't pretend concern for my welfare.' Aphanie scowled at him as she took a chair.

Lord Rousharn sat beside her while Lord Cullough bridged the gap, half-booted feet planted wide. A long-standing correspondent with Rousharn and his wife on matters of natural philosophy, he was also known to Charoleia and so had cautiously agreed to host this meeting in the interests of peace.

Aremil was relieved to see Lady Derenna seat the orphaned girls at the high table. They all looked frightened and miserable and he doubted this conversation would offer much comfort. He realised Derenna had lost weight, sunken cheeks making her expression more severe than ever.

'Let's be done with this masquerade.' Duchess Aphanie folded her arms. 'What indignity do you intend for us now?'

'Your Grace, you requested this meeting.' Aremil glanced at Lord Rousharn.

The nobleman's letter had insisted that Aremil accede to Aphanie's stipulation that they meet within Sharlac's boundaries. The duchess insisted that Aremil come in person or forfeit his role as intermediary between the remaining dukes and the exiles and rebels.

Had Lord Rousharn told her that Aremil's physical infirmities made him wholly unfit for such responsibility? He never hid his own opinion on that score.

So determination to prove the arrogant noble wrong had goaded Aremil into making this journey. Along with Charoleia's insistence that finding some settlement with the dukes was an increasingly urgent necessity.

'Have you retrieved my son Jaras's ashes?' the duchess demanded. 'No, of course you haven't.'

Had she come here simply to force a quarrel? Aremil wasn't about to gratify her.

'Your Grace, I outlined your present choices in my letters.' He addressed Duchess Aphanie with careful calm. 'Those manors you brought to your marriage remain your property, to provide for you and your daughters.'

Now that Charoleia had assured Aremil that those manors were too widely scattered, and their tenant lords too cautious, to support any uprising to restore the duchess to her castle.

'Since at least two of them are now vacant, you may live in whichever you choose,' he continued, 'or you may go to Tormalin, where Emperor Tadriol has offered you his protection. I've no doubt you'd also find a welcome in Caladhria if you wish to go there.'

Aphanie was most welcome to follow her late husband's vassals and those lords who'd abandoned her dowry manors across the Rel.

'What of my husband's property?' The duchess looked at him with burning hatred. 'My children's plundered inheritance?'

'Madam,' Aremil interrupted curtly, 'the dukedom is no more. Sharlac will be one province in a peaceful Lescar. Estates that your husband confiscated will be returned to their rightful owners. His hereditary properties will be divided among however many of his blood we can find.'

Initially Aremil had baulked at that suggestion. Then Charoleia had listed all the outer branches of Duke Moncan's family tree. The more hands stretched out for festival bounty, she pointed out, the fewer coins landed in each one. None of Moncan's remote cousins would inherit enough of his land or revenues to fuel ambition for more. Aremil had agreed, even though the tactic reminded him how dukes had sowed division down the fractious generations.

'So you wash your hands of us?' Aphanie was still glaring at him. 'How long before some mob hacks off our heads and rapes my innocent daughters? Should we fear some knife in the night? Poison, to mimic some wasting disease?'

'Wasn't poison His Grace of Parnilesse's preferred choice? When he had waited too long for his father to die?' Aremil was provoked into speaking too fast. As he felt spittle slip from his mouth, he saw Lord Rousharn turn away, repelled.

'I will not entrust my daughters or my own safety to the likes of you.' Aphanie looked equally disgusted. 'I am elevating Lord Rousharn to be Duke of Sharlac,' she proclaimed.

That was scarcely a surprise. Rousharn had been arguing that Sharlac needed a regent since their first meeting. Derenna had been quick to suggest her husband should serve. Since they had sheltered Aphanie and her children, Rousharn had styled himself the duchess's castellan.

Aremil and Tathrin had laughed, mocking the title as hollow as the burned-out shell of Sharlac Castle. It wasn't so amusing now.

As Aremil struggled to clear his throat, he recalled his conversation with Branca. Once he was certain of his voice, he managed a half-smile.

'On whose authority, madam?'

Aphanie looked incredulous. 'I am dowager duchess.'

'My lord?' Doubtful, Aremil turned to Lord Cullough. 'Could such a decree have any legal standing?'

'I can't think of any precedent,' said Cullough, clearly troubled. 'Such circumstances have never arisen—'

'I must propose a convocation of Sharlac's nobility, on the Tormalin model,' Lord Rousharn said swiftly, 'to confirm any such elevation.'

'That would seem rational,' Cullough said slowly.

Rationalism: the favoured philosophy of those Lescari nobles who found scholarship a safer and more rewarding occupation than the pursuit of ducal favour and advancement.

Rousharn and Derenna had long been foremost among such intellectuals. Indeed, their avowed Rationalism had persuaded many Sharlac and Draximal vassals to stay by their own firesides when their overlords raised their battle standards.

So Aremil wasn't going to get very far arguing against this apparently logical proposal. As a new notion occurred to him, he stifled a crooked grin and addressed Duchess Aphanie.

'Then you are abdicating all your daughters' claims.' He nodded sagely. 'I am glad of it, for their sakes.' He turned to Lord Cullough again. 'Presumably anyone with a claim to Duke Moncan's honours will also have to step aside?' Every single one on Charoleia's long list.

'That would seem necessary.' The crease between Cullough's brows was deepening.

'You agree to my husband's elevation?' Derenna spoke up from her seat at the end of the table.

'We undertook to remove the dukes to save Lescar from their oppression.' Aremil looked straight at her. Charoleia always advised that when dodging a question. 'We never intended replacing that tyranny with our own.'

Is that what you intend? Now his gaze silently challenged her.

'There must be authority,' she insisted, 'otherwise we risk Parnilesse's anarchy.'

Was that guilt he saw in her eyes? Or fear that her commitment to the obligations of rank had led her down a false path? Before Aremil could decide, Derenna turned to hear a whispered question from Garnot's younger daughter.

'Summon your convocation if you must,' Duchess Aphanie told Lord Cullough scornfully. 'Meanwhile, *Duke* Rousharn will stand as my daughters' guardian, without prejudice to their claims to their father's honours.'

'I also stand as guardian to Duke Garnot's orphaned daughters,' Rousharn assured the grey-haired noble more courteously.

'Won't their elder sisters, and their brothers by marriage, have something to say about that?' Aremil wondered aloud.

Though those households had been among the first to flee for Caladhria when Carluse Town was besieged. That prompted another thought.

'This convocation of nobles,' enquired Aremil, 'how many would need to attend to make their decisions binding on all the rest?'

'You're just making difficulties,' snapped Aphanie.

'No, that's a pertinent question.' Lord Cullough rubbed the back of his neck. 'This will need careful consideration.'

With an exasperated exclamation, Aphanie rose to her feet. 'This meeting is concluded.' Snapping her fingers at Derenna, she stepped down from the dais.

'My lord. Lord Aremil.' Lord Rousharn swiftly bowed to them both and hurried after Aphanie. Derenna was still encouraging her confused charges to follow.

As Aremil watched the women scurry down the hall, he chose his words carefully. 'Was Her Grace always so . . . confident?'

'She was never much of anything,' Lord Cullough said frankly, 'which suited Duke Moncan very well.'

Aremil didn't pursue that. It was enough to see Lord Cullough's misgivings.

The rotund nobleman heaved himself out of his chair. 'I shall see them safely on their way. Then you and I should talk further.'

'I am at your disposal, my lord.' As the nobleman walked slowly after his departing guests, Aremil wondered how he might seed further doubts in Cullough's mind.

The tapestry hanging behind the high table flapped as Failla slipped through the door concealed behind it, pulling it closed after her.

Aremil reached for the schoolroom slate and pencil that Serafia had found for him before he left Carluse. He had to admit it was a good idea, even if the squeak of the pencil set his teeth on edge. 'How much of that did you hear?'

'Enough.' Failla jabbed the poker viciously at one of the logs smouldering in the hearth. 'You notice she didn't ask about Litasse?'

Aremil contemplated the door closing behind Aphanie and her retinue. 'Nor did Rousharn or Derenna.'

'When they've been insisting that we know where she is ever since the Battle of Pannal.' Failla shook her head. 'Or hinting we've foully done them to death, concealing our guilt along with their bodies.'

'So they've found out where she is,' Aremil concluded. 'Can we assume Duke Iruvain is with her?'

Failla shrugged. 'Until we know for certain he isn't.'

'What do you suppose they're planning?' Aremil mused. 'We're still reading all Aphanie's letters?'

'The ones that we know she's sending,' Failla pointed out.

'Should we start intercepting Rousharn's correspondence?' Aremil wondered distastefully. 'And Derenna's?'

'Their household is very loyal.' Failla frowned. 'Any newcomer sent to join them at our bidding will be very closely watched, out of natural curiosity if not outright suspicion.'

'Charoleia might devise some useful scheme,' Aremil mused.

'If Rousharn and Derenna discover a spy, we risk them breaking with us completely,' Failla warned.

'I fear that's inevitable, and sooner rather than later.' Aremil coughed and winced. 'But so be it. It's time we began setting the pace,' he said decisively. 'Captain-General Evord wielded the whip hand all through his campaign. We need to do the same to forge a lasting peace. We must send someone to Caladhria, to find out exactly where those absent Sharlac and Carlusian lords have washed up, as well as Duchess Litasse. Once we know that, we can decide how best to stick a spoke in their wheels, before Duke Iruvain or anyone else can stir up the Caladhrians to interfere.'

'Charoleia will know who to watch most closely,' Failla commented.

'She would be invaluable in Relshaz or Abray.' Aremil sighed, provoking another tiresome cough. 'But if she leaves Tormalin, we won't know who's whispering in the Emperor's ear. She must convince Tadriol to keep his legions east of the Asilor.'

Failla nodded reluctantly. 'Then Kerith will be best placed to advise on Caladhria.'

Aremil's pencil scraped the slate. 'You and I will write to your Uncle Ernout. He must enlist every influential Carluse guildsman to convince the guildmasters of Sharlac to shout down Aphanie's plan.'

'That will only happen if we offer something better.' Failla betrayed a hint of uncertainty. 'If we convince everyone that a better future lies ahead, not simply a return to the same old follies.'

'Then we must offer something more than vague hopes.' Aremil tapped the slate pensively. 'I don't imagine the guildsmen will accept a parliament of nobles like the Caladhrians, any more than the lords will yield to a magistracy governed by merchants such as they have in Relshaz.'

Failla nodded. 'And after all Reniack did for our cause, the commonalty won't stand for being trampled underfoot.'

Aremil scrawled another erratic note. 'I must consult Lord Cullough's library for histories and political philosophies.'

'I'm sure Branca could offer some suggestions,' Failla ventured artlessly.

'No doubt, if she weren't helping Charoleia.' Refusing to meet Failla's eyes, Aremil continued writing. 'While Tathrin's most urgent task is crushing those renegades in Wyril.'

'He knows that full well.' Failla's gaze slid to the south-facing windows. 'The sooner there's an end to bloodshed on Lescari soil, the sooner folk will believe we truly offer peace.'

'There'll be more pyres lit before we see calm in Parnilesse,' Aremil predicted grimly. 'Tathrin will have a fight on his hands with Reniack.'

But he couldn't resist a mercenary's vulgarity. 'Still, I imagine Sorgrad and Gren will have a few notions on how to piss in our erstwhile friend's ale.'

Chapter Ten
Tathrin

Carif,
in the Dukedom of Parnilesse,
29th of For-Winter

He had been told this rocky coast was exposed to the severest weather surging up from the Southern Sea. The reality was worse than he'd imagined. As they followed the narrow path along the cliff edge, he couldn't stop shivering. The incessant cold and damp seemed to have penetrated the marrow of his bones.

Glancing down towards the roiling grey waves, he saw a small harbour with a rocky breakwater making the best of a scant natural inlet. A few masts rocked at anchor and Tathrin's stomach gurgled queasily.

At least they wouldn't be returning by sea, risking the wild surf along Parnilesse's rocky coast before a sail barge retraced their more sedate journey along the River Dyal, bringing them back to Triolle.

'We could find some breakfast down there.' Gren pointed at the weather-beaten black-tarred roofs. 'There must be a dockside tavern.'

Sorgrad shook his head. 'We'll just be delayed.' He spared Tathrin a thin smile. 'You're no ale-draper's lad barely worth a second glance now. You're the hero who saved Ashgil from brigands. By the time we've got clear of the gossip in these taverns, we'll have missed our quarry.'

'I know.' Tathrin contemplated the little harbour. He'd always heard Carif called a port but the reality was nothing like he had imagined. Relshaz, the only other seaport he'd ever seen, was an estuary city of low-lying brick, houses white with plaster cut through with canals connecting the sprawling streams of the Rel.

Here in the Carifate, as they called it, steep hills ran down to the sea. These little anchorages were dotted along the coast, wherever some break in the cliffs offered salvation to hapless vessels. Between the warehouses and the abrupt dark rock of the quayside, Tathrin saw a shingled strip barely wide enough for two wagons to pass without their wheels scraping.

He gestured towards a leaping-fish flag flying from the closest masthead. 'Are we enlisting any of these brethren?'

Sorgrad shook his head. 'We won't persuade a shipmaster to risk his vessel in the winter storms. Besides, they'll be keeping a weather eye out for Duke Orlin's mariners on the horizon.'

Tathrin had noted the square tower on the cliff beyond the harbour. Surrounded by a high wall, it had three rows of windows visible and a watchman's turret jutting from the roof. No ship could anchor here without someone seeing it coming.

He recalled the speculation in the tavern where they'd spent the previous evening. He'd learned that the mercenary sailors whose ships defended the Carifate claimed all this broad rocky bay between Parnilesse's southernmost cape and the promontory to the north, which in turn sheltered the broad inlet that the dukes had long since claimed for their own. It seemed the shipmasters of Maubere were still doggedly patrolling the Gulf of Lescar, for their own profit if not their dead liege lord's.

'Perhaps we should come back this way,' he said thoughtfully, 'to see if Reniack's made any headway recruiting ships for his cause.'

'Not unless he's handing over a good share of Duke Orlin's treasury.' Gren shot Tathrin a grin. 'Even in fair weather, sailors only whistle for a wind when you give them a fistful of gold.'

'Let Reniack waste his coin.' Sorgrad strode onwards. 'Ships will be no more use to him than they would be to us.'

Tathrin hoped the Mountain Man was right. He knew Aremil was concerned that the Emperor would see Reniack as an even graver threat if he learned that the rabble-rouser could summon up ships to carry his call to arms to Solland and the Tormalin shores beyond.

Regardless, they had no coin to spare for greedy sailors. They had little enough to offer the warriors they really needed, at least until they could refill their war chests by reclaiming whatever plunder the renegades had piled up in Wyril.

If they couldn't do that? Then everything they had worked so hard for, all the blood that had been shed, would have been for nothing. Tathrin set his jaw. Such an outcome could not be allowed.

How long would the journey to Wyril take? Ten days? At best, if they could march straight up the highway to Deflin and then cut westward. As long as the weather favoured them and if they weren't delayed by having to fight their way through the chaos that Reniack had brought to Parnilesse.

The sooner they could leave here the better. Tathrin lengthened his stride along the steep cobbled path. 'Can't we find some horses to save on time and shoe leather?'

It had taken them half a day to walk back to the coast from Carif's heart, where they had headed after first making landfall at another little harbour. That had been more what Tathrin expected from this notorious city of mercenaries, with merchants and moneychangers and paved streets and, according to Gren, the very best brothels this side of Selerima.

Initially Tathrin had wondered at the lack of any apparent defences ringing the buildings, till he noticed that every inhabitant, man or woman, kept a sword to hand night and day. Then he'd realised the full extent of the enclave. It reached a full day's ride inland from the coast, as far as an ancient ditch and turf rampart dug by Saedrin only knew who. Tathrin calculated the whole district probably had twice as many inhabitants as any other Lescari town. That helped explain why no Duke of Parnilesse had sent his militiamen across the Carifate boundary inside ten generations.

'How about it, 'Grad?' Gren prompted when his brother didn't respond to Tathrin's question. 'Saddle sores instead of blisters?'

'You've the coin to spare?' Sorgrad glanced at Tathrin. 'Wouldn't you rather have more swords to help retake Wyril?'

He ground his teeth in frustration. 'All right. Where are we heading now?'

'The Hollow Yew, then we'll call in at the Eagle Crag,' Sorgrad said promptly. 'After that, we'll see who's trading at Redgull's Rookery.'

'The Yew's just beyond that ridge.' Gren pointed.

Tathrin shaded his eyes with his hand and gauged the distance. It left him wishing they could stop for a second heartier breakfast down on the dock, after their daybreak cheese and hard biscuit. But Sorgrad was right. They couldn't spare the time.

After the swift ferocity of the autumn's campaign, Tathrin burned with frustration at the slow pace of progress this For-Winter. It was like wading through mud. So much could happen in Wyril in the next ten days. So much could already have happened since he left Ashgil. Failla might be safely away with Aremil now but that was scant comfort.

He could already have attacked Wyril, if Captain-General Evord had agreed to march. But the Soluran was steadfast in his refusal. No company from the army that had thrown down the dukes would march again under his command.

Tathrin must lead an army newly recruited to bring peace to Lescar. The ordinary men of the different dukes' militias must be free to rally to the gold and cream standard with a clear conscience. Victory at Wyril would unite them still more.

That said, Evord had agreed they needed experienced swordsmen at this new army's core and acknowledged Tathrin had nowhere else to look for them but here.

He contemplated the prospect inland, as the narrow path zigzagged up to the ridge. Solitary towers dotted the landscape, similar to the one on the cliff but larger in scale. Haphazard hovels built from crudely shaped boulders squatted around them. Each knot of buildings was ringed with stone-walled fields and a few black cows browsed the tough pasture. One small enclosure held a lonely pig, its littermates gone for bacon and sausage.

Tathrin couldn't help voicing his doubts. 'Are you sure we'll find swords worth having all the way out here?' If not, they were wasting more precious time.

Sorgrad nodded. 'More to the point, you'll find men willing to march into the teeth of the winter. Mercenary companies big enough and rich enough to hold their ground in the heart of the enclave won't stir until next spring, no matter what you offer. We'll find companies in these outlying towers who've had a bad year through no fault of their own.'

'They'll still be worth their salt and silver,' Gren assured Tathrin. 'No captain can hold any tower in the Carifate without good men to back him.'

'Captains facing a lean winter should be interested in mending their fortunes,' Sorgrad added, 'before some lieutenant challenges for their command.'

Tathrin nodded. Walking on without further conversation, they finally crested the ridge, his calves aching. The turfed ground fell away to offer shelter from the storms. Rough tracks branched off a gravel road, straggling towards more towers. There was one unexpectedly close, only just in the lee of the land.

A harsh voice called down from the watchman's turret. 'Who goes there?'

'Silk Maspin, and his brother, Dirk.' Sorgrad waved a hand at Gren. 'And their good friend, Tathrin Sayron!'

'Where are you headed?' the sentry demanded.

Tathrin didn't know what authority the man had to ask that, but guessed he had a crossbow ready if he didn't like the answers.

'The Hollow Yew,' Sorgrad obligingly called back.

'Any feuding we should know about?' Gren shouted up.

'Just the usual smouldering.' With a wave, the watchman retreated into his turret.

'On we go, long lad.' Gren picked up the pace.

'With your name going ahead of us,' Sorgrad said with satisfaction.

As they passed the squat tower, Tathrin saw two youths already running inland. 'Why did you ask about feuds?' he asked Gren.

'Quarrels always fester in winter camps.' Sorgrad shrugged. 'There'll be some willing to trade the risks of a winter campaign against staying amid the dogfights.'

Further on, Tathrin saw the running boys disappear into a sprawling building as different from his own father's inn as he could imagine. There was no yard for wagons or stabling for horses. As roughly built as the local cottages, it was just bigger, enclosing three sides of a square with doors on all sides ajar, even in this cold and rain.

'The Hollow Yew.' Sorgrad indicated a long-dead tree in the drinking den's courtyard. It bristled with the hilts of daggers driven deep into the wood.

'Ale or white brandy?' Gren pushed at a half-open door.

'Small beer.' Tathrin wasn't about to cloud his wits.

Sorgrad scanned the long room, half-filled with men and women. 'White brandy and ale for Ekarre Amber-Eyes.' He glanced at Tathrin. 'We're off to a good start already.'

A few inquisitive faces looked up. Men and women were dressed alike in dun breeches and sturdy boots, long-sleeved tunics buttoned tight against the chill. Cloaks draped on benches and chair backs ranged from good broadcloth in muted hues to heavy furs and a few gaudy silk capes offering more bombast than protection from winter weather.

Tathrin was relieved to see the tavern's customers return to their conversations. Most were cherishing a half-empty tankard rather than drinking hard. The rattle of bones beyond the tavern-keeper's long counter elicited cries of success or chagrin. Smaller tables around the hearth were given over to silent games of white raven.

Gren rubbed his hands. 'I should try a few throws of the runes.'

'White brandy,' Sorgrad repeated, 'and ale.'

He led Tathrin towards a man sitting beneath a leaded window, his back against the whitewashed wall. Round-faced, he looked more like a merchant travelling the Great West Road than some leader of swords for hire. Though his eyes were indeed striking: a hazel so pale they were almost golden.

The three with him looked like the mercenaries Tathrin was used to – two men and a woman as muscular as both, her hair cropped brutally short. All four wore the same badge, a pine marten's mask.

'Maspin.' The woman nodded, her eyes hard. 'Where's your pain in the arse of a brother?'

'Buying you all a drink.' Sorgrad gestured towards the counter. 'I hear you need friends to help drown your sorrows.'

'We didn't have friends to get us a hire with that Soluran,' the woman said resentfully. 'Not like you, from what I hear. Slick as oiled silk like always, you bastard half-measure.'

Unperturbed, Sorgrad looked at Ekarre. 'So just how bad was your summer?'

'We were set to spend the season chasing Dalasorian horse thieves back over the River Drax for three lords holding lands around Maerden.' One of the other men spoke, a noteworthy scar on his neck half-hidden by a rusty beard. 'Only by Midsummer Solstice, we'd barely seen two heaps of horseshit.'

Because those Dalasorians who so enjoyed plundering Sharlac's borders were enlisting with Sia Kersain's troops. Tathrin quietly took a seat.

'We were paid off early.' The last man scowled, sweeping back shoulder-length hair with a scarred hand. 'Still left all wrong-footed, when Sharlac Castle went up in flames.'

'No sniff of Jackal Moncan facing such a threat.' The woman took that as a personal affront.

Gren appeared with a tray carrying a blue glass bottle, pottery goblets and five tankards of ale. He set his burden down and filled the goblets, the sharp scent of strong liquor rising. Tathrin hid his face in a tankard of ale in case anyone saw his satisfaction at their conspiracy's success.

'Before we could catch Lord Cassat and get his seal on a contract, he was dead as mutton outside Tyrle. Then this Soluran threw down Triolle's duke and Lord Geferin with him.' Ekarre was torn between exasperation and admiration. 'With Duke Orlin killed and Parnilesse and Draximal both like to go up in flames, coming home seemed the safest bet.'

Sorgrad cupped untasted brandy in his hands. 'A truly unfortunate year.'

'Not for you.' The bearded man made a show of looking them up and down.

Indeed, Sorgrad was as dapper as ever and he had advised Tathrin to make every effort to match him. Even Gren was tidier than usual and wearing silver and gold rings, not at all his usual custom.

'So what are you doing here?' Ekarre's long-haired companion asked sourly.

'As you say, Parnilesse is going up in flames.' Sorgrad lifted the goblet to his lips. 'We want to know who this man Reniack's got throwing oil on the fires. If they're really looking to set Draximal ablaze. We want to know who got washed down the River Anock after the battle at Pannal, and we'll take whatever news you have to sell about comings and goings between Parnilesse Town and Marlier or Relshaz.'

Ekarre nodded slowly. 'Lord Roreth of Triolle washed up dead and stinking downstream, a few days after the battle.'

'They say his head sold for its own weight in gold in Parnilesse Town.' The woman jerked her head inland.

'What's that news worth?' the long-haired man sneered. 'You don't seem burdened with heavy purses.'

'Heavier than yours,' Gren assured him.

'There'll be fighting enough to mend our fortunes if Emperor Tadriol ships his legions over the Asilor.' Ekarre tipped a goblet of white brandy into one of the tankards.

'I wouldn't wager on that happening,' Sorgrad said.

'What have you heard?' The woman glared.

'This and that, from Lady Rochiel.' Sorgrad was still looking at Ekarre. 'She's in Solland for the winter.'

Tathrin recalled that was one of Charoleia's many different names, each one with a convincing history behind it. That news certainly dampened Ekarre's hopes.

'Never mind,' Gren said cheerfully. 'This Reniack wouldn't be paying you to fight anyway, not when he can whip guttersnipes into battle for free.'

'That's what you reckon?' The woman looked suspiciously at him as she fortified her own ale.

'Don't you?' Gren retorted.

The two other men exchanged a mordant look before drowning their disgust in their tankards.

'You could look for honest work elsewhere in Lescar.' Sorgrad smiled. 'For more reward than just paying your way over winter till merchants come hiring along the high road next spring.'

'That'll be the best you can hope for.' Gren nodded. 'There won't be another fighting season in Lescar.'

'So you say.' But the woman's retort lacked conviction.

'What sort of work?' Now Ekarre looked like a merchant intent on negotiation.

Sorgrad set his goblet on the table, barely tasted. 'Did you hear some of the companies mustered for Duke Secaris turned renegade after his death?'

'Bonebreakers, Swallowtails, Reskin's Prowlers, Boot Snakes and the Triple Knot.' Gren ticked them off on his fingers. 'They've overrun Wyril—'

'We know that,' the woman interrupted. 'Haven't you heard? They're setting up their own dukedom.'

Tathrin wasn't sure who she was mocking – the renegades or the two Mountain Men.

Ekarre cut off her reply with a gesture. 'The Soluran's recruiting to crush the renegades?'

'No.' For the first time in the conversation, Sorgrad turned to Tathrin. 'But my friend here is. Those renegades will be put to the sword for their crimes just as soon as the assizes sit at Winter Solstice. Then we'll see to it that Ferdain of Marlier and Secaris of Draximal pack their bags. After that we'll be coming for Reniack so ordinary Parnilesse can have a voice in their own future without him shouting them down or worse.'

'So you say,' the woman scoffed again.

'When did you last bet against my brother and win?' Gren asked with interest.

Tathrin cleared his throat and reminded himself of the speech he'd rehearsed, and delivered in the five taverns Sorgrad had led him into yesterday.

'Lescar will be free of the dukes before next summer,' he assured Ekarre. 'But there's no freedom without the strength to defend yourself. Anyone looking at the Carifate sees that. Only what's to become of the Carifate without the dukes to hire the companies and lavish gold and silver on their squabbles?'

He held Ekarre's pale gaze and saw the same veiled uncertainty that the captains he'd already talked to had betrayed.

'The Soluran's going home.' He gestured vaguely westwards. 'Those mercenaries with ties to Ensaimin or Dalasor will do the same, along with any who can claim Relshazri blood. But what about those of you born and bred in Lescar, two and three generations back?'

'Three out of four of your men,' murmured Sorgrad.

'You've fought for the dukes because that was the best you could make of your situation. You had no other choice.' Tathrin looked earnestly at Ekarre. 'You're still as much Lescari as the rest of us. Don't you deserve some share in the coming peace?'

'Served on a silver platter?' the woman asked sarcastically. 'Ringed with steaming sausage?'

Tathrin ignored her, still addressing Ekarre. 'Every Lescari town will need a Watch to keep the peace and its own company of militia to give greedy Caladhrian barons or arrogant Tormalin legions pause for thought. I want to enlist experienced men as their sergeants-at-arms. I want to enlist Lescari men and women. You know how to fight, how to train men to fight—'

Ekarre interrupted. 'What do we get out of it?'

'Gear and food while you're serving, and whatever stipend these towns can afford.' Tathrin looked steadily at him. 'Don't expect to get rich.' He spoke over a mutter of disgust from the crop-headed woman. 'But you can expect a grant of land, a smallholding or a shop maybe, once you've served ten years. A settled future, for whatever family you might have.'

'Better than starving in a ditch when you're too old and blind to hold a sword,' Gren observed.

'Ask around till you find someone who saw the autumn's funeral pyres,' Sorgrad suggested. 'Who can say how many of the dukes' militias won't be going home?'

'Rewards will be waiting for those who prove worthy,' Tathrin promised.

Ekarre didn't look convinced but he was clearly interested. 'Proving that how?'

'Help drive these renegade curs out of Wyril,' Tathrin said bluntly.

'Take your share of that loot and welcome,' Gren added.

'Is this an open invitation?' the scarred and bearded man asked suspiciously.

'No.' Tathrin held his gaze. 'Only to men and women born on Lescari soil, who've served in companies that get the nod from my friends here.'

'And Lady Rochiel.' Sorgrad smiled. 'You can spread that word, as far as you like.'

The long-haired man cracked bony knuckles. 'There's plenty won't like it.'

'We'll convince them otherwise,' Gren said with happy malice.

Sorgrad shrugged. 'I don't imagine they'll rally a full company to argue the point, not when they see that picking a quarrel with one Lescari town means picking a quarrel with them all. The days of the dukes stabbing each other in the back are gone.'

'We've already enlisted men and sergeants from the Wyvern Hunters,' Tathrin continued, 'also from the Gallowsfruit, the Tallymen and the Shearlings.'

'The Sundowners,' Gren added, 'and the Wheelwrights.'

'Who else are you talking to hereabouts?' Ekarre asked slowly.

'You don't need to worry about that,' Sorgrad assured him. 'Just consider what's best for your own future.'

'We march north from the northern entry in the rampart, the morning after tomorrow.' Gren looked around. 'So, who's for a few hands of runes?'

No one answered.

'You don't think you'll be waiting with your thumb up your arse?' the crop-haired woman challenged Tathrin.

He pretended to consider the question before answering. 'No, I don't.'

Hopefully that confident reply would satisfy Sorgrad. Tathrin had been practising. The Mountain Man had said time and again on their journey that this scheme would be stillborn if he ever betrayed doubts.

So Tathrin refused to contemplate the possibility of no one answering this call. He had also balanced that likelihood against the chances of disgruntled mercenaries turning up at the rendezvous to rob and fight those willing to enlist. If the worst came to the worst, they'd just have to rely on Sorgrad's magic to escape and argue later with the Archmage's spy Jilseth.

The scarred and bearded man looked at Ekarre. 'It's interesting, but maybe we should see if Reniack makes us a better offer.'

'That won't happen,' Sorgrad assured him.

'Why don't we ask him?' The woman smiled spitefully.

The sound of horses filled the courtyard. Tathrin stiffened as the idleness in the drinking den evaporated. Men and women were already on their feet. Some moved to look into the courtyard or made ready to leave through the outward-facing doors. Knives and short swords appeared on all sides; not yet menacing but laid ready on tables and benches.

Since there was nothing else he could do, Tathrin sat and contemplated his tankard of ale. Sorgrad drank his white brandy while Gren produced a pouch of rune bones and threw a few casual trios on the table.

A door darkened as two figures entered. Every eye in the place fixed on the newcomers.

'Good day.' Reniack greeted the entire room before pausing momentarily as his gaze reached Sorgrad. 'Master Maspin.'

'An unexpected pleasure.' Sorgrad's tone gave the lie to his words.

'Master Jettin.' Gren's words were less of a welcome than some unspecified, ominous threat.

Tathrin glared at the young Vanamese adept. How dare he turn the very Artifice they had relied on against them?

Jettin must have been watching their journey and betraying every move to Reniack, otherwise the rabble-rouser could never have got there so fast.

Unless . . . A new fear chilled Tathrin. Had the Vanamese youth been trespassing on his thoughts, without him even being aware of it?

All Tathrin could do now was hope Aremil sought him out quickly enough to see the straits they were in. Ideally, before Sorgrad was forced to use his magic to save their necks. Though he had no idea what his distant friend could possibly do to help.

Chapter Eleven
Aremil

**Satheron Manor, near Wellan,
in the Dukedom of Sharlac,
29th of For-Winter**

'Have you–' Failla broke off as she entered the parlour. 'Why didn't you ring?'

Aremil tried to draw a breath to answer but couldn't stop coughing. He was powerless to resist when she leaned him forwards to rub his back as though he were a fractious child. He couldn't decide which was more infuriating.

At last the spasm subsided. The handkerchief he had used to stifle the wracking cough felt ominously damp. Forcing himself to look, he found the linen was wet with spittle not blood. He managed a cautious sigh of relief.

'You have a fever.' Failla tested his forehead with a cool hand. 'Go back to bed.'

'My cough gets worse if I lie down.' Aremil forced the words out, his throat still raw.

'But your cramps are soothed.' Failla eased him back against his cushions. 'Those set you coughing.'

'I'll take more poppy tincture,' Aremil retorted through clenched teeth.

'Which kills your appetite.' She wasn't yielding. 'You scarcely eat as it is.'

'I'm hardly out ploughing fields.' Aremil curbed his irritation. He didn't think he could stand another bout of coughing.

'You're as stubborn as a Gidestan mule.' Plucking the sodden linen from his hand, Failla produced a dry kerchief from the folds of her periwinkle dress. 'I'll fetch a tisane. Perhaps the steam will ease your chest.'

'Thank you.' Aremil tried to sound grateful.

'You're welcome.' With something perilously like a snort, Failla left.

Aremil sat motionless, concentrating on breathing as steadily as he could. He knew he had a fever but he couldn't afford to be nursed in bed.

To begin with, Lord Rousharn would use such frailty against him, luring more adherents to his proposal for a landowners' convocation. Whereas Lord Cullough was writing to Sharlac nobles near and far. Disliking Duchess Aphanie's high-handed manner, he was inviting any and all suggestions for establishing a lasting peace for Lescar. Each day brought more replies for him to discuss with Aremil.

Then there was Branca's news from Solland. Every day saw more sworn men drafted by the Tormalin princes who held lands along the River Asilor. Emperor Tadriol had returned to Toremal. Was he in the capital making ready to call all Tormalin's legions to arms?

How long would mustering that force take? Would Charoleia know? Reaching for his slate, Aremil stifled another infuriating cough and made a note. He must ask Branca.

What news would Kerith have from Carluse? Now they knew which nobles had made such haste to Caladhria, the scholar and Master Ernout were heartened to discover most guildmasters regarded such flight as cowardice rather than prudence. Most merchants had little interest in seeing their erstwhile overlords return from exile. Which was all very well, but if Tathrin's errand in the Carifate succeeded, Lescar's towns still needed to pay taxes and levies to reward their new defenders. How readily would the common folk accept a renewal of their obligations with Reniack's defiance still echoing in their ears?

Aremil glanced at the timepiece above the mantelshelf. It was a silver willow tree with a brass leaf sliding down the scale marked on its trunk. A calendar was incorporated into its leafy crown, with numbered slips of ivory and enamelled moons changed daily by whichever servant had charge of the household almanac.

Aremil smiled, recalling Tathrin's oft-voiced frustration with the vagaries of the lengths of the seasons, as decreed differently by each committee of priests and scholars in the cities where the various calendars were printed, with a day added here or subtracted there to match some pairing in the dance of the moons.

Perhaps they should institute a Lescari Almanac, with the turn from each season to the next decided by strict arithmetical division of the year. That would satisfy Tathrin's mathematical mind.

Aremil sighed, nearly provoking his cough. They only had eighteen days until the Winter Solstice when quarterly rents were paid. When the assizes should be held, to administer justice in Raeponin's name. When the priests of Poldrion led the solemn rites to honour all who had died in the preceding year. People would throng to the shrines, seeking to placate malign fate before the hungry days of Aft-Winter. Those gatherings could turn into riots if they didn't have some new rule of law to offer Lescar.

Aremil scrawled a further note. Could they get their hands on some share of the quarterly rents? Saedrin save them, they needed money for their own expenses. Lord Cullough would never be so crass as to expect his guests to pay for their lodging, but Aremil was very well aware that those tradesmen supplying Carluse Castle would expect Kerith to settle their bills. Whatever her other resources, Charoleia must be incurring considerable debts in their service. Then there were these hoped-for mercenaries from the Carifate. Whatever Tathrin promised by way of future recompense, they still needed to be sheltered, fed and equipped, along with the Lescari town militias.

But he couldn't reach Tathrin, Kerith or Branca today. Not tormented by this accursed scratching in his throat and the heat of fever behind his eyes. Such ailments would prompt a wizard to lose control of his magic, perilous for all around and merely one reason why the mageborn were so readily shipped off to Hadrumal. On the other side of the coin entirely, it was impossible to work Artifice without absolute concentration. Aremil had learned to rise above his usual bodily discomforts to focus his enchantments but that was proving impossible with this current malady.

The parlour door opened. Failla entered with a steaming tisane glass in its silver holder on a small tray.

Aremil was surprised to see her hands shaking as she set it on the table by his chair. 'What's the matter?'

'You have visitors. Lord Cullough—' She glanced over her shoulder, apprehensive.

'Master Aremil.' The nobleman appeared in the doorway, his placid expression troubled.

'Let me pass.' Though the man following him was entreating rather than demanding.

The voice reminded Aremil of his much-missed nurse, Lyrlen, who never lost her Draximal accent even after twenty years and more in Vanam.

Aremil sat silently as Lord Cullough ushered a man and a woman into the parlour.

'His Grace, Duke Secaris of Draximal.' The Sharlac noble bowed low. 'Her Grace, Duchess Nisina.'

Failla sank in a dutiful curtsey before retreating behind Aremil's chair. Neither newcomer gave her a second glance. They were both staring at Aremil.

All he could do was stare back. These were his parents, not that he recognised them. He didn't even remember them. He certainly didn't know what to say.

Duke Secaris wasn't overly tall, nor strikingly robust. Aremil had always attributed his own slender frame to the wasting effects of his infirmities. With a shock, he saw he owed a good deal of his physique to his father, just as he had inherited his straight brown hair. But the dark eyes he saw each day in the mirror gazed from his mother's face.

Aremil couldn't stand to meet Duchess Nisina's gaze, so full of anguish. He looked away, ashamed.

They looked so old. Why had he not expected that? Dukes often married late, and decades ago, when battles had ravaged central Lescar, noble heirs like Secaris, Garnot and Gerone had been too busy leading men into battle to procreate. Acquiring wives and begetting children were the preoccupations of peace, when such hopes for the future weren't so vulnerable as hostages.

Then Aremil looked a second time and saw that while Secaris and Nisina were grey-haired, the smooth skin of youth lost, the deepest lines in their faces were of grief, not age. Both wore mourning, in silk the hue of a raven's wing.

Duke Secaris looked at Aremil's crutches beside his chair before glancing at Lord Cullough, uncertain. 'I thought you said he—'

No, I'm not the imbecile you believed me to be, when you sent me away with Lyrlen, to relieve your embarrassment by conveniently dying.

Aremil swallowed the challenge that leaped to his tongue. But at least neither of them looked at him with the disgust that Lord Rousharn was so unable or unwilling to conceal.

He cleared his throat as best he could. He'd be bitten by Poldrion's demons before he'd stumble over his very first words in this conversation.

'Forgive me.' Failla swiftly reached for the tisane glass and removed the pierced silver ball containing the steeping herbs. She laid it on the tray.

'Do you hate us so much?' Duchess Nisina's voice broke on a sob as she twisted a black lace handkerchief. 'Did you have to kill him?'

'Cassat was only doing his duty.' Duke Secaris stared unseeing out of the window.

'I don't hate you,' Aremil protested. 'I never hated Lord Cassat.'

Truly, he was shocked to realise, he felt nothing at all for them. While he was sorry for their evident grief, from simple common humanity, he found that it didn't affect him nearly so much as the thought of Serafia's loss, and he'd never even known her lost love, little Kip's father.

He didn't hate the duke and duchess's lost son. Indeed, he'd mourned the loss of whatever relationship he might have had with his unknown brother, were they ever to meet. Now he realised that regret was equally foolish. There was simply no connection between him and these people.

Duchess Nisina wasn't listening. 'Is that why you plotted this horrible revenge? Because we gave him what should have been yours?' Her handkerchief tore, twisted beyond endurance.

'We have always provided for you. Didn't you know?' Duke Secaris asked desperately.

'I know.' Aremil's mouth was as dry as ashes. He glanced longingly at the tisane but it would spill if he tried to lift it.

Failla made a move but he glared at her, forbidding. He'd be cursed if he'd let her raise it to his lips, a helpless invalid.

'We could never have raised you as our heir. Parnilesse and Carluse would have allied against us before you even reached manhood.' Now the Duke was pacing back and forth across the coldly sunlit window. 'I did write to you, before Cassat marched on Tyrle and since, though you've never answered.' Secaris hastily checked himself. 'Perhaps my letters haven't reached you through all this upheaval.'

He was doing his utmost to be fair. That cut Aremil more deeply still. The lie he wanted to tell scalded his throat. 'No. That's to say—'

'Master Aremil has so many calls on his time,' Failla answered swiftly.

'No.' Aremil cut her off. She wasn't going to lie for him. 'Forgive me. I received your letters but I haven't found myself able to read them.'

'I don't understand.' Bemusement shaded the sorrow in Secaris's gaze as he halted. 'What has all this been for?'

'For a Lescar where mothers don't weep for dead sons.' Aremil spoke before he could help himself. 'Where the weak and vulnerable are cherished and protected.'

'We gave you the best life we could!' Swift anger roughened Secaris's reply.

'Believe me, I bear no grudges.' At least the helpless jerk of Aremil's head emphasised his words. 'I know I have been much more fortunate than most in my situation.'

'We won't name Matrim as Draximal's heir.' Duchess Nisina was still wrapped in her fear and grief. 'Don't send your soldiers to kill him. Show his sisters mercy. If they quit any claim on Draximal, let them marry into Tormalin and swear not to pursue their children. They're good girls, truly, and Matrim never hoped to rule.' She stumbled over her pleas, terrified tears pouring down her cheeks.

'I will cede the rule of Draximal to you and we will go into exile,' the duke said stiffly. 'As long as you promise to end this slaughter of innocents, I will swear whatever oaths you demand.'

'Your Grace!' Aremil tried to curb his anger. 'Whatever you think of me—'

Wracked with emotion, a tremor ran down his arm. His hand jerked and knocked over the tisane. Failla bent to gather up the glass and its holder, sopping up the spill with her apron.

Aremil wanted to tell her to leave it. He opened his mouth but his chest was too tight. If he spoke, he knew he'd start coughing.

'You say you're hoping for something better?' Duke Secaris was searching his face. 'You and whoever helped bring all this misery upon us? What is your plan for Lescar?'

'We will devise a fair system of governance.' It took every scrap of self-control that Aremil could muster to answer clearly. 'Through debates with nobles and scholars committed to peace, and with the guildmasters' and merchants' councils, and with the priests who administer the shrines and their charities, to give the most humble a voice.'

'What right have commoners and craftsmen to say who rules them?' Duke Secaris was genuinely perplexed. 'The natural order cannot be denied.'

Aremil would have tried to explain but a cramp was tightening around his chest like a leather strap. His temples throbbed with a ferocious headache.

'That's a discussion for another time,' Failla said with scarcely veiled anger.

Provoked, Secaris was glad to vent his frustration on her. 'His parents should have first claim on his time.'

'I can't bear this.' Bursting into noisy weeping, Duchess Nisina stumbled blindly for the door.

'Let me help you.' Lord Cullough hurriedly offered his arm. 'Let me summon my wife.'

His voice faded as he escorted the sobbing woman down the corridor. With an incoherent exclamation of anguish, Duke Secaris followed, kicking the door closed with a slam.

Failla turned to Aremil. 'Are you all right?'

He closed his eyes and leaned back, nodding mutely. Sweat prickled beneath his shirt and he felt vilely light-headed. The parlour had felt cold all morning. Now it was stiflingly hot. Could Failla open a window? Could he ask her without succumbing to murderous coughing?

'I'll get you another tisane.'

Aremil heard her gather up the tray and hurry away. Then he felt an unwelcome urgency in his bladder. He gripped the arms of his chair in frustration.

No. He wasn't going to wait like a helpless child, and risk soaking his breeches and the cushions beneath him. At very least he could get himself to the discreet closet across the hall, to find the relief of a chamber pot.

Aremil reached for his crutches, banging them against the table. He hissed, exasperated by his clumsiness, and had to stifle another brutal cough. Wincing, he swallowed a putrid taste in the back of his mouth.

Tucking the crutches under his arms, he forced himself to his feet. Too fast. He found himself unable to do more than stand motionless as the room swayed around him.

The dizziness subsided but now his head ached worse than ever. How by all that was sacred and profane was he going to work any Artifice today? Irritation only exacerbated the pounding in his head. Should he take more poppy tincture? But the medicine impeded aetheric enchantments in its own way, slowing his wits as well as his digestion.

He took a cautious step, cramps tormenting his weak legs. He shifted his crutches, first one then the other, and took another stubborn step.

Instead of the carpet, his soft shoe found something hard and round. It slid away, taking his foot with it. He had no hope of keeping his balance. As his other ankle turned beneath him, his crutches slipped away. Aremil fell hard onto the floor.

All the breath was jolted from his chest. He fought in vain to draw air into his burning lungs. Success, on the edge of oblivion, only provoked an agonising convulsion of coughing. His gorge rose. Fresh terror seized him. If he vomited as he struggled to breathe, he could very well choke to death.

His vision blurred. The last thing he saw was the silver tisane ball gleaming on the carpet. That had been his downfall. Then darkness overwhelmed him.

Chapter Twelve
Tathrin

Carif,
in the Dukedom of Parnilesse,
29th of For-Winter

'How've you fared since we last met?' Sorgrad asked Reniack genially.

Gren glowered. 'We didn't expect to see you here.'

'I'll wager you didn't,' Jettin said smugly.

At Ekarre's nod, the Pine Martens silently rose and moved away.

Tathrin rubbed the back of his neck, though he supposed he shouldn't be surprised by a sudden headache. How were they going to get out of this? Any revelation of Sorgrad's wizardry would put paid to any hopes of recruiting mercenaries for their militias. It could turn the whole Carifate against them, given how often he'd heard hired swords agree that the only good mage was a dead mage.

What if such hostility encompassed all who'd fought with the Soluran, and who now held some semblance of power in Carluse? This could all rebound on them to Reniack's considerable benefit.

'We've been in Inchra.' Matching Sorgrad's conversational tone, the rabble-rouser took a seat at a nearby table. 'We've allies commanding the town council there as well as in Brynock now.'

'Ready to direct Parnilesse's future for the good of all,' Jettin interjected as he sat down, 'not just the noble-born and wealthy.'

'Like your dad?' Gren raised golden eyebrows. 'Isn't he wealthy? And what about folk who don't want your hands on their reins?'

Before the scowling youth could reply, Reniack's gesture cut him short, just as Sorgrad's glance warned off Gren. The younger Mountain Man turned away, throwing ostentatiously casual trios of runes onto the table before him.

The three-sided bones rattled, each landing with one engraved rune upright, another showing reversed. Half of the symbols were reckoned stronger than the others; Water quenched Fire, the Harp's resonance outlasting the cry of the Horn. The Wolf hunted the Deer while the Oak overshadowed the Pine. Depending how the heavenly rune fell, though, with the Sun, the Greater Moon and the Lesser the only runes that had no reverse, sometimes the weak could still overcome the strong.

Tathrin contemplated Reniack's shaven head. What did the rabble-rouser intend by making his mutilated ears so noticeable? Because Tathrin knew his every move was shrewdly calculated.

'You were in Inchra when you heard we were here?' Turning his head, Sorgrad snapped his fingers towards the bar counter. 'More brandy, if you please.'

'We were on our way back to Parnilesse,' Reniack corrected him. 'And yes, word soon reached us. We have a good many friends hereabouts.'

'Don't we all?' Sorgrad smiled at the girl bringing clean goblets and another blue bottle. Handing her a silver mark, he poured a drink for Reniack and for Jettin before saluting them with his own cup. 'Saedrin send you good health.'

Tathrin was relieved to see the tension in the drinking den evaporating. Conversations returned to their previous informality and swords and daggers were mostly sheathed. When a hard-faced woman went to leave, Reniack's minions let her pass through the door without comment.

Reniack and Jettin were both dressed like the mercenaries who accompanied them, their badge a unicorn's head. Tathrin did his best to count them all. As well as a couple of men on each door, a handful or so leaned on the tavern counter while another trio lounged around a table a few strides away.

'You must have had a few days' hard riding,' Sorgrad observed.

'How did you enjoy your voyage?' Jettin asked Tathrin. 'I see you managed not to spend it hung over the ship's rail spewing up your guts. Congratulations.'

Tathrin smiled and nodded. He had barely suffered any seasickness, unlike the nausea that assailed him whenever Sorgrad's arcane mastery over the air shifted them from place to place.

And now it was certain that Jettin was using Artifice to spy on them.

'The weather favoured our journey.' Reniack continued talking as if the younger man hadn't spoken. 'We'll take our ease on the way back to Parnilesse,' he told Sorgrad with a confident smile, 'making sure to enlist every village and hamlet between here and there to our cause.'

'And after Winter Festival?' Sorgrad contemplated the goblet in his hands. 'You'll make your representations to Hardrew and Quirton?'

'They'll soon fall into step,' Reniack assured him. 'If they know what's good for them.'

Sorgrad looked up and smiled. 'Don't let us keep you from your business.'

Reniack stared back unblinking. 'Your business here is concluded. Get on your ship and sail away.'

'I'm sorry.' Sorgrad sounded genuinely contrite. 'But your writ doesn't run in the Carifate.'

Tathrin wanted to know what the mercenaries within earshot might be making of this exchange, but didn't want to draw attention to himself by looking around.

'You and your friends betray all freeborn Lescari.' Reniack leaned forwards, his expression ugly. 'That bitch Charoleia is talking terms with Tormalin's Emperor—'

'She's doing her utmost to keep his Imperial Majesty's legions from stamping you into the mud,' Sorgrad countered.

'Horseshit,' sneered Reniack.

So Jettin was also using his Artifice to spy on Charoleia, if he knew she had met with Emperor Tadriol. But Tathrin wondered how much the young adept was really learning if he truly believed she was ready to betray them. He must ask Aremil—

'Let Tadriol come,' Jettin challenged. 'We'll fight every prince of Tormalin!'

'Parnilesse will be free,' Reniack said with a nod. 'We'll carry that freedom to Triolle and Draximal—'

'And to every last corner of Lescar!' Jettin asserted.

'—and we will have our revenge,' Reniack concluded with menace.

Tathrin realised they were seeing the Parnilesse man in his true colours.

He had seen Reniack wearing everything from rags fit for the gutter to a silver-buttoned doublet and breeches, as much at ease in any garb. Now he realised the rabble-rouser had always been playing a role. He was as consummate an actor as the men and women who strutted in Vanam's fabled playhouses. Reniack's every step had been calculated, whether he was striding barefoot through the streets, proclaiming the rights of the humblest to shelter and justice, or piously attending some shrine confraternity meeting, seducing merchants into seditious dissatisfaction with their liege lords.

Now Tathrin saw something new in his eyes. Reniack had discarded all pretence. With his head shaved to grizzled stubble and his beard cropped short, the barrel-chested man looked like some tavern brawler, driven by a brutish love of violence.

Was it that simple? Had they been so mistaken, so deceived? For all his high-flown claims, was Reniack simply out to avenge his own lifetime of suffering and insults as the son of a Carifate whore? The more noble-born his victims, the more vicious he seemed to be towards them. Tathrin wondered if such a base-born appetite for vengeance could ever be sated.

Sorgrad's cold blue gaze fixed on Jettin. 'I don't know what you think you know, lad, but you're wrong.'

'You think Charoleia would let Trissa's death count for nothing?' Gren's lip curled. 'Like some hackle-finch discarded for advantage in a game of white raven?'

Reniack smiled unpleasantly. 'I might have believed she was true if I didn't know the cripple has been lured back to his birthright.'

'Whatever do you mean?' Sorgrad managed to sound faintly amused.

Reniack shared a malicious look of pleasure with Jettin. 'Your friend Aremil has had a most affecting reunion with his noble parents, this very morning.'

'He's quite overwhelmed.' Jettin laughed spitefully.

Tathrin tensed. He knew how tormented Aremil had been by Secaris of Draximal's unopened letters. No wonder he hadn't reached through the aether today if he had been brought face to face with the duke and duchess. But what had really happened? Could Jettin hear what was said when he looked through the aether? Tathrin was beginning to doubt that. He must ask Aremil.

'You knew he was Draximal's heir and you never thought to tell me.' Reniack spat his contempt into the sawdust smeared across the floor.

'You didn't let us know what you planned for Duke Orlin.' Sorgrad glanced at Jettin. 'You owe us a reckoning there, lad.'

Jettin stiffened defiantly. 'You've no notion what I've learned since we last met.'

Now Tathrin recalled Aremil telling him that Kerith and Branca feared Jettin was experimenting with Artifice's more problematic enchantments.

Gren wagged a finger with a smile. 'You'd be surprised what I know about your sort's talents.'

It was remarkable, Tathrin reflected, just how menacing Gren could seem while apparently being so amiable. Suddenly Jettin wasn't looking quite so bold, running a defiant hand through his tangled curls.

'You leave the lad alone,' Reniack chided. 'You don't want your own secrets known, Master M— Master Maspin.'

Gren glanced at his brother and turned back to his rune stones, casting another spread of three.

Tathrin recalled Branca saying there was some lost link between Artifice and the ancient symbols of the Storm, the Calm, the North Wind from the Mountains and the Zephyr, the Southern Sea breeze.

Thus far, Vanam's scholars had concluded the weather runes distinguished different aetheric enchantments. Some had physical effects just as a storm shook a tree's branches. Calm, serene enchantments rendered an adept immune to physical assault. The cold wind from the Mountains symbolised an adept forcing an unwilling mind, just as Kerith had done to Failla. Subtle southern breezes hinted at aetheric abilities to influence another's behaviour, all unsuspected.

So what exactly could Jettin do? And what had happened to Aremil?

'I don't know what your boy's told you,' Sorgrad told Reniack, 'but Master Aremil has no interest in restoring the old order.'

Tathrin shifted on his stool.

'Need a piss, long lad?' Gren enquired.

Tathrin caught the glint in the Mountain Man's cornflower eyes. 'Yes, as it happens.'

Jettin laughed. 'A tapster's son who can't hold his ale?'

'We'll show you the latrines on your way to the dock.' Reniack got to his feet. 'If I see you in Parnilesse again,' he added, 'I'll have all your throats cut.'

'Not man enough to do it yourself?' Sorgrad rose up and cracked his knuckles. 'How about Duke Orlin and Duchess Sherista?'

'Oh, I had their blood on my hands,' Reniack assured him, 'warm and—'

Sorgrad's punch silenced his brutal boast.

As Reniack stumbled backwards, his nose bleeding, a wiry ally strode forward, his sword half-drawn.

Sorgrad was quicker, already holding the three-legged stool he'd been sitting on. Before the wiry mercenary got his blade clear of its scabbard, Sorgrad clubbed him round the head. The man fell like a poleaxed steer. That gave the man at his shoulder pause for thought, just long enough for Sorgrad to down him with the stool as well.

'Kill them!' Reniack said thickly through his broken nose.

More men were approaching, weapons drawn. Gren was ready, holding a bench to batter anyone fool enough to come within reach.

Tathrin spared a breath to look around the tavern. No one was coming to their aid. Those closest were simply moving away, careful of their ale.

He saw that Jettin looked aghast and recalled what Aremil had said – that Kerith and Branca feared Reniack's villainous character was overwhelming the younger man's will. Drawing a dagger, Tathrin reached for the young adept. Perhaps, if they could get him away from Reniack—

Before Tathrin could grab him, Jettin realised his peril. He stumbled backwards, shoving chairs into Tathrin's path.

He kicked them away, taller and stronger than the young Vanamese. They might just get out of here if he could get his blade to Jettin's throat. Just as long as Reniack valued him as highly as he should.

But where was he? Tathrin blinked. He couldn't see Jettin at all. All the approaching men were now blurred, as though he peered through rain-streaked glass.

Reaching for his sword, he couldn't find the hilt. Tathrin groped frantically at his hip but his numb fingers closed on empty air. Someone shoved hard at his shoulder, sending him staggering backwards. But there was no one there. Even reeling like a drunkard, Tathrin could see that much.

He nearly fell headlong on the sawdusted floor, stomach hollow and mouth dry. Twisted shadows flickered around him. He flailed frantically with his fists, all the while terrified that he would feel a blade biting into his flesh. The steel plates sewn into his jerkin might protect his vitals but his arms and legs were unarmoured. Which phantasm held the sword that could be the death of him?

Whatever was amiss didn't affect his ears. A nervous laugh cut him to the quick. Jettin thought this was funny?

Fury burned through Tathrin's fear. Before he realised he had reached for it, his hand closed on his sword hilt. He ripped the long blade free and swept it around at waist height. That should keep his would-be killers at bay.

Abruptly his vision cleared. Gren had already laid three men on the floor, groaning amid the filth. A fourth, bearded and burly, had grabbed the other end of the bench.

Tathrin winced. Gren was strong but the bearded man could have taken on Reher the blacksmith back in Carluse. The bearded man grinned and hauled, using all his height and weight. Gren simply let go and the man fell back with a crash to stun himself on a table's edge.

Sorgrad was ringed by four murderously intent men. Each had a dagger, as did Sorgrad, though he'd discarded the stool.

Tathrin choked on a warning as the man behind Sorgrad made his move. Distraction could be fatal. But somehow, someone's glance had betrayed that attack to the Mountain Man. As the man lunged, Sorgrad stepped backwards, stooping down. So much taller, the mercenary couldn't curb his rush forward, sprawling helplessly across Sorgrad's back.

With some shift of his weight, Sorgrad used his hips like a wrestler and threw the man into the attacker on his off-hand. They fell hard in a tangle of limbs and furniture.

The remaining pair grabbed Sorgrad's arms. With one on each side as he straightened up, they apparently robbed him of any freedom to move. To Tathrin's horror, Sorgrad seemed to sag with defeat.

Then he saw that all Reniack's men had hold of was Sorgrad's hands. The Mountain Man ducked and twisted completely around, stepping right under his own dagger. Pulled off balance, his startled attackers stumbled into each other as Sorgrad's hands crossed. The mercenaries' heads clashed with a sickening thump. One fell, knocked senseless. The other collapsed with Sorgrad's dagger embedded in his shoulder.

Tathrin saw Ekarre and his long-haired associate had Reniack himself in a painful hold. As the rabble-rouser struggled, he winced and yielded.

Jettin turned to run.

'No you don't, lad.' One of the drinking den's customers blocked the young adept's path. 'You want to play here, you play by our rules. Stand your ground or take your beating.'

The disinterested mercenary shoved the young adept straight into Gren's embrace.

'No, please,' Jettin begged.

Gren's hands were closing around his neck. Jettin could only struggle for a moment before he was strangled into unconsciousness. Gren let him fall to the floor.

'No!' Tathrin shouted, seeing the Mountain Man reach for a dagger.

'Enough!' The tavern-keeper walked out from behind his counter, a heavy cudgel in one hand. 'That'll do,' he warned one of Reniack's men who was trying to rise despite Ekarre's female lieutenant's boot planted on his chest.

'You and yours are fairly beaten.' The tavern-keeper glared at Reniack and around the room at his minions. 'Take yourselves off or that unicorn badge will be shit on across the Carifate. You know the rules.'

'This isn't over.' Reniack spat a fine spray of blood at Sorgrad.

'No indeed.' Sorgrad smiled through the bruises darkening on his face.

'You three have till sunset to conclude your business and be gone.' The tapster jabbed a forefinger at them.

'We welcome your forbearance.' Sorgrad's courteous bow prompted chuckles from the onlookers.

'Get the boy!' Reniack slapped one of his bloodied men and pointed at Jettin, now lying behind a fallen table where Gren had apparently rolled him.

Tathrin moved to bar their way. 'He's—'

Gren laid a firm hand on his arm. 'He's one of their own and they've claimed him. That's the rules.'

Unwilling, Tathrin stepped back as one of Reniack's henchmen hoisted Jettin up, limp as a leaky wineskin.

As the defeated mercenaries filed out, the drinking den's customers began righting the tables and chairs. The tapster returned to his counter and threw a broom to a sullen youth. Another lad appeared to strew more sawdust on the spilled ale. Tathrin coughed on the reek.

'Come on. We're not done here yet.' Gren urged him towards the table where Sorgrad was once again sitting with Ekarre and his companions.

Tathrin dropped onto a stool. 'I never knew there are rules in a tavern brawl.'

'Just to keep it fair.' The long-haired man grinned.

His bearded colleague nodded. 'If you knock one of their lads off the board, we don't let him back into play.'

'Just like a game of white raven?' Tathrin shook his head in disbelief.

'Why else do you think I started a fight?' Sorgrad winced as blood trickled from his split lip.

'If they'd caught us outside, we could have been outnumbered.' Gren ran a hand through his bloodied hair. Fresh bleeding glistened in a gash above his ear.

'I can put a stitch in that,' the woman offered.

'What now?' Tathrin demanded.

'We carry on.' Sorgrad looked surprised that he needed to ask. 'Then we go north to the rampart the day after tomorrow and march with all the mercenaries who've shown the good sense to take up our offer.'

'Reniack won't attack us again or his name really will be shit in the Carifate,' Gren agreed.

'Who does he think died and made him High King?' growled the scarred and bearded man.

Tathrin wondered how far and how fast this tale of Reniack's unguarded arrogance would spread. He caught a glimpse of satisfaction deep in Gren's eyes and wondered if that had also been part of the plan, when he had started the fight. But could such news do Reniack's cause much harm beyond the idiosyncratic confines of the Carifate?

'Will you help us find the sergeants we need,' Sorgrad asked Ekarre bluntly, 'to bring lasting peace to Lescar, who deserve the rewards that will bring?'

'What do you people plan for the Carifate?' the long-haired man asked, more curious than challenging.

Sorgrad shrugged. 'We have no plans for the Carifate. Folk can live here in peace along with the rest of Lescar or they can go to find some fight to earn their coin elsewhere.'

'Reniack can say what he likes about having everyone bow their neck to his yoke,' Gren agreed, 'but that's not going to happen. There won't be another fighting season after this winter, not inside Lescar, and that includes Parnilesse.'

'There's a fair amount we can't tell you,' Sorgrad apologised. 'But you know the quality of Lady Rochiel's word.'

Tathrin watched the mercenaries exchange glances before coming to some unspoken conclusion.

'We'll help you drive those renegades out of Wyril,' Ekarre said finally, 'for a consideration. Then we'll see where that leaves us.'

'For a handsome consideration,' the woman amended.

'You can't say fairer than that.' Sorgrad snapped his fingers at the tapster. 'Ale and white brandy, if you please?'

'*Tathrin?*'

He closed his eyes, startled by the unfamiliar voice in his head.

'*What's happened to Aremil?*'

Kerith sounded inexplicably afraid. That sent shivers down Tathrin's spine. But he was no adept. He couldn't hold a conversation through the aether without actually speaking aloud and he certainly couldn't talk here.

Tathrin rose to his feet. 'Excuse me, I do need the privy.'

'I'll watch your back.' Gren already had a dagger in one hand. 'In case Reniack's left any scum hiding behind the pisspot.'

Once they were outside, he quickly led Tathrin to a stinking wooden ease-house. 'Keep your voice down,' he warned before closing the door to stand guard.

'*When did you last speak to Aremil?*' Kerith demanded.

'Not since yesterday morning.' Now Tathrin could feel the scholar's fear, not merely hear it in his words. Apprehension gripped him. 'If something's happened, Jettin may well be behind it. He said something about Aremil being overcome. He's mastered some arcane enchantments—'

About to try explaining what had happened in the bar fight, Tathrin found he was alone with his thoughts. The scholar had gone.

Tathrin was even more unnerved. Had something happened to all their adepts? Had Jettin recovered sufficiently to somehow deny them their conduits through the aether?

Could he persuade Sorgrad to scry for Charoleia and Branca? Or would provoking the magewoman Jilseth simply make matters worse?

Chapter Thirteen
Branca

**The Rope Walk,
Solland, in the Tormalin Empire,
30th of For-Winter**

THIS DOCKSIDE DISTRICT wasn't so very different from Vanam's. The wind carried the taste of salt, unknown in her lakeside home, but the business of maintaining and repairing ships was the same.

Rhythmic sawing drifted from workshops shaping spars and blocks. The tang of hot metal cut through the morning chill along with the stifling reek of molten pitch. Ships' storekeepers hurried from chandlery to grocery while sailmakers carried bolts of canvas as wide as they were tall.

The brick-built warehouses were quieter, waiting to open their wide doors to the bales and boxes unloaded and dragged on broad sledges that skimmed iron rails driven into the dockside.

In between the waterside and the warehouses, the Rope Walk cut an undeviating line. It had been laid out to provide the longest unbroken cables that the lay of the land would allow. The shallow roof sheltered the endless lengths of hemp yarn laid out by the prentice lads, while the open sides let the breeze carry the equally endless dust away. The chill didn't bother rope-makers sweating over the spinning handles that drove the whirling gears that twisted rope from countertwist strands.

As long as no one hampered their work, the rope-makers were content to allow passers-by to pause beneath the long roof. Such visitors brought them news from all the rest of the docks. Prudent craftsmen and tradesmen took their breaks here, sheltered from summer sun or winter sleet and too far from their workshops to be too readily called back to work.

No one looked twice at Branca in her dowdy gown and cheap frieze cloak, just another wife or daughter running some errand.

'Mistress.' Tecaul was a lean man, not so much aged as cured like a Derrice ham by the salt and wind off the sea.

'Good day.' Branca smiled and handed him a packet wrapped in oiled cloth along with a discreet purse.

The evening tide would see another consignment of freshly printed broadsheets cross the Gulf. Once they reached Relshaz, curiosity about events in Lescar would be satisfied according to Charoleia's wishes. Branca had already dispatched a subtly different package to a ship heading for Derrice and the other west-facing ports of Tormalin.

As Tecaul departed, she took a last clean breath of the breeze and steeled herself for the stink of courier dove dung. That was a necessary evil when she escorted the crates of courier birds delivered by ships from Talagrin only knew where. She took them to the silent old man tending his loft in a backstreet. He knew Charoleia as Mistress Lanagyre and occasionally betrayed a secretive smile when he handed Branca a bag of the silver message holders that fastened to the birds' legs.

'*Are you alone?*'

'Kerith?' Taken unawares, Branca spoke aloud. She looked around but thankfully no one had noticed.

'*Have you spoken to Aremil?*'

He was sitting in the Carluse chamberlain's office at Aremil's desk. Always stern-faced, Kerith looked more dour than ever.

His inexplicable dread stabbed Branca like a knife.

'Wait a moment.'

She made her way to the remote end of the Rope Walk, where empty seats were scattered for the women who secured the ropes' ends with needle and twine. Branca sat in a chair wrought from a half-barrel.

'Not for a day or so.' Now she had a firm hold on her Artifice, she could reply without actually talking. She opened her shabby reticule, as if she were searching inside for something.

Kerith hesitated, worrying her still more. '*He has been taken ill.*'

'At Satheron Manor?' Branca felt the chill wind cut right through her.

Aremil had seemed unusually distant when they had exchanged what little they'd learned since their last conversation, but she had thought that was her own fault, for keeping him at arm's length for so long. She'd tried to persuade herself it was for the best. But if he had been concealing some illness—

'*He has a high fever and a putrid cough and since he collapsed, Failla cannot rouse him.*'

Branca caught a glimpse of some other sickbed, where an old woman gasped her last for lack of coin to buy her medicine. Was that Failla's recollection or Kerith's?

'Does Lord Cullough have a household physician?' demanded Branca. 'Or a skilled apothecary to call on?'

'*Failla wants to bring him back to Master Welgren.*'

Branca was cruelly torn. There was no one she would rather trust to care for Aremil, but how dangerously might he suffer on such a journey through the worsening weather?

'Is that wise?'

As she silently voiced her concern, she felt the full force of Kerith's own doubts. But there was something more.

'Sorgrad? You want magecraft to bring him back?'

Wouldn't that fall foul of the Archmage's edict? Branca shivered. She had no wish to encounter Jilseth again, Planir the Black's merciless mouthpiece, whom Sorgrad had so blatantly defied in the nightmare of Adel Castle.

'*I have talked to Master Welgren, and he thinks it could be safely done by slow stages, if Failla sees him warmly wrapped and sustained with honeyed water and soup—*'

'Kerith!' Branca tried to curb her fears. 'What are you not telling me?'

'*There may be something more.*'

She heard Kerith's voice as if from a great distance. All around, the bustle of the dockyard continued, oblivious to her distress

'*I sought Tathrin through the aether when I couldn't find Aremil. He told me something strange. Jettin knew that Aremil had fallen ill before any of the rest of us.*'

Branca didn't understand his apprehension. 'We've suspected Jettin of spying on us all.'

'*But I'm utterly unable to find Aremil. Even when someone is sleeping you know Artifice can touch them!*'

In her mind's eye, Branca saw Kerith pacing around the chamberlain's room.

'How hard have you tried?'

'*You think I should force him? Break down his defences?*'

Kerith's fury stung like a slap to her face. Branca was shaken by a sudden vision of the pillared hall so integral to Aremil's Artifice. Stained glass lay in shards on the floor and a double door at one end had been smashed to kindling. Windswept darkness lay beyond.

'*Didn't you hear me? I can't even find him!*'

'Forgive me!'

Branca knew how utterly Kerith detested what he had done to Failla, forcing her to confess she had betrayed their conspiracy to Duchess Litasse's spy. But surely this was different?

'*If you think you can find him, if you wish to try rousing him through Artifice—*'

In a searing instant, Branca saw Kerith knew all her fears. How she dared not venture so deeply into Aremil's sleeping thoughts. Then he would see completely into her self-loathing over her part in the spy Pelletria's death.

With a gasp, Branca recoiled, wrapping every veil of Artifice she could around her innermost self.

Why had no one warned them of this unwanted intimacy? How many other secrets were kept by Vanam's scholars, supposedly so adept with Aetheric lore?

She caught an echo of such thoughts from Kerith, but subtly different.

'Jettin? What makes you think he knows something of this?'

'We thought we would learn so much about Artifice by using it across these distances, in service of this honourable endeavour. At least we have proved the old adage: there are none so truly foolish as the wise.'

Kerith's abiding wrath at Jettin's betrayal was now tainted by fear that the younger scholar had mastered some truly dangerous Artifice. In the next instant, Branca saw what Jettin had done to Tathrin in that Carifate tavern. Like Kerith, she had no notion what enchantments the younger adept had worked to bewilder Tathrin like that.

'If I had known where this path would take us, I would never have set foot outside Vanam.'

His bitter chagrin was painfully close to her own treacherous thoughts in the blackest watches of the night. But Kerith's thoughts also rang with defiant anxiety.

'This betrayal may not all be Jettin's fault. He has spent so much time in Reniack's company. He was always the one to reach him with Artifice when Reniack was apart from the rest of us.'

'Perhaps.' Branca wouldn't have entertained this notion in Vanam, understanding more theory of Artifice than its practice. But now? 'But he has still betrayed us, spied for Reniack and attempted worse.'

'Because he's been unduly influenced by the man's ideas. You know the force of his personality!'

She felt Kerith's obstinate conviction that some excuse could be found for Jettin and did her best to curb her own anger. Though if the young adept had done something to hurt Aremil—

'We should talk to Sorgrad and Gren about these Mountain Artificers, the *sheltya*. Perhaps their tales will offer some clue.' She knotted her fingers in her lap. 'In the meantime, I will see if I can find Aremil.'

'Very well.'

The brusqueness of Kerith's departure couldn't hide his lingering shame. The scholar felt both responsible for Jettin's perfidy, and guilty that he had somehow failed the younger man.

Branca pressed her lips tight together. Let him fret. She had graver concerns. What had happened to Aremil?

She made certain no one was watching her. No, mid-morning's labours were still in full flow.

'*Al daera sa Aremil sast elarmin as feorel.*'

But the lyrical syllables of the enchantment didn't take her to that empty hall. Instead, she stood outside looking at a smoothly crafted wall of grey stone. The dark oak of a double door bristled with iron studs. Boards had been crudely nailed across it. She saw crescent-moon dimples where hammer blows had dented the wood.

Kerith had only imagined windswept darkness beyond this door. There seemed to be sunlight for her, filtered through the watery overcast of winter.

What was behind her? Branca's scalp prickled beneath the linen cap she wore despite Charoleia's objections.

She withdrew sufficient of her consciousness from this eerie Artifice to remind herself that she was safe in Solland. She still sat on the barrel chair in the shelter of the Rope Walk. No one had spared her a second glance.

Returning her full attention to Aremil's hall, Branca forced herself to turn around. She saw only emptiness ahead. The milky sky reached down to an unknowable horizon where it met the flat ground. Pale gravel stretched in all directions.

Branca swiftly turned to consider the hall again. It was more modest than it seemed from within; plainly built without aisles or porches, with a steeply tiled roof.

She knew something of Lescari architecture, after all the manors and towns and castles she'd seen on her travels through the summer and autumn. This didn't look familiar. Was it some recollection of the Draximal mansion where Aremil had spent his early childhood?

Was there any other entrance? Or something to be seen from the far side? She took a step and her booted foot crunched on the gravel to break the oppressive silence.

Branca checked herself. Walk widdershins around a shrine and the Eldritch Kin would see you and follow you home. That's what the old tales said. Attract their curiosity and you'd live to rue the day. That's if you were lucky. If you weren't . . .

'Nonsense,' she said aloud.

This place wrought of Artifice was hardly the realm of those shadowy folk, encountered by those bold, foolish or unlucky enough to step through the arc of a rainbow or to stumble through a tear in the twilight.

All the same, she turned to go the other way.

'What's nonsense?' Jettin asked with interest.

'What are you doing here?' Branca was shrill with shock.

'The same as you, I imagine.' Jettin contemplated the outside of the hall. 'Where is our ailing friend?'

'Don't you know?' Branca asked before she could help it.

'Don't you?' Jettin looked at her with interest.

'I know what you did to Tathrin.' She glared at him.

'Do you?' Jettin folded his arms across his chest.

She noted he was dressed for winter travel, wearing a heavy cloak over a long-sleeved leather jerkin with a thick flannel shirt beneath. His buff breeches and iron-braced boots were splashed with mud.

'Do you know *how* I did it?' He challenged her with a cold smile.

Branca was perturbed by the hardness in his gaze. Back in Vanam, his eyes had been so lively with merriment.

'Have you mastered such enchantments?' She couldn't hide her desire to know that much. 'Or was that attack some collision of luck and instinct?'

Jettin shook his head, his black curls shorn. 'That's for me to know and you to find out.'

Irritation drove out Branca's unease. 'We're swapping taunts like brats in a dame school? Is that the scholarship you learned from Mentor Tonin?'

'Mentor Tonin doesn't share half that he knows,' snapped Jettin. 'Why should I share what I've learned with him?'

'Where did you find this supposed lore?' Branca coloured her question with scepticism just short of disbelief.

Jettin succumbed to her lure. 'Parnilesse.'

'Parnilesse?' Branca was incredulous.

Jettin thrust his jaw forwards, darkly stubbled. 'It's just over the river from Tormalin. Emperor Tadriol has been searching out aetheric lore lurking in noble archives, in search of a magic not subject to the Archmage's writ.'

Branca uneasily recalled Mentor Tonin saying much the same. She nodded but did not speak, hoping to tempt Jettin further.

He nodded, satisfied by her apparent capitulation. 'Duke Orlin was no fool, for all he was a murderous brute. He was paying his own spies to steal lore from Tormalin. We found some interesting tomes when we took possession of Parnilesse Castle.'

'Now you're using these enchantments against friends, in Reniack's interests?' Branca scowled. 'What would Mentor Tonin think of that?'

Jettin shrugged. 'I don't care.'

The weight of truth in his words oppressed her dreadfully.

'Why not? What do you want?'

'Freedom.' Jettin moved closer. She could feel his breath on her cheek. 'To be free to explore my magic as I see fit, to go where I want and do as I choose, without you or Kerith or Tonin or my father or anyone else telling me what to do.'

'You're still doing Reniack's bidding.' Though Branca realised she saw no shadow of the rabble-rouser following Jettin, heard no echo of his words. She refused to yield. 'Will you claim the same freedoms that Minelas enjoyed?'

She flung every vile recollection at Jettin; all the renegade wizard's depravity that she'd discovered when she had been forced to sneak into his mind, to turn his thoughts from the pleasures of torturing Trissa and Charoleia to reminiscences of earlier murders.

Branca bludgeoned the younger adept with the dead mage's arrogance; his belief that his elemental talents lifted him above any mundane-born, that he was entitled to whatever rewards he desired, treating innocent girls as his playthings to be discarded when he had broken them.

She didn't know if she'd ever be free of the stains of Minelas's corruption. How could she ever share such repellent knowledge with Aremil?

Jettin took a step backwards but Branca didn't see what she'd sought in his eyes. Instead she saw derision.

'You chastise me for unwarranted Artifice? When you slid inside a man's head and deceived him so utterly that you made him your witless puppet?'

Before Branca could protest, the young adept was gone, leaving her alone in this desolation.

Had she made things better or worse? At least Branca found she believed Jettin, when he said he knew nothing of what had happened to Aremil.

But where was he? She closed her eyes to reject this uncanny emptiness.

Hearing a stealthy noise, she reopened them. What was that whisper at the very edge of hearing? Not a voice but something else.

Branca looked this way and that but saw nothing that hadn't been there in the nothingness before.

Was something hidden by the building? Had Jettin known what it was and fled? Or had he sent something here to attack her? Could his newfound Artifice do that?

She strode around the corner of the building. Whatever Jettin might try, she'd faced worse when she had used her Artifice against Minelas. How dare he rebuke her for that? Had he risked his life in this undertaking to free all of Lescar?

There was nothing around the corner but the featureless far side of the hall. Branca marched onwards but her boot skidded on the gravel. Looking down, she saw the ground was darker here. Halting, she watched it grow darker still.

Water was steadily seeping through the stones. Points of light glittered, then puddles began running together into glistening sheets.

Was this some manifestation of Aremil's illness? Was it some unpleasantness of Jettin's, directed at her or at Aremil?

Now the water was soaking the dusty leather of her boots.

Branca cut short the liquid syllables of her Artifice echoing in a remote recess of her mind. She blinked to clear this place from her vision and see the busy dockyard once more. She must tell Charoleia—

But the Solland Rope Walk was nowhere to be seen. Branca couldn't even feel the unforgiving wood of the barrel where she sat. She was trapped in this arcane emptiness with cold, clear water seeping through her boot buttonholes to soak her woollen stockings.

The overcast sky was darkening. Dark billows of cloud bulged with rain. How much faster would the waters rise? How could she get away?

Branca ran back to the door of the hall. It was still securely barred. She pulled at the nailed planks, a futile effort.

'Aremil!' she screamed.

A rising wind snatched her words away. It swirled around the hall, buffeting her coming and going. The waters ruffled to lap noisily at the stonework. Dust blown from somewhere stung her eyes.

Branca pressed her back against the door, shivering in the biting cold. On the far horizon, lightning seared a purple sky.

She remembered a childhood storm which flooded half the low-lying districts of Vanam. The worst weather in three generations had lashed the lake and all the towns around it for five incessant days.

Hundreds had died, drowned in the tempest's first fury or from the cold in the following nights. Those towns that escaped more lightly hadn't been able to help. Vanam's harbour was choked with wreckage from broken boats. Streets were impassable where gales had felled chimneys and ravaged roofs.

Branca recalled the paralysing terror as she and her family fled to the slopes of Vanam's hills below the walls of the upper town. Those lofty gates had swiftly been closed. She remembered her father slipping on his crutches, cursing the university and all its scholars with the foulest obscenities he knew. Her mother had held Branca's hand so tight that she'd feared the bruises would never fade.

Those with carts and horses reached the heights first. Those with family and friends living in such fortunate districts found shelter. Branca and her family had been forced to huddle with the other paupers in the wooded gullies where Vanam's feral pigs foraged amid the city's refuse. They had finally returned to find their humble house half-destroyed and their sodden belongings comprehensively looted.

This time she would drown when that deadly squall arrived.

'*Seldiviar ayemar ekelrath!*'

Branca yelled her defiance at the storm. All at once, she was safe beneath the Solland Rope Walk.

She pressed a trembling hand to her breastbone. If she believed in any gods she would thank them. She certainly owed Mentor Tonin her gratitude for that passing mention of a mysterious incantation tied to the notion of Calm which occasionally had a quelling effect on other enchantments.

But if she told Mentor Tonin about this, she would have to explain how comprehensively Jettin had rejected his training and example. What would happen to the young adept then?

Had he truly meant to kill her? Branca struggled to believe it, recalling Kerith's stubborn advocacy for the youth. She forced herself to breathe more calmly and felt her racing heart slow.

Assuming that had been some spite of Jettin's, how had he found her terrified memory? Or was that his own recollection? Where had Jettin been, when that catastrophe struck Vanam? Wealthy as his father was, they still lived in the lower town—

'Good day, Mistress Branca.'

Startled, she saw a slender young man approaching, as soberly dressed as any clerk. Only a silver and enamel spray of honeysuckle gleamed on his collar. Yadres Den Dalderin.

She hastily gathered her wits. 'Good day, Esquire.'

'Are you taking the sea air?' His amusement told her he doubted that.

'Just running a few errands like yourself.'

'Quite so.' He bowed and offered her his arm. 'Shall we take the air together?'

Branca rose and felt her stocking feet squelch. They were sodden and cold, even though her boots were as dry and dusty as before.

She hastily thrust aside that shock as she searched out some nugget of information she knew Charoleia would be willing to share.

'Have you heard the latest news from Triolle?' She feigned amusement. 'The longer Iruvain lolls in Adrulle, the more loyalty to him melts like snow in a thaw.'

The duke had Charoleia to thank for the tales of his drunken idleness being whispered in every chimney corner. Her broadsheets printed in Solland had nearly the reach of Reniack's.

Yadres Den Dalderin pursed thoughtful lips. 'My uncle tells me Lord Leysen of Sharlac is now Duchess Aphanie's private courier to Duchess Litasse.' He glanced at Branca. 'Shall we see what your mistress might know of this noble?'

'Why not?' She took his arm.

That was at least as urgent news as telling Charoleia of Jettin's newfound audacity.

Chapter Fourteen
Litasse

The Mistle Wreath Inn,
Adrulle, Caladhria
34th of For-Winter

SHE LOOKED DOWN from the window seat into the bustling street, searching in vain for any courier.

These delays were as infuriating as the incessant squeak of the swinging inn sign. Even before all this, some missive too long or insufficiently urgent to warrant a courier dove's dispatch could spend as many as fifteen days making the round trip between Triolle and Sharlac. But now, when her mother's correspondence must first be smuggled out of Lord Rousharn's demesne, then covertly passed to Lord Leysen, then carried along the Great West Road to Abray before finally being sent down the River Rel to Adrulle? Karn had warned her that even a slip of paper fine as onion skin could take twenty days to travel in either direction.

He could do it faster. Litasse was convinced. He would steal fresh horses and evade whatever bandits roamed the roads. But that would take him away and she had no one else to rely on here, certainly not her husband. So she must just wait patiently for her mother's letters.

At least she could wait in comfort thanks to the coin her mother had already sent. If this apartment overlooked the noisy street rather than the peace of the inn's rear gardens, the rooms were warm and clean with polished panelling and mistletoe motif embroideries.

Best of all, she had her own bedchamber with a door to lock against Iruvain. His room was on the other side of this parlour while Karn slept on a truckle bed in here between them. And it seemed her husband wasn't quite shameless enough to bring his would-be mistresses to this well-respected inn. Not now that something of his standing as Triolle's duke had been re-established by her mother's money.

Though Karn told her Iruvain still spent his evenings drinking with foolish Carluse and Sharlac nobles, all drunkenly reassuring themselves they would soon reclaim their domains.

Litasse didn't care. If his insobriety became the stuff of gossip, so much the better. Whatever might be rumoured about her own adultery, she would soon enjoy more sympathy than censure as Karn discreetly spread word of Iruvain's recklessness around the back stairs.

She crossed the room to put another split log on the fire and set the iron tongs back in the basket, careful not to smudge her red gown. Her wardrobe still only held three dresses.

Litasse went back to the spacious bay window to gaze at the dressmaker's over the road. When would that insolent slut of a seamstress finish the gown she had commissioned for the Winter Solstice?

How would they spend the festival? How rowdily did Caladhrian merchants and barge-masters celebrate? Which exiled Lescari nobles might invite them to some more elegant evening of feasting and dancing? Litasse sighed. Her own purse wouldn't run to the most modest entertainment, never mind anything remotely ducal. Doubtless Iruvain would blame her for that.

She gazed over the snow-dusted rooftops and smoking chimneys towards the unseen estates of Caladhria's barons. Could they expect any invitations there? She doubted it. After writing endless courteous letters to the wives and daughters of her father's erstwhile allies, she had yet to receive a single reply.

Hearing a step in the corridor, she swiftly reached for her lace-making pillow. Whoever entered would see a portrait of womanly virtue.

It was Karn. 'Your Grace.' His bow was perfunctory as he offered her letters.

'At last.' She tossed the pillow aside with a clatter of ivory bobbins. 'Have they been tampered with?'

'The ones coming through Sharlac Town are definitely being read.' Karn passed her a sealed parchment packet. 'But they don't know about Lord Leysen's wife's orders to her favourite spice merchant.' He handed her a thinner, grubbier letter.

Throwing the thicker packet on top of the lace pillow, Litasse snapped the seal on the single sheet. Deciphering it was a slower business. It would be quicker with pen and ink but she wouldn't take that risk even with a fire to burn the evidence.

'Lord Rousharn of Nolsedge?' She looked up at Karn, appalled.

He frowned. 'Lady Derenna was deeply involved with the exiles' plots in Vanam—'

'He's to be elevated to my father's rank?' Litasse's hand shook so hard the parchment rattled. 'What right has my lady mother to make so free with my inheritance!'

She bit her lip as Karn took the letter, intent on reading the coded words himself.

'Why did she not assert her own rule as dowager?'

Karn didn't answer, still intent on the page.

Litasse couldn't decide what was more infuriating – his silence or what she knew full well about her mother.

When had her mother ever asserted herself? When had she ever controlled her own fate? Duchess Aphanie's life had been guarded and guided by her father, her brothers and her husband. She had fully expected to live out her days cherished by her adored sons. Such were the expectations she had taught her daughters.

Litasse recalled Lord Rousharn from occasional meetings in her Sharlac girlhood. He soon dominated any gathering with his height and his readiness to state his position on any question. He was always ready to argue with anyone inclined to the contrary. No wonder her father disliked him. No wonder her mother had yielded so feebly to his control of her affairs.

Though Rousharn didn't expect his women to be silent helpmeets, Litasse thought bitterly. In her outmoded gowns and haphazard jewellery, Lady Derenna had been as free with her opinions as her husband. Far from rebuking her, he praised her independence of spirit as their repellent children were raised with a scandalous lack of discipline.

Litasse gazed unseeing out of the window. 'So my witless mother has dashed any hope of reclaiming my position in Sharlac.'

'Don't weep, Your Grace,' said Karn quietly. 'Not yet.'

'How so?' Realising a tear had indeed trickled down her cheek, Litasse angrily wiped it away. She had done enough weeping for a lifetime.

Karn looked thoughtful. 'Lord Rousharn has binding ties with Tormalin. With Duke Secaris's long-standing friendships across the border, their alliance could offer Tadriol and his princes some hope of peace along the Great West Road. While Parnilesse is held by murderous thieves, merchants will surely send their goods by land, not along that hostile shore.'

'Will that make a difference?' Litasse couldn't see how. 'There's still anarchy in Carluse and Triolle and this renegade cripple from Vanam claims to be Draximal's heir.'

Karn smiled briefly. 'He has been struck down by illness.'

'Since when?' Litasse demanded. 'How do you know?'

'Master Hamare still has friends in Carluse Town and Abray.' Karn patted the front of his humble brown doublet. 'So let's consider what our Caladhrian friends will make of Tormalin influence waxing in Sharlac and Draximal.'

'My mother long planned to marry my sisters into noble houses across the border,' Litasse said slowly. 'Duke Secaris has more daughters than sons now.'

'Won't that appal our Caladhrian friends?' Karn suggested. 'Won't they see the sense of supporting Duke Moncan's rightful heiress, his eldest legitimate daughter?'

'Won't they just sit tight and count their coin and sell their wares to whoever will pay?' Litasse demanded bitterly. 'That's all they've done thus far.'

Karn nodded. 'But now there are bandits prowling Lescar's highways. Copses shelter mercenaries thrown off the muster rolls, militiamen who fled the autumn's battles.' He gestured in the direction of the river. 'Caladhria's barons will be hard pressed to send their goods east by land without help from Sharlac and Draximal and that would mean acquiescing to Tormalin demands. Unless Emperor Tadriol's influence in Draximal was balanced by Duke Moncan's daughter ruling Sharlac in her own right.' He paused. 'If this would-be Duke Rousharn is cast down, you'd take Carluse's orphaned daughters under your wing. Supporting them through you would see Caladhrian interests on both sides of the Great West Road protected.'

Litasse desperately wanted to believe all this. Reluctantly, she shook her head. 'Caladhria's barons will look to Duke Ferdain and Marlier first.'

'Ridianne the Vixen turned her coat to support this Soluran.' Karn scowled as though that was a personal insult.

'She's broken with him now,' Litasse pointed out. 'She's sitting tight with the remnants of her army, defying anyone to cross Marlier's borders.'

Karn was still scowling. 'The barons will soon see she's a toothless bitch if those ruffians plaguing Lescar band together, stealing boats and raiding across the Rel.'

'Is that likely?' Litasse asked, uncertain.

'Quite likely, I assure you.' Karn's face cleared. 'Then Caladhria's interests would demand that the barons take action, and upholding Duke Garnot's daughters' interests would do so. None of them will want Marlier seizing Carluse if the Vixen does get off her fat arse to fight. Duke Ferdain would dominate the entire eastern bank of the Rel from the coast to the bridges at Abray.'

'But I would be beholden to Caladhria for my restoration.' Litasse had serious doubts. 'To whoever commanded the forces the barons lent me.'

Karn rubbed his chin. 'Not if His Grace your husband commanded that army.'

'So I must remain shackled to him,' Litasse said unguardedly.

Karn looked at her, all innocence. 'Battlefields are dangerous places, Your Grace. More than one final victory in a campaign has been dimmed by the loss of a captain-general.'

'No—'

Before Litasse could protest that wasn't what she was proposing, the parlour door crashed open. Iruvain strode in. Karn retreated to the fireside, every measure the unobtrusive lackey.

'Make ready to travel, my lady wife.' Iruvain laughed, too raucously. 'You're celebrating Solstice in Marlier this year.'

'It's barely mid-morning,' Litasse observed with contempt, 'and you're already drunk.'

'And you're an adulterous whore, but we've had this conversation before.' Iruvain smiled unpleasantly. 'Shut your mouth and pack your bags and do as you are told, bitch. Or you can go begging barefoot on the streets, or sell yourself, whichever you see fit, Your Grace.'

Litasse bit down on her anger. 'What does Duke Ferdain offer? Will his Vixen lead her army to reclaim Triolle?'

Iruvain's finger wavered in front of her nose. 'You're going to Marlier, my lady wife, and that's all you need to know.'

'You're not coming with me?' At least that was good news.

Now Iruvain smiled with spiteful pleasure. 'I will celebrate Solstice in Ferl where I shall address the Caladhrian parliament. What do you think of that?'

'I think you had better be sober when you do.' She took a quick step back to avoid his slap. Clear-headed, he might have succeeded but the wine was blunting his reactions.

Over his shoulder, she glimpsed Karn's disdain. For the briefest moment, Litasse was tempted. Karn surely knew how to kill Iruvain without anyone accusing her. If she was ever to be free of him, to regain her place in Sharlac—

Iruvain's next words drove such thoughts from her mind.

'I've had a letter from Her Grace your mother.' He reached inside his lilac doublet.

The wool was already stained with wine and grease, Litasse noticed with irritation. Was her coin to further replenish his wardrobe?

'And a letter from His Grace Duke Rousharn of Sharlac.' Iruvain waved a second parchment with malicious satisfaction. 'I will convey his compliments to Caladhria's parliament and assure them he will restore peace to Lescar and see me and Secaris and Ferdain secure in our rightful places.'

Litasse couldn't restrain her fury. '*Lord* Rousharn cannot speak for Sharlac.'

'He can when your lady mother gives him your father's seal and her own approval,' Iruvain taunted. 'She can't want a whore ruling Sharlac, even one she whelped. So you will go to Marlier and tell Duke Ferdain that he can join us and secure a fat portion when we carve up Carluse. Or he can cower beneath his Vixen's paw and wait for whatever scraps we see fit to throw.'

'Don't you think I should honey those words a little?' Litasse asked sarcastically.

'You can lie back and let him lick your honeypot for all I care,' Iruvain retorted. 'Just as long as you make him see sense.'

Litasse folded stubborn arms. 'What army will enforce this peace that Lord Rousharn is so sure he can regain?'

'Tormalin's legions.' Iruvain looked surprised she needed to ask. 'Which will get Caladhria's barons' attention. They had better match Tadriol's forces, if they don't want to be sucking the old cow's hind teat come the end of summer.' He scowled. 'The price will be handing over southern Parnilesse to his Imperial Majesty, but that'll be fair recompense to see Lescar's dukes restored.'

He smiled with sudden smugness. 'The fate of the High King's crown can finally be settled. Everyone will see I am the truest claimant. The Vixen's treachery has discredited Ferdain and who could trust his sons, raised alongside her pack of bastards?'

'The High Kingship?' Litasse couldn't believe her ears. 'You'd renew an empty quarrel that's blighted Lescar for generations?'

This time she wasn't fast enough to escape his slap. 'Shut your mouth,' he snarled, 'and be grateful I can't throw you into the gutter where you belong while I need your mother's support and her open purse.'

Pressing a hand to her stinging cheek, Litasse saw Karn was thinking the same as her. This might be the reverse of the plan they'd devised but every coin had two sides and spent the same whichever was uppermost.

This scheme of Iruvain's could well work and where would that leave her? The disgraced wife of a resurgent duke, with no value in her bloodline and a whole gaggle of unwed maidens now with rightful claims on Carluse and Draximal, and somehow, somewhere, there must still be an heir or heiress to Parnilesse.

Iruvain took her silence for acquiescence. He looked down, the wine-borne brightness in his eyes dulled. 'This morning hasn't only brought good news. Roreth is dead.'

'How—?' Litasse began.

'At Pannal, you foolish slut.' Iruvain raised his fist.

Litasse took a step back, still pressing her hand to her face. 'How did you find out? What's happened to his body?'

She blinked away unexpected tears for her brother-by-marriage. When Lord Roreth had failed to reappear, she'd wondered if he had run away. Perhaps he had fled to that new land across the ocean, where the Tormalin Empire had founded their colony. Litasse had half-hoped he had, thereby escaping the burdens of his birth.

'His body was found in the river.' Iruvain choked on grief and outrage. 'Those vermin in Parnilesse Town have stuck his head on a gate spike and thrown his corpse to the dogs.'

'That's vile.' Litasse retreated to the window seat and sank onto the tapestry cushions.

'They will pay, I promise you.'

At least Iruvain's wrath wasn't directed at her any more. This might even be the goad he needed to truly act like a ruling duke.

'May I read my mother's letter?' She let the tears slide down her face. When Iruvain forced a quarrel, making her cry usually convinced him he'd won. If the swine would leave her alone, she could think all this through.

'As you wish.' Iruvain tossed both parchments onto the table. 'See to it that all our belongings are packed, for your journey and my own. I have other business to attend to.'

As he strode out of the room, Litasse wondered how long it would take him to find a bottle. Though perhaps he had some excuse today.

But Roreth was dead and no one could save him from Poldrion's demons while his mortal remains lingered to tie him to this world. Litasse must think of her own future.

Karn stood by the table, examining the letters from her mother and Lord Rousharn.

'What now?' she asked him helplessly.

'We continue with our own endeavours.' The gaunt spy was examining the letters' wax seals. 'I can't be certain this has been lifted,' he concluded, 'but it's the same as the one on those letters from your mother.' He nodded to the parchment packet still lying by the lace pillow. 'This is written in her usual cipher and we know they have the key to that too.'

'So these rebels are reading all Lord Rousharn's clever plans?' Litasse contemplated her unopened letter with loathing. But she would have to endure her mother's self-serving justifications for this heinous betrayal of her father and her dead brothers. Still more hateful, she must find some way to reply, to keep her rightful share in Sharlac's gold flowing. 'What good does that do us?'

'They're chasing their own tails at the moment,' Karn said thoughtfully, 'rounding up hounds in the Carifate to flush out the rats they've let nest in Wyril.'

'Who cares?' Litasse's exasperation swelled to anger. 'What do we do now?'

'Iruvain and Rousharn are making all their plans around Solstice. If we set our own endeavours in motion sooner, we'll still have the whip hand.' Karn looked steadily at her. 'If you give me leave to go to Relshaz, I can drop a few words in the right ears and some coins in the right palms to set the dead grass alight across Caladhria, Carluse and Marlier.'

Litasse remembered a childhood coach journey across the wolds of Sharlac. The land had been blackened in all directions, scorched by just such a ferocious fire. Her face must have betrayed her doubts.

'Your Grace, to reclaim your rightful inheritance, we must do whatever it takes.' Karn clearly had no qualms. 'You say you want to be revenged, on all of these rebels, for your father's sake and your brothers'. Iruvain has dishonoured you and, forgive me, so has Her Grace, your mother. This is how you can be free of them all.'

Litasse remembered her father telling her how the grass would grow again now that the fire had passed. It would be richer than before and bright with glorious flowers.

She touched her cheek, to see if Iruvain's blow had left a bruise. Her marriage had been a wretched bargain and her own mother had been the one to make it. Hamare and Pelletria were dead, leaving Karn as her only ally.

'I don't have much ready coin,' she said reluctantly.

'I can deal with such necessities,' Karn assured her. 'Triolle has old friends in Relshaz, and debtors.'

Litasse decided she need not ask for details. Hamare always said men such as himself saved their masters and mistresses from petty concerns.

'I will have to go to Marlier,' she said at length. 'You must come and find me there, when you've concluded your business in Relshaz.'

CHAPTER FIFTEEN
Karn

Relshaz,
40th of For-Winter

HE WOULD HAVE to choose his words carefully when he returned to Litasse. It was better not to lie outright, just to be sparing with the whole truth. Master Hamare had been adept at such skilful evasions and for the first time, Karn was really appreciating his teacher's artistry. If it was no great task to let Iruvain deceive himself, Litasse was as shrewd as she was beautiful.

Karn must see to it that she didn't know what could hurt her. Whatever he did was in a just cause. He owed it to Master Hamare's memory to see Litasse happily settled and mistress of her own destiny.

Whereas Iruvain had betrayed Hamare by mocking everything that the intelligencer had discovered about these Vanam plotters. Karn had long since decided he owed Triolle's duke no more loyalty. If the opportunity presented itself, he might as well cut Iruvain's throat, he decided. Though he wouldn't distress Litasse with such uncomfortable knowledge, given she always shied away from an opportunity to voice her undoubted desire for her husband's death.

Karn stepped over a man sprawled across the entrance to an alleyway. The addict was drooling and mumbling in the thrall of the tahn berries he had eaten. Illusions would keep him warm until the cold night killed him.

Litasse's tender conscience amused Karn, even if he didn't understand it, any more than he understood the genuine love that she and Hamare had appeared to share. Karn accepted such passions were real. They just weren't for him.

His unerring path took him past numerous workshops and manufactories. The Relshazri didn't merely buy and sell all manner of goods brought down from Ensaimin, Caladhria and Dalasor. They made plenty more coin by turning wood and leather into furniture, and brass and steel into weapons. Weavers blended linen thread from the north with Aldabreshin silk before handing their fine fabrics to tailors, upholsterers and other craftsmen.

He may have loved someone once, Karn mused. His mother perhaps, in that peasant childhood he could barely recall, before warfare had destroyed it and his father had sought to kill them all, to save them from slower starvation.

The old fool hadn't even managed that, leaving Karn alive in a ditch of corpses. Since then he'd had no use for love and little enough for friendship. If such emptiness left him free to kill without concern, that was all well and good.

The scent of the sea grew stronger as the white plastered walls grew higher. He had reached the merchants' compounds where exotic luxuries and narcotic spices from the Aldabreshin Archipelago were stored. Guards watched from their gatehouse cubbyholes and upper windows glowed where sharp-eyed men and women were totting up their profits.

Karn briefly considered robbing a counting house. Without swords to back him, though, without taking the time to gauge his victim's comings and goings, it would be hideously risky. The Relshazri paid their dues to the Magistracy to maintain an inconveniently astute and persistent Watch.

No. The Magistracy reserved an inconveniently unpleasant fate for thieves, and besides, Litasse would have no one to call on at all if he was captured here. There were other ways to get coin and she need not be troubled with those details either.

He was passing an unbroken high wall topped with vicious shards of glass. A long building within loomed black against the Lesser Moon, so nearly full, and the waxing half of the Greater. Karn heard faint coughing and sobbing drifting out through the barred windows along with the stench of soiled straw.

More fool them for being caught, or for being fool enough to protest their innocence instead of running as fast as they could. Anyone with any sense knew what passed for Relshazri justice was more concerned with profit than proof.

Leaving the lock-up behind, Karn crossed a wide paved expanse where sturdy wooden pens stood empty in the moonlight. A few scraps of cloth had been tied around the posts. Did anyone ever come looking, in search of some pathetic token left by husband or son, wife or daughter?

What good did that do, when such debtors and defaulters, thieves and deceivers had already been sold off to some Aldabreshi warlord, to live out their days as slaves in his domain, never to be seen again?

He did wonder how those condemned to that new life brought such rags and tatters as they were herded into these enclosures. The Magistracy's jailers stripped and washed all such merchandise before market so the purchasers could see just what their coin was buying. The sales of nubile girls were always popular with male spectators.

Karn walked across to the warehouses on the slave market's far side. The reek of human misery seeped from beneath their doors. Stealthy, he listened carefully at each entrance for the shuffles and murmurs of those condemned within finding some transient release in sleep.

At the far corner of the market he found a building left open to the cleansing breeze. Karn walked cautiously inside, alert for any hint of a presence within the barred cages. Nothing stirred, not even a rat.

Everything had been swept bare, and recently. That posed some interesting questions. Some of the answers he could think of might prove more interesting still.

His eyes soon grew accustomed to the shadows with the moonlight filtering through the high barred windows. He picked out a wooden stair drawing a sloping line across the darkness to the rear. Karn climbed it without a sound.

Once at the top, he pressed an ear to the tight-fitted door and listened for a long moment. His searching fingers found the brass plate of a skilfully crafted lock. It was doubtless one of the finest that money could buy in this wealthiest of cities. He could probably defeat it but that would take time and he begrudged every moment just now.

He retreated silently down the stairs, past the slave cages and out through the arched doorway. Moving more swiftly now, he went to the rear of the building. With every finger-width of river mud so precious to the Relshazri, he had to sidle along the narrow alley dividing it from the one behind.

Good. Karn pressed his back against that building and pressed his hands and booted feet flat against the ruddy bricks in front of him. Shifting, twisting, his limbs always braced to stop himself falling, he climbed slowly but surely upwards. Invisible in the deep shadow between the buildings, the only sound he let slip was a faint scuff now and again.

He reached the narrow louvered window he had seen from the ground. Bracing his legs still more securely, he slid one hand between the slats and the frame and then drew his dagger with the other, to lift the catch inside and twitch the shutter open.

Something scraped in the darkness within; furniture on bare boards. White light flared and died. Someone was squeezing a spark-maker, trying to light a lamp.

Karn launched himself headfirst through the window. He rolled lithe as a playhouse tumbler, back on his feet before the lamplight swelled. Before the man cowering in the bed's quilts could yell for help, Karn had the dagger at his throat.

'Hush.' Karn smiled. Though this hadn't been much of a gamble. Any slaver living above his own pens was unlikely to be married, and the whores who plied this trade didn't linger with customers when they could be selling their bodies elsewhere.

'Please,' the man begged, shivering.

Karn knew his smile was doing little to ease the wretched man's terror. These days his face was so drawn, he looked more like a death's-head.

It would take half a year of good food and rest to restore the handsome looks that he'd used so effectively in Master Hamare's service, to cozen and seduce men and women alike. There were so many situations when violence didn't answer in the search for information.

In the meantime, he would use the fear that his gaunt visage prompted to best advantage.

'I have some business that's best done discreetly.' Sitting on the end of the bed, Karn sheathed his knife with ostentatious care.

'What?' Sitting straight-backed, his empty hands prudently spread, the man didn't waste time on pointless questions.

Karn nodded downwards. 'I see you've sold all your stock, and recently too, from the stink still fading there. That's some achievement in the middle of winter. None too many Aldabreshin galleys risk the open seas at this time of year.'

'A good merchant can always find a market.' The slaver relaxed a little, tugging a quilt up around his shoulders.

'I like to deal with shrewd men.' Karn nodded sagely. 'Would you be interested in more stock?'

'I might be.' The man's dark eyes narrowed. The lamplight showed he had the copper skin of mingled Archipelagan and mainland blood. 'What can you offer?'

Karn smiled. 'I would need to know your market, so I can make sure to find you what you need.'

'You're not Caladhrian, by your accent,' the slaver said warily.

Karn shook his head. 'No, and I'm not concerned where my customers come from, as long as their coin is sound.'

He was already beginning to suspect what the man was going to say next.

'So you wouldn't be overly troubled by dealings with corsairs?' The slaver folded his hands slowly, still not wanting to provoke this unexpected visitor.

Karn's smile broadened. 'It wouldn't be the first time.'

'They'll take any walking, breathing body to chain to their

galleys' oars.' The slaver stumbled over his words, breathless with relief. 'They don't pay much but they wear them down to shark bait fast enough. So they're soon back looking for more, even in the depths of winter.' He grinned. 'Buy up whatever other dealers are left with, after the Aldabreshin have stopped sailing, and a shrewd man can still make a handsome profit.'

'What about women?' asked Karn. 'Children?'

The slaver looked more eager. 'I get a better price for those, as long as they're not diseased.'

Karn drummed his fingers on his scabbarded dagger. As the movement and noise drew the slaver's eye, he didn't see the blade Karn had palmed from its sheath up his other sleeve.

He swept a fold of the heavy quilt up and over the slaver's face. The man struggled, frantically fighting back. But Karn was on his feet, bearing down with all his weight. The padded fabric fatally hampered the desperate man's efforts.

Karn clamped one hand over the slaver's mouth and nose to smother him. The dagger in his other hand finished the job. He stabbed down hard, unerring, the razor-edged steel slicing through cloth and wadding to bite deep into the slaver's neck and chest.

The man went limp beneath him. Karn waited a few more moments to be quite certain his victim was dead, then stood back to contemplate his handiwork. These were the killings he preferred: swift and silent, with no risk of blood on his clothes to betray him. There was always the Relshazri Watch to consider and he still had a great many things to do.

Picking up the lamp from the bedside table, he knelt and looked under the bed. No strongbox there, which was hardly a surprise. He swiftly searched the bedchamber, and after that the windowless living room with its locked door to the warehouse stair.

No, nothing. He came back into the bedchamber and searched more slowly, more methodically. His patience was rewarded by finding a hidey-hole underneath a clothes chest.

Karn contemplated the lock but decided against taking the time to pick it. Fetching a brass candlestick from the inner room and a quilt from the dead man's bed, he smashed through the hinges, using the cloth to muffle the noise.

He lifted a strongbox out from among the splinters. It was pleasingly heavy and he shook it to be further rewarded with the solid clink of coin.

That suited him very well. Aldabreshin gemstones would be worth more but coin spent far more easily. With the corsairs raiding the Caladhrian coasts as far north as the Gulf of Peorle, he'd wager this would all be good gold and untainted silver.

That would pay his would-be slavers enough to keep their mouths shut until they had left for Caladhria and Marlier. Once they began raiding the farms and hamlets, Karn would soon see which ones he could trust, who had the stomach for slave-raiding, and who would need a timely knife in the back to keep this particular secret secure.

Karn found the dead man's keys and pocketed them. Returning to the living room, he ate meat and bread left in a wire mesh box to foil Relshaz's ever-present flies. Seeing half a glass of wine left in a wide-necked flagon, he savoured that as well. Picking up the money chest, he let himself out, carefully locking the door behind him.

Testing the weight of the strongbox again, he hid it beneath his cloak and went out into the night. He might even have enough coin to hire a few honest swords, which would give him something useful to tell Litasse.

Karn strode away, well satisfied. If one slaver was profiting by trading with corsairs there would be others doing the same. He could sell the homeless and dispossessed that his recruits rounded up and make sure such slaving was blamed on the exiles and rebels.

A few raids launched into Caladhria, with their plump women and ruddy-cheeked children thrown into chains for a life of debauchery, and the barons would soon raise an army to back Iruvain, without any need to rely on this so-called Duke Rousharn of Sharlac. Who was of course married to one of those very rebels from Vanam. Karn would soon find a way to convince Iruvain the man wasn't to be trusted.

Marlier would suffer too. Karn owed Ridianne the Vixen an ill turn. He had so very nearly died when that bitch Charoleia had sent men to kill him, inside Ridianne's own camp. She'd made no amends, never even shown any remorse. So now she could pay the price for that and Duke Ferdain of Marlier with her. Karn never forgot or forgave an insult.

He spared a moment to wonder what had become of Charoleia. At least one of her maidservants was dead at Minelas's hands, so that was something on his side of the ledger. But he still owed that other dumpy little slut a brief lifetime of pain before she died.

If the little Vanamese hadn't foiled him, when he'd tracked the scent of Derenna's deceits and so very nearly caught them, even with his festering wound barely healed, he might still have been in time to warn Sharlac, to warn Master Hamare.

But Hamare had been killed while Karn lay insensible, wracked with the fever that had come so close to killing him and left him with scars to horrify any future bed mates, even when his good looks were restored.

Hamare had been murdered on Charoleia's orders, by those blond bastards of Mountain Men who'd stolen her away from Adel Castle, thanks to their cursed wizardry.

He was certain the Mountain Man wasn't the only one with magic at his fingertips in their enemies' camp. Karn sometimes wondered what the Archmage's vengeance might be, if he ever discovered all the secrets of the rebels' magecraft, and called Planir the Black's wrath down upon them.

He would have to find a way to achieve that without putting Litasse in jeopardy. Though with Minelas dead, Karn would defy anyone to prove that he had recruited the renegade mage. After all, he had made sure there was no one left alive to link them, even before the wastrel had first set foot in Triolle.

He let slip a sigh of exasperation. As futile as Litasse's remorse might be, he knew it was heartfelt, all the more so once she learned of Minelas's inconvenient appetites.

Didn't she realise what control that should have given them over the duplicitous wizard? But no, and Karn knew that Litasse's guilt would compel her to abject confession if she was ever challenged again by that magewoman who'd so inconveniently appeared in Adel Castle. So he had to save her from that particular folly. Not least to save his own neck from whatever penalty the Archmage might impose.

Besides, he would rather wreak his own revenge on those Mountain Men. Karn strode swiftly through the silent Relshazri night towards the tavern district. If those exiles thought they had the upper hand, he relished the prospect of showing them their mistake.

His only concern was that those particular rebels who owed him their deaths for Master Hamare's sake might inconveniently get themselves killed in whatever skirmishes were going on around Wyril, before he could cut their hearts out himself.

Chapter Sixteen
Tathrin

Wyril,
in the Dukedom of Draximal,
44th of For-Winter

TYRLE GREW RICH on linen and Wyril grew rich on wool. Tathrin recalled his father once telling him that. He shivered. One of the town's famous striped blankets would be welcome about now. The night was bone-numbingly cold.

'Stay down,' Gren warned, a few paces ahead.

Tathrin was already stooped as low as possible, scurrying through the meagre shadow cast by the wall running along the lane. The pack beneath his cloak dragged awkwardly at his shoulders.

Both moons were slightly smaller than full; the Greater waxing, the Lesser waning. It was the best night for a battle that For-Winter would offer. Which made it the worst for approaching the town unseen. Well, every rune landed with one upright face and one reversed. He could only hope the persistent snow flurries would hide them from any sharp-eyed sentry on the wall.

Frustration burned Tathrin's throat with a mockery of warmth. Whatever its uses tonight, this snow had cost them at least a day on the road coming north through Parnilesse. There were so few horses travelling from town to town or from farm to market, and still fewer wagons, that long stretches of the highways had become impassable. Some drifts had been so thick they'd had to swap their swords for spades and dig.

The weather hadn't been their only foe. Few wandering bandits dared challenge his company recruited from the Carifate but they had twice encountered more determined opposition, from mercenaries cast adrift from shattered companies who'd made common cause with militiamen abandoning their allegiance to Parnilesse, Triolle or whoever.

Gren's breezy assertion that fights helped everyone keep their hand in was scant consolation. Granted, as Sorgrad had pointed out, those freebooters weren't doing Reniack's bidding; swift interrogations had established that. Tathrin still ground his teeth, recalling the casualties they could so ill afford.

He had hoped to see more men and women at that rendezvous by the Carif rampart, convinced to stake a claim on Lescar's future. Sorgrad had reckoned they'd done as well as he'd expected but Tathrin still fretted. Did they really have enough seasoned warriors to strengthen their eager but green contingents freshly enlisted from Lescar's towns, thanks to the efforts of Master Ernout and his allies among the guildmasters and craftsmen? Reher the Carluse smith had proved a particularly effective recruiter.

'Hold up.' Behind them, Sorgrad called out softly. 'Wait for the stragglers.'

He didn't sound in the least cold, Tathrin heard, aggrieved. Gren wasn't bothered by the weather either, doubtless thanks to their Mountain blood.

Hunkering down in the wall's shadow, Tathrin shifted his feet to make sure he could still feel his chilled toes wriggling inside his thick socks. The last thing he needed was Maewelin's nip from the frost. Every morning saw another handful of his meagre force limping along, betrayed by inadequate boots.

Never mind the weather. How would those untested lads from Losand and Sharlac, Carluse, Ashgil and Dromin, from Triolle and Adel, meet the challenges of battle? He'd had very mixed news from the different town militias who had joined up with them over these past two days. Every sergeant-at-arms reported being harried by haphazard gangs on their journey. Some contingents had acquitted themselves well. A couple had been cut to pieces.

That was another challenge to add to his list. Tathrin sighed. Once he had seen Wyril retaken from the renegades, and somehow dealt with Reniack and brought Parnilesse back into Lescar's fold, he must put an end to all this brigandage.

But first things first. Swirling snow stung his eyes as he peered at the dark bulk of Wyril's walls. The town was well defended. It was Draximal's second largest and Duke Secaris's most westerly stronghold, where his territory drove a blunt wedge between Carluse and Triolle. High walls overlooked strong gates commanding the roads running north-east to Draximal Town, south-east to Deflin and the Parnilesse border, more southerly still to Triolle and south-west away towards Tyrle.

This was the road they had used for their approach, after cutting across to find their assembled militias lurking where Carluse and Triolle's lands butted up against Draximal's border. Kerith had done his job well.

In happier times, Tathrin reflected, all those towns and every village in between had been glad to buy Wyril woollens. Would there be anyone left to return to card and spin the wool and weave the cloth after all the tribulations this region had suffered?

'Can you see any lights?' he asked tensely.

'Not this side of town,' Gren replied, satisfied.

Tathrin allowed himself some cautious hope.

Sorgrad appeared at his shoulder. 'Let's move.'

Tathrin glanced back to see their small force was all assembled. At his nod, Gren led them onwards.

Some distance back, they had slipped away from the highway that ran from Tyrle to Draximal. The road followed this shallow ridge running from south-east to north-west. The town itself claimed the gentle slope running down to a shallow, gravelly river whose waters washed wool and drove Wyril's fulling mills, before running away to the Vale of Ashgil and the other streams that flowed on into the River Dyal.

Snow crunched beneath Tathrin's boots as he moved quickly along this slope. These broad meadows were the tenter-grounds, where vast lengths of freshly napped blanketing were hooked onto frames to dry. Though there was no cloth hanging stiff in this frost and the long wooden racks had been stolen away for firewood.

They drew closer to the town. There was still no shout from the battlements, no sentry seeing them plain as spilled ink on a page as they hurried across the moonlit snowfield. Bent almost double, Tathrin dashed across the last stretch of open ground. Reaching the black shadow cast by the walls, he breathed just a little easier.

But now he looked in vain for the lesser gateways that pierced the walls. The weavers tending their cloth hung to dry in these meadows had long been accustomed to use their own entries. Tathrin had been surprised, but Ekarre and other mercenaries who had travelled this road had explained such passages were securely locked and barred in time of peril. Besides, none were wide enough to admit more than one person at a time, so they hardly invited an all-out assault.

Sorgrad still reckoned that's how these renegades had got in. After the disaster of the battle for Tyrle, with Lord Cassat dead and any loyal Draximal militia scattered, there would have been no one watching these walls, ready to send armed men to defend any threatened doorway.

If he was right, would renegade mercenaries be lying in wait for anyone else seeking to exploit that same weakness?

Tathrin looked back over his shoulder. 'When did we last see scouts from the town?'

'Dawn yesterday.' Sorgrad shrugged. 'Verista's Pine Martens cut their throats.'

Tathrin could only hope Ekarre's lieutenant hadn't let some witness flee to report those murders. Though that would be unlike her. He had rarely come across a mercenary so single-minded, once she had decided to throw in her lot with them.

'Which way?' He pressed his back against the masonry, glad to stand upright. The double-handful of men with them were all now lined up against the wall.

Gren stripped off his gloves to run bare fingers across the stonework. 'This way.' He ran lightly down the slope.

Tathrin followed and slipped on treacherous ice. Only Sorgrad's bruising grip saved him from a nasty fall.

'More haste, less speed, long lad.'

'How far to the entry?' Tathrin asked curtly.

Sorgrad's unerring fingertips read the signs he'd chipped into these stones before they had withdrawn with the dusk to find Tathrin's rough-hewn army.

'It's the next one along.'

Sorgrad and Gren had crept alone through the snowy dawn shrouded in grubby linen, to lie hidden in a ditch all day. Scorning the deadly lethargy that cold so easily be forced on less hardy men, they had determined which of these unregarded gates showed no sign of use.

'In here.' Ahead, Gren had already ducked into an archway, a glimpse of darker shadow in the blackness of the wall.

Tathrin heard a faint rattle akin to keys. Gren soon pulled the heavy oak outwards. He had sworn nothing short of the costliest work from a Mountain locksmith could foil his finely honed skills, numb fingers or not.

'Mind your head, long lad.' His grin caught the faintest glimmer of light from within.

Tathrin ducked as he entered the passageway running right through the thickness of the town wall. Firelight flickered along the glistening stones. He could see the glow through an iron gate barring the far end so town watchmen could see if the outer door had been compromised. No one was keeping watch tonight. Still, Tathrin could hear none-too-distant shouts and his heart quickened.

'Keep moving.' Sorgrad pushed at the pack on his back.

Tathrin hurried on and heard the oak door close behind them. All their small force was now in the tunnel. Despite the cold, sweat beaded his face. If anyone saw them, they were caught like rats in a trap.

He heard a grunt of discomfort behind and recognised a stifled oath as Reher's. Master Ernout had set the Carluse blacksmith the challenge of recruiting and captaining the town's militia. Tathrin didn't imagine he faced many arguments. He smiled unseen. Reher was even taller than he was and far wider in the shoulders. He must barely fit through this narrow entry.

Gren was already working on the lock securing the iron lattice. Once again, his larcenous skills triumphed. Like the outer door, this opened towards them, all the better to foil invaders by handing the advantage to the town's defenders. But there was still no one looking out for Wyril's interests tonight.

Gren emerged into a street dappled with fire-lit shadows running along the entire inner face of the wall, uninterrupted by buildings. 'Try to look like you belong here.'

Tathrin hurried after him to find the flurries of snow were subsiding to leave the night crisp and cold.

Sorgrad was hissing final orders to the men behind him. 'Don't follow the walls too closely. Spread out and lose yourselves in the alleys.'

The men swiftly obeyed, hunchbacked with the packs beneath their cloaks. Like Sorgrad and Gren they had all been hand-picked for having at least some knowledge of Wyril's layout, whether their visits had been as honest tradesmen or as mercenaries taking Draximal's coin for some troubled season or other.

Within a few moments, Tathrin and the two Mountain Men lurked alone in a stinking ginnel. No lights showed at any window of the terraced houses on either side. The only illumination was a burning heap of refuse outside a weaving shed.

Gren chuckled. 'That should help things along.'

'How soon?' Tathrin looked at Sorgrad.

The Mountain Man threw back his hood, listening intently.

Those earlier shouts had faded away. All Tathrin could hear was the thudding of his anxious heart. After what felt like half an age, the seventh chime of the night rang raggedly through the moonlight.

'Not long.' Sorgrad's smile was as cold as the uncaring stars. 'Come on.'

Tathrin followed him through the back-alleys. Every house was dark. Here and there doors stood open or smashed. Shutters hung askew. Surely there couldn't be any innocent townsfolk left in Wyril? He desperately hoped not, given what was to come.

They turned a corner and found themselves facing an irregular square of unexpectedly grand houses. They looked more thoroughly ransacked than any buildings Tathrin had seen yet.

'Don't say a word.' Sorgrad quickly pulled his hood back up.

Gren's hand had already gone for his sword hilt beneath his enveloping cloak.

Around an ill-tended sprawl of embers, men were lighting crude torches, sharing them out. An avid circle of mercenary men and women ebbed and shifted. Dogs snarled, brindled beasts and piebald. Some were fighting their leashes, others recoiled from growled threats. Drool glinted in the firelight.

A gang of burly men wrestled with a young bullock. One tied the end of the rope around its neck to a chain looped around a fountain basin in the middle of the square. As the other men flung themselves clear, the bullock was left plunging and struggling against the tether. Despite the cold, foaming sweat smeared its flanks.

Someone yelled and the dogs were let loose. Confused, several attacked each other. Shouting men hauled them apart, throwing the hounds bodily at the bullock. Others thrust their torches into the faces of dogs trying to flee.

Straining so hard that the rope cut into its neck, the bullock thrust a horn through a piebald hound's flank. The wretched creature yelped as the bullock tossed it to its death. Two others seized their chance to go for its throat. More were nipping at its heels. Every time a bite drew blood, the crowd roared drunken approval.

Swallowing his revulsion, Tathrin followed Sorgrad and Gren to another dark alley offering sanctuary. As they reached it, a man stumbled out of the shadows. Oblivious to the cold in shirt and breeches, he saluted them with his bottle of white brandy.

'Fair festival!'

Trepidation twisted Tathrin's stomach. Did these renegades carouse night and day? Could they reach their goal undiscovered? How would their other men fare, sneaking through the town?

'Celebrating Solstice early?' Gren waved the man on with a cheery laugh. 'Good luck to you, friend!'

'He won't see midwinter.' Sorgrad picked up the pace as the drunk disappeared into the mêlée around the bull-baiting.

Glad to leave the brutality behind, Tathrin lengthened his stride. He could smell spilled liquor, piss and shit in every doorway. There was no savour of cooking meat or any other homely scent. These renegades had plundered the town and picked the surrounding country as bare as a crow-scavenged carcass.

His own stomach rumbled disapprovingly. For the past three days, they had marched on dry biscuit, cold bacon and cheese grudgingly doled out by the quartermasters and no one was expecting to feast in Wyril.

'Here we go!' Gren halted, looking upwards.

A fiery ball soared overhead. Tathrin followed its course down into a huddle of houses. As the first startled shouts rang out, more spheres drew blazing arcs across the moonlit sky.

'Move!' Sorgrad urged him on with a merciless thump.

Tathrin ran after Gren, trusting his knowledge of Wyril's streets. The frosted cobbles were slick beneath his feet.

He braced himself for a challenge. Surely someone would wonder why they were turning their backs on this inexplicable incident. Where were they heading, if not to help put out the fires? He could already hear cries for buckets being raised by those still sober enough to recognise the peril of fire amid these narrow streets of close-packed houses.

There it was: the Tyrle Road Gate. Tathrin drew his sword as he followed Gren.

The rising tumult in the town's centre was beginning to draw people out of nearby taverns. Tathrin picked out badges on jerkins and cloaks. The Bonebreakers' cloven skull grinned back at him. There would surely be mercenaries here who'd seen how effectively the rebels had used trebuchets at Tyrle.

'What's amiss?' a woman shouted, a billowing cloak draped over her ill-fitting gown.

Tathrin just shrugged and forced his way past two bleary-eyed drunks leaning on each other as they gawked.

What he was about to do sickened him. But they hadn't been able to come up with any other plan, not with the limited forces at their disposal. They must rid Wyril of these renegades, to be free to deal with Reniack and to scour the rest of Lescar clean. Only then would they see a lasting peace.

They had to do that fast, according to Branca. Charoleia was warning that the clamour among the Tormalin princes would soon force Emperor Tadriol to intervene.

Tathrin recalled something else his father had said. The hardest journey is only a series of steps. He set his jaw. He had come too far to give up now, whatever it might take to see this dreadful night through.

'Who goes there?' A man swaddled against the cold stepped out of the shadowed archway.

So the Bonebreakers had set a sentry. Sorgrad had said they were the best of this treacherous rabble.

Gren was already there, his blade slicing through the torchlight. The man's blanket tangled around his sword-arm and he died on a gurgle of surprise as Gren's thrust slid deep into his chest.

Tathrin spun around in case someone had noticed. He saw the open expanse inside the gate was now filling with people but they were all looking at the fires taking hold in the heart of the town or at the blazing missiles still raining down.

'Watch the battlement stair.' Sorgrad was already unbolting the little postern set into the gate.

Tathrin glanced at the doorway to the spiral steps and then back at the gathering mob. Would they be expecting an assault undermining the walls, as had happened in the first assault on Tyrle, after trebuchets had bombarded the town? There must be some renegades here who had escaped that battle. How long before some of them decided they were better off quitting the town rather than trying to fight the fires? Those who'd marched with Lord Cassat's ill-fated attempt to retake Tyrle would surely recall his appalling death, struck by just such blistering alchemy.

Was there another sentry up above? How long before he saw the militia companies now marching up the road? There was no hiding that number of men.

'Warm enough for you?' Gren asked cheerily. 'Don't fret. We'll soon get your blood flowing!'

'Hopefully not on the cobbles.' As Tathrin muttered that thought aloud a blast of cold air raised the hair on the back of his neck.

He spared a glance to see that Sorgrad had unlocked the postern. The first contingent of Lescar's new army swiftly slipped through the narrow entrance, led by the Pine Marten woman Verista.

Tathrin looked carefully at Sorgrad. There was no hint of magelight around him, not even a glint in his eyes to raise Tathrin's suspicions. The Mountain-born wizard wasn't even looking at the rising flames but at the milling crowd.

That relieved one of Tathrin's fears. If the Archmage sent his spy Jilseth to search Wyril for some stain of magecraft, they couldn't accuse Sorgrad. This conflagration really was instigated by the infamous alchemy of Aldabreshin sticky fire thanks to one of the darker-skinned Shearlings.

At least Tathrin was confident Reher wouldn't use his own half-taught wizardry. Now that the blacksmith had learned his magebirth was known to Hadrumal, he knew any further transgression would win him a summons from the Archmage that he wouldn't be permitted to ignore.

Tathrin gripped his sword more tightly. He had no more time for such distractions. Bonebreakers were seeking each other out amid all the confusion. One of them noticed what was going on in the gateway.

As the man gestured and yelled, a Pine Marten sergeant hurled a dagger with deadly intent. It fell short and anyway, the man had already got his companions' attention. The renegade gang advanced, drawing steely blades.

'Steady, lads,' warned Verista.

Tathrin and Gren quickly withdrew as the Ashgil militiamen crowded close, gripping their newly hafted halberds.

The Pine Marten sergeants flanking the men at the front locked their shields with those on either side. Resolute, the line advanced to hold the inner edge of the arch.

Chapter Seventeen
Tathrin

Wyril,
in the Dukedom of Draximal,
44th of For-Winter

THE BONEBREAKERS' ASSAULT was fast and furious. The Lescari line held firm. Their sergeants shouted encouragement as swords jabbed over and under their adamant shields. Halberds used their longer reach to good effect and the Bonebreakers fell back, bloodied and dismayed. Some collapsed to the cobbles, gasping, forced to crawl away.

'Come on, long lad. They don't need our help.' Gren darted for the narrow stair leading up to the battlements.

Keeping his sword close, Tathrin ran after him. Thankfully they found the narrow spiral lit by candle lanterns.

Who had lit those? As Tathrin wondered, Gren threw open the door to the gate's highest turret. Tathrin ripped his sword across the startled face of the Bonebreaker who'd been dozing aloft. He died like his comrade below before he could raise a shout.

Tathrin flung the man's blood from his blade as he used his other hand to unfasten his cloak. It was hard to believe he had ever felt cold tonight. Hearing a footfall, he spun around, sword ready.

'All clear.' It was Sorgrad.

Tathrin walked out onto the open battlements on top of the gatehouse. As he looked eastwards, Gren surveyed the fortifications running west. No danger threatened. There was no one else up on these walls. Not yet, anyway.

Tathrin slipped the heavy pack off his shoulders, momentarily savouring the relief. But there was no time to waste. He quickly joined Sorgrad and Gren in securing ropes around the outward-facing mullions. They dropped the woven ladders they had carried to waiting archers below. Lightly armoured, the bowmen climbed swiftly, their weapons and quivers slung on their backs.

With that last task done, Tathrin studied the town. Fires were spreading, fast and furious. Townsfolk might have organised bucket chains or begun tearing down threatened houses to save the rest. These renegades were so drunk, so feckless, they merely fled the flames.

Such flight brought them to the gates, all now successfully captured by Tathrin's army. He could see signal torches marking out the dark circle of the walls, lurid green thanks to more Aldabreshin alchemy. The Draximal Gate, the Deflin Gate, the Triolle Gate. He heaved a sigh of relief, his breath smoky in the cold air.

Sorgrad was watching the confused mob below. The Bonebreakers were advancing again, more cautiously this time, still determined to force their way out of the town.

'They'll soon sober up,' Gren predicted, 'when they realise we're not coming in to attack, just keeping them penned them up inside.'

'Just as long as we can do that.' Tathrin looked again at the signal torches. This night had to see an end to these renegades. They couldn't let them loose to simply regroup and continue their depredations.

He was still revolted by this cruel plan, even if he had helped to devise it. As long as the runes rolled in their favour, and he had helped weight them as far as possible, this would be slaughter, pure and simple.

He reminded himself that these Bonebreakers and all the rest had murdered countless innocents. However brutal, this could be considered some kind of justice, like the sentences meted out at Losand. The Guild Councils there had decreed Duke Garnot's mercenaries should be hanged from the town's walls. With Wyril's guildsmen dead or fled, this army drawn from all Lescari would pass judgement in their name.

At his elbow, an eager crossbowman cranked his weapon. 'Give us a look.'

Tathrin stepped aside as more archers scrambled over the outer mullions.

The renegades below scattered as bolts and arrows began raining down. The Lescari contingent holding the gateway stood firm, safe from the murderous missiles.

The fires were gaining more ground even though no more pots of stickily sodden, flaming rags were smashing on roofs or in alleyways.

How long before the Bonebreakers launched a third assault on the gate, despite the archers up above? As soon as they realised they were fighting for their lives, Tathrin guessed bleakly.

What would Aremil think of this? Would he have argued against such a barbaric plan? Or would he have agreed with the brutal necessity, as Tathrin had been forced to? Either way, he imagined he'd see the truth reflected in his friend's thoughts when Aremil finally learned what they had done. When he recovered from his illness.

Tathrin refused to contemplate any other outcome. He knew Failla had nursed his friend with every possible care on that agonisingly slow journey back to Carluse Castle. Master Welgren was tending him now and the apothecary had saved the lives of men despaired of on the battlefield. Curing a winter ague was hardly beyond his skills.

Granted, this had been an unusually persistent fever but it had finally broken once Aremil could be properly cared for in a bed. After that, well, however strong his will, there was no denying his bodily weaknesses. They must leave him far less able to recover as swiftly as someone more robust like Tathrin. No wonder Aremil had been sleeping ever since, only rousing briefly for some sustenance. It was ludicrous to imagine he'd be able to master any Artifice this side of Winter Solstice.

Though Tathrin couldn't entirely shake the suspicion there was something Kerith wasn't telling him, in their brief, brusque exchanges across the aether. He would be glad to get back to Carluse once this distasteful task was done; to see Failla and to see Aremil for himself.

'Watch out!' The crossbowman beside him ducked as an arrow sliced through the night.

Some Bonebreaker had found a bow. More arrows followed. So had the Bonebreaker's friends.

Tathrin crossed to the outer face of the wall. Down below, he saw a couple of wounded Ashgil militiamen being helped back out through the postern. They were tended in comparative safety as fresh men slipped inside to reinforce the shield wall still holding the archway.

'Hear that?' Gren shoved at his shoulder to get his attention.

'What?' Then, faint in the distance, Tathrin heard hollow thudding.

'Someone's sober enough to remember those little doors,' Gren observed cheerfully.

Tathrin managed half a grin. Because those oak doors piercing the walls opened outwards, from a jamb of carved stone recessed into the masonry, all the better to resist an enemy's battering ram from outside.

So the first militiamen to follow, once his chosen band had slipped unseen into the town, had been ordered to hurry along the walls, to hammer wedges and spikes under and around each lesser door between the main gates, to frustrate all attempts to open them up from within.

So now it was the renegades who were desperately trying to wield some improvised ram in the cramped confines of those passages. While Lescari militiamen were waiting outside like cats at a mouse hole, lest any of them succeed.

'Ready?' Gren called.

'Steady,' warned Sorgrad.

Tathrin joined them where the wall-walk around the battlements reached this wider platform on top of the gatehouse. None of the handful of men now running towards them wore the cream and yellow kerchief of Lescar's army. That made them the foe.

Gren ducked low to stab the first in the groin and Sorgrad's blow swept the man away through the crenellations. Tathrin used his greater reach to smack his blade hard into the side of the following man's head. If he wasn't already dead as he fell, he would be when he hit the cobbles.

A bolt from the crossbowman now leaning over the corner of the gatehouse took the next one in the neck. The renegade close behind shoved his stricken comrade bodily at Gren. The brothers stepped back, forcing Tathrin to retreat. The last two renegades advanced.

'Where do you think you're going now?' Gren demanded, incredulous.

A fair question, it distracted the first man for the instant it took Sorgrad to stab him through the thigh. He collapsed to his knees, lifeblood spurting over the stones. Seeing the last only wore a leather jerkin, Tathrin swiftly ran him through the heart.

He stooped to clean his sword on the man's cloak. It bore a bird badge. 'Swallowtails?' He glanced at Sorgrad.

'And Triple Knot.' Gren cut the complex woven token of cord from another dead man's shoulder.

Straightening up, Tathrin assessed how much fighting was now joined up on the battlements. As fast as his army had been to seize the gatehouses, they had known some renegades would reach the various stairs that ran up inside the walls to access the heights.

But reaching the wall-walk still left those renegades with nowhere to go but risk the killing drop to the snowfields beyond, unless they'd had the forethought to bring a rope. These Swallowtails and Triple Knots had precious little room to fight to retake the gatehouses, whether or not they were still trying to hold the town or simply wanted to use the invaders' own ropes to escape.

In the ruddy light of the consuming fires, Tathrin saw skirmishes flare up around the battlements. Men toppled into the darkness, some screaming, some limp and silent. How many of those were his own?

Down below, the Bonebreakers resumed their assault on the militia holding the archway. Once again they were beaten back towards the encroaching flames. How long would it take, Tathrin wondered bleakly, before all the renegades were dead, whether by fire or sword?

Would any of them surrender? Would any of the Lescari soldiers let them, passing up the chance of revenge for all the endless years of suffering such mercenaries had inflicted on their hapless land? No, he didn't think he'd be dealing with many prisoners, come dawn.

'Tathrin!' Sorgrad pointed through the sooty orange glow towards an unnatural blue flare.

'Where's that?' Tathrin answered his own question. 'The Deflin Gate.' A second blue light kindled, and a third.

'They've forced it open.' Sorgrad shook his head.

'Or had it opened for them.' Gren already had a leg over the battlements, his sword sheathed. 'Andarise always was a greedy bastard. That's a Tormalin gold crown you owe me.'

'Only if you find his pockets full of silver,' retorted Sorgrad.

'The reserve will have seen that signal.' Tathrin was seeking reassurance as much as offering it.

'Let's go and make sure.' Gren disappeared down a rope, lithe as a squirrel.

Better safe than sorry. Tathrin followed him down the ladder.

Good fortune could still confirm the justice of their cause. If Sergeant Andarise had proved a broken reed, whether his men had opened the Deflin Gate for whatever gold or silver the renegades were throwing at them, or if they had been overwhelmed, at least some trusted mercenaries had managed to signal a warning of that calamity.

Trusting his gloves to save him from rope burns, Tathrin slid down the last few spans of the ladder. Landing with a thud, he ran after Sorgrad and Gren, as fast as he could on snow trampled hard and slick.

He had insisted their reserve force wait between the Triolle and Deflin roads, to give them the best possible chance of intercepting any renegades who managed to break through a gate. He had held back many of the most experienced mercenaries to strengthen that contingent: Shearlings and Tallymen, allied with the Triollese militia who'd most distinguished themselves on that arduous march north to Ashgil.

Just as long as those warriors weren't too stiff and slow after waiting in the winter cold. As long as they could catch whatever force of renegades was making a dash for freedom along the Deflin Road. Otherwise all this long murderous night could have been for nothing. When he finally saw the Triolle Road Gate ahead, the cold air burning his lungs, Tathrin tasted bile at the back of his mouth.

He spat it out and shouted at the Adel militiamen tending their wounded in the soiled slush. 'Every third man fit to fight, follow me!'

That gate was still securely held but he could not risk stripping away all its defenders lest whatever renegades remained within got some second wind.

The stretch of wall now separating them from the Deflin Road Gate was longer still. They ran on. Gren veered to avoid bodies spilling out of one of the narrow passages piercing the wall.

Tathrin saw two men slam the oak shut and brace themselves against it while a third jammed it closed with a broken sword. He could only assume they were his own and ran past without a word.

Blue light cast eldritch shadows across snow stained with blood. Bodies sprawled still and broken. The fight for the Deflin Road Gate had been fierce. Who had won?

Tathrin saw that only half of the double gate stood open. The other door was still resolutely closed, jostling figures within the archway silhouetted against the burning town. Tathrin could hear shouting but he couldn't make out the words.

A man ran from the shadows, brandishing a blade. Tathrin saw the militiaman's yellow and cream kerchief and tugged at his own, knotted around his neck.

'Peace for Lescar!' His words were lost in a cough as the wind swept smoke into his face.

The oncoming militiaman hadn't seen the kerchief any more than he'd heard Tathrin shout the day's battlefield password. Yelling ferociously, the man swept his arm back, ready to bring the blade crashing down.

Tathrin stepped in close and punched him hard in the chest, sending him staggering, sword flailing uselessly.

'Peace for Lescar!' he snarled at the man. 'What's happened?'

'Captain Sayron?' The hapless man gaped. Hastily gathering his wits, he gestured towards the gate. 'Reskin's and some Boot Snakes, veterans, they rushed us on horseback. They got through, and some on foot, but we drove the rest back,' he insisted.

'Where's Sergeant Andarise?' Even as he asked the question, Tathrin changed his mind. 'Never mind.' He turned to the men who'd followed from the Triolle Road Gate. 'Half of you, strengthen them here. The rest, with me!'

At least the escaping renegades had left an easy trail to follow, hobnailed boots and hooves alike pocking the unsullied snow. Each sapping step should slow men and horses both. Tathrin could only hope so.

He hoped his own strength would hold out long enough to catch them, and that of the men valiantly following him through this endless night. Even Sorgrad and Gren were looking grimly weary now.

Tathrin led his small force into the darkness. They soon left the blue reflections of Aldabreshin torches and the ochre glow of the burning town colouring the snow. He struggled to pick out the line of the smothered road across the moonlit ground ahead. The countryside was latticed with hedges and patched with copses, black against the white.

What had the escaping renegades decided? Would they be lying in wait to attack? Hiding up in hopes of dawn? Or getting as far away as they could?

'Horse!'

As Sorgrad shouted, everyone halted.

A handful of mounted men appeared from the far side of a coppice, black cloaked against the cold.

Men surged up behind Gren and Tathrin. Halberds bristled, one blade cleaving the moonlight perilously close by Tathrin's head. Lescar's militias had learned hard lessons on defending themselves against cavalry over these past few seasons.

Instead of charging them, or taking to the hazardous fields in hopes of cutting around to the town, the riders slowed to halt a prudent distance ahead. The foremost threw back his hood, moonlight gleaming on his shaven head.

Sorgrad shoved a halberd pole aside and stepped forwards. 'Hanged Man?'

Now Tathrin saw the pale smudge of a badge on the riders' black tabards: the gibbeted corpse of the Gallowsfruit blazon.

The tall mercenary captain rode closer. 'Captain-General Evord's compliments and we hold the Deflin Road. You may conclude your business in Wyril.'

Sorgrad laughed. 'He must know your birth festival's Winter Solstice, long lad. He's brought you an early gift!'

As the weary warriors behind Tathrin raised a ragged cheer, the Hanged Man grinned wolfishly. 'Juxon's Raiders have camped on the Draximal Road and the Sundowners hold the Tyrle Road. Wyvern Hunters block the way to Triolle.' He fixed Tathrin with an unreadable look. 'Captain-general's compliments and he would like a word with you.'

'Gladly.' Relief left Tathrin light-headed. He turned to the men clustered behind him and picked out a burly halberdier wearing a badge made from half the Wheelwrights' blazon and half of the rebellion's ring of hands. 'Sergeant, take these men back to the Deflin Road Gate.'

The man sketched a brief salute. 'Gladly, Captain.'

'How far—' But as Tathrin turned to talk to the Hanged Man, the handful of mercenaries were already riding away into the night.

'So we're on our own two feet. Come on, long lad. ' Sorgrad began loping after them. 'Don't keep Captain-General Evord waiting.'

Tathrin opened his mouth to protest, then forced his leaden feet to a jog instead.

'How lucky is that?' Gren trotted at his side, grinning from ear to ear. 'He just happens to be marching north and he's run into all this trouble on the road. One of those Boot Snakes must have sorely offended Halcarion.'

Tathrin was certain luck had nothing to do with it. Evord took great pains to know what was going on, sending out scouts and gathering news from far and wide, even without the benefit of

Artifice or Charoleia's subterfuges. Any number of reports would have reached him during their march north through Parnilesse and he'd always known Wyril was Tathrin's next objective.

Then he wondered how much further he could go before he fell asleep on his feet and sprawled headlong in the road. Thankfully, he saw the horsemen riding ahead meet another mounted contingent. A banner snapped briefly open and he caught a glimpse of a bird's widespread wings.

Sorgrad halted. 'Solura's gyrfalcon.'

Tathrin stood dumb and exhausted as the Soluran captain-general and his personal troop rode up.

'Captain Sayron.' Evord looked down, curiosity blended with mild disapproval. 'Where is your horse?'

'My horse?' That surprised Tathrin. 'Captain-General, I have been fighting through streets and along battlements.'

'Why?' Evord raised steely grey brows.

Tathrin didn't know what to make of this. He was standing in the middle of a snowy night, covered in blood and muck. Captain-General Evord sat on his horse, armed and armoured for a hazardous winter's journey. Yet the Soluran was engaging him in placid conversation, like two scholars debating some point on either side of a fireplace.

He gestured at the fiery glow lighting up the night. 'To take Wyril back from the renegades.'

'I understand the aim of your campaign,' Evord assured him. 'My congratulations on a well-executed assault. But why do I find you here on foot, leading an inconsequential pursuit? Where is your banner? Where are your gallopers and runners?'

Tathrin saw the youthful lieutenants in Evord's personal troop regarding him with veiled curiosity. Someone somewhere choked back a chuckle. Dagaran was there on a piebald cob, looking ruefully sympathetic.

'It is not a captain-general's business to be chasing all over a battlefield,' Evord reproved him. 'You should be holding some vantage point at a safe distance, to direct your forces according to reports reaching you. Which can only reach you,' he added, 'if your banner shows your sergeants where you are.'

Chagrin goaded Tathrin to incautious words. 'Forgive me, my lord. I am no such great hero—'

'Heroes don't win battles–' Evord surprised him with a grin '–any more than great men decide the course of history. But the right man in the right place can determine the course of a battle, with all the good or ill that follows from that victory or defeat. You're the right man to command Lescar's armies. This night's work proves that. So I expect to see you in your rightful place, Captain Sayron, to make best use of your undoubted abilities. Not where an unfortunate arrow or some bold fool with a blade could end all Lescar's hopes along with your life. I would take it very much amiss if such an entirely avoidable mishap undid all my hard work this autumn,' he added sternly.

'My lord.' Exhausted and uncomfortably aware that Evord was correct, Tathrin settled for a respectful bow.

'We spread ourselves along all the roads in hopes of finding more forage as we marched.' Evord looked over Tathrin's head towards the burning town. 'We will continue on towards the Great West Road at first light. But do call on me to share some breakfast before we go.'

Tathrin managed a crooked smile. 'Provided I can find a horse, my lord.'

'Quite so.' Evord nodded. 'You'll be writing to Mistress Charoleia, to tell her how you've fared?' Now Tathrin saw a gleam of amusement deep in the Soluran's icy pale eyes. 'My compliments and she may be interested to know that King Solquen intends to repay Mandarkin impudence on his northern borders, as soon as the snow melts in the mountain passes. These companies that I march with will accompany me on that task.' He paused. 'If she doesn't already know.'

Tathrin's smile broadened. 'I couldn't guess what Charoleia does or doesn't know, my lord.'

Evord nodded before snapping his fingers at a couple of the mercenary lieutenants. 'Your horses for Captain Sayron. Double up to ride back to camp.'

Tathrin saw the two young men weren't best pleased but they knew better than to argue. These places riding with Evord, all the better to learn the arts of battle, were eagerly sought.

'Thank you.' He accepted the reins of a fine bay horse while Sorgrad took possession of a raw-boned grey.

Evord smiled. 'I'll see you at first light, Tathrin.'

At the Soluran's nod, the whole troop wheeled around and melted into the night.

Tathrin heaved a sigh. 'Let's get back.' He urged the bay horse back towards the burning town. He fervently hoped the fighting was nearly done. Would it be possible to snatch some sleep before dawn and what must surely be his last farewell to Evord?

He was grateful for the Soluran's presence but still more pleased that the captain-general's mercenaries had been given so little to do. This truly was a Lescari victory.

Gren chuckled. 'I wouldn't like to be that young Wyvern Hunter, telling Arest how he lost his mount.'

'That'll teach the fool to snigger when Evord's schooling our long lad.' Sorgrad's sideways glance was warmer than his words.

Tathrin's thoughts were already moving on. He must indeed compose a report for Branca to pass to Charoleia. Could she already know what King Solquen of distant Solura was planning for the spring? Did her reach truly extend that far?

Chapter Eighteen
Branca

The Three Fountains Inn,
Solland, in the Tormalin Empire,
Winter Solstice Festival, First Day, Morning

This first morning of festival, so Charoleia informed her, was when the most fashionable in the town paid the season's respects to Ostrin. Branca looked dispassionately at her reflection in the long mirror. While she would never be a beauty, she was elegantly gowned in maroon wool, pleasingly coiffeured and jewelled. If these Tormalin despised her Vanam accent, they couldn't scorn her wardrobe.

She recalled a question she'd seen in Tathrin's thoughts. 'Where do you suppose Captain-General Evord and his mercenaries will be spending the festival?'

Charoleia was sitting on her daybed, sifting through the morning's delivery of letters and the messages Branca had fetched at dawn from the old man with the courier dove loft.

'They'll still be on the road,' Charoleia remarked absently. 'If they make good time, they should reach Abray in time for the Solstice.' She looked up. 'When does Tathrin leave Ashgil?'

'Today,' replied Branca. 'He'll be in Carluse the day after tomorrow.'

She knew he was as eager to see Failla and Aremil as he was to leave the blackened shell of Wyril. How could the town ever be rebuilt now it had become a funeral pyre? Branca shared his doubts.

'It seems the common folk of Draximal are delighted to see Wyril rid of those renegades.' Charoleia was studying another letter, smiling. 'Since their own liege lord so signally failed to act, they're increasingly inclined to contemplate a future without dukes or kings. Duchess Nisina's decision to take her daughters and son across the river to spend the festival in Ashery seems like a further betrayal.' She read a short passage aloud: '"Even those most loyal to Duke Secaris see no prospect of peace if he abdicates to a cripple who's lived all his life in exile and is now laid so low by sickness that his very life is despaired of."'

Branca shivered at a fearful vision of cold wind blowing dead leaves through Aremil's pillared hall. 'That isn't true.' But how much longer could it be before Aremil slipped beyond Welgren and Serafia's ministrations?

'No,' Charoleia agreed, 'but as long as we don't deny it, the more damage Duke Secaris does to his own cause by insisting that's how he will come to terms with us.'

Branca closed her eyes. Repellent though that calculation was, she could see how it served their purposes. It was worthy of Charoleia.

'Is there any news from Parnilesse?' Branca had also seen how urgently Tathrin sought some insight into tackling Reniack without setting Lescari against Lescari as the dukes had always done.

'Nothing noteworthy.' Charoleia's satisfaction momentarily dimmed. 'Forgive me,' she continued briskly as she locked the letters inside a casket beside her. 'Are you ready?'

'Indeed.' Branca took the casket, hid it in the false bottom of an entirely different chest from the one whose secrets Emperor Tadriol had seen, and fetched her scarlet cloak and sable muff.

Coils of ivy and sprays of yew were embroidered around the snowy hem of Charoleia's white velvet cloak. Her silk dress beneath was the same rich green and emeralds shone among the curls of her wig.

As they went down the stairs she glanced at Branca, her violet eyes bright with purpose. 'Now we're securing our hold on Draximal as well as Triolle, Carluse and Sharlac, I'll give some thought to cutting Lord Rousharn off at the knees. Remind me to write to Lord Trenaval, near Maerden, when we return. I believe he'll recall Rousharn's youthful rashness to His would-be Grace's discredit.'

'I'm sure he and Derenna are doing what they believe is right.' Much as she detested the bull-necked Rousharn for his treatment of Aremil, Branca still regretted Derenna's loss to their cause. It couldn't be denied that they were still reaping the benefits of the noblewoman's earlier arguments persuading vassal lords not to answer their lieges' summons.

'No doubt.' Charoleia shrugged. 'Now, what we need is some festival gossip that offers some clue as to how to deal with Parnilesse. We mustn't forget Marlier either, for all that the Vixen's gone to earth.'

They reached the inn's entrance hall, thronged with merrymakers. Charoleia broke off to exchange compliments and congratulations. Her step was brisk, her manner lively. Her scars were only visible when she stripped off her wigs and cosmetics at the end of each busy day.

When Branca's guilt nagged at her in the dark silence, when all other voices were stilled.

'Where are we going?' she asked quietly as they emerged from the inn's front door.

'To see the lanterns.' Charoleia carefully negotiated the steps. While Solland enjoyed far milder weather than most of Lescar, frosts persisted underfoot in the depths of midwinter.

This street lined with drapers' shops would take them to Ostrin's shrine. The flagstoned paths were so crowded that some men were risking their polished boots along the cobbles. Branca would have done the same but for her high-heeled shoes.

'Oh, look!' She paused to feign admiration for an array of embroidered stockings in a window.

Where Vanam's warehouses served their customers from tables set amid their stores of lace or buttons, Tormalin merchants laid out finery on their deep sills to lure those passing by. Step inside in this wealthy district and attentive vendors would instantly offer a seat and obsequious service.

'Fine work,' approved Charoleia, 'but Master Vitrie has finer. Oh, forgive me.' She stepped back to allow a grey-haired gentleman to examine the stockings through an inquisitive eyeglass.

'Fair festival, ladies.' He bowed and retreated into the crowd.

'You're right.' Branca turned her back on the window. 'Let's see what's offered elsewhere.'

They passed by several more shops before Charoleia paused in front of a display of gaudy feathers in silver and jewelled fans. Paper crackled as she opened the note that elderly esquire had slipped into her muff.

Branca gazed idly along the street, an apparently bored companion. No, she saw no one watching them. 'Well?'

'All manner of precedents are being kicked around Toremal's law courts and libraries. Advocate Tathel cannot find a conclusive argument that explicitly bars Tormalin's Emperor from intervening in Lescar.' Charoleia didn't sound too perturbed. 'On the other side of Raeponin's scales, his opponents cannot find any action since the rise of the dukes that would offer Tadriol the most flimsy justification.'

'Let's hope they'll continue wrangling right through to Aft-Spring.' Branca knew that's what Charoleia was seeking.

'By which time we must have a settlement for the warmongering princes to choke on.' Charoleia dropped the crumpled paper into a nut-seller's brazier where it burned to unreadable ashes. 'Which means dealing with Parnilesse and with Ferdain of Marlier,' she said with some asperity.

'With Aremil still unwell, I'm not at all sure Failla is asking the right questions of her uncle and his allies. I want to know what lies behind this recent spate of banditry in Carluse. Then there's the Caladhrian parliament meeting in Ferl, and it will take me days to find out what's deliberated there. I could wring Master Gruit's neck for having Kerith driven out of Abray, if we knew where the old fool had gone.' Shaking her head, she walked onwards. 'But if we leave here, who will keep a hand on Tormalin's reins?'

Branca had no answer for that. But she had seen a lackey waiting outside a sweetmeat emporium. His honeysuckle badge was as bright as an evening star on his dark blue jerkin. Pausing to find a handkerchief in her pocket, she nodded at the shop. 'I believe we're out of candied violets.'

'So we are.' Charoleia snapped her fingers for a crossing sweeper.

As they followed the lad's diligent broom, Branca found him a silver penny.

'Candied violets?' Charoleia frowned as the sweet-seller's lad opened the door. 'Wouldn't you prefer honeyed almonds?'

'Actually, I would.' Branca supposed she should hardly be surprised that Charoleia had noticed.

'Relict Den Sarascol!' As they entered the shop, Yadres Den Dalderin turned with every appearance of surprise. 'And your charming companion. Fair festival to you both.'

He was dressed in the height of Tormalin fashion. Indeed, Branca thought, emulating Charoleia's expert eye, he was trying a little too hard with so much lace at his shirt cuffs and collar, those jewelled rings on every finger and such florid silver buckles for both his knee-breeches and his shoes.

'Dear boy,' Charoleia cooed as Branca curtsied. 'Fair festival.'

'Are you going to see the lanterns?' Yadres extended one arm to Charoleia and the other to Branca. 'Shall we walk there together?'

'Why not?' Charoleia laid her hand on his forearm.

'Thank you, but the flagway isn't wide enough for three abreast in this crowd.' Branca also preferred to keep her hands warmly in her muff.

'Will you be visiting the pleasure gardens after seeing the lanterns?' Yadres asked brightly as they left the shop. 'There's to be a concert and a marionette show.'

'That sounds delightful,' agreed Charoleia.

'It will be my honour to escort you.' Yadres smiled somewhat fatuously before gesturing to his lackey. 'You there, go and find your own amusements for the afternoon. I'm sure there's some festival ale you'd rather be drinking.'

'As you command, Esquire.' The man grinned and slid off into the crowd.

Not for the first time, Branca wondered what the other sieurs made of Yadres; those formidable princes who governed the great houses of the Tormalin Empire.

Did they think Eofin, Sieur Den Dalderin, advisor to the Emperor, had chosen wisely when seeking an apprentice among his considerable quantity of nephews and cadet cousins? Or did they dismiss Yadres as no more than he seemed: an amiable youth trustworthy with some letter or simple task but too lightweight to be privy to his uncle's secrets? How hard did they look instead for some stealthier enquiry agent?

They turned down a glass-roofed arcade where coaches couldn't follow and fewer pedestrians seemed to have business. As the crowd around them thinned, Yadres glanced at Charoleia.

'My uncle tells me the renegades are burned out of Wyril.'

No messenger could have carried that news by hand to the Tormalin capital, not even by riding several horses into the ground. So as Branca and Charoleia suspected, there were still Tormalin spies in Lescar cherishing their last few courier birds.

Charoleia smiled winningly. 'As we've always told your uncle and his dear friend, we're committed to bringing peace to Lescar.'

'You told us the Soluran was leaving for home.' Yadres wasn't smiling now. 'That he wouldn't lead men into battle again.'

'He was leading his men and those mercenaries still with him north to the Great West Road.' Charoleia met the young man's gaze unperturbed. 'What other route would you have him take in the midst of winter?'

Yadres shook his head. 'Do you take my uncle for a fool? The Soluran's men killed those renegades.'

'Perhaps a double handful, but no more than that.' Charoleia slid her hand free from his arm.

'Those few who'd escaped the trap that Captain Sayron sprang in Wyril,' added Branca.

'That's not the tale told in Toremal's tisane houses,' Yadres insisted.

Charoleia continued through the pillared walkway. 'Then please tell your uncle to tell his gullible friends that he knows for a certainty that Captain-General Evord is on his way home to

Solura. He's taking those mercenary companies with him, intent on taking King Solquen's coin when the fighting season arrives in the Wildlands.'

Branca knew Tathrin still suspected Charoleia had some hand in that. She wouldn't mind knowing the answer to that question herself.

'You may assure your uncle and his honoured friend that Lescar's army will secure Lescari peace and prosperity from this festival onwards.' Charoleia paused to look sternly at Yadres. 'There will be no more mercenaries in Lescar to excuse Tormalin's legions intervening to save their hapless neighbours.'

'Other than the ones your Captain Tathrin Sayron has recruited in the Carifate,' countered Yadres.

Charoleia shook her head as she continued walking. 'Tathrin has recruited men and women of Lescari birth, willing to stake their lives on Lescar's peaceful future, to serve as sergeants and captains for Lescar's town militias and Watch contingents.'

Yadres pursed his lips. 'Doubtless those militias will be glad of Tormalin's legions' assistance in curbing the anarchy sweeping through Parnilesse.'

'Parnilesse is hardly suffering the upheavals you seem to imagine,' Branca objected. 'Captain Tathrin established that much on his march north from Carif.'

Yadres shrugged. 'Those who seized Parnilesse Castle have imposed their will on the Guild Councils of Brynock and Inchra and executed those who oppose them. Their next step will be to subjugate Hardrew, and after that Quirton. As long as they hold all those towns, they have mastery over every villager and yeoman in between who needs a market to sell produce and buy household goods.'

Unfortunately Branca couldn't argue with that. If Reniack's reign of terror had proved less widespread than they'd feared, Tathrin had found that the dread of his men's reprisals had the common folk thoroughly cowed.

She also knew he feared how much more brutal Reniack's rule might become once the quelling cold of winter had passed.

'As I have been at pains to assure your uncle,' Charoleia told Yadres sharply, 'now that we've brought peace to Wyril, bringing freedom and concord to Parnilesse is our most urgent priority. I have every faith in Captain Tathrin.'

'Unfortunately, the Convocation of Princes has now agreed that Tormalin intervention is the best guarantee of Tormalin interests.' Yadres betrayed exasperation, but not with Charoleia.

Branca wondered if that was an echo of his uncle's feelings. And of Emperor Tadriol's?

'After seeing the Soluran take up arms again,' the young nobleman explained, 'those princes who suspect King Solquen's malign interest in our affairs have made common cause with those who fear Parnilesse's anarchy will soon spill across the Asilor. They agree prevention is better than cure.'

'I wouldn't wish to belittle that honoured assembly's wisdom, but such interference will do more harm than good.' Neither Charoleia's face nor tone betrayed the intense annoyance Branca knew she must be feeling. 'Captain Tathrin is more than capable.'

'Perhaps he is,' Yadres allowed, 'but he cannot be in two places at once. Who will be dealing with all the fresh unrest in Carluse and Marlier if his attention is turned to Parnilesse?'

'All what unrest?' Charoleia coloured her response with amusement as well as disbelief.

Yadres heaved a sigh and halted. 'Madam, I am truly surprised that you need ask. These past ten days have seen homes and farms burned all along the Marlier bank of the Rel. These past few nights have even seen incursions into Caladhria by these mercenary brutes.'

He abandoned the usual pretences of their conversations entirely. Branca could see Charoleia was as taken aback as she was.

'Mercenaries from Marlier's winter camps are raiding Caladhria?' the older woman demanded.

'No one knows where these curs have sprung from.' Yadres shook his head. 'Ferdain of Marlier is utterly outraged. He is calling on Caladhria's parliament to muster an army at once, as well as writing to every friend he has in Tormalin's Convocation.' He lowered his voice, glancing around to be sure no one was within earshot.

'My uncle tells me Duke Ferdain is offering generous inducements to the Sieur Den Breche. Gold to show Marlier's goodwill has apparently already been dispatched, along with the firm assurance of more once the first legions cross into Parnilesse.'

Branca couldn't help asking: 'Why does Ferdain want Tormalin's legions in Parnilesse?'

Yadres looked askance at her. 'So they can march on to Draximal and Sharlac after securing that dukedom, while Caladhria's barons send their men to drive your Captain Tathrin's companies out of every town in Carluse and Triolle. If they have their way, come the spring, your captain will have every battle that the Soluran won last year to fight all over again.'

He returned his attention to Charoleia. 'The Sieur D'Orsetis is getting letters from Duke Iruvain, begging him to back Den Breche in the Convocation's debates.'

'What's Iruvain offering?' Charoleia demanded.

'Lots of pleas and promises but no gold as yet.' Yadres' grin relieved a little of the tension. 'My uncle says D'Orsetis won't move till he has silver in his hand, so that gives us a little time.'

Charoleia wasn't amused. 'Den Breche has fewer friends than he imagines but D'Orsetis' voice will carry a fair distance. That's before Secaris of Draximal begins asking for aid to reclaim his dukedom too.'

'I don't imagine Duchess Aphanie will be slow to plead her case,' Branca commented reluctantly.

'Quite so,' Yadres agreed.

Charoleia halted at the end of the arcade. 'What will Tadriol need to stop Tormalin's legions marching?' she asked bluntly.

Yadres had a ready answer. 'You say Duke Orlin's murder and all that's followed is the work of comparatively few men? Give his Imperial Majesty proof that he can lay before the princes of the Convocation. Bring those men responsible to answer for their heinous crimes. If you uphold the rule of law, there's less case to be made for Tormalin's legions doing so. But you have to act fast and you must show some firm plan for the peaceful governance of Lescar, while your friends curb whatever banditry's plaguing Marlier and Carluse,' he warned.

'Once Caladhria's barons send an army over the Rel, Tormalin's legions will march.'

'Indeed.' Charoleia nodded.

Branca felt a pang for Tathrin. She could already imagine his weariness, when she had to tell him there was no respite in the demands made of him and his army. And how were they to come up with some new rule of law for Lescar without Aremil's scholarly contribution? She felt hollow inside. Were they ever going to see a conclusion to all their endeavours?

'I must give all this careful consideration,' Charoleia said after a long moment. 'You may call on me the day after the Solstice, to discuss how we might proceed in all our best interests.'

'Then I'll wish you both fair festival till then.' Yadres offered a courteous bow. 'I hope you enjoy the concert.' He smiled with sudden charm. 'I would take it as a personal favour if you were to tell anyone who asks that I accompanied you there.'

He bowed again and went out of the arcade.

Branca watched him stride across the broad square beyond. 'Where do you suppose he's going in such a hurry?'

'I don't know and I really don't care,' Charoleia said frankly. 'Now let's see these cursed lanterns and get back to the inn to start writing letters. We need more news and quickly if we're to make any kind of plan.'

She hitched up the hem of her cloak and walked swiftly across the square. Branca hurried along beside her.

'Fair festival, good ladies.' Even before they had crossed half the expanse, an eager priest approached with an enamelled ceremonial urn.

Seeing Charoleia was wrapped in thought, Branca hastily searched her reticule for some more silver pennies.

'Health and happiness for the year to come.' The priest approved the rattle of coin into his little urn with a smooth benediction before hastening to intercept a family crossing the square.

Branca wondered what had brought him to this life. Country priesthoods were often held by lesser noble sons, the office inherited in lieu of some share in those lands where the shrine had stood from time before memory. Some such lordlings merely mouthed the festival litanies but others found true purpose in the charities and education that shrine fraternities offered the local populace. Master Ernout had proved adept in finding such priests to argue the cause of peace and prosperity in Lescar, even if sacrificing the dukes might be needed to secure it.

Town shrines were a different matter, at least in Vanam. Branca had found priests and priestesses there equally divided between those driven by genuine dedication to their god or goddess, and those whose piety went no deeper than devotion to the food and shelter their sacred robes secured without the need for strenuous labour.

She contemplated the vast building ahead. The Solland shrine to Ostrin that sprawled in all directions was no mere temple of pious hopes for healing. While it showed a graceful outward face, blessed with the most expensive, most Rational architecture, the halls enclosing the hot springs and accommodating the sick had grown with each generation, thanks to priests more concerned with the demands of the suffering than with their own comfort and prestige..

The main gate to the shrine's precincts rose in the centre of a long colonnade. Ostrin's statue was honoured above the entrance. Six niches adorned the precinct wall on either side, harmoniously set within the pillars, housing exquisite statues of the other gods.

Today, great silver lanterns glowed in the shadows of the colonnade. Each one showed three facets, like a rune, all painted with scenes from winter fables. There was Trimon on his travels, Talagrin at his hunting, and Larasion amid her clouds. If she didn't recognise all the myths alluded to, Branca recognised each god and goddess as she and Charoleia walked slowly along the colonnade, both of them silent amid the volubly admiring throng.

As well as the lanterns, the colonnade was adorned with pine boughs that recalled more ancient celebrations. Branca breathed in the evergreen scents and felt horribly homesick for Vanam. How were her family celebrating the Solstice? Had they received the letter she'd sent with one of Charoleia's dispatches?

The older woman finally spoke as they passed the last lantern. 'I believe I may just see a path through this maze.'

'How so?' Branca looked around to make sure no one was listening.

Charoleia lowered her voice as they left the colonnade. 'All Caladhria's news washes downstream to Relshaz. A woman called Mellitha Esterlin can help us there.'

Branca knew that name. 'But she's a wizard,' she said, uncertain.

'Quite so.' Charoleia smiled. 'She can scry and tell us all about these goings-on in Marlier without Planir having any grounds for an objection.'

'Are you sure?' Branca remembered what Aremil had told her of Tathrin's meeting with the Relshazri magewoman. That's where he'd first met the Archmage's enquiry agent. 'Isn't she a friend of Jilseth's? Won't this Mellitha tell her everything she discovers?'

Tathrin had no doubt that both women served Hadrumal's interests above all others. In the hidden recesses of his thoughts, frankly, Branca knew he feared them.

'Quite so,' Charoleia said again. 'Better yet, I believe Madam Jilseth will prove just the person to help us allay Emperor Tadriol's concerns.'

Branca stared, quite unable to fathom this.

'I'll explain, all in good time.' Charoleia began walking briskly in the direction of the inn. 'First we have to find out exactly what's afoot in Marlier.'

Chapter Nineteen
Litasse

Marlier Castle,
Winter Solstice Festival, Third Day, Evening,
Souls' Ease Night

She had waited till nearly midnight. Now the castle was quiet, after the exuberant relief of the first day of festival and before the more desperate revelry of the last to bolster everyone's spirits against the hungry days of Aft-Winter. This middle night, the longest and coldest of the year, was given over to commemorating the beloved departed even by those who seldom set foot in a shrine year round.

Not that spirits seemed particularly high this festival. Litasse had noticed guests drinking in moderation, talking quietly among themselves. What were the Marlier nobles discussing? But she had no loyal maids to listen at keyholes, to gather scraps of conversations from stairwell shadows.

Reaching an unfamiliar corridor, she hesitated. Which way now? Litasse didn't think she'd ever learn her way around this rabbits' warren. The dukes of Marlier's castle sprawled this way and that across the broad hill that it dominated.

A jousting ground had been added here; there, a further courtyard to accommodate some newly married heir in anticipation of his children. The original keep had fallen into disfavour many generations ago, so a second great hall had been built. New ducal accommodations had soon followed, not to be outdone by its splendour.

Marlier's dukes remained mindful of the perils of war. The outermost curtain wall had been rebuilt several times to enclose these successive renewals. The remnants of older fortifications were seldom entirely demolished though. Rather, they were incorporated into stables or kitchens or storehouses; whatever the castle was now deemed to lack.

After growing up in Sharlac Castle, where the four-towered keep was neatly flanked by twin turreted gatehouses marking the limits of the rectangular outer ward, all Litasse saw was disharmony and confusion.

Though she wasn't lost now, she realised with relief. This corridor led to Duchess Adarise's Hall. She cared nothing for that long-dead duchess but she knew the old keep beyond housed the castle's shrine to Poldrion.

Litasse ran along the corridor, her slippers silent on the carpet. Prudently shielded lanterns shone beside each closed door but she could have found her way without them. Only just past its full, the Greater Moon's clear light poured through the tall leaded windows. The cloudless sky was bright with stars scattered around the fading quarter of the Lesser Moon.

The door to the old keep was unlocked. Litasse stayed alert for Duke Ferdain's cat-footed night watchmen, but none prowled these echoing stone stairs. Plucking at the skirt of her black velvet gown, she hurried upwards. The longer she was absent from her chamber, the more likely she'd be missed by one of Marlier's suspiciously attentive maids.

She halted outside the shrine. What if someone else was in there? Litasse squared her shoulders. She outranked any noble lord or lady, all but Duke Ferdain and his duchess herself. Why should she explain herself, any more than she should excuse her absence to mere servants? She would remember her dead on Souls' Ease Night and Poldrion's demons could bite anyone suspecting worse of her.

There was no one in the shrine to provoke her ire. A single, massive white candle burned before Poldrion's statue. The glow burnished the ducal funeral urns on shelves running around the walls.

Litasse sat on a velvet stool. Where were the vessels holding the ashes of her younger brother Kerlin, of her dead father? Were her mother and sisters weeping over them?

Jaras's urn had been lost, his remains doubtless scattered, when the exiles sacked Sharlac Castle. How did usurping Lord Rousharn explain away that desecration to her foolish mother? Litasse ground her teeth.

But no, this wasn't a time for such grudges. It was her duty tonight to beseech Poldrion's care for her brothers and father, on that fateful journey to the door to the Otherworld. There they would beg for Saedrin's mercy as they confessed their transgressions in this life. He would open that door for the virtuous or the truly penitent and usher them across the threshold to oblivious rebirth.

All the priests agreed, those sworn to Poldrion and every other deity: when someone was reborn into the Otherworld, or born here after dying in that unknown realm, they had no recollection of any life lived before. That's what the priests said anyway. Necromancers who claimed otherwise, who claimed to speak to the dead, were beaten bloody until they recanted.

Could it be true? Would her father acknowledge his faults before Saedrin, mightiest of the gods? Or would he deny the arrogance that had driven him to attack Duke Garnot time and again, year after year, at the ultimate cost of her beloved brother Jaras's life?

Could he justify his selfish grief at that loss, shutting himself away so these rebels and exiles had been able to attack? Or was he still suffering in the darkness of the void until he repented his obstinacy? Were her guiltless brothers still loyally at his side or had they gone on ahead to find peace?

There were no answers for her here. The god leaned on his ferry pole, cloaked in black mystery. Litasse couldn't see his face and was glad of it. Most such statues resembled a gaunt, aged man but in Sharlac Castle's shrine, curious worshippers peering beneath Poldrion's hood met the bottomless gaze of a skull. Litasse had loathed it from a child.

Tears pricked her eyes. She would give anything to see the horrid thing again. The motionless statue silently rebuked her. Why say so, when she had nothing to give?

A still more unwelcome thought wormed its way into her contemplations. If she were to encompass some vengeance for Hamare and Pelletria's deaths, they would never know about it. That much was certain, whether the priests and their fables were true or if the Rationalists were in the right when they insisted folk had only one life to lead as honestly as they might.

Wouldn't that leave any such revenge as hollow as these urns that surrounded her?

'Fair festival and ease for your grief.'

Litasse gasped, her heart thumping. She sprang to her feet, affronted. 'Excuse me. I'll leave you to your devotions.'

The woman in the doorway chuckled, making no move to let her pass. 'There's no one to see us talking at this time of night.'

'We have nothing to say to each other,' Litasse retorted frostily.

She had no business with this whore. No, Ridianne was worse than a whore. As well as trading her own body for coin, she bought and sold the services of countless others, as Marlier's captain of mercenaries. Even on this sombre night, she flaunted her disgraceful occupation, wearing boots and breeches and a full-skirted coat in the Tormalin style over a lace-trimmed shirt.

'You look like a kitten bristling at a farmyard hen who's just stolen its mouse.' Closing the door, Ridianne leaned against it. 'I thought you might like to know – we've every hope that Tormalin's legions will be crossing the river Asilor into Parnilesse within days. After that, we expect they'll press on to secure the crossings over the Anock.'

'Then you will fight?' demanded Litasse.

Ridianne shrugged. 'Perhaps, perhaps not.'

'How can you expect to win if you do not fight?' cried Litasse.

If this woman wouldn't stir her fat carcass, how were her and Karn's plans ever to prosper?

Ridianne simply smiled. 'Look at that rune reversed. As long as I don't fight, I can't lose.'

'That's a fine excuse for cowardice,' Litasse shot back.

Ridianne's face hardened. 'You might be more courteous, as His Grace's guest.'

'I feel more like a prisoner,' snapped Litasse. 'I've received no letters since I arrived and whenever I have asked for a courier, I'm told no one is available. My every conversation is watched and noted.'

'You think this makes you a prisoner?' The candlelight picked out the silver in Ridianne's roughly cropped hair. The ferocious red that had earned her title of Vixen was long since faded. 'I could have you locked in a dungeon and loaded with chains, if you'd like to know the difference?' Her eyes glinted.

'You have no such authority.' Litasse took an involuntary step backwards. 'You're nothing but Duke Ferdain's mistress!'

'These past twenty years and more.' Ridianne's smile curved like the edge of a sword. 'You think that makes me nothing? I say that as one whore to another.'

Litasse blushed furiously. Was that what Marlier ladies were saying, as they whispered behind their hands? 'You have no authority over me,' she managed to say.

'Perhaps, but who's to stop me chastising you?' Ridianne raised her unkempt eyebrows. 'I am my own mistress, if you please. I haven't put my fate into any man's hands since my first husband died and his fool of a son threw me penniless out of my home. Can you say as much, for all your foolish pride?'

Litasse lifted her chin defiantly. 'Our situations are entirely different.'

'Doubtless you like to think so.' Ridianne waved a careless hand. 'But Duchess Hidarin and I understand each other. I'm not taking anything she wants for herself, and the whole world knows Ferdain and no other fathered her children.'

Litasse longed to argue with this abominable woman, but she had seen Marlier's duchess at this festival. Hidarin exchanged amiable courtesies with her husband when their duties coincided but both were more intent on celebrations and entertainments with their separate retinues. The duchess would return to her own fortified residence by the lake at Saltebre as soon as the Aft-Winter weather permitted.

Ridianne grinned as she saw Litasse struggling to find a retort. 'So kindly write to Iruvain, so he may tell Caladhria's barons that Tormalin's legions will soon be marching. I'll guarantee your letter's safe delivery.'

'Why by all that's holy should I trust you?' spat Litasse. 'You've already betrayed Lescar. You turned your coat against Triolle and Parnilesse and planted your standard alongside the Soluran. I wonder Duke Ferdain didn't have you flogged until your bones showed!'

'I have no great loyalty to Lescar.' Ridianne was unperturbed. 'My choices were simple: see my own forces cut to pieces for no one's benefit but Orlin of Parnilesse's, or yield and live to fight another day. Ferdain knows I always look out for Marlier's interests and Hidarin knows I'll see her children's interests as well protected as those of my own.'

Litasse trembled between anger and fear. 'I don't understand.'

'No, I don't suppose you do,' Ridianne agreed, 'you and Iruvain both, caught up in your passions and follies. Well, don't bother your pretty feather-head. Just write to Iruvain and tell him once Tormalin marches, now that the Soluran has definitely left the field, we have a chance to crush these rebels and see some order restored.'

'What order will that be?' Litasse laced her fingers together so tightly her hands ached.

For the first time Ridianne looked puzzled. 'You and your husband can return to Triolle and settle your differences or live apart, as you see fit. This Duke Rousharn looks strong enough to hold Sharlac and we'll divide Carluse between the three of us.'

'And the eastern dukedoms?' asked Litasse

The stout mercenary woman shrugged. 'If Secaris of Draximal remembers where he left his manhood, he's welcome to his patrimony. Or if we must surrender his domains to that cripple these exiles have foisted upon him, so be it. I don't doubt Tadriol of Tormalin will seize Parnilesse, but as long as the legions come no further west than the Anock, we can live with that.'

'You will all return to business as usual?' Litasse asked

scornfully. 'You and your hirelings will go back to taking merchants' gold to see them safely along the roads or down the Rel?'

Ridianne laughed. 'Pray tell, Your Grace, what else do you expect? What else do you want beyond gold and trade and peace? Didn't you learn anything from Master Hamare? Or was his tongue too busy to hold a sensible conversation with you?' Her amusement vanished in a threatening glare. 'Saedrin save us but I wish he was still here to advise us, and to send his spies into the enemy's camps. You say I betrayed Lescar, Your Grace? You did all of us a far graver disservice when you stuck a blade in him. Triolle could have stood your loss five times over rather than be deprived of his counsel.'

'I didn't kill Hamare,' Litasse burst out, 'and I'll have revenge for his death, and recompense besides, for everything that I've lost, for the ruin of my hopes, in Sharlac and in Triolle.'

She didn't know what made her more furious – this vile woman or the realisation that angry tears were sliding down her cheeks. She wouldn't stand for this whore pitying her weakness.

'I'll wish you well with that.' Ridianne was unmoved. 'In the meantime, let's play the runes as they roll. I'll send a courier for your letters tomorrow at noon. And now, if you please, where exactly is your man Karn?'

'Why should I tell you?' Litasse defied her. 'So you can see him stabbed in the back again?'

'Don't blame me for whatever quarrels followed him into my camp.' Ridianne's face hardened. 'And if you want to balance accounts, he left a lad dead behind him, according to the poor fool's tent-mates. Karn values anyone else's life as little as he values his own. Would you like him to answer for that at Duke Ferdain's winter assizes?'

Litasse bridled, indignant. 'You'll take the word of vagabonds over Karn's? He is the Duke of Triolle's intelligencer!'

'You seem very sure of him.' Ridianne angled her head. 'How many of Master Hamare's duties does he now fulfil?' Her insinuation was unmistakable.

Litasse gasped. 'Don't you dare spread such lies!'

Such gossip reaching Iruvain's ears would see him beat her senseless, if not lifeless.

'Then don't offer me scullery-maid insults,' Ridianne suggested. 'You're all alone here, Your Grace, without even that hired knife Karn. I will find out what he's about, even if you don't choose to tell me. When I do, just remember I can see him broken any time I like. If he has any hand in this current mischief, I'll see it cut off at the elbow, at very least.'

She broke off to frown at Litasse. 'But you have no idea what I'm talking about, do you?'

Litasse could only stare dumbly back.

Ridianne shook her head, exasperated. 'I really don't care if you're sheathing his blade in your scabbard twice-nightly. All I need is your handwriting and your seal on a letter to let Iruvain know where he stands.' She jabbed a ringed forefinger hard at Litasse. 'His Grace your husband is quite as bereft as you are. Without my mercenaries and Caladhrian aid, he has no hope of regaining the castle he fled like a scolded scullion, still less of re-establishing dominion over his dukedom. Marlier has far more friends in Caladhria that Triolle does, so don't imagine you can plan any campaign without Ferdain's approval, which is to say, without mine. You might point that out to your gracious lord. Be ready for my man at noon.'

Without even the suggestion of a bow, Ridianne departed the shrine.

As the door swung closed, Litasse sank back down onto the stool. She felt weary to the point of faintness. She was so truly, heartily sick of people telling her what she could and could not hope for, what she should and should not do.

The draught from the door had set the candlelight dancing around the silent polished ranks of Marlier's ducal dead. Litasse watched the shimmers settle as she contemplated her situation.

Could the spring or the summer to come possibly see her and Iruvain restored to Triolle Castle? Could she endure it, if the price was some accommodation with this Lord Rousharn, to secure Emperor Tadriol's aid? Even if it meant, Saedrin save her, coming to terms with these exiles who had killed Hamare?

If that was how all the runes finally rolled, would she have gained anything at all to make up for the loss and fear and grief that she had suffered? Would it have been worth all she had done or allowed to be done in her name?

Litasse shivered, though the shrine was not overly cold. How keenly did Ridianne want to know where Karn might be? What might she do to find out? What could Litasse tell her? She had no clear idea where he might really have gone, after his departure for Relshaz.

She had still less idea what he might be doing. Though echoes of their last conversation rang uneasily in her memory. Whatever it might take to reclaim her inheritance; that's what they had agreed.

Litasse gazed through the solid door after Ridianne. Had Karn truly killed a man in her camp? Whoever that had been, was someone mourning his loss tonight? Or desperately refusing to give him up for dead, despite his long, silent absence?

Why would the Vixen lie about such a thing? If she was honest with herself, alone in this shrine, on this most sombre of nights, Litasse knew Karn was capable of such brutality. He had beaten and robbed that fool of a girl in Adrulle without a second thought. He had been ready to stick a knife in that vile wizard Minelas, back in Adel Castle. He wouldn't even have blinked as the blade sank in. Saedrin save her, she had agreed he should do it, even before those rebels had intervened.

Litasse looked up at the statue of Poldrion. If she ever found herself on his fabled barque, as the priests all promised, perhaps she should just throw herself over the side into the void, surrender to the mercies of his demons and save them all some time.

Perhaps she might, if that day ever came. Wallowing in self-pity meanwhile would hardly improve her situation.

Ridianne was right, unfortunately. She was alone here. Litasse certainly couldn't hope to leave unless Iruvain's prospects improved. At the moment they were both being shifted around like carved forest birds on a white raven board. How long before they were sacrificed, for the benefit of someone of greater value to Marlier or Caladhria? Someone like this upstart Lord Rousharn who was still busy stealing her father's dukedom?

If she were ever to become mistress of her own destiny, she had to begin finding answers to all these questions. Even without friends or allies here, even without Hamare and Pelletria, she still had the skills and stratagems they had taught her.

Litasse clenched her fists. What was going on? What did Ridianne suspect Karn was up to? Was the Vixen right, or was Karn busy with some other scheme entirely?

Chapter Twenty
Karn

The Silver Gull, Relshaz,
Winter Solstice Festival, Fifth Day, Evening

He seldom gave a second thought to the men and women he had killed; for his own youthful purposes amid the chaos of Lescar's wars and later at Master Hamare's order in Triolle's service. But Karn was forced to conclude that the undoubted necessity of killing Downy Scardin, back in the early days of Aft-Autumn, was proving cursed inconvenient now.

He smiled charmingly at the olive-skinned girl bringing a tray to their table. As she set down the green-striped glass decanter and shallow little cups, he held up a golden Tormalin crown. Her sooty eyes brightened. His drinking companion didn't react but Karn knew he'd noticed. Shanish would assume plenty more such coins kept company in Karn's plump purse.

Good. He didn't want to spend any more time than he must trailing around these taverns and brothels where mercenaries idled. It was taking him far too long to recruit a second wave of brigands. If only he could have gone straight to Scardin, returning to Relshaz after setting his first murderous cohort loose in Marlier to plague that bitch Ridianne.

Karn would have paid whatever price the information broker demanded, with the gold the corsairs' slavers had paid for those startled peasants. That would have been by far the quickest way to learn what had been going on elsewhere.

But he had cut Downy Scardin's throat to break the scent that might tie him to Minelas and now the best Karn could do was pick up rumour and hearsay while he sought out the fighting companies wintering here and judged who looked ripe for a clandestine return to Lescar, untroubled by inconvenient scruples.

'It's midwinter, Browd.' The other man leaned forward to pour the pale liquor. 'I don't know where half my men are at present. I wouldn't expect anyone back to sign their names on the muster roll until the turn from winter to For-Spring.'

Karn considered standing up, as if to leave, but Shanish didn't have the air of a man trying to drive up a price. He truly wasn't interested. Karn savoured the spicy scent of the distilled metheglin. He might as well learn what Shanish knew before he moved on.

'The Firebrands don't want to steal a march on the rest?' He feigned surprise. 'The dukes of Marlier and Triolle won't be dallying. They'll drive these exiles and rebels out of Lescar before we see Spring Equinox.'

'They won't do much without men to back them.' Shanish shrugged. 'I can't see many captains persuading their men to risk hanging from some battlements like Wynald's Warband did at Losand. The Red Hounds took a thrashing when Garnot of Carluse was beaten and the Brassnecks too.' He set down his cup with a shake of his head. 'Trimming her sails to weather the storm didn't much help Ridianne the Vixen either. After that battle at Pannal, Alsar's Eaglets and the Flintstrikers can barely muster enough swords to call themselves a company.'

Karn couldn't deny it. Every step and skirmish of the autumn's campaign was still the stuff of gossip all around Relshaz. He refilled Shanish's cup.

'The Soluran's marched north once and for all.' He had learned that much from the tittle-tattle that swept along the coast from Triolle to Relshaz's docks. 'You know he's been paying off his men since the start of For-Winter. All Lescar has left is old men and beardless boys with blunt halberds in one hand and soggy cocks in the other.'

'That'll be the only thing they have in their breeches. Every dukedom bar Marlier must be as empty as a picked pocket by now.' Shanish grimaced, and not at the excellent metheglin. 'Or raked out like the ashes of Wyril. Who wants to suffer the same fate as the Bonebreakers and the Triple Knot?'

It took all Karn's years of practised deceit to shrug with indifference. It took still more effort not to ask what in the name of Talagrin's hairy arse Shanish meant. What had happened at Wyril?

'Wyril's not Triolle or Marlier.' He hoped that meaningless truth suggested he knew more than he did.

'Maybe so, maybe not.' Shanish still looked dubious. 'The only way you'll get men signing up to follow your flag, whether you're recruiting for the green grebe or the triple swords, will be to stack your coin that high.' He pointed at the bottle on the table. 'Tormalin gold too, none of your lead-weighted silver.'

'If that's what it takes.' Karn feigned unconcern. 'You know the Tormalin legions will cross the Asilor any day now? Caladhrian barons and their cohorts will be marching to the bridges over the Rel. These rebels and exiles will be cracked like a nut in a vice.'

'If you have so many allies, why hire swords?' retorted Shanish. 'I hear the Caladhrian barons are dragging their heels.'

'You know their folly of a parliament dithers like a girl choosing between three dresses.' Karn took an unhurried sip of his liquor. 'But they will back Triolle, I promise you.'

'So you say.' The bald mercenary turned away as a troupe of dancing girls emerged from the tavern's back room. A man carrying an Aldabreshin serpent-flute followed and his apprentice flourished a sweetly tuned branch of silver bells.

Shanish wasn't taunting him, Karn saw, nor even trying to tempt him into betraying secrets. The mercenary captain was merely certain of what he'd heard. Certain he had no interest in fighting in Lescar.

Karn felt like a man trying to find a path without a lantern on a moonless night. He didn't like it. He'd heard nothing from the Caladhrian town of Ferl, which was enjoying the dubious honour of hosting Caladhria's Winter Parliament of barons.

Arriving in Relshaz barely a chime ago, on the last of the stolen horses he'd ridden nigh to death, Karn had hurried to the most reliable of Master Hamare's former enquiry agents. The woman wasn't there and her house was shuttered tight. The neighbour's startled maidservant had no idea where the woman had gone.

He hadn't bothered searching out any others. Without the spymaster's coin, without the regular deliveries of courier doves to carry their urgent news back to Triolle Castle, that network of eyes and ears was as gone as a cobweb lost to a housemaid's duster.

Shanish was watching the dancing girls avidly. As they swayed and twirled to the jingling bells and lilting flute, their dresses, entirely composed of silk ribbons, slipped and shifted. Karn made sure he looked just as eager as any other man for tantalising glimpses of naked breasts and buttocks. In truth, he saw nothing to arouse his disinterested lust.

If he were alive, Downy Scardin would know every word and whisper passing between the Caladhrian barons. The fat man would also know just how thoroughly Duke Iruvain was hitting his own thumb with what he fondly imagined was the hammer of his eloquence. If he could only be there in Ferl with Iruvain, listening, interpreting and advising, Triolle's chances of securing Caladhrian support would be doubled or trebled.

Karn drank, the liquor's aroma momentarily overwhelming his senses.

If he was in Ferl, he would cursed well know what had befallen those mercenaries who'd taken Wyril. The last he had heard, the renegades were holding the town, well able to defy whatever ramshackle companies the exiles were recruiting from the Carifate.

But he couldn't be in two places at once. Not even a wizard could manage that.

Karn scowled inwardly. He would still have owed Downy Scardin a beating, if the man was alive. He'd have taken whatever information the fat man could offer up to save his neck. That would be some recompense for the miserable failure that wizard Minelas had proved to be.

He refilled his cup and emptied it in a single swallow. He hadn't even had the satisfaction of gutting the useless mage. The lesser of those two cursed Mountain mercenaries had stolen that particular pleasure. It might only be a pennyweight's grudge against the incalculable loss of Master Hamare, but Karn would settle both debts with a length of steel in the ribs. He downed another drink.

'That's a sound notion, my friend.' Shanish did the same. 'Warm the innards before Aft-Winter's chill.'

'Let's see out the festival in style.' Karn slapped his jerkin and the fat purse beneath chinked. 'Where might a man find a lively game of runes among friends?'

That was one way to sniff out mercenaries in need of coin. Fumble the runes to favour some awkwardly indebted lieutenant and he could find new boon companions before night's end.

'Try the Spiked Collar,' Shanish suggested, 'or the sword school above the Plaited Pennants.'

'Wish me luck.' Karn gestured towards the bottle. 'Enjoy your evening. I'll see you here tomorrow?'

'And the next few days.' As the music stopped, Shanish beckoned to a milk-skinned dancer in cherry-pink ribbons.

Her quick step told Karn that the fool had been lavishing his coin on her all festival. The Firebrands must have had a successful year defending Caladhria's coasts against the corsairs.

Karn left him to his lechery. With luck he'd remember the metheglin and the Tormalin gold and mention Browd of Triolle's generous purse to someone more desperate for coin.

But Karn no more trusted to luck than he trusted to ice in a thaw. Deterring a hopeful slut with a forbidding look, he slipped through the cheerfully inebriated crowd to the tavern door.

The night was raw with a salt wind blowing from the sea. Karn turned up the collar of a Saltebre merchant's cloak as he strode through the white-walled streets. The man didn't need it on his way to a life of servitude in the steamy heat of the Archipelago.

He paused for a moment, listening. Had he heard a soft following step? Or just garbage tossed by the wind?

Karn walked on, his hand resting on his sword hilt underneath the heavy wool. If an air of purpose didn't deter footpads, that blade would settle any argument.

He passed the alley heading for the Spiked Collar and took a turn in quite a different direction. There were a few other scents to follow before he endured rune-play with drink-sodden mercenaries.

Crossing the narrow bridges that arched over the criss-crossing canals, he left the central tavern district for quieter, residential streets. By the time the last lamps were quenched, he had left these prosperous dwellings with their gardens and fountain courts behind.

Now he reached the noisy, crowded tenements where the poor sought some respite from their labours in Relshaz's workshops, and around the docks and the wharfs. The paved roads narrowed and white-plastered walls were stained with shadowy mould.

Karn walked more slowly, cutting unexpectedly through back alleys before returning to his intended route. If anyone was pursuing him, he knew how to spot the signs. But he was soon satisfied that the passers-by were hurrying elsewhere, intent on business of their own.

Refuse choked the gutters as the paving gave way to bare mud. These were the sagging hovels where the truly destitute washed up. The stench of the river, the stink of human and animal filth all hung heavy this far from the cleansing breath of the sea.

Karn rapped on a black-tarred gate in a wall leprous with flaking plaster. No one answered. He knocked again and then a third time.

'Who's there?' A voice rose over the warning growl of a dog. More than one dog.

Karn contemplated his choices among his aliases. He wouldn't be here long enough to need to cover his tracks. 'Browd, for Egil the Toad.'

The dogs filled the silence with curious whines accompanied by the rattle of hefty chains.

'Wait there,' the voice eventually said.

'Gladly.' Karn looked around to make sure no one was approaching.

After a short while, bolts rattled and the gate grudgingly opened. 'What do you want?'

A short, stocky man blocked the entrance, warmly wrapped against the chill. He was well enough muscled to easily restrain the two thick-necked black dogs coupled by a chain.

The animals looked up at Karn with suspicion to equal their master's. Even with the clouds from the sea subduing the waning Greater Moon, their pelts shone with good health and grooming.

Karn glanced up and down the dilapidated street. 'Can we talk somewhere more private?'

'No,' the man said bluntly.

Karn shrugged. 'I'm looking for men to venture into Lescar—'

'Lescar's dukes are all spitted and roasted.' Egil raised a hand to close the gate.

Karn stopped it with a firmly planted boot.

'You can move that or lose it, friend,' warned Egil. 'Ebony's not been fed tonight.' The off-hand dog's lip curled in a snarl.

Karn didn't shift his foot. 'If the cockerels are spitted and roasted, who's guarding their flocks of hens? Where are all the scattered chicks running in hopes of cover? A man with an eye to the poultry market could make a tidy sum, if he moved quickly.'

The glint in Egil's eye told Karn that he had understood his meaning. The man soothed the rumbling dog's hackles with a broad hand.

'Provided no one turned up to dispute ownership of the flock,' he allowed.

'Work fast and no one would know where to lay a claim,' Karn pointed out. 'So such a man would need a few helping hands to set his nets discreetly.'

Egil angled his head. 'He would want to be certain his new friend had a ready market for these fowl.'

'You need have no worries on that score,' Karn assured him. 'Would you care to know—?'

'Details don't concern me.' Egil looked down at his dogs, which both pricked floppy ears. 'Where might such men find this hen-hawk roosting?'

Karn could see the Toad was already considering which desperate mercenaries he'd sell this opportunity to. 'Why don't you see who's interested in making good money in a penniless season? You suggest somewhere safely out of the way for them to meet me tomorrow at sunset. I'll call here beforehand and you can tell me where.'

There was something he didn't quite trust in Egil's eyes, even more than usual. So he would take his own sweet time approaching here and wherever Egil told him to go. He might even make his way over the rooftops where no one would be looking. It would be as well to be sure the man hadn't found some larger pay-off by setting a snare for him.

The stocky man glanced up and down the silent street. 'You'll pay me for such services?'

Karn crossed his arms. 'You'll get your share of the profits.'

'With no guarantee you'll catch more than a few feathers on the breeze?' Egil shook his head. 'That won't keep me warm through Aft-Winter.'

'Then I'll bring something to stuff your comforter tomorrow.' Karn hid his exasperation.

'Call back around mid-afternoon.' Egil pushed at the gate to conclude their conversation. The dogs obediently retreated.

Karn made as if to withdraw his foot before apparently recalling a trivial question. 'I'm hearing curious tales about this business in Wyril. What do you make of it all?'

'You don't know what happened?' Egil's laugh prompted a bark from one of the dogs. 'Fancy that.' He grinned unpleasantly at Karn. 'What's the truth of it worth?'

Karn considered the weight of the purse hidden within his jerkin. With a swiftness that made both dogs snarl, he pulled it out and sliced the strings around his waist with a dagger he'd palmed from his sleeve. He was pleased to see that blade's appearance took Egil by surprise.

He tossed the purse and it landed with a thump. One of the dogs sniffed it suspiciously. 'There's plenty more where that came from.'

Egil made no move to pick it up. 'That could all be copper cut-pieces.'

'But it isn't.' Karn matched Egil's disagreeable smile. 'I told you. Selling fowl down the river is a profitable trade.'

Egil patted the dog that was looking upwards, its muzzle pressed against his thigh. 'Make hay while the sun's shining, my friend. Wyril has fallen to the exiles' and rebels' new captain, Tathrin Sayron. He trapped all the freebooters inside the walls and set the town alight. I hear barely a handful got out alive and they were cut down on the roads.'

Who was this new captain? Karn had heard that name before, though his recollection carried no hint of such ruthlessness. 'I heard he was recruiting in the Carifate. What companies were prepared to do that to their own?'

Other mercenary captains would be baying for the blood of those responsible. Any amount of brutality against peasants was excusable but undue savagery against other mercenaries was not. It only invited retaliation from a crushed company's allies and such battles offered no profit for anyone.

Could he use this news to Triolle's advantage? But why hadn't Shanish been full of outrage at such an atrocity?

Egil was shaking his head. 'This captain wasn't recruiting companies, just men and women who could make a fair claim to be Lescari-born. He's promising them land and livelihood in this new Lescar free of dukes and their quarrels. He swears there won't be another fighting season, so if they don't want to find themselves begging on the roads, they should throw in their lot with him.'

Karn could scarcely believe it. 'He's found enough folk to suck up this dream-smoke to make himself an army?' An army formidable enough to make Shanish think twice about venturing into Lescar?

'He's found enough sergeants-at-arms.' Egil's hollow laugh prompted an unhappy whine from his dogs. 'They're drilling fine new regiments of Lescari militia, all strutting like cocks on a dunghill. They've been enlisting volunteers in every town since the start of For-Winter. They'll have twice the number after festival now they have the conquest of Wyril to brag about.'

'Militiamen,' Karn sneered.

Egil shrugged. 'Corner the mangiest shithouse rat and it'll take on a dog five times its size, especially if it's fighting to protect its nest. Enough of them together can bring down a mastiff.'

'Or a vixen,' Karn commented. 'What does Marlier make of this?'

'That's a good question,' agreed Egil. He nodded at the dog and took the purse it retrieved for him. He weighed the coin in his hand and looked at Karn. 'Bring me the answer to that and I'll let you have half of this back.'

Karn shrugged. 'Maybe I will, maybe I won't.'

'As you see fit.' Egil nodded. 'Call back tomorrow and I'll tell you where to find your hunters.'

He closed the gate. As Karn walked away he heard the bolts slide securely home.

What did all this news mean for the plans he'd laid out for Duchess Litasse? Karn tried to think every new twist through but found he was simply too tired.

Not too tired to go gambling, especially when the other gamesters would be all the wearier, that much less observant. Now Karn would make sure the runes favoured him, refilling his own purse after paying off Egil for this perplexing news.

Would the Toad find enough unscrupulous men to go plundering Marlier's peasants and Caladhria's prosperous villages? Or would all Relshaz's mercenaries prove as reluctant as Shanish to risk themselves in Lescar?

Regardless, it was now all the more urgent that Caladhria's barons and Tormalin's legions marched quickly to quell the unrest in Marlier and Parnilesse. Karn spared a moment to regret that he didn't have the time to go to Ferl, or to Toremal, to hurry that turn of events along.

Still, whoever this rebel Captain Tathrin Sayron was, he was still only one man. He couldn't be in two places at once, any more than Karn could. He breathed a little more easily as he recalled another titbit of gossip around the taverns. That other Vanam exile, the other instigator of this rebellious plot, still lay close to death. Once the man succumbed, these exiles' ambitions would suffer a fatal blow.

Chapter Twenty-One
Failla

Carluse Castle,
9th of Aft-Winter

How many eyes were covertly watching as she walked across the open bailey? How much had changed since she was the duke's mistress, to be tactfully ignored by most, tacitly scorned by servants loyal to his duchess? Now the household accorded her measured respect; for defying Duchess Tadira and Lord Ricart, for her defence of Carlusian interests amid the exiles' plots.

The price she paid for that was always being observed, as soon as she left her garret room. Friends, old foes and those indifferent or undecided noted her visits to the erstwhile chamberlain's office where Kerith shuffled letters and ledgers, to the innermost keep where Master Welgren tended the suffering. She was surrounded by apprehension and expectation, occasional blunt questions, more frequent indirect appeals and mute, speculative glances.

Failla changed her mind. She wouldn't go to see Kerith just yet. She would visit Aremil instead. Yesterday, Master Welgren had planned some fresh brew to stimulate his senses. Ostrin send there'd been some change for the better.

She followed the dark line across the cobbles where the snow was trampled to slush. The great hall's door stood open; bombastic centrepiece of this range of buildings rebuilt in ornate Tormalin style, to proclaim Garnot's wealth on his accession to the dukedom. Failla hurried through the empty, echoing hall.

Steps descended from the far door to the lawns of the inner ward, still swathed in pristine white. Ahead, the inner keep had been the ducal sanctuary. Rebuilt in an elaborate style, its furnishings proclaimed Garnot's artistic sensibility, with fabrics, ceramics, glassware and metalwork brought from southernmost Aldabreshi, and from Inglis to the distant north-east. The finest artists had been commissioned to decorate its plastered walls and ceilings. Failla ran up the central stone staircase, an architectural marvel in its own right.

Above, the elegant reception rooms had been stripped of their finery to accommodate pallets for the sick. Master Welgren had fewer patients now but those remaining were the most grievously injured. Walking soft-footed between the sleeping men and women, Failla exchanged silent smiles with the townswomen nursing them. She sighed as she noted a sheet-wrapped corpse awaiting removal with the infinite patience of the dead. Though that grievous news would at least release one family from the agonies of hope.

She had seen that pain in Tathrin's eyes, when he had visited Aremil every morning and evening of the festival. Master Welgren had hoped Tathrin's presence, his voice, his grip on Aremil's hand, might rouse him from this eerie sleep. But Aremil hadn't stirred and all Failla could do was take Tathrin to her bed and offer whatever comforts her warmth and love might provide.

Then Tathrin had been forced to leave, to bear all the burdens of his next perilous venture alone. Failla couldn't even send him her own love and assurances. She couldn't contemplate conveying such intimacies through Kerith, as she had done with Aremil's goodwill. If only he would wake up.

Taking a resolute breath, Failla opened the door to the room in the keep's south-east corner. Once this had been Garnot's presence chamber, with portraits of his ancestors admiring him from the grey walls. Now the cobalt and white floor tiles were cracked and chipped, the marble table cluttered with instruments and medicaments. Two plain beds replaced the luxuriously upholstered chairs; one for Welgren and one for whichever patient had most constant need of his attention.

'Oh.' She halted, taken aback.

Kerith sat watching Serafia as she carefully spooned bacon broth between Aremil's slack lips. He lay propped on feather pillows, as limp as the doll that their Aunt Derou had sewn for Anilt's festival gift. The faintest suggestion of soiled linen hung in the air beneath the scent of dried flowers.

'He swallows.' Kerith shook his head, mystified.

'Master Welgren says that's proof he wants to live.' Serafia refilled her spoon.

'How long can his body endure this?' Kerith's stern face twisted with apprehension.

Serafia hesitated, soup trickling back into the bowl. 'Master Welgren fears a sudden decline cannot be far off.'

Failla tried to curb her irritation as she entered. 'He says not to betray such misgivings in Aremil's hearing.'

Kerith rose to his feet. 'Is there news? From Parnilesse or Marlier?'

'No,' Failla snapped. 'I came to see Aremil.' She moved closer and brushed a lank strand of hair from his pale forehead. Was it her imagination or did she feel some slight pressure against her fingers? Was he was responding to her touch?

'Branca must attempt to rouse him,' she said suddenly.

Kerith had gone to the tall leaded window that overlooked the fountain. He rounded on her. 'You, of all people, would propose such a thing?'

In that instant, Failla recoiled from a dizzying vision. It was night-time in the keep, a chance encounter on the servants' back stair. Kerith was embracing Serafia. Failla could feel all his longing, desperate to ease the ache of his loneliness. She could feel Serafia's blood rush through her veins, physical desires repressed for so long burning deep within her. As Kerith's hand tightened on her waist, Serafia guided it upwards to cup her modestly bodiced breast.

Then Kerith's tense passion was overwhelmed by guilt and self-loathing. All he could feel was Failla's hurt, her terror and humiliation as he forced his questing mind into her memories. He had used his Artifice to strip bare all she had done to seduce Duke Garnot, every shamefully erotic detail of their intimacy, as he sought to find out what she had done to betray Tathrin and Aremil when the Triolle spy-woman had threatened Anilt.

Tearing himself away, Kerith had nearly fallen headlong down the stairs, leaving without a word. His last backward glance showed Failla a glimpse of Serafia standing appalled; at herself for yielding to such temptation, at this sullying of memories of her dead love, Elpin, and worse still, stricken by Kerith's rejection.

'No!' Failla protested, shaken.

'Then what?' Serafia demanded.

Failla hastily gathered her wits. Kerith was staring at her, his jaw clenched. Did he realise what she had just seen? Serafia simply looked bemused. Failla breathed more easily. Her cousin surely couldn't have felt any echo of that riot of emotions in Kerith's mind. She guessed he didn't know the whole truth either. She couldn't imagine he'd still be able to meet her eyes if he did.

'Not Artifice.' Failla managed to speak more calmly. 'But when Tathrin and Sorgrad and Gren have done what they must in Parnilesse, Branca will be free to leave Solland. Her voice, her touch might rouse Aremil when no other's will.'

'Ostrin bless that thought.' Serafia filled the spoon afresh and touched the broth to Aremil's lips.

'What's that?' Kerith asked sharply.

'What?' Failla looked around to see him pointing at a letter set on Master Welgren's marble table.

'When did this arrive?' Kerith went to pick it up. 'Weren't there other letters? You said there was no news.' His tone was accusatory.

'I didn't bring that with me,' Failla protested.

Kerith glared at her. 'It wasn't there before.'

Serafia interrupted Failla's angry retort. 'Surely who it's from is more important than who brought it?'

'Let's see.' Kerith snapped the seal vindictively, unfolding the paper with an angry rattle. His expression yielded to confusion. 'It's from Mellitha Esterlin.'

'The magewoman in Relshaz?' Failla recalled Tathrin's tale of meeting her in a brothel.

'It's dated this morning.' Kerith glanced up from the letter to look askance at the table. 'She must have used her wizardry to send it here.'

'What does it say?' Failla demanded half a breath ahead of Serafia.

Kerith frowned at the writing. Finally he answered them both.

'It seems Jilseth, that magewoman who answers to Planir the Black, has been scrying after Karn, Litasse of Triolle's enquiry agent. Apparently he's been busy in and around Relshaz this past half-season. Mellitha has been using her own sources to find out exactly why.'

Failla recalled Tathrin's tale of the horrors of Adel Castle. 'He recruited that renegade mage.'

'Indeed.' A humourless smile momentarily lightened Kerith's expression. 'Both magewomen are watching him from afar to be sure he makes no more such mischief.'

'So what is he doing?' Failla couldn't believe the villain was simply enjoying the seaport's debaucheries.

Now Kerith was scowling again. 'Jilseth and Mellitha believe he's behind a good deal of this brigandage plaguing Carluse and Marlier. He's encouraging penniless mercenaries who've washed up in Relshaz to try their luck to the north. They say it won't take many more raids across the Rel to bring the Caladhrian barons to their senses.'

He looked up at Failla. 'They'll send their own forces across the river, in support of the exiled dukes and their heirs, unless Tathrin and his army can deal with Parnilesse promptly enough to march for Carluse and Marlier and put these bandits to the sword themselves.'

'Would the Caladhrians truly do that?' Serafia looked uncertain. 'Before their next parliament meets?'

'Mellitha believes so.' Kerith nodded. 'She says the Solstice vote to wait and see was carried by a bare handful of voices.' His scowl darkened. 'If only I was still in Abray. There would be so much more I could do.'

'These bandits aren't just attacking travellers. They're raiding hamlets and farmsteads.' Serafia's eyes were troubled. 'I hear entire families cannot be found. What about Lathi and her children? Shouldn't we send word for them to come here?'

'You should ask Aunt Derou to write.' Failla forced the words through the selfishness tightening around her throat. If Lathi came to Carluse, all Anilt's love would focus on the woman she'd called mama since she was born.

'Give me the letter.' Failla held out her hand. When Kerith made no move to oblige, she snapped her fingers impatiently. 'I will take it to my Uncle Ernout. He can alert Reher and the other guildsmen and send covert word to craftsmen in Marlier. If they know this is a Triollese plot, intent on bringing Caladhria to invade us, they should prove more willing to work with Carluse. They can all begin hunting these bandits down instead of simply trying to avoid them on the roads.'

For a long moment Kerith looked at her unblinking. 'I'll let Tathrin know he and Sorgrad must conclude their business in Parnilesse as soon as they can.' He handed over the letter.

'Indeed.' Failla tucked the paper inside the little reticule she carried.

'Do you hear that?' Serafia said softly to Aremil. 'Then Branca can come to see you.'

But Failla saw the broth trickling unheeded down his chin. Feeling despairing tears prick her eyes, she walked swiftly to the door. 'I will be back soon.'

Leaving the inner keep, she only paused in the central range to fetch a cloak from her garret room. Hurrying across the open bailey, she nodded briefly at the militia sergeant commanding the gatehouse. After the hollow planks of the bridge over the ditch that separated the castle from the town, the previous night's fresh fall of snow muffled her boots on the cobbled road.

She could see servants busy sweeping it onto the mounds that already lined the main street running down the steep hill to the town gate. It would be a long, cold season before they saw a thaw to flush the gutters.

Some were enjoying themselves. One harassed lackey outside a prosperous merchant household threatened two young children with his besom. Jumping on the heap, they were scattering fresh clods of white over the path he'd just brushed.

As Failla drew closer, the man stopped sweeping. Their game forgotten, the children drew nearer to his protective presence, breath misty in the cold. The man upended his broom to study its birch twigs. Was he one of those who still believed she was an unregenerate slut?

Regardless, Failla politely inclined her head. 'Good day to you.'

Whatever the man murmured, his tone was civil. She knew the house belonged to a cloth merchant who had traded with Duke Garnot and other lords across Carluse with methodical detachment. No one could accuse him of being their lapdog. Now Master Bessier was keeping his own counsel close, like so many in the town. If Caladhria did invade and restore Lescar's dukes, they would doubtless argue they had never supported such rebellion. Whichever runes landed upright, such men sought to protect their wealth and families.

Did they have no concept of sacrifice for the good of all? Failla huddled inside her cloak, recalling the warmth of the sable cape that Master Gruit had provided for their masquerade as wealthy Lescari in Abray. But that had been lost when she had risked her neck to sneak back into the castle.

Then there was the coin she had hoarded, as she turned every gift, every indulgence won from the duke into more readily traded gold and silver. First she had sought to provide for herself, knowing that sooner or later Garnot would turn to a fresher, younger mistress.

Then she had lived for the day when that money would buy her a swift and secret departure, to reclaim Anilt and build a life as far away as possible. But she had given that gold to Corrad, the castle's horsemaster, as she had promised when she appealed to him, one of the few men who could sway the garrison against Duchess Tadira.

Yet these merchants still hoarded their coin and their treasures and turned a blind eye to everything else. It enraged Failla. To be free of all pretence, with Anilt acknowledged as her own, she would be content to live in a hovel, barefoot and dressed in rags. As long as they lived in a Lescar where no dukes claimed anyone's fealty.

Then Failla smiled inside her cloak's collar. Tathrin would never allow her or Anilt to sink into such poverty. Such nonsense about living barefoot was a pointless flourish of rhetoric, worthy of Master Reniack. Her smile faded at the thought of the rabble-rouser, and of Tathrin, departed on his perilous quest into Parnilesse eight long days ago.

She missed him so dreadfully. Abandoning all pretence, he had shared her room through the five days of festival. They had celebrated the anniversary of his birth alongside everyone else in the castle household who'd been born in some past For-Winter. With his silver ring on her finger, they had danced with the wedded and betrothed in Duke Garnot's great hall.

They could wed when all this was over, so she must do all she could to bring on that day and not fret about him in the meantime.

Further down the hill, the walled gardens and spacious merchant dwellings gave way to closely packed grey stone houses. Householders and shopkeepers were busy with shovels and brushes clearing snow. Her uncle was sweeping around the gate in the low fence that surrounded the ancient flint-walled shrine.

As always, the door stood open. As ever, the dark oak was hidden beneath coins and rags nailed to it, tokens of pledges and entreaties that the townsfolk had brought to Saedrin, whose ancient statue stood within. Now the shrine's doorposts were equally covered with patches and halved and quartered coins. Failla couldn't recall seeing that before.

'I should see if the boys can knock some of that down.' The priest was looking up at the thatch, piously maintained despite the fear of fire that saw every other building tiled or shingled. Successive snowfalls had built up into a thick layer, as white as Ernout's uncovered head. His only concession to the cold weather was a thick flannel shirt under his faded, shabby jerkin.

'You should,' Failla agreed. Saedrin save anyone standing underneath those bristling eaves if a great slab broke loose.

'Till then, let's get warm, my dear.' With a smile, he set down the broom and they walked round to the brick-built house behind the shrine. Failla was pleased to see the old man was finally moving without stiffness. It had taken him a long time to recover from the kicking and beating that Duchess Tadira's henchmen had inflicted.

'Go through to the kitchen.' Ernout opened the front door. Rather than follow her down the panelled hallway, he turned into the schoolroom.

Failla caught a glimpse of the boys within. They had all drawn their stools close to the modest fire, many still wrapped in their cloaks. They turned, young faces drawn with apprehension, stilted conversation abandoned.

She recalled her girlhood, when all Uncle Ernout's persuasive authority had been needed to still the youths' exuberance. So many of those boys were dead or gone, Poldrion only knew where. Or they had returned maimed, like Milar, who so desperately loved Serafia. But now Serafia was drawn to Kerith. Could that possibly be love or just base, lonely lust?

'I didn't expect to see you today.'

Aunt Derou looked up from her darning as Failla opened the kitchen door.

The warmth from the black-leaded range embraced her, along with the chatter of little children. Three girls knelt on a rag-rug playing with battered wooden animals. Two boys were skidding brightly coloured blocks across the tiled floor. At least they were free of the cares weighing down the older children.

'You can watch the little ones while I see what's to be had in the victualler's.' Derou rose from her chair, prudently placed between the scampering children and the hot range. She set the oiled wool stocking and her needle out of reach on the windowsill and took her dark-blue cape from a peg by the door.

'Will there be anything fresh?' Failla knew every trader in the town was despairing of replenishing stocks with none of the usual wagons and pack mules on the roads.

'I don't imagine so.' Buttoning her cape, Derou raised the hood over her tidily pinned grey braids and shook off slippers to step into her boots. 'But there'll be gossip, and we don't want despondency spreading like mould in a damp cellar.'

As Derou closed the kitchen door, Failla hung up her own cloak and took the chair between the children and the range. She saw one of the little boys contemplating the enticing flickering behind the iron bars. 'You play with Yeni, Kip.'

The lad, Serafia's fatherless son, looked at her, mischief still bright in his eye. Then he sighed and went to join Yeni making a rickety wall with the wooden blocks.

Failla saw one of the girls regarding her with some curiosity. Her own daughter, Anilt. She held out her open arms. 'Chick?'

With a shy smile, Anilt came to return her hug. Did the child truly understand she was her mother? Failla buried her face in the little girl's curls and breathed in the familiar fragrance of the herbs Derou used against moths in her linen chests.

If she didn't, no matter. There would be plenty of time to become a family, Failla told herself fiercely, once Lescar's peaceful future was settled. When Anilt would never know any father but Tathrin. When she would stare down all the curious eyes and dare them to whisper their suspicions behind their hands.

They had to secure this peace, for the sake of all Lescar's women and children; for her redoubtable aunt and the women she had met in Ashgil. Their families deserved a future free from any duke's tyranny.

She must repay those women's faith in her, as privation pinched their children's cheeks. As they nursed sons and husbands through wounds and ailments borne home from the autumn's battles. As the old and frail succumbed to winter sicknesses all the more punishing in such a hungry season.

'That game should stop them fretting for a while.' Ernout entered the kitchen with a smile of satisfaction. 'What news from the castle?' He pulled a chair closer to the range and stretched his bony hands to the warmth.

Failla reluctantly loosed her hold as Anilt wriggled and the little girl hurried back to her friends and their giggling game. 'We have unexpected allies in Relshaz.' Unlacing her reticule, she handed over the letter.

Ernout leaned back and shoved his feet towards the range. 'Don't tell Derou. She scolds me worse than ever, for lack of Vrist to chide.'

Failla saw he had gone outside in his embroidered felt slippers. Sodden, they steamed in the heat. 'Have you heard from him?'

For all his sufferings at Tadira's orders, her cousin, Derou's youngest son, had insisted on marching with Reher and the Carluse contingent. Failla wondered if his nightmares of that dungeon, shackled to a corpse had begun to fade.

'He came safely through the battle for Wyril, Saedrin be thanked.'

The old priest read Mellitha Esterlin's news. Failla watched Anilt's carefree game.

He refolded the paper precisely and offered it back. 'What do you make of this? You and your allies in the castle?'

Failla took the letter and stowed it safely away. 'Will this persuade Marlier's guildsmen to work with Carluse's, to hunt down these brigands?'

'It may just tip the scales. They see Ashgil secured and Wyril reclaimed and Triolle holding its own without any need for a duke.' Ernout nodded slowly. 'I'll write to Reher and Milar. They'll know who's most inclined to our cause over there.'

Failla felt a pang. Milar was striving so hard to bring peace to Lescar. If he couldn't hold a weapon with his useless crushed hand, he was still Reher's lieutenant, as the two of them rallied and trained Carluse Town's militia. One day, Failla knew, Milar dreamed of Serafia setting aside her grief for Elpin and rewarding his unwavering devotion.

But it seemed Kerith had stolen a march on him; another reason for Failla to hate the scholar, not that she needed one.

'I will write to those of Marlier's shrines served by men and women of good faith.' Ernout raised a warning finger. 'Who are sorely troubled by all these current uncertainties. You must propose some lawful governance for Lescar as soon as a thaw opens the roads.'

Failla bit her lip. 'As soon as Master Aremil recovers.'

'Serafia tells me he fares no better.' Ernout shook his head. 'I pray for him daily.' He sighed. 'As long as he lies senseless, Draximal wavers like a river barge that's lost its rudder. The Guilds and the shrines grow more dissatisfied with Duke Secaris's flight by the day but see no one else to take the helm. They see Emperor

Tadriol's legions massing and I hear tell that this murderous rabble in Parnilesse have been raiding across the river now, to rob and plunder Tormalin lands.'

'We hear the same,' Failla admitted reluctantly. 'Reniack is buying loyalty with bread and meat and his stores are running as low as everyone's at this season.'

Ernout shook his head. 'Draximal may yet welcome Secaris back, if they believe that will secure their safety, as they fear Parnilesse's anarchy will spread to engulf all of Lescar and bring in the Emperor's wrath from the east while Caladhria's barons march from the west.'

'Tathrin has a plan to foil Reniack,' Failla assured him, 'and to leave Parnilesse free to determine its destiny.'

Ernout pursed his withered lips. 'What does he propose?'

'I can't tell you. I don't know.' Despite herself, Failla's voice shook. 'Since Jettin turned spy for Reniack, Charoleia says the fewer people who know the details, the better.'

Was that really the truth, or did they still not trust her, Sorgrad and Gren and Charoleia herself?

Ernout surprised her with a grin that deepened his wrinkles. 'I cannot approve of that lady but only a fool would wager against her.'

'Indeed.' Not for the first time Failla wondered what had passed between Charoleia and the priest, when she had taken that urn to his shrine, containing her dead maid's ashes; Trissa, her friend and confidante. Tathrin had agreed something lightened the grief in Charoleia's violet eyes.

Ernout's thoughts had moved on. 'Let's hope young Tathrin's plans prosper.' He patted her hand. 'I'd like to see you a spring bride and Derou tells me she approves.'

'Bless Drianon for that.' Failla smiled. Did Ernout guess she had been braiding ribbons into her hair, imagining Tathrin cutting her wedding plait short, their offering to the mother-goddess's altar?

'Have you met his family?' Ernout enquired.

'Not yet.' Failla gazed into the glowing range.

Tathrin had written letters from Triolle, from Ashgil, to tell them he had come unscathed through the fires of Wyril. But he'd had no reply. Would his parents ever forgive him for rejecting that safe life in Vanam they had sacrificed so much to secure for him? For taking a dishonoured woman to wife?

Would she first meet them carrying the urn of his ashes, if this hideously dangerous plan was the death of him?

Chapter Twenty-Two

Tathrin

Parnilesse Town,
10th of Aft-Winter

IT WAS QUITE different from Carluse and Triolle. Tathrin couldn't really compare it to Sharlac. He'd barely seen anything beyond the panic, smoke and slaughter engulfing the castle there.

They were riding down the Inchra Road. Ahead, Parnilesse Town's walls were formidably high and Duke Orlin had plainly forbidden so much as a pigsty to be built outside. A grassy bank below the masonry slid into a broad ditch now choked with snow. Beyond that the ground had been cleared for two plough-lengths. Anyone approaching would be spotted long before they came within bowshot of the vigilant turrets.

Tathrin coughed as the capricious wind shifted. He was heartily sick of this journey through the most dismal days of the year. 'I take it that stink's the marshes?'

Sorgrad had explained how the higher ground that thrust Parnilesse's rocky coast out into the sea fell away in a long escarpment here. Brackish swamps stretched towards the River Asilor, with one safe channel cutting through the mire to bring ships to the deep pool at the base of the scarp.

'Do you suppose Branca and the scholar are baffling Reniack's lad by now?' Gren looked ahead to the great gate looming over the road.

'Let's hope so.' Apprehension knotted Tathrin's guts.

He had seen how reluctant Kerith was to use his Artifice against their erstwhile colleague, when the Adept had shared the latest news from Carluse. Would that unwillingness fatally undermine that aspect of their stratagem? Would Branca have the strength to frustrate Jettin's aetheric spying on her own?

'We'll know soon enough.' Sorgrad was unconcerned. 'Less chatter. Let's close up with the others.'

Tathrin urged his weary horse forwards. Sorgrad and Gren encouraged their shaggy ponies with broad Parnilesse accents.

He was saying as little as possible, uncomfortably aware of the Caladhrian intonations, common in Carluse and Marlier, which marked him as a stranger here. Parnilesse speech held more closely to the Tormalin spoken across the border.

As they caught up with the travellers ahead, though, a couple of faces turned to offer tired smiles. There were all too few on this road; just these apprentice carpenters who'd braved the menacing weather to pay festival visits to their families in nearby farmsteads.

Whatever they might have thought of his accent, they had welcomed Tathrin's honest face, the breadth of his shoulders and his razor-sharp sword. No one paid much heed to Sorgrad and Gren. No one had, since Serafia had dyed their fair hair muddy brown. Along with voluminous cloaks to hide their battle-hardened muscles, they adopted hangdog, fearful expressions, befitting two runts accustomed to ill-treatment.

Tathrin had been impressed. Their masquerade hadn't faltered once. Though Jettin's Artifice presumably saw through any such feints. Would armed men be waiting for them?

The carpenters kicked their weary horses into a trot. No one wanted to be locked out when the gates were secured at sunset. Tathrin had learned that Reniack's regime still held to a good many of Duke Orlin's practices. The ominous shadow of the gate soon enveloped them.

'Anyone you recognise?' Sorgrad looked upwards, not at the crossbow-wielding guards but at the severed heads thrust on bristling spikes.

The faces were surprisingly well preserved. Queasily Tathrin recalled Gren explaining how such ghastly trophies were boiled in brine and vinegar, to slow rot and deter hungry crows.

Gren contemplated the array for a moment. 'No.'

Two of the carpenters exchanged greetings with the halberd-wielding gate-wards. Gren rode forward to humbly tug at the cloak of another prentice woodworker. The lad had been reasonably civil since Gren had lost the pathetic contents of his purse to him, suffering remarkable ill-luck with the runes.

After a short exchange, Gren reined his pony back until Tathrin and Sorgrad drew level.

'That's Orlin's youngest brother Brehard, his wife, her two brothers and their children,' he said grimly. 'Duke Orlin and Duchess Sherista grace the gate on the Carif Road.'

Sorgrad nodded before glancing at Tathrin. 'Lead the way, long lad.'

As a gate-ward advanced, Tathrin squared his shoulders and rehearsed his most convincing Parnilesse tones.

'I hear Tormalin's Emperor wants our land for his own. I'll lend my sword to the fight for freedom.'

The man looked unimpressed. He had the bearing of someone well used to the burden of his chain-mail hauberk beneath that thick tunic of felted black wool, though Tathrin didn't think he was a mercenary. Most likely he'd been sworn to Duke Orlin's militia before Reniack persuaded him to betray that allegiance.

'Where are you from?' The man's halberd was ready if not precisely threatening.

'Nylmaris.'

Sorgrad had assured Tathrin that this village, in the disputed forests west of Quirton, had barely two-score houses and more goats than people.

'Never heard of it.' The gate-ward glowered at the Mountain Men huddled on their scrawny ponies. 'Who are they?'

'We met on the road.' Tathrin feigned embarrassment. 'But if we're fighting for brotherhood . . . ?' That was a recurring theme in Reniack's crowd-pleasing pamphlets.

'Every man deserves his day in the sun,' Gren piped up like a hopeful child, 'not to shiver all his life in the shadow of a nobleman's banner!'

'True enough.' The gate-ward still didn't look overly welcoming. 'Have you coin to pay your way? All charity ended with the close of the festival and we won't stand for beggars on our streets.'

'We came to help not to burden you.' Tathrin shifted his cloak. Let the man think that bulge in the belly of his jerkin was a fat purse.

'Try the Yellow Thrush.' The gate-ward stepped back, his halberd relaxing. 'On Looping Lane, south of the castle.'

'Thank you.' Tathrin urged his horse forward.

Sorgrad and Gren's ponies' hooves echoed in the confines of the gate. 'Take the second street bearing right,' said Sorgrad quietly.

Tathrin did so, hoping it wasn't too obvious he had no notion where to go. He wondered wryly if that would baffle Jettin.

'Cut through that alley between the bakehouse and its wood store,' Sorgrad instructed next.

As they made their way through the town, Tathrin was relieved to see sufficient riders and coaches on the streets to make their presence unremarkable. Men and women crowded the paths on either side and tavern doors stood open despite the chill. As much debate as drinking was going on inside.

Were all these people united in supporting Reniack? Could their plan succeed in the face of such opposition? Tathrin could only hope so. There was no going back now.

He tried to see Parnilesse Castle but could only catch glimpses of its brooding bulk. The buildings in between reminded him of Duke Garnot's renewals of Carluse. False gables hid plain roofs behind curved adornments, while fussy wrought-iron balconies caged every window.

Gren chuckled softly. 'Don't they know Tormalin nobles favour Rationalist architecture now?'

'Lescar's dukes are always a generation behind the times,' murmured Sorgrad.

Tathrin inadvertently jerked his horse to a halt as the next turn brought them into an open square. Parnilesse Castle stretched all along the far side. It had no lofty towers like Triolle Castle or the advantage of higher ground like Carluse Castle. That counted for nothing when a fortification was so vast, so many buildings enclosed within its formidable wall.

Fire-baskets illuminated the gate and torches blazed all along the frontage. Militiamen with halberds patrolled the battlements above. Only a fool would even contemplate challenging this vigilant stronghold in the very heart of the town.

Tathrin felt cold, not merely chilled by the breeze from the unseen marshes.

'Lots of mouths to feed,' Gren commented, 'with all these newcomers crowded in. No wonder he's been sending raiding parties across into Tormalin.'

'Those raids haven't prospered overmuch, according to Charoleia,' Gren said thoughtfully. 'I wonder what Reniack has laid by for a siege. Folk can't eat fine words.'

Tathrin felt a little warmer. Every bone lands to show two runes.

Sorgrad gestured across the square. 'Go past the shrine to Dastennin.'

The other buildings ringing the square were temples dedicated to the various gods, all embellished with architectural flourishes. They rode past the shrine to Trimon, darkly shuttered. Tathrin was used to such sanctuaries standing open, a lantern offering the traveller god's protection through the night. Had the Forest Minstrel's priests always been so unwelcoming here?

There were stocks in front of Raeponin's shrine. Seven figures sat still and silent, lightly dusted with snow. Tathrin's horse fretted at the insidious stink of death. He looked at the god of justice's tight-shut shrine and wondered who had sat in judgement on these men.

Gren's pony was less fastidious. He rode closer to read the placards nailed to the planks trapping the dead men's feet. 'Condemned as cowards, apparently.'

'Let's be on our way.' Sorgrad nodded towards a halberd-wielding watchman heading in their direction.

'Was it stoning or the frost that killed them?' Tathrin felt the corpses' glassy stares pursuing him. Were those deaths he must account for or add to Reniack's tally?

'If it was the stoning,' Sorgrad observed, 'these people are so dedicated to Reniack's cause they'll kill their own dissenters.'

'Or so scared they'll kill to prove their loyalty,' Gren countered, 'so they're not the next accused.'

'Regardless, Tormalin's legions face a hard fight in harder weather,' Tathrin said grimly. 'Is this the Carif Road?'

'It is,' Sorgrad confirmed.

There were fewer taverns along this highway cutting southwards through the town. That was a double-edged blessing. Fewer folk spilled out of doorways to stare at passing riders. Those who did stopped to watch them with unnerving intensity.

Sorgrad urged his pony into a trot. As Tathrin's reluctant horse followed suit, the clip of steel-shod hooves echoed back from the stone row-houses. Curious candles appeared in windows.

They could only trust in the gathering dusk. The Greater Moon was gone from the sky and with the Lesser still a few days short of its first quarter, this was the darkest night until late For-Spring.

It took far longer to traverse the town than to reach the castle from the Inchra Gate. The high road swung close to the scarp and Tathrin saw narrow lanes cutting down to the unseen harbour below. The wind blew stronger still.

Eventually he saw a black barrier dotted with torches ahead. The town wall marched down the scarp to embrace the pool below and the Carif Gate kept watch both on the marshes and the road. It was a major fortification, now securely barred for the night. Anyone knocking for admittance would have a long, cold wait for dawn.

Gren turned into a lane where no window showed a lamp. Tathrin followed Sorgrad after him.

'A nice present for someone in the morning.' Gren slid lightly from his saddle and tied his pony's reins to a gate. Shrugging off his heavy cloak, he secured it over the animal's hindquarters. Sorgrad was doing the same.

Tathrin dismounted and found a woodshed that offered his horse some shelter. He shivered as he gave the beast his own cloak but he had scant need of it now.

He hurried back up the lane. As he unbuttoned his jerkin, he caught a sniff of the potent flask that Master Welgren had given him. Nervously investigating, his cold fingers felt only a little seepage into the swaddling cloths.

At the end of the lane, Gren was looking warily for any movement within the silent houses. 'Ready?' His smile caught a glint of fugitive moonlight.

'One moment.' In the shadow of a holly bush, Sorgrad peered into his cupped hands. Water seeped between his fingers, the faintest trace of emerald radiance vanishing as the drops hit the ground.

How soon would they be explaining themselves to the Archmage? Surely Jilseth was keeping the same unrelenting watch on Sorgrad that Kerith said she had focused on Karn?

Tathrin unscrewed the flask and dampened the rags. 'Master Welgren said to hold it away from you,' he warned Gren.

Master Welgren only used this potent blend of mandragora, poppy tincture and henbane when he had to cut into the belly or chest of a patient otherwise certain to die. He also acknowledged physicians had likely killed more patients with this soporific than they had cured with its aid.

Sorgrad shook the last drops of water from his hands and took a cloth from Tathrin. 'One man up top and three below.'

Tathrin clamped his jaw shut as white light blinded him, as painful as thumbs shoved into both his eyes. Dizziness snatched away all sensation; of the ground beneath his feet, of the coldly insistent wind, of the brass flask in one hand and the soft cloth in the other. He couldn't even smell that intoxicating dampness—

Then they were standing on the Carif Gate's topmost turret.

Gren kicked the startled sentry hard in the side of the leg and the man collapsed onto his knees. Before he could shriek with agony, Gren stifled him with the potion-soaked rag. The sentry struggled, clawing at Gren's hands. To no avail. In a few moments, the man hung limp.

'Careful!' Tathrin was alarmed.

'This way.' Sorgrad opened the door to the stair, listening intently with a dagger drawn.

Tathrin followed him downwards. Gren brought up the rear, pausing only to lock the door behind them.

Sorgrad's arrival in the guardroom prompted angry shouts of alarm. Tathrin rushed after him. Sorgrad vaulted a sturdy table to kick one guard against the wall. Landing deftly, he stuffed his rag into the man's startled mouth.

Tathrin shoved another sentry who had sprung up from a seat by the fire and the man stumbled over his toppled stool. Tathrin grabbed his sword-arm, preventing him from drawing the weapon. He pressed the rag hard over the man's face with his other hand. Coughing, light-headed, he realised his mistake. He held the man at arm's length till he slumped to the floor.

Gren had grappled the remaining sentry, who'd rushed for the guardroom's other door. Shorter but stronger, the Mountain Man bore him to the ground. Gren clamped a hand over his mouth to silence him but Tathrin saw he no longer held a rag.

Blood glistened as the man bit Gren's fingers. Gren drove a brutal knee into his groin. As the sentry abandoned his struggles to huddle around his agony, Sorgrad grabbed a handful of hair to haul his head back. Tathrin pressed a fresh stifling cloth over his nose.

'Bastard.' Gren shook his chewed hand.

'Get a rag around that. Not one of Welgren's!' Tathrin hated to think of that concoction mingling with someone's blood.

'Get the ladder rigged.' Gren was already ripping a strip of linen from his unconscious victim's shirt front. As he staunched the wound, he went to bolt the doors on either side of the room that led out onto the wall's high battlements.

Tathrin went to the windows overlooking the road to Carif. For a heart-stopping moment the stiff catch wouldn't yield.

'Smash the glass.' Sorgrad was unwinding a fine rope ladder from around his waist.

'Not yet.' Tathrin redoubled his efforts and the catch gave way with a petulant squeal. Cold wind swirled and he tasted the threat of snow.

Gren shook out a linen bag he'd had tucked in his shirt and tied its drawstring securely to his belt. Sorgrad was tying the rope ladder to the crosspiece bracing the heavy table's legs. Tathrin listened for boots approaching along the battlements.

Sorgrad tossed the ladder out through the open window. Gren swung one leg through the stone mullions. Tathrin made certain the unconscious sentries hadn't stirred.

He half-wished they would, so he would know he hadn't killed them. What of the man on the open roof? Would he freeze to death in his torpor before he was discovered?

Sorgrad was leaning out of the window to watch Gren climbing down. 'He's there.'

One of the door handles rattled. 'Pik?' A puzzled voice tried the handle again. 'Who's in there?'

Tathrin glanced at Sorgrad who raised a warning finger to his lips. Tathrin shot back an exasperated glare.

'Pik! Idnan!' The voice was growing angry. 'Is this some kind of joke?'

Tathrin heard another voice, more querulous. The door shook beneath the assault of a determined shoulder. He wondered how long the bolts would hold.

Then an outraged shout rang through the night.

'They've seen him.' Sorgrad stepped back from the window and took firm hold of the rope ladder. 'Help me.'

As Tathrin gripped the deceptively slender hemp strands, the door shook under another assault. The bolts rattled loosely, screws dragged askew in the wood. Tathrin saw a long splinter fall away. Someone had an axe.

Sorgrad hauled the ladder upwards. Tathrin matched his rhythm to retrieve Gren as fast as possible.

'Hold hard!' The younger Mountain Man's head appeared. 'Take these cursed things!' His expression was as black as the night outside.

Tathrin braced himself to hold the weight of the ladder with Gren and his burden while Sorgrad pulled the bulging sack in through the window. Gren clambered awkwardly after it, hampered by the cord still tying the burden to his belt. Dropping it was out of the question.

Tathrin looked apprehensively at the door. The axe was biting deep. He caught a glimpse of the shining blade before the assailant ripped it free.

'Let's not wait to introduce ourselves.' Sorgrad wrapped a swirl of azure magelight around his upraised hand.

Blinding giddiness overwhelmed Tathrin. He had to endure the loathsome sensations far longer this time. When his boots struck solid ground, nausea surged up his throat. He pressed his hands to his mouth as he staggered. That was a mistake. After the disorientating magic, even the lingering trace of Welgren's potion on his fingers nearly made him empty his stomach entirely.

'Tathrin?' A hand grabbed his forearm.

With a monumental effort, he regained his balance. A deep breath of cold air, faintly perfumed, went some way to restoring him.

'Branca.' He forced his eyes open.

They stood beside a fountain, now dry for the winter. Coloured glass lamps threw soothing light across this peaceful courtyard. The windows surrounding them were snugly curtained, outlined here and there by firelight within. He heard distant music and the memory of a fine dinner lingered on the air.

'Well done, long lad.' Gren sounded honestly impressed. 'Twice in one night and you didn't throw up once.'

Tathrin utterly failed to find a witty riposte. At least going without food or drink since noon had been worth it.

'Is that them?' Branca was looking wide-eyed at the lumpy sack.

Gren cut the cord with a slash of a dagger and handed it to her. 'I have the honour to present Duke Orlin of Parnilesse and his duchess, the honoured Sherista, along with several of their children.'

Now Tathrin wondered if Branca was about to be sick.

Chapter Twenty-Three
Branca

The Three Fountains Inn,
Solland, in the Tormalin Empire,
10th of Aft-Winter

SHE HELD THE sack with its disgusting contents well away from her dress. 'That door, if you please? Up the stairs.'

As Tathrin obliged, she was thankful so few guests remained at the inn. Every room had been taken for the festival but now war with Lescar was all but confirmed, nobles who might have lingered through Aft-Winter had returned to more safely distant residences. They reached Charoleia's sitting room unseen.

''Grad, Gren.' From her daybed she extended a welcoming hand.

Branca debated where to put her repellent burden. She didn't want to leave any lingering, stinking stain.

Sorgrad kissed Charoleia's hand before contemplating her critically. 'You look better than you did.'

Gren simply stooped to hug her, saying something in the Mountain tongue. Charoleia returned his embrace, replying in the same language.

Momentarily surprised by this display of emotion, Branca chided herself. Charoleia and the enigmatic brothers had been comrades and co-conspirators for more than two decades, travelling back and forth between the ocean coast of Tormalin and the westernmost reaches of Ensaimin and beyond. How else could Sorgrad use his magic to come here, if he hadn't already visited the inn like any other traveller?

'Let's keep that by the window.' Tathrin removed the cushions so she could rest the bulging sack on the broad wooden sill. 'How are you, Branca?'

'I'm well, thank you.' Branca quickly turned to address Charoleia. 'Shall I send word to Esquire Den Dalderin?'

She had thought it would be easier to meet Tathrin in person, without the need to hide her thoughts from him. But as his eyes searched her face, she saw he wanted to raise matters she had no wish to discuss. But how could she avoid that, lacking the unquestioned control she had when they were linked through Artifice?

'No need. I sent a note after dinner.' Charoleia extricated herself from Gren's embrace.

'You were so confident we'd succeed?' Tathrin tried to make a joke of it but Branca saw his surprise equalled her own.

Charoleia smoothed lace ruffled by Gren's affection. 'If you'd arrived empty-handed or not at all, I would still have tried to persuade young Yadres that it's in Emperor Tadriol's best interests to limit the Tormalin legions' advance.'

Sorgrad was at the mantelshelf, finding a long wax taper. 'Do you have something I can use to bespeak Jilseth?'

'Here.' Branca had laid out everything Charoleia had requested on the table. Her hand shook as she tipped wafer cakes onto a plate and passed their silver salver to Sorgrad.

The last time she had seen wizardry, Charoleia and Trissa were imprisoned by that depraved mage Minelas. She had barely managed to hide herself away in Adel Castle, her Artifice strained to breaking point, terrified, cold and bruised after that villain Karn's assault when he had captured them. Jilseth, the Archmage's cold-eyed adviser, had threatened Sorgrad with unspecified retribution if he ever used his mastery over the elements to influence the course of the Lescari wars.

'Don't fret, pet,' Sorgrad said softly. 'There's no law against magic in Tormalin.'

Branca did her best to smile but catching a glimpse of Gren's scowling face only reminded her more vividly of that gruesome night. Usually so genial, the younger Mountain Man looked as brutal as when he'd gutted Minelas like a fish.

Sorgrad glanced at the taper and it kindled with arcane scarlet flame. He brought his hands together until the magefire reflected in the polished silver plate. The Mountain mage concentrated on the mirrored glint. No longer leaf-like, it blossomed into a scarlet circle. The burning ring widened, a flicker of ruby brightness swirling round and around its outer edge. Beyond it, the silver shone, untarnished. Inside the magewrought circle the metal grew darkly opaque.

'Jilseth?' Sorgrad looked through the fiery ring. 'How are you this evening? How's the Aft-Winter weather in Hadrumal?'

'I am well enough and the fog is as thick as usual. I take it you wish to explain yourself?'

Branca shifted in hopes of a clearer view but could see no hint of the distant, waspish speaker beyond the sorcerous blackness.

'So she has been watching us,' murmured Tathrin.

'I have an invitation.' Sorgrad smiled charmingly into his spell. 'We would like you to help us persuade Emperor Tadriol not to send his legions into Lescar.'

'How often must you be told?' Incredulity strained Jilseth's annoyance. 'Every Archmage has forbidden the use of magic in the dukes' wars.'

'The dukes are gone, or as good as,' Sorgrad said crisply. 'We're not in Lescar now and I don't propose to use any more magic tonight. We have need of your particular talents.'

Branca missed Jilseth's reply as Gren growled under his breath. Charoleia held out her hand with a few words of his mother tongue. Gren went to sit on the end of her daybed.

Sorgrad was talking over Jilseth's objections. 'The argument against magic in Lescar has always been that it would make battles more lethal. You can use your craft to save countless lives. If the legions' campaign carries them clear across Lescar, how many hundreds of innocents will fall victim to winter's cold, to hunger, to sheer despair, never mind the bloodshed of battle?'

His voice hardened, striking a faint echo from the silver. 'How long before I find a family frozen to death in a ditch, their mouths full of dead grass? A father who's smashed his starving children's skulls before hanging himself from the doorframe? Shall I scry those visions for Planir and tell him you scorned the chance to turn such misery aside?'

'You wouldn't dare!'

But everyone heard the hesitation undercutting Jilseth's protest.

Sorgrad replied with low menace. 'Ask Usara what he thinks I'll dare.'

Branca couldn't place that name, though she thought she'd heard it before. Regardless, it clearly had an impact on Jilseth.

'We need not rouse him. Where are you?' she demanded. 'In Toremal? Tell me—'

'We're in Solland.' Sorgrad spoke swiftly over the magewoman. 'I'll come to Hadrumal myself and fetch you. Unless you're too much a coward to trust to my aberrant magic?'

'For a man who wants a favour you are abominably rude!' The scarlet ring of the spell flared with Jilseth's anger.

'Meet me in the Boar and Elder, just as soon as suits your convenience.' Sorgrad dismissed the spell with a contemptuous snap of his fingers.

Branca stared at the silver salver. She expected to see it blackened with soot, the surface irreparably distorted. But the metal shone, pristine, as if it had just left the inn steward's polishing cloth.

'I don't know how long it'll take her to find Planir.' Sorgrad was addressing Charoleia. 'She won't come without telling him that something's afoot. But I'll go now, to be sure I'm waiting for her.' He grinned suddenly. 'You never know what interesting gossip I might pick up in Hadrumal's best tavern.'

With that, he was gone. Branca had expected something akin to the blinding light that enveloped her when Sorgrad's magic had carried them away from Adel Castle. Instead, she was left wondering if she had imagined that azure flicker.

'Is everything ready?' Tathrin turned to the table with its curious collection of bottles and bowls.

'Charoleia explained what we would need.' Despite the cosiness of the room, Branca shivered. 'You've seen necromancy worked?'

'In Relshaz, once.' Tathrin hesitated, looking at Gren.

The younger Mountain Man sat hunched on Charoleia's daybed, looking mutinously at the carpet. She spoke soothingly in the archaic tongue of his people.

'What is his objection?' Branca asked quietly.

'I'm not entirely sure,' admitted Tathrin. 'He pays scant heed to his gods but Mountain folk set great store on bones being returned to their own soil.'

'I see,' Branca said, uncertain. Hadn't Gren dug up bones from a long-forgotten battlefield, to convince Duke Garnot that Failla had truly been kidnapped and murdered, to ensure he wouldn't pursue her?

Gren looked up and glared at them both. 'Only the *sheltya* should seek guidance from the bones of the dead and seldom enough at that, at Solstice and in times of great trial. Hadrumal's wizards have no notion of what they're corrupting.'

'If there were any other way, we would take it, but there isn't.' Charoleia was sympathetic but implacable.

Tathrin was equally resolute. 'We said we would do whatever it took.'

Somewhat to Branca's surprise, it was Gren who looked away first, his face still dark with disgust.

'Never mind,' she said quickly. 'I'll see for myself soon enough.'

'Will Jettin?' Tathrin looked around, as if searching for unseen eyes.

'I've no sense of him through the aether.' Branca paused to make certain no fresh presence lurked at the edge of her thoughts. 'Kerith and I stopped harrying him as soon as I saw you arrive in the courtyard. But he has become remarkably subtle in his Artifice. Do you want me to try and find him?'

'No.' Tathrin quickly shook his head. 'We don't want him to suspect we've any interest in him now.'

'Very well.' Branca didn't hide her relief. Jettin was becoming increasingly ferocious in his aetheric assaults. Contacting Kerith had become like trying to shout through a gale to someone a plough-length away.

Her reprieve was short-lived.

'Have you tried to reach Aremil recently?' Tathrin asked.

'No.' Branca turned away. 'Now, Yadres Den Dalderin—'

'Branca.' Tathrin's firm hand restrained her. 'You're the only one who can reach Aremil. We're certain of it, me and Failla—'

'I have tried,' she protested, 'but at this distance—'

'Then go to Carluse.' Tathrin wasn't about to yield. 'If you're there to hold his hand, to speak to him in person—'

'I will go, when I can,' she promised. 'But I'm still needed here.'

Tathrin looked sternly at her. 'You can be there in the blink of an eye with Sorgrad's help, and back again within the day. We need him, Branca. You know that.'

But did Aremil need her? Had the growing affection between them been severed once he learned she had killed that old woman? Had she destroyed it herself, with her wretched rejection, so guilt-ridden?

How many more times did she need to visit that barred and shuttered hall, waters lapping ankle-deep around its foundations, before she accepted that he was gone somewhere, somehow, far beyond her reach?

What would she do when all hope was lost? Wasn't it better to wait and to hope that he might one day return?

She shook off Tathrin's hand. 'I cannot go back to Carluse while Kerith and I must maintain all our aetheric communications, and frustrate Jettin's spying.'

Tathrin grasped her shoulder, forcing her to face him. 'Aremil could help you counter Jettin and relieve your other burdens besides. Then there's this question of Lescar's governance. If we're to save everyone from another year of pointless warfare, we must propose a settlement and soon; to the remaining dukes, to Emperor Tadriol and the Caladhrian parliament. Aremil knows a hundred times more than I do about political philosophies and systems.'

His firm expression wavered and Branca glimpsed the uncertain scholar Tathrin had been. But the trials of this past year had honed his determination, just as surely as swordplay and tough living had hardened his face and body.

'We all need Aremil, Branca, and Saedrin save us, I miss him. Don't you? I long to have him tell me that we were right to start all this upheaval. To tell me that we're doing what we must, however hard it is, to bring about a better future for all Lescari. I need to know that he still believes that. Then I can tell him that I still believe it, when it's his turn to be torn by doubts.'

Branca busied herself rearranging wine glasses. 'There's no reason to suppose I could reach him with my Artifice, even if I went to Carluse, not if Kerith can't.'

'Branca!' Tathrin's irritation stilled her hands. 'He loves you. You love him. You can't tell me that won't help!'

'I—' Tears blurred her vision as the stifled ache of Aremil's absence blossomed beneath her breastbone.

'Are you so ashamed of what you've done?' Tathrin stepped closer, low-voiced. 'Are you so scared of what he might see? When you only did what you had to, to save yourself, to save Charoleia and Trissa? Do you really think he could hate you for that?'

'He's already seen it.' Branca could barely speak.

'Did he drive you away when he did?' Tathrin shot back. 'No, and he won't, any more than he's denied me as his friend, for my violence in this war. I've done far worse than you, Branca. Don't tell me you haven't seen it when you've touched me with your Artifice. I killed two men just for trying to steal my horse, when all they wanted was to escape the battlefield's slaughter. Don't tell me they deserved that!'

Branca found she couldn't escape Tathrin's memories of the battle at Pannal. This was far worse than confronting him through Artifice, where she could have denied both his memories and her own.

She tried to move away but only knocked over a carafe with her hand. Tathrin caught it before it spilled wine across the table.

'It's easier to forgive myself because I know Aremil doesn't hate me for such deeds,' he said gently. 'It doesn't mean I don't bitterly regret what I've been forced to do.'

He took Branca's hands in his own. His fingers were cold and calloused.

'Failla doesn't blame me, any more than I fault her for her choices. She knows that I love her, no matter what. Instead of staying mired in the past, we both look to the future. You're the only one who can give Aremil such peace of mind. He's the only one who can give it to you. Please, go to Carluse and use your Artifice to find him, wherever he has gone. Otherwise he's going to die, and soon. If you don't believe me, ask Serafia. Ask Failla. Ask Master Welgren.'

Appalled, Branca looked up to see that awful truth plain on Tathrin's face. Before she could reply, a polite knuckle rapped on the sitting room door.

'Gren, if you please.' Charoleia sat up straight.

Branca turned away to the window as the Mountain Man opened the door. She heard Charoleia speak.

'Good evening. Please, come in. Would you like some wine, Esquire? Branca?'

It took all her resolve to turn back to face them all. Though she saw no one was actually looking at her. Yadres Den Dalderin hovered on the threshold, regarding Gren with consternation. Few of Solland's elegant salons included warriors in battered leather and chain mail.

'Angovese red, Esquire.' Tathrin was already pouring the fine vintage.

'Thank you.' As Den Dalderin accepted the glass, he looked Tathrin up and down. 'I don't believe we've been introduced?'

'Tathrin Sayron.' The Carlusian bowed with more elegance than Branca expected. 'Of Lescar.'

'Yadres Den Dalderin.' The noble youth returned the courtesy. 'Of Zafer, a little town of still less account.'

Charoleia snorted with laughter. 'Of Toremal, and deep in the Sieur Den Dalderin's councils, when that noble prince advises the Emperor.'

Yadres merely answered her with a smile before addressing Tathrin once again. 'I take it you bring vital news?'

'I don't know.' He shrugged.

Perplexed, Yadres looked to Charoleia. 'My lady?'

'May I?' She extended an elegantly beringed hand and Branca gave her a glass of wine.

Charoleia took a sip. 'His Majesty must satisfy those noble houses who insist the legions should stop this chaos in Parnilesse from spilling across the Asilor. We accept that. She smiled. 'Indeed, we shall be grateful for Imperial assistance. However, we've no more desire to see Tormalin rule re-established across Lescar than his Majesty wishes to become entangled in such a hare-brained undertaking. Even if the legions were to crush all Lescar under their boots, the cost to the Empire, the disruption to the exploration of those new lands across the ocean, could not possibly be worth it. Not when Lescari resentment and resistance would flourish like thistles with the spring, year in and year out.' She arched her brows at Yadres. 'Don't you agree?'

He inclined his head, though his tone was non-committal. 'You are as well informed as ever.'

'Would it help Emperor Tadriol to restrain his noble princes,' Charoleia wondered, 'if we could show you exactly who was guilty of Duke Orlin and Duchess Sherista's murders? This man has also instigated all these recent raids across the river into Tormalin. If that man could be captured, tried and hanged, wouldn't that quench the zeal of those princes so eager for battle? Every advocate would agree such an execution would be sanctioned by law. Unlike wholesale conquest, where three precedents clearly forbid it for every two that might argue in its favour.'

Branca recalled the carefully copied documents that Charoleia had received from Advocate Tathel; thick bundles threaded through with white ribbons bearing the Imperial Archivist's lead seals.

Yadres looked dubious. 'One man overthrew Parnilesse's duke acting entirely alone?'

'Hardly single-handed,' conceded Charoleia, 'but cut off the head and the rest of the snake will die.'

'These are your witnesses?' Yadres looked curiously from Tathrin to Gren.

'No.' Charoleia took another sip of her wine. 'You'll learn exactly what happened from the duke and duchess themselves.'

'What?' Yadres was baffled.

Charoleia looked steadily at him. 'Emperor Tadriol has used magic to determine guilt before now, even if no charges were ever levied against the Relict Tor Bezaemar.'

While that was another name meaning nothing to Branca, they all saw Yadres freeze with shock. Branca could only guess Charoleia referred to some notable scandal.

Charoleia smiled sweetly. 'Make sure to tell Tadriol everything that you see and hear tonight. Gren, show the esquire our witnesses.'

Still scowling, Gren fetched the sack from the window seat. He dumped it on the table without a thought for the pristine cloth.

'Duke Orlin.' He drew out a ghastly bearded head, his fingers tangled in its lank silver hair. 'Duchess Sherista.' Her once lustrous skin was as discoloured as her husband's, her closed eyes gruesomely sunken pits. Whatever had been done to preserve them had left her black hair oddly brindled.

'Saedrin save us.' Yadres was as pale as his linen shirt. He emptied his glass in one swallow. 'But how—?'

'All will become clear, I promise,' Charoleia assured him.

But how exactly were the dead going to speak? Branca saw their mouths had been sewn shut. That must have been done after death, to stop their jaws flapping loose. Queasy, she noted the ragged flesh around their severed necks as Gren thrust Reniack's repellent trophies back into the sack. How hard had those deaths been?

Glass clinked in the awkward silence as Tathrin poured the esquire more wine. Branca took a glass for herself and watched Gren retreat to a distant chair, his blond brows still knotted in a scowl.

Tathrin cleared his throat. 'Did you celebrate the festival with your family, Esquire?'

'Alas, I didn't have that pleasure.' Yadres dragged his gaze away from the sack on the table. 'Did you?'

'No.' Tathrin grimaced. 'Though I was able to be with my betrothed.'

Branca wondered if it was her imagination, or could she really smell a breath of corruption rising from the bag concealing the cadaverous heads?

Chapter Twenty-Four
Branca

The Three Fountains Inn,
Solland, in the Tormalin Empire,
10th of Aft-Winter

THE CLICK OF the timepiece's arrow down the scale to the quarter-chime snapped through the room like a cracking glass.

Before it moved again, the opening door startled them all. Tathrin was there to stop it with a booted foot, his hand hovering by his sword hilt. He threw the door wide, relieved. 'Sorgrad!'

'Good evening.' The Mountain Man entered and swept a bow worthy of the Imperial Court. 'Esquire Den Dalderin?'

'Indeed.' Yadres glanced at Charoleia.

She gestured towards the unremarkable young woman who followed Sorgrad into the room. 'May I make known to you Jilseth Disimonea, wizard of Hadrumal and adviser to Planir the Black?'

'D'Isimonea?' Yadres looked more closely at the magewoman. 'Of Derrice?'

'Four generations ago,' she replied coolly.

Branca wouldn't have imagined the magewoman was of Tormalin descent. Her skin was pale, her eyes grey and her silky brown hair was shot through with auburn in the lamplight. Such mingled bloodlines were far more typical of Ensaimin.

'I take it this is why I am here?' Walking to the table, Jilseth opened the bag to hold up the duke's lifeless head. She examined it without apparent qualm.

Branca retreated to stand beside Tathrin. Yadres had moved closer to Charoleia's daybed, leaving the table to Sorgrad and the magewoman.

'Madam Jilseth is a necromancer,' Charoleia explained.

'What will her skills show us?' Wide-eyed, the young noble watched Sorgrad emptying a flagon of oil into a deep earthenware bowl.

'I have no idea.' Charoleia shrugged. 'Isn't that proof of our honest intent?'

'You haven't already—?' Yadres gestured helplessly with his empty glass.

Jilseth answered without looking round. 'Necromancy can be worked only once with any earthly remains. So I recommend you all pay close attention.'

'Let's see what Duchess Sherista can tell us.' Sorgrad handed her the dead woman's head. 'Whatever Duke Orlin's crimes, her death must be pure murder.'

Branca saw a muscle quivering in his clenched jaw. For all his composure, she realised he disliked this as thoroughly as his brother.

Even she was struggling to remind herself that she didn't believe in Poldrion's demons. That this callous preservation of the remains of the dead was condemning them to untold tortures. The children too.

Jilseth lowered the duchess's head into the viscous oil and swept her hands across the the bowl in an intricate pattern. The magewoman had dreadfully bitten fingernails, Branca noticed inconsequentially.

The unpleasant smell she had noticed earlier grew stronger. Steam rose from the earthenware bowl and thickened, lingering unnaturally around the rim. Whatever magic was being worked deep within the oil cast up shimmering amber light that reflected off the slowly swirling steam that was following Jilseth's guiding hand.

Now smoke rose from the bowl, acrid in the back of Branca's throat. Striving to ignore the scent of scorched flesh, she heard the oil faintly bubbling. She bit her lip. The inn's staff had assured her this was one of their kitchen's strongest pots. But what if so much oil caught fire?

The tales she had heard as a child clamoured in her memory; of wizards and their incautious pupils seduced by unbounded arrogance and thus suffering agonised deaths. She glanced at Sorgrad. Could his magic save them from unrestrained sorcerous fire?

Golden radiance flowed from Jilseth's hands; tendrils weaving the mingled smoke and steam into an insubstantial mass of light and shadow. Reflections sparkled in the magewoman's eyes. A miniature vista formed in the hollow heart of the magic.

'What is that?' Yadres' wonder overcame his revulsion.

'Come closer, if you wish to see.' Jilseth's hands didn't slow.

Despite herself, Branca was intrigued. Charoleia rose to her feet and they all moved to stand around the table. Only Gren stayed stubbornly hunched on his seat.

The necromantic vision reminded Branca of the ceramic dioramas fashionable among the wealthy Vanamese. As she had helped her mother clean and polish their houses, she was fascinated by the hunts and dances, peopled by figures no taller than her finger, motionless in their domes of glass.

This was a wholly different scene. Branca guessed they were seeing Duchess Sherista's bedchamber. It was an eerie sight, a night-time picture painted from glints and shadows hanging in the ensorcelled air, defying this brightly lit room.

A spark flared in the darkness. A lamp had been lit beside the seductively canopied bed. It showed two people roused from sleep by a servant rushing through a doorway at the fraying edge of the magic.

Jilseth gestured and the sphere expanded. Tathrin would have been hard put to encompass it with his arms now. The threads of grey and gold drew the merest veil over the figures hastily dragging dressing gowns over their nakedness.

The duke was silver-haired and bearded, heavyset, his paunch dark with body hair. The duchess was still slender despite her dutiful childbearing though no corsets disguised her sagging belly or her drooping breasts in the intimacy of this bedchamber.

Despite all she knew of Orlin's brutality, the persistent rumours that he had poisoned his father, Branca couldn't help but pity them. Her eyes were irresistibly drawn to the dead duke's head, lying disregarded on the top of the sack. No one deserved to be reduced to such carrion.

'Can we hear what's going on?' Yadres forced the request through clenched teeth.

Jilseth shot Sorgrad a venomous glance. 'You never asked for that.'

'If you can't do it . . .' The Mountain mage shrugged.

'Don't insult me.' Colour rose on Jilseth's cheekbones as she thrust her fingers into the margins of the swirling magic.

Faintly at first, then strengthening, warning shouts stumbled over each other. The castle was under attack. A mob had taken the gates. The battle at Pannal was lost and the Soluran's army was coming to kill them.

More figures rushed through the doorway, more voices shouting at once. These newcomers were guardsmen not servants. Branca saw several were wounded and all carried bloodied weapons.

Duke Orlin was demanding a sword. Duchess Sherista clutched his arm, heedless of her disordered clothing, her night plait unravelling around her shoulders. Her hysterical shrieks were unintelligible.

Branca shivered, intensely grateful that this elemental magic couldn't carry the emotional burdens of aetheric enchantments. It was bad enough seeing all this without feeling the woman's terror as well.

Was that why Gren was so wary of the *sheltya*? Could they raise such visions complete with every sensation and emotion with their unknown Artifice? That was a truly appalling prospect. She thrust it hastily away.

The duke silenced the clamouring guards with a commanding sweep of his hand. He kissed Sherista with fierce passion before shoving her into the merciless grasp of an armoured man.

'There's a passageway,' Tathrin breathed.

'Parnilesse Castle's riddled with them,' murmured Charoleia.

Branca saw a second guardsman wrench open a wooden panel half-hidden by the duchess's dressing table, a wondrous confection of angled mirrors in gilded frames. The armoured man dragged Sherista towards it. Even through the muffling magic, her piercing screams clawed at Branca's ears.

One guardsman gave the duke his sword, drawing a dagger instead. Another was struggling out of his hauberk, desperate to offer his lord some armour. It was too late. A man fell backwards through the doorway, blood spraying from a gaping wound in his neck.

Four followed. No, seven. More. Branca couldn't tell. The room was filled with fighting men, swords flashing in the lamplight. A guard died, a blade thrust through his eye. Another plunged his own weapon deep into an invader's chest, only to lose his head to a halberd's scything stroke.

More invaders carried blazing torches. One threw his burning brand onto the rumpled quilts. Flames shot upwards to devour the lacy canopy.

'There's Reniack!' Tathrin jabbed a finger at the elemental vision.

Abruptly, the magic wavered, the figures obscured by smoke. Voices dissolved into meaningless snarls.

'What did he do?' Yadres demanded.

'Nothing!' Tathrin looked horrified.

'Wait!' Jilseth's face was remote in the amber magelight. 'The magic can only reflect what Sherista experienced herself.'

The smoke cleared and they now saw a fraction of the bedchamber framed in the passage's doorway.

Duke Orlin was on his knees, disarmed, his hands raised in supplication. Reniack stood over him, grinning with frenzied delight. All they could hear was Sherista's hysterical screaming as her desperate guardian dragged her down the passage.

Reniack kicked Orlin hard in the chest. The grey-headed man fell awkwardly, his gown tangled around his legs, his nakedness exposed. Reniack stamped hard on his groin, grinding his boot down. As the duke writhed in agony, the rabble-rouser bent to grab his dishevelled hair.

He spat in the nobleman's face before shaking him as viciously as a dog shakes a rat. But even Reniack's unreasoning hatred didn't lend him the strength to snap Orlin's neck, so he shouted at one of his cohort. The man slapped a sword into Reniack's open hand.

The rabble-rouser thrust it deep between Orlin's throat and his shoulder. Blood gushed from the wound. Reniack still had hold of Orlin's hair. He hauled the dying man upwards, sawing clumsily with the unsuitable blade. Orlin thrashed violently with his failing strength. Blood poured down his naked chest to soak his brocade gown, pooling around his pale thighs.

Branca turned away with Sherista's despairing, disbelieving screams still ringing in her ears.

'So that's the guilty man?' Yadres swallowed hard and stepped back from the table.

'Wait,' Jilseth ordered. 'We must see this through to the end. Once the spell is done, there's no recalling it.'

Yadres looked revolted. 'There's more?'

'Sherista isn't dead yet,' Jilseth said, strained.

Reluctant, Branca turned back. Swirling blackness obscured the heart of the spell. The guards were dragging Sherista along an unlit tunnel, the woman's panic-stricken sobbing reverberating in the confined space. Then a door opened in the darkness and they were in another room.

'Where's this?' demanded Tathrin.

Charoleia replied with measured sorrow. 'It's the nursery wing.'

Branca saw a schoolroom filled with servants, already dressed for travel. They clustered around a bevy of noble children: a youth on the verge of manhood, two girls separated from him and each other by a year or so and then, markedly smaller than the rest, a little boy wailing in the arms of his nurse.

The toddler struggled to reach his mother. She shoved away the maids desperately forcing clothes upon her. The room was all confusion, everyone shouting or crying. Only the guards who had followed Sherista had any idea what to do. They began barricading the door they had come through and rushed to the windows to assess the chaos below. Firelight outside flickered on the leaded glass.

Urgently beckoning, liveried lackeys threw open double doors at the end of the room. Branca glimpsed a long hallway and a stairwell, lanterns glowing in the depths.

Then those hapless servants recoiled with horror, desperately slamming the doors. The guardsmen rushed to help. One man smashed a table, to wedge broken pieces under the doors. He died on his knees as a halberd crashed through the panel and ripped into his head.

As soon as the doors gave way, the guardsmen were hacked to bloody pieces. The servants fought heroically but bare hands, flailing cloaks and lengths of broken wood were no match for swords and halberds.

Duchess Sherista and her children stood huddled, ringed by loyal corpses.

Branca could barely breathe as the rebels paused, merely attacking with obscene taunts.

'Jettin . . .' Yet somehow she had expected this.

He strode into the schoolroom at the head of a bloodstained phalanx. His face shone with savage fervour, as brightly as Reniack's had. At his gesture, his men ripped the terrified family apart. Two held the frantically struggling duchess while a single brute subdued each weeping child.

One man grinned with evil intent and tore open the elder daughter's hastily laced bodice. As Sherista screamed, Jettin threw up his hand, not at her, but at the would-be rapist. The man collapsed, clutching his head. Blood spilled from his eyes and choking mouth.

Branca's heart thudded in her chest. Jettin had learned how to kill with his Artifice. The enchantments threaded through with all the savagery of the Storm rune truly had swept away all his principles.

The rebels looked awestruck at their dead comrade and warily at the youthful Vanamese. The duke's daughter stood paralysed by fear as another man grabbed her shrinking shoulders. Terror held her siblings in thrall. Only Sherista was still fighting to break free of her captors.

'Kill them all!' Jettin's command cut through her hoarse curses.

Branca found no consolation in the swiftness of the children's executions. Each was turned to face the wall and dispatched with a blade to the heart before their heads were severed with brisk butchers' strokes.

Sherista was still struggling. In some vain hope of saving herself or simply to embrace her slaughtered family? It hardly mattered. The invaders hacked her to pieces. She fell amid their booted feet, blades scything down, and blood spraying up. The elemental vision dissolved into red-tainted blackness.

The stinking smoke stung Branca's eyes and made her stomach roil. She did her very best not to vomit.

'Madam mage!' Tathrin stepped quickly around the table as Jilseth wavered on her feet.

Ashen-faced, the magewoman continued shaping the spell with her hands. 'Once the spell is broken, none of this can be recalled.' The first vision reappeared: the sleeping duke and duchess, all unknowing in their peaceful bedchamber. 'If you wish to see anything more, I must sustain it.'

'Must we, now we know the guilty men?' Revolted, Yadres looked to Charoleia. 'You can identify them for His Majesty?'

She nodded. 'Reniack Ragged-Ear of the Carifate and Jettin Aniseth of Vanam.'

'This was not justice, whatever Orlin's crimes. Their lives are forfeit, along with any others we can tie to this slaughter.' Yadres' implacable expression looked incongruous above his fussy, fashionable garb. 'We'll see their heads stuck on spikes above Parnilesse Town's gates. You have my word on that.'

Now the duke and duchess were roused once again.

Branca wished she could protest or offer some plea for the young adept's life. But there could be no excuse for Jettin. Not even Kerith could argue that now. Even if Reniack's warped passions had infected the youth all unawares as they communicated across the aether, Jettin had been master of his own decisions, as much as Reniack had been of his.

Duke Orlin's brutal death reappeared in the magic.

Branca was still more troubled. Just how grievously had Jettin abused his knowledge of Artifice? Had he used aetheric enchantments to tip these men's hatred and resentment for their duke into the madness that sanctioned this wholesale murder and so many noble deaths besides? Branca feared so. She struggled to believe even Reniack's eloquence could stir Parnilesse's men to such wickedness.

She glanced at Jilseth, doggedly sustaining the gruesome spell. Sherista and her guards burst into the schoolroom, desperation on every face.

Fear soured Branca's throat. The Archmage forbade elemental magic's use in Lescar's wars, for fear of the unbounded damage it might do. No one had paid much heed to aetheric enchantment, a mere curiosity for harmless scholars. What might the wizards of Hadrumal do now, once they learned these insidious evils had been wrought with Artifice?

Tathrin turned to Yadres. 'We believe Lescar's army can bring these men to answer for their crimes. We believe we have that right. We ask the Emperor to respect it. Please, let us prove to the noble houses of Tormalin and all of Caladhria's barons that such murder was never our intent.'

'Will punishing these few end all this madness?' Yadres was torn between hope and doubt.

'It'll be a start,' growled Gren from his seat.

'Won't some other agitator jump up to take Reniack's place?' Yadres was still dubious. 'He has allies clear across Parnilesse.'

'No more than one man in a hundred,' Charoleia said firmly. 'I can offer proof of that.'

'If Tormalin's legions march in, as Reniack has long sworn they would, to chain us all under the Emperor's yoke, then yes,' acknowledged Tathrin, 'his allies could well rally opposition, in the name of their martyred leaders.'

He shook his head, determined. 'But not once Reniack has been beaten by Lescari forces united to throw off ducal tyranny and any other oppression that seeks to replace it. Not when we offer the honest folk of Parnilesse a peaceful future alongside all Lescari, with a voice in their own governance–' Tathrin shot Branca a meaningful glance '–instead of cowering with Reniack's boot on their neck.'

'I believe—' Yadres paused for a long moment, his gaze looking inward. 'Tadriol should be able persuade the Convocation to give you one chance to deal with Reniack. If you lose, the legions will march without delay.'

'We can do it,' Tathrin promised, 'if you just give us a little more time.'

'Before the end of Aft-Winter?' Yadres pressed him.

'Do you want me to sustain this much longer?' Jilseth demanded through gritted teeth.

Duke Orlin's children were being murdered once again.

Yadres hastily bowed. 'I've seen enough.'

'Thank you, madam mage. You may leave the dead in peace.' Sorgrad poured white brandy and pressed the glass into Jilseth's nail-bitten hands.

The spell vanished to leave only the disquieting scent of cooked meat. Visibly drained, the magewoman accepted Sorgrad's supportive arm to a chair beside the fireplace.

Steeling herself, Branca went to the table. Charoleia forestalled her, drawing a cloth over the oil-filled bowl. 'You don't want to see.'

Branca certainly didn't. Recollections of pigs' heads that her mother boiled for brawn already tormented her. She didn't think she could ever eat that dish again.

'Let's sweeten the air.' Sorgrad snapped his fingers at the scented candles Charoleia had told Branca to request from the inn's housekeeper. The wicks kindled with honest yellow flame.

'I must write to my uncle and to the Emperor.' Yadres Den Dalderin strode around the room, unable to settle. 'Madam mage.' He addressed Jilseth with the deepest reluctance. 'If there should be any question, if any further evidence is needed, to be laid before the Convocation of Princes—' He halted to look at the duke's lolling head.

'As long as Archmage Planir sanctions it,' Jilseth said wearily, 'I will undertake the necessary necromancy for Tadriol. I won't see all this effort wasted,' she added with something of her usual acidity.

'Can we at least leave the children untroubled?' Gren demanded suddenly.

Branca pressed her hands to her mouth, revolted by the notion of committing those little heads to the sorcerous oil.

Yadres nodded swift agreement. 'Let's set them on an honourable pyre.'

'And Sherista,' Branca said quickly. 'If this spell cannot be worked again?'

'Of course.' Yadres looked helplessly at Charoleia. 'Do you know a discreet priest?'

She nodded. 'We can trust Drianon's priestess in the shrine on the Ashery Road.'

Gren sprang to his feet. 'I'll take them there tonight.'

Branca wondered what had befallen the murdered children's bodies. Had they been somehow burned in secret, in hopes of freeing them from demon-haunted darkness to make that last journey to Saedrin's door? Did loyal Parnilesse grieve in secret; for fear of Poldrion refusing the innocents passage till all the flesh tying them to this world was destroyed?

If by any remote chance there was some truth in those myths, wouldn't the memories of their own deaths and their family's slaughter be more torment than any demon could inflict? Her hand shook as she lit more scented candles and placed them around the room.

A new thought struck her. Were funeral pyres actually used to deny whatever magic raised such ghastly phantasms, whether wielded by necromancer or aetheric adept?

She sighed, setting the candle flames dancing. There was so much they didn't know about Artifice. What folly it had been, to think they could use it for their own purposes, never imagining these consequences.

Tathrin walked over, leaving Charoleia and Sorgrad, Jilseth and Yadres by the fireplace discussing the letters they must write.

'Jettin must pay for his crimes,' he said sombrely.

'I know.' Branca had been trying not to think about that. She gazed into the candle flame. 'You'll need my help, and Kerith's, and I must see what I can do for Aremil.'

The thought of him waking to this clawed at her heart.

Chapter Twenty-Five
Aremil

Carluse Castle,
20th of Aft-Winter

PEACE AND QUIET. Leisure to read and to think. No one to disturb him. He looked up and savoured the emptiness of the torchlit hall. Light and shadow vacillated amid the intricately carved vaulting, the stone as yellow as butter.

But he must make best use of his time, he guiltily reminded himself. He applied himself once again to the book open on the reading slope pulled close to his chair. Beeswax candles on the branched stand behind his shoulder burned steadily, untroubled.

Marol Afmoor's *Geography of the East* was a remarkably tedious book; a pedantic catalogue of every town, demesne and fiefdom that had once offered fealty to Toremal's ancient Emperors. Could it possibly be of use when devising some new governance for Lescar? Possibly, and the only way he would find out was by re-reading the thing. Stifling a yawn, he turned the page and tried to make some sense of the differing accounts of Eyhorne's foundation.

A carriage rattled past the window, its shadow flitting across the hearth rug. Aremil looked up, surprised. This was usually a quiet street. Most of Vanam's scholars preferred to walk or to summon carrying-chairs. They seldom lodged far from the university halls to which they were accredited, their narrow houses clustered between the upper city's libraries.

He waited but no knock sounded at his door. Good. He tugged at a cushion to settle himself more comfortably and stretched out his legs to the warmth of the fire. Transferring the weight of the book to one hand, he turned the page. Sieur D'Isellion's *Annals of the Empire* offered a caustic dissection of the failings and failures of Nemith the Last. If nothing else it should offer some hints as to what to avoid in a political settlement for Lescar.

The silver timepiece on the mantel struck five soft chimes. Noon. Lyrlen would be bringing some soup, perhaps a dish of nourishing pottage. His stomach growled with pleasurable anticipation. She always took such good care of him.

He frowned at the page. Was this correct? Surely the fatal Tormalin advance into Dalasor, in hopes of plundering Gidesta's unhewn riches, had been well under way by the fifth year of Nemith's reign. He set the book down on the table at his elbow and rose to search the tightly packed shelves beyond the fireplace. There was a copy of Mentor Fidocal's *Chronicles of the Chaos* somewhere.

He set the bulky book on the trestle-table between the pillars of the side aisle and swiftly leafed through the pages. This fragment from Den Segurie's Annals was interesting. That noble family's interests in Halse went back further than he realised.

Could he find some other record to confirm it? He should note down the details. With this research filling his days, it was folly to rely on memory alone. Mentor Tonin always said as much.

As he reached for pen and paper, he nearly knocked the inkwell over. Catching it up, he took an involuntary step back, the heel of his boot loud on the flagstones. Aremil swallowed his horror at the thought of explaining such damage, such carelessness, to those archivists who had loaned him these irreplaceable records.

Sunshine poured through the plain leaded windows. Dust motes danced and sparkled, the light burnishing some scrap of gilding on a faded book's binding.

He looked guiltily at the tomes he had heedlessly left open, even piled askew on top of each other. He should return those volumes to the chests shoved out of the way between the table's trestles.

Dusk came so early on these winter evenings. He would light the lamps himself though. No need to disturb Lyrlen in her kitchen. He tossed the crimson-bound collection of travellers' tales onto the upholstered settle and rose to find a taper on the mantelshelf, stooping to the smouldering coals.

Once lit, the faceted glass globes made the room cosier still. Glimmers warmed the golden frame of the painting over the fire, the silver timepiece below it and the decanter and goblets on the table beside his comfortable chair.

He contemplated the tray. Wine would be most welcome. But he should keep his head clear, at least till he had learned all he could about the settlement between the Merchant Guilds that kept Inglis such a peaceful and profitable town. Could they build such a consensus in Lescar? Or had the Gidestan town only done so because it was so remote, in such inhospitable country?

Taking up the crimson book, he settled himself in his fireside chair. He would ring for a tisane in a little while. Ginger root and lemongrass would stimulate his wits.

'Aremil?'

He looked up, surprised. 'Branca?'

She was at the far end of the hall, the postern in the studded door ajar.

'Oh, Aremil, at last!' She hurried towards him, hampered by stiff petticoats beneath her maroon silk gown.

'Are you all right?' He dropped the *Chronicles of the Chaos* onto the trestle table and hastened to her.

'Aremil, listen to me.' She held his hands tight. 'You've been here far too long.'

What was she talking about? Then he saw the stained-glass windows were dark. He swallowed a guilty qualm.

'We were supposed to meet for dinner?' He squinted at the silver timepiece hung on the closest pillar. For some reason he couldn't make out the silver hand that caressed the scale of chimes. 'Shall we eat at the Forked Pennant?' he said briskly. 'Then see what the comedy players are giving at the Looking Glass?'

'We're not in Vanam.' Branca surprised him by dropping his hands and grasping his shoulders instead. 'You have to leave here.'

'Don't be so foolish.' He fought an impulse to break free of her insistent hold.

'Where is this place?' She actually shook him. 'Which hall are we in, which library?'

That was absurd. 'It's—'

No, this was absurd. He couldn't recall. 'Mentor—'

He attempted a gesture towards the side aisle. 'I have borrowed all these books—'

'Who from?' demanded Branca. 'Who carried your letters to ask for their loan?'

He stared at her, bemused. Her elegant gown was no more, replaced by a travel-stained riding dress and muddy boots. Her clutching hands were rough with chilblains and her hair was tousled.

'Lyrlen—' No, that wasn't right.

'Who brought the books?' Branca persisted. 'Aremil, did you see anyone bring them through that door?'

He stared down the hall. There hadn't been a door. The end wall had been a smooth expanse of masonry. That was impossible, wasn't it?

'Where did that timepiece come from, Aremil?' She thrust a finger at the silver ornament.

He frowned. 'My house in Vanam.'

'That's right.'

He saw tears in her eyes, her chapped lips trembling. 'What's wrong? I—' His legs buckled as inexplicable weakness overwhelmed him.

Branca caught him around the waist. 'You must sit down.'

He could feel her trembling, exhausted. They barely managed to reach his wooden chair beside the branched candle-stand.

Aremil looked in vain for the reading slope that he had pushed aside to stand up. 'I don't understand.'

The carved wood was hideously uncomfortable. What had happened to his softly accommodating chair by the fireside? Closing his eyes, he leaned his head back.

'Aremil!' Branca said sharply. 'Tell me where we are!'

Why was she pestering him when he was so tired, so hungry?

'I want to go home,' he said involuntarily.

'You left Vanam at the end of For-Autumn,' Branca prompted. 'Where did you go?'

'I went to Losand,' he remembered, surprised.

'Who did you travel with?' Branca challenged.

That took a moment's thought. 'Master Gruit and Mistress Charoleia.'

'Where are they now?' she asked quickly.

'They're—' They had all met with Evord and Tathrin in the upper room of the timber-framed Merchants' Exchange. Why was he studying all alone in this remote stone hall? Aremil opened his eyes. 'This isn't Losand.'

Branca was looking intently at him. 'When did you last see Master Gruit and Mistress Charoleia?'

'In Carluse.' Candle flames sputtered in a chilling draft. 'Charoleia's been hurt.' Worse than hurt. She had been tortured. Aremil stiffened, horrified. 'Trissa is dead!'

'Yes.' A tear glistened on Branca's cheek. 'And Gruit?'

'He fled Abray,' Aremil slowly recalled, 'after embezzling the funds to supply Tathrin.'

How did he know that? How could he have forgotten?

Anxiety seized him. 'Where's Tathrin?'

How could he have forgotten his friend, marching with the Soluran, risking his life while Aremil sat surrounded by books?

'He's in Parnilesse,' said Branca, 'with Sorgrad and Gren.'

'Charoleia is in Solland.' Aremil wasn't sure how he knew that either. 'You were there too.'

'That's right.' Relief was allaying the fear in Branca's eyes. 'Where are we now?'

Aremil knew that he had left Losand. Where had he gone after that? Why couldn't he recollect? This was becoming ridiculous. Or it would be, if it wasn't so unsettling.

'Carluse?' he ventured. 'No.' There was another journey he couldn't call to mind.

But Branca was nodding with a smile. 'You're in Carluse.'

Voices echoed all around; male and female, anguished and angry. The candles flickered madly.

'*Do you hate us so much?*'

'*Did you have to kill him?*'

'*We always provided for you.*'

The flaming torches bracketed on the pillars died. Black smoke spiralled upwards to thicken the shadows in the vaulted roof.

'*Don't pretend concern for my welfare.*'

'*So you wash your hands of us?*'

'*How long before some mob hacks off our heads and rapes my innocent daughters?*'

The postern door slammed shut. Bolts drove themselves home with a screech of metal.

'No!' Branca exclaimed, horrified. 'Aremil, please, we must leave.' She thrust his crutches at him.

He stared uncomprehending at the leather-padded props. Couldn't he stand on his own two feet? No, he couldn't. Now he saw his wasted legs, his awkwardly twisted shoes. Breath tightened in his chest and he felt a threatening cramp.

How could he have forgotten? He was a cripple. Abject misery twisted his face into untold ugliness. A spasm shook his hands lying helpless in his lap, striking his knuckles hard against the wooden chair.

'Oh, my poor love.' Branca's voice broke on her distress.

Treacherous tears escaped him. 'Leave me alone.'

'How would I explain that to Tathrin?' Branca pulled him forward. 'To Failla and Master Welgren?'

She was trying to force the crutches under his arms, pressing his feeble hands onto the grips.

'We need you, Aremil. Lescar needs you!'

Now he remembered. 'Lescar needs new governance. That's what I'm doing here.' Sudden anger blazed. 'Why won't you leave me alone to work?'

Hot wax dripped from the candle-stand to puddle on the floor. The air was stifling.

'If I do that you will die!' Branca glared at him through her tears. 'Will you force that grief on me and Tathrin? Will you fail every Lescari looking to us to end their misery? When you promised to throw down the dukes and set up the rule of law in their stead?'

Aremil pointed a shaking hand towards the tables of books. 'I have found precedents—'

The books weren't there. There was no side-aisle, just a blank stone wall. He looked up to see a low vault of plain grey masonry.

'We must leave.' Branca hauled him upwards. 'Or you will be locked in here alone!'

This time Aremil didn't resist. Even though the torches had guttered, he could still see the far end of the hall. The great entrance had vanished, leaving only a narrow iron door.

Aremil didn't know what had happened but something was very wrong. He threw all his feeble strength into getting to his feet. The crutches felt unfamiliar but he knew that for a falsehood now. Calluses on his hands matched the worn leather grips. He swayed, light-headed.

'I'll make sure that you don't fall,' Branca promised.

His legs nearly failed but he held himself upright long enough to swing one prop forwards. Gritting his teeth, he forced the second to join it. Breathing heavily, he shifted his recalcitrant feet.

Step by ungainly step, he made his way towards the distant door. Branca's outstretched arms embraced him without ever touching. As they drew nearer, he was relieved to see the way out was bigger than he had first thought. He wouldn't have to risk stooping and losing his balance.

An abrupt thought halted him. 'If Tathrin is in Parnilesse—' Guilt choked him. 'If I've been locked away in here . . . ?'

His crutches skidded beneath him. His feet were cold and wet. Aremil looked down, alarmed to see water seeping through the joints between the flagstones.

He threw himself through the door and fell hard into the darkness beyond.

* * *

'I have been speaking to Tathrin by means of Artifice and so has Kerith.'

Dazed, Aremil realised Branca was talking to him. He tried to reply but his tongue was sticky against his teeth.

'Drink a little of this,' a different voice suggested.

A gentle arm around his shoulders raised him up and he felt a cup at his lips. Aremil opened his mouth to be shocked by the chill of ice crushed into currant cordial. At least it cut through the vile taste clogging his throat.

He managed to open his eyes, though his lashes seemed stuck together. Trying to speak, he coughed.

Serafia lifted him upright to save him from choking. Aremil realised he was in bed, clad only in a nightshirt. Worse, he was diapered like an infant.

'Do you know where you are?' Branca sat on a stool close by.

'In Carluse Castle.' Aremil recognised Duke Garnot's disapproving forebears on the pale-grey walls. 'This is Master Welgren's room.'

'You have been mortally ill.' Serafia plumped his pillows before leaning him back against them.

Aremil looked at his hands. Always thin, now they were skeletal. The mere effort of sitting up left him trembling with exhaustion. 'For how long?'

Branca leaned forward to fold his hand in her own. 'Fifty days, near enough.'

Aremil stared at her, disbelieving. 'Why am I not dead?'

Branca's half-smile cracked her painfully chapped lips. 'You have Serafia's nursing to thank.'

'I am most grateful.' Though Aremil found it hard to meet the Carlusian woman's eyes, humiliatingly aware of the damp linen around his groin.

Serafia shrugged, setting the cup of iced cordial on the marble-topped table. 'You rallied from time to time, otherwise there would have been little I could have done.'

'I don't remember anything.' Aremil was baffled. 'Not since we were in Wellan.'

'You caught a winter ague,' Serafia explained. 'It went to your chest.'

'Failla brought you back here as slowly as she dared.' Branca tried to smile but her eyes brimmed with tears. 'Fever gripped you for ten days.'

'After Master Welgren cured that, you slept.' Serafia stirred the cordial with a silver spoon. 'But we couldn't rouse you to do more than swallow soup.'

'Are you hungry now?' Branca asked, concerned.

Aremil turned his face away. 'I deserted you all.'

'No,' protested Branca.

'I'll find Master Welgren.' Serafia hurried to the door.

Aremil wanted to look at Branca but he couldn't bear to see her pity. Worse, now he was recalling his conversations with Duchess Aphanie and those strangers who were his parents.

He had shirked all those challenges, retreating into some enchanted delusion when everyone else was risking life and limb. When he couldn't even stand on his own two feet.

'So long asleep?' He fought to keep his voice level. 'Then I take it everything is settled?'

'Hardly!'

Branca's exclamation reclaimed his attention.

'We have secured Wyril,' she said briskly. 'There's peace in Carluse and Triolle, for the most part anyway. No one pays much heed to Would-be-Duke Rousharn up in Sharlac.' She hesitated. 'Duke Secaris and his family have fled to Tormalin so the Guilds and the priests are keeping order in Draximal. But everyone is still waiting for us to show them a path to a peaceful future.'

The task he had so shamefully abandoned.

'What of Marlier and Parnilesse?' he asked slowly.

Branca took a long moment to reply. 'Bandits are plaguing both banks of the Rel. Master Ernout has his Woodsmen tracking them to their lairs to drive them out of Carluse. We believe this is all Iruvain of Triolle's doing, though Ferdain of Marlier doesn't know it. He sent Iruvain as his envoy to Caladhria's Winter Parliament.'

'To bring the barons into this war.' Aremil grimaced, helpless on his pillows. 'What is the Vixen doing?'

Though his body was frighteningly weak, he was relieved to find his wits were rallying.

'She keeps her own counsel as thoroughly as she ever did.' Branca laughed without humour. 'While Ferdain sits on his hilltop bleating for help from Caladhria.'

'Will the barons answer?' Aremil couldn't guess. How much had happened while he'd lain insensible? He could have pounded the quilts in frustration but barely had the strength to clench his fist.

'Kerith still has friends in Abray who don't hold Gruit's misdeeds against him. They believe the border barons might send their own household soldiery to Marlier in the spring, if they think helping to crush these brigands will restore their own peace.'

Branca gently stroked his wasted hand. 'So before the spring arrives, we must drive out these bandits ourselves, and show Caladhria that Lescar can manage its own affairs. We need a new settlement between nobles and commoners, between townsfolk and yeomen.'

'If we can offer Marlier something better than Ferdain's rule, with every other dukedom standing shoulder to shoulder,' Aremil said slowly, 'could we see them turn against him without a drop of blood shed?'

'Saedrin save us from another massacre like Parnilesse,' Branca said fervently.

Aremil gasped as screams deafened him – a woman and her children!

'What is it?' Branca leaned forward anxiously.

'I'm recalling Duchess Sherista being murdered,' Aremil said shakily, 'though I've no notion how.' Then he recalled something else, far more urgent. 'Tathrin is in Parnilesse. He's going to fight Reniack!'

'Within the next handful of days, and he will defeat him,' asserted Branca. 'Then we must convince Emperor Tadriol that the Lescari can secure their own peace.'

'I've never met Tadriol the Provident.' Curiosity began to win through Aremil's self-recriminations. 'I've never even seen his likeness. How do I know what he looks like, and the tone of his voice?'

'I've met his Imperial Majesty.' Branca released his hand. 'You cannot have been so lost to us as we feared.'

Looking up, he saw tears trickling down her cheeks.

'I'm so sorry. You were all alone and I should have helped you.' She could barely whisper. 'I should have come sooner but there was so much to do, for Charoleia and Tathrin. When I did come, it's taken me so long to find a way in—'

'I failed you when you needed my comfort after Adel.' Aremil tried to reach for her but didn't have the strength.

'I should have let you.' Her tears fell onto the rumpled quilt.

Aremil was too exhausted to argue. Silence spread to fill the room. But now they shared that silence. Before, it had divided them.

Summoning all his will, refusing to acknowledge his weakness, he sat up. 'My love—'

'I know.' She shifted her stool, to sit with her forehead leaning against his, their fingers intertwined.

After a few moments Branca moved, to rest her head lightly on his shoulder. 'You're wondering how Tathrin's faring.'

He brushed a kiss against her cheek. 'You're wondering what's to become of Jettin.'

Chapter Twenty-Six
Tathrin

The Hardrew Road,
North of Parnilesse Town,
24th of Aft-Winter

SUNRISE AND ANOTHER battle ahead. How long before peace truly dawned over Lescar? How many would lie dead before nightfall, across these sere fields shrouded in winter mists?

Tathrin looked up at the sky, where both moons lingered in the pale blue, Great and Lesser both at their full. There wouldn't be another night so bright till the latter third of For-Summer. But it had passed as they advanced unchallenged.

Where were Reniack's forces lying in wait? Captain-General Evord would have sent out scouts. The Soluran took great care choosing his ground for battles, securing a commanding view of the fighting, all the better to direct his regiments to counter the enemy.

But Tathrin had no gallopers and hadn't risked sending out scouts. They had barely enough men to threaten the Parnilesse forces convincingly.

Their route followed a bank raised half a man's height above the meadows. Even leafless in winter, dense lines of osiers blocked his view in all directions. Some traced the deep ditches that drained this sodden ground, reclaiming the mire for spring grazing and summer hay. Others marked the solid earthworks that curbed the worst winter floods, when the wind-driven pumps and elm sluice gates were forced to admit defeat.

Tathrin contemplated the contingent marching along the narrow track ahead of his small command troop. These Deflin men were untested in battle but trained and drilled by Shady Moth sergeants. The men and women formerly of that company had acquitted themselves bravely in the battle for Wyril.

He had thought galloping through battles carrying urgent messages was daunting. But being responsible for governing the ebb and flow of the fighting, the man to whom every company captain looked for guidance? The prospect filled him with cold dread that the watery sun couldn't counter even at its zenith.

How close an aetheric watch was Jettin keeping on their advance? Tathrin hadn't felt any whisper of Artifice brush against his thoughts. Regardless, he was convinced the young adept would be spying.

Unless he was watching the Tormalin legions. Unease chilled Tathrin further. Could he have been so mistaken in Reniack's intent? Was the rabble-rouser looking east instead of north?

Did Reniack honestly believe he could launch some full-scale assault across the River Asilor without Tormalin's legions retaliating? Was he so desperate to keep his henchmen loyal with largesse now that Parnilesse's granaries and larders were bare? Or could he be counting on that retaliation, to unite doubters and dissenters against an undeniable enemy?

Or did he know how reluctant Tadriol was to become embroiled in Lescar? Did he imagine the Emperor might pay him off? Were his arrogant raids merely a bluff?

Little birds warbled in the sedges and the osiers rustled in the gentle breeze.

Tathrin shook off such fruitless speculation. They were committed and his whole concern must be his marching men and women, drawn from all corners of Lescar including Parnilesse.

Even though Quirton was well inside Duke Orlin's erstwhile lands, Tathrin and his army had found a cautious welcome there.

This far to the north and east of his domain, Orlin's hand had rested more lightly. His brutal murder and the slaughter of his family won little understanding, even among those who sympathised with Reniack's aspirations.

Freedom was one thing; anarchy quite another. These merchants and yeoman valued peace, which would allow them to trade with their prosperous Tormalin neighbours and with similarly minded Draximals across their forested border.

Tathrin smiled wryly. Reniack's pamphlets and broadsheets were still helping rally men to the cream and gold banner, though that must be far from his intent.

As they had waited in Quirton for the Lescari army to march from Deflin to Chinel and southwards, Gren had discovered Reniack's envoys were distributing his writings in the town and its environs.

They were demanding that the guildsmen yield to the new order in Parnilesse of their own free will. Otherwise Reniack's devoted followers would compel their obedience, in the name of the silent commonalty. They'd already succeeded in Brynock, Inchra and Hardrew, so the night letters nailed to shrine doors proclaimed.

According to Gren, plenty of Reniack's supporters were already insinuated into the nearby villages, set to secure them with the minimum of fighting. Then his henchmen could declare he was simply serving the downtrodden poor, as he'd done across so much of Parnilesse.

Then he would reward all those unfortunates, whether they had supported him or not. According to Reniack's writings, Tormalin's great houses had profited so long from Lescari misery that now it was only justice for Parnilesse's free men and women to settle that debt in wheat and meat. They should unite to refill their empty storehouses, to fill their children's empty bellies.

But first, Tathrin decided, Reniack's attention would be wholly on their advance. He would see defeating Tathrin as a wonderful opportunity to secure his hold on this dukedom. With this fledgling army defeated, he could begin his challenge for the rest of Lescar.

He would know they were advancing down the Hardrew Road. Since they had not attacked, skirting around to leave the town in his allies' hands, they were clearly intent on Parnilesse Town itself. He would have Jettin watch their every move. That's what Charoleia and Sorgrad agreed.

Tathrin twisted in his saddle to see Sorgrad riding a few paces behind. The Mountain Man was polishing a silver dish with a twist of his cloak. He grinned as he stowed it away. 'Don't fret, long lad.'

Tathrin could only trust Sorgrad wasn't foolish enough to be scrying. Jilseth was still adamant that wizardry was forbidden within Lescar's borders. It had taken all Charoleia's eloquence to convince her to let Sorgrad take Branca to Carluse by magical means, and she had still insisted that he return by horse, to rejoin them in Quirton.

They had left the magewoman with the Emperor and his retinue, ready to use her own magic to see if Lescari forces would prevail today and allow the Tormalin legions to march back to their barracks unbloodied.

After that, Archmage Planir had agreed Jilseth should remain in Tadriol's company, to convince the Convocation of Princes of Reniack's guilt with whatever necromantic evidence could be wrung from Duke Orlin's cadaverous head. Charoleia had warned that belligerent border princes still favoured claiming Parnilesse lands, even if the wholesale reconquest of Lescar was a step too far for most.

Was Jilseth watching Jettin as well to make sure no Artifice affected the day's outcome? Tathrin ground his teeth. He had come to fervently dislike the dispassionate magewoman, with her insistence on balance and fairness. Did she consider this pain and death of no more account than a game of white raven?

What was his father wont to say? Life's not fair and the sooner you learn that, the happier you will be.

Gren's horse appeared at his elbow. 'Anyone looking over your shoulder?'

'Not that I can tell.' Tathrin wished he could be certain if Jettin was spying on them.

'Any word from our girl?' Gren pressed closer, chewing a currant cake.

'Branca? No.'

Tathrin was only getting the briefest of updates from Carluse. Branca was nursing Aremil, constantly vigilant for any aetheric assault by Jettin. She was convinced the renegade adept had been foiling her initial attempts to breach Aremil's imagined sanctuary, that Jettin had sought to swamp Aremil with his malice right to the last.

Kerith was preoccupied with banditry along the River Rel. Whenever they spoke across the aether, he would remind Tathrin how urgently he must address the issue of Marlier, as soon as Parnilesse was settled. Tathrin got the distinct impression the scholar didn't want to contemplate Jettin's treachery, still less discuss it.

When would this endless, exhausting campaign finally be done?

'You think too much.' Sorgrad's dun mount drew level with Tathrin's bay. 'You know what we've got to do.'

'Indeed,' Tathrin said curtly. 'How far to this bridge on the Moss Lode?'

These lodes, the deep, steep-sided channels into which all the lesser ditches drained, determined every route through this inconvenient landscape. The few bridges that crossed them would choke any army's advance. Reniack must be counting on that.

'It's just past that last line of trees.' Gren pointed.

As they advanced through the osiers, Tathrin saw banners appearing to either hand. Though the Lescari army had advanced on as wide a front as possible, every route for leagues around inexorably converged on the Moss Bridge. The Pine Marten sergeants had taken Ashgil's company by a more southerly route while the Shearlings' captain had rolled the losing rune, condemning the Triolle men to the frozen furrows of the northerly fields. Tathrin hoped he hadn't lost too many to twisted ankles. He would soon know, as the cream and gold banner summoned runners reporting each company's strength.

Reniack and his forces must be waiting to attack once Tathrin's army advanced beyond the bridge. Swift horsemen would have summoned the rabble-rouser's most fanatical allies from Brynock and from Inchra. His most ferocious supporters would have marched in hurried pursuit from Hardrew, intent on cutting off any retreat for Tathrin.

Reniack would be confident his men could defeat Lescar's long-scorned militiamen, even if their threadbare cloaks bore freshly embroidered badges, blending their town's insignia with the different tokens they'd adopted from the rebellion's standard.

At least, that's what Tathrin very much hoped. They had done everything they could to convince Reniack that they were marching into his trap unawares. Kerith and Branca had played their weary, distracted parts convincingly. Sorgrad had teased Jettin for days with that silver dish, even pouring water into it from time to time, only to quench his thirst.

The Moss Bridge lay straight ahead, as hump-backed as a hissing cat. A wind-driven pump stood beside it; four posts capped with a little tiled roof that sheltered the woven-reed sails fixed vertically around the central pillar. Breezes coming from the sea, or rolling down from Dalasor's grasslands, would spin them to drive the pump as the seasons turned.

'*He has no idea what you're planning.*'

Branca was sourly amused though Tathrin winced at her fatigue.

Kerith's voice echoed inside his head, taut with regret.

'*He's on the far side of the bridge and Reniack's with him.*'

Then all sense of the two of them vanished, so abruptly as to leave him dizzy.

Tathrin gathered his reins and his wits. Sorgrad had won his wager. He'd said Reniack would calculate how far and how fast the Lescari army must march and conclude the Moss Bridge was the place to stop them.

His men must be hidden in the weed-choked fields beyond the bridge. But what precisely was he planning? Would he wait for all Tathrin's troops to cross? Or only allow the first half of the Lescari army over? Were Reniack's Hardrew forces already close on their tail to attack those left behind?

The Deflin men led by the Shady Moths were arriving at the bridge. Instead of crossing, they slid down both sides of the raised road and spread out along the steep banks that held back the Moss Lode's waters.

Tathrin raised a hand and his command troop halted, the cream and gold banner flapping softly. To the north, the Ashgil company scrambled up to crouch amid the dead grasses, alert for any foe on the far embankment. To Tathrin's other hand, the Triolle men were doing the same.

'How blunt's that sword of yours?' Gren was running a whetstone along his blade.

'Ask Sorgrad.' Tathrin shrugged. 'He sharpened it last night.'

Despite the hard frost, the sun was warm on his face. They waited, with their horses mumbling their bits, clinking against yellowed teeth.

Tathrin half-wished for something to break the silence, even as he reminded himself that the longer they waited, the better.

Finally men appeared on the embankment at the far end of the bridge: Reniack, Jettin and a trio of their supporters. So far, so good.

'How baffling,' mocked Sorgrad. 'They're offering battle and we don't take it.'

'They're well within bowshot,' mused Gren.

Tathrin wished he hadn't said that. Some bold crossbowman loosing a bolt in defiance of his orders could lose this battle for them all.

No such missile was loosed. They watched Reniack and Jettin confer, then the tallest of the nameless warriors disappeared from view. The ground beyond the lode was appreciably lower than the fields on this side, the road nowhere near so elevated. The man reappeared with an armful of frost-bleached sedge.

They watched Jettin advance to the crest of the bridge. He waved the fronds for lack of the green branches that normally signalled a request for a parley.

'Interesting,' Gren observed, 'how treacherous scum always expect other folk to abide by custom.'

'I'm more concerned with Emperor Tadriol knowing us for honourable men.' Tathrin nodded to the Shady Moth carrying the cream and gold standard. The man dipped it twice, the gold fringe brushing the dusty track.

He rode on with Sorgrad and Gren. Reniack and the tall man joined Jettin on the bridge. Custom dictated three aside in a parley.

'Are there horses below the embankment?' Sorgrad asked quietly.

'I can't see,' Gren growled, frustrated.

Tathrin contemplated the stocky rabble-rouser. Reniack seemed at ease, thumbs hooked into the belt cinched tight over his chain-mail hauberk. Jettin glowered, the sedge fronds in his hand twitching like a cat's tail.

Tathrin avoided even glancing at him. He didn't know if meeting the adept's gaze would leave him more vulnerable to Artifice but he wasn't about to risk it.

They reached the bridge but did not dismount, to stay on a level with the men on the crown of the arch.

'You wish to surrender?' Tathrin asked Reniack.

The rabble-rouser laughed. 'You should be looking for terms.'

'How so?' Tathrin had to keep them talking for as long as he could.

'You're trapped like witless sheep!' Reniack couldn't restrain his triumph.

'How so?' Tathrin repeated, derisive.

Reniack's brow creased. 'You cannot imagine we'll allow you to cross this bridge.'

'We hold this side of the lode, so we have an impasse. Perhaps we should discuss our differences,' Tathrin offered. 'Even resolve them? We began this campaign as allies.'

'When I still believed you had the stomach for it,' Reniack spat, contemptuous. 'I thought the Soluran had the stones to see the job through, but he let Garnot of Carluse run, time and again. Just as you've let Duke Secaris flee.' He jabbed a menacing finger at Tathrin. 'You say you came to do away with all the dukes' injustices? Hand over Duchess Aphanie and her brood, along with this lord she thinks to anoint as Sharlac's new oppressor—'

'Lord Rousharn,' Tathrin interrupted. 'Lady Derenna's husband. Won't you spare his life for her sake? Or will you hang her alongside him?'

Reniack continued as if he hadn't spoken. 'When you've proven your good faith, turn over your forces to my command. Once we march on Marlier to cut Duke Ferdain's cowardly throat, along with all his spawn and his treacherous bitch, Lescar will truly be free!'

He knew they would refuse. Tathrin saw that. All Reniack wanted was some justification for the day's bloodshed. But the pretence of reasoning with him would draw out this conversation.

'Is Aremil to go to the scaffold?' he protested. 'You condemn a crippled man for an accident of parentage?'

Reniack took a wrathful step. 'He deceived us from the outset—'

'Something's wrong.' Jettin looked over his shoulder.

Tathrin nudged his horse forward a pace. 'You lied and dissembled and—'

'They—' Jettin sank to his knees with a cry of pain. 'I can't see!'

Reniack drew his sword. 'Call off your adepts!'

'No adepts of ours abuse Artifice like Jettin.' Now Tathrin coaxed his horse backwards.

That left Reniack at a clear disadvantage if he ran down the bridge to challenge three mounted men.

'This parley is over!' As Reniack retreated, dragging Jettin, the third man drew his sword and spread his arms wide to bar their way.

'They have horses.' Gren had edged aside, to see the road beyond the embankment.

Someone hidden behind the bridge yelled out. Reniack's man turned. Then something caught his eye and he looked down into the lode.

'Shit.' Sorgrad spurred his horse up the steep bridge.

'The water!' The man managed a baffled shout before Sorgrad's sword slammed into his head. The man staggered against the low parapet. He toppled over, screaming as he fell into the water with a resounding splash.

'Come on!' Tathrin urged his horse forwards.

Reaching the crest of the bridge, he saw Reniack's allies staring aghast into the lode. It wasn't the loss of their comrade that appalled them. The water was sinking fast, to leave the dark walls glistening in the sunlight.

'They're getting away.' Gren pointed with his sword.

Reniack and Jettin had mounted. Tathrin lashed his horse with a rein. It sprang forward as his command troop galloped after him, every man hand-picked by Sorgrad and Gren.

Captain-General Evord wouldn't approve. But Tathrin was the man with this particular task, here and now.

He spared a backward glance to see Deflin's contingent take control of the bridge, and Lescar's army surging up the banks of the lode, yelling abuse and defying Reniack's men to attempt the crossing.

Looking ahead, Tathrin saw Reniack's forces appear. As he'd suspected, they'd hidden in the ditches on either side of this road. He ducked, the bristles on his unshaven cheek catching his horse's mane as arrows sliced the air overhead.

These fields were glistening. Water seeped through tangled dead grass and the straight line of a ditch blurred beneath a rising flood. Now the road ahead was crowded as Reniack's warriors sought drier ground. Men cast aside their heavy cloaks and sodden cloth fanned out like the wings of fallen birds.

Tathrin and his galloping men forced a path through their confusion with brutal boots and swords. They were gaining on Reniack now and Jettin rode close beside him, one hand pressed to his head. Tathrin guessed Branca was repaying him for Aremil's woes.

Ahead, the next bridge was a simple affair of planks and rails crossing a ditch heading for a distant lode. Now seething water washed silt across the boards.

Jettin's mount shied, fighting its bridle. All the adept's horsemanship had deserted him. The horse reared with alarm as the first plank was ripped loose from the bridge by the flood.

'Surrender!' bellowed Tathrin. 'You have nowhere left to go.'

The rabble-rouser wrenched his horse around to face them. Blood dripped from its mouth. 'What have you done?' he screamed.

'Broken the pumps and blocked the sluices.' His eyes white-rimmed, Jettin subdued his horse with violent hands.

Sorgrad and Gren flanked Tathrin. The rest of his hand-picked troop were beating back those trying to rally to their leaders' aid. Most of Reniack's men were floundering down in the fields where the water was now thigh deep. It lapped at the edges of the roadway.

'Both moons at their full bring the highest tides between now and For-Summer,' Tathrin shouted. 'The rains cannot flow to the sea so they've flooded all the drained land behind you as far as the Inchra Road. Your way back to Parnilesse is blocked. Your allies from Brynock cannot reach you.'

'Our Hardrew men will cut you to pieces,' the rabble-rouser hissed.

Tathrin shook his head. 'Not before the Carluse militia company hamstrings them from behind.'

'They went west!' Jettin choked. 'To hunt bandits in Marlier!'

'That's what Kerith had you think.' Tathrin looked at Reniack again. 'Just as Branca stopped your boy seeing the Chinel men taking barges down the Asilor, to land north of Parnilesse once you had passed by. Quirton men showed them how to raise this flood and still leave a path to pursue you. You're the ones trapped like rats in rising water.'

Reniack's eyes blazed. 'Our allies in Parnilesse Town—'

'Will surrender to the Quirton militia, if they have any sense.' Tathrin curbed his own horse's disquiet at the creeping water. 'Emperor Tadriol doesn't want your kind ruling Parnilesse. His galleys have carried Quirton guildsmen into the pool beneath the town, along with boatloads of those who've fled your vision of freedom for sanctuary in Tormalin.'

For the first time, Reniack's certainty faltered. He glanced over his shoulder to see the wooden bridge now reduced to four barren posts. He glared at Jettin. 'Get us out of here!'

The younger man stumbled over the cadences of some aetheric enchantment. 'I can't!' He looked at Tathrin, desperate. 'I never imagined things would go this far!'

Tathrin hardened his heart. 'Surrender and you'll stand fair trial for the murders of Orlin and Sherista.'

'Or I can save the hangman a length of hemp.' Gren levelled his sword.

'I bend my neck to no man!' Reniack spurred his horse at Tathrin.

Tathrin gripped the saddle with his thighs. He hated fighting on horseback, so he had practised every day. Gren had been beating him black and blue while he got the measure of this skill.

Reniack's sword met his with a scrape of steel and they exchanged a flurry of blows. Tathrin swiftly realised Reniack was merely hacking at him, blind with fury. Tathrin easily parried his strokes. What he needed was a decisive thrust. But whenever he saw an opening, Reniack's steed involuntarily frustrated him, even though it was no warhorse, terrified, snorting bloody foam.

Tathrin's mount snapped viciously at it. This bay had come through more battles than he had, according to the Shady Moth's erstwhile horsemaster. As Tathrin parried and thrust, the horse deftly shifted beneath him.

Reniack's blows became more ragged. The rabble-rouser was red-faced and breathing hard. Tathrin saw that he had lost a stirrup and spurred his own horse harder. Reniack's steed shied away.

Tathrin drove his sword at Reniack's face, only for the man to throw up his arm. Tathrin's blade skidded across the links of the rabble-rouser's mail, ripping into one of his mutilated ears.

Reniack's roar of pain was too much for his panicked horse. Bit clamped between its teeth, the animal reared up. So terrified, it reared too high. Its hooves slid in the mud, skidding beneath its hocks. Screaming, it toppled backwards.

Reniack threw himself from the saddle for fear of being crushed and fell hard onto the road, the water too shallow to soften the impact. The horse crashed down, hooves flailing as it rolled into the flooded field.

Amid the chaos of the skirmish, Tathrin contemplated Reniack in an instant of cold clarity. If he surrendered, he would be an unspeakably troublesome captive. Friends and allies would smuggle his writings out of whatever prison held him. When he was tried for his crimes, his self-justifying speeches would breed more confusion and discontent.

Would that end even after he was hanged? That was the only possible outcome. Tathrin saw Duke Orlin's brutal murder, Duchess Sherista fighting for her children.

His vision cleared and he saw Reniack grope for his sword. The man struggled to his knees. Tathrin rode forward, prompting his horse to a trot. As Reniack staggered to his feet, Tathrin drew back his arm. His horse broke into a canter and Tathrin swung the blade with all his strength behind it.

The razor-edged steel caught Reniack between his helm and the throat of his hauberk. His head bowled along the waterlogged road. The breeze snatched away a spray of blood before his body collapsed in the mud.

Cursing, Tathrin pulled his horse up by the wrecked bridge. Where had the head disappeared to amid those wild waters? Tadriol wanted it spiked on Parnilesse Town's gate. How much trouble could Reniack's cronies be if they could cling to some hope that he had escaped?

No matter. He had to win this battle and more men that Reniack would still have to die. But as Tathrin wheeled his horse around, he saw his command troop prevailing on the causeway. Beyond, all along the embankment, Reniack's men were surrendering. It was that or drown, just as Tathrin had intended.

A horse dodged and he saw Gren fighting Jettin on foot. To Tathrin's surprise, the adept looked as proficient with a sword as he was with his enchantments. He parried, once, twice, and even attempted a counter-thrust as he twisted his blade free of Gren's.

Tathrin looked for some hint that the Vanamese wanted to yield. If Kerith was right, if Jettin had been in thrall to Reniack on account of the Artifice linking them, now that Reniack was dead—

Jettin fell with a scream in a welter of scummy water. He clutched his thigh with bloodied hands. Gren kicked the adept's sword away and raised his own blade for a killing blow.

Tathrin's mouth was too dry to shout. Besides, misguided was still guilty under every law-code from Tormalin to Solura.

Though Tathrin didn't believe Jettin was misguided. Whatever Kerith might want to believe, Branca insisted Jettin could have resisted if he didn't like what he saw in Reniack's thoughts. The rabble-rouser certainly couldn't force Jettin to hack Duchess Sherista to pieces. Reniack wasn't the adept.

More merciless still, Sorgrad and Gren insisted their *sheltya* would kill the lad out of hand. How could they bring him to trial, before Raeponin's shrine or any other court, when he could twist the sympathies of those judging him? To go free to improve his aetheric understanding, to refine his attacks on vulnerable minds?

So Tathrin simply looked on as Gren lowered his sword and watched Jettin's struggles grow weaker. After an eternity that could have only been a few breaths, the young adept lay motionless in a slough of reddened mud.

Sorgrad appeared on foot at his horse's shoulder. 'Do you think Planir will understand if Jilseth starts telling tales?'

As Tathrin looked down, he saw a flash of green magelight in the flooded field. Reniack's head spun through the air to land beside his body, the last dregs of his lifeblood seeping into the rising water.

Sorgrad stooped to retrieve it. 'Do you suppose this little gift will persuade the Tormalin Emperor to ship some men to Marlier for us?'

'What?' Tathrin stared at him.

Sorgrad grinned. 'We've still got Duke Ferdain on our dance card.'

Chapter Twenty-Seven

Litasse

Marlier Castle,
26th of Aft-Winter

FERDAIN'S BROAD SHOULDERS disappeared around the corner. 'Your Grace!' She hastened down the hallway.

The maidservant dogging her footsteps scurried after her with a strangled bleat. 'Your Grace?'

Litasse ignored the foolish girl. She had wasted half the morning looking for this 'chance' encounter with the duke.

Ferdain stopped and his escort of young nobles deftly withdrew to leave the sun-dappled carpet empty between them.

Most had their new doublets sewn from the same silver velvet as the duke's. If not, they copied other details of his dress; Aldabreshin opals on their buttons, silver Caladhrian shoe buckles. She hid her contempt for their fawning with her sweetest smile.

'Your Grace?' Duke Ferdain bowed. 'I trust you're keeping well?'

'Very well, Your Grace.' Litasse's curtsey graciously acknowledged their equality of rank. 'Though I would ask one favour,' she added quickly as he turned to depart.

'If it's in my power.'

Litasse detected a wariness in his dark eyes. She gestured towards the blue sky beyond the leaded windows. 'After so many days within doors, may I beg you for the loan of a horse?'

Ferdain smoothed his silky beard. 'The beasts will be fractious, my dear, after so many days in their stalls.' He wagged a playful finger. 'His Grace your husband would be justly furious if you suffered some accident while you are my guest.'

With some effort, Litasse kept smiling. 'Iruvain would be the first to assure you that I am a most competent horsewoman.'

Ferdain nodded amiably. 'It will be my honour to see you both mounted when His Grace returns. I believe we will enjoy his company for the celebrations at the turn of For-Spring?'

'Indeed.' Litasse hid her anger. This was the first she'd heard of that. 'But that is twelve long days away.'

One of the lordlings spoke up hopefully. 'I would gladly accompany Her Grace to see that she comes to no harm.'

'I must not distract you from your duties to your liege lord,' Litasse replied with faint reproof. She didn't recall his name but the callow youth had tried to entice her into flirtation several times.

'I could spare him.' Ferdain shot the youth a mildly disapproving glance. 'But I can only entrust Your Grace to my horsemaster's personal care.'

Litasse simply waited, her expression winsome.

'I shall ask Master Hamber to choose a suitable mare.' Duke Ferdain smiled more warmly. 'A lad can ride the fidgets out of her, then Hamber and the horse will be at your disposal as long as the weather stays fair.' He snapped his fingers at the importunate young noble. 'Lord Jainen, carry my message to the stables.'

'You are most kind, Your Grace.' Litasse sank into a grateful curtsey.

'Think nothing of it.' Duke Ferdain was already turning away, his retinue hurrying to follow while the disgruntled Lord Jainen headed for the stables.

Litasse was left in the hallway, the maidservant fidgeting behind her. She ignored the stupid chit.

Twelve days and Iruvain would return. What had he been doing all this time in Caladhria? Every morning she waited in vain for some letter. Had he written or not? Were such missives being kept from her, to be read while she remained in ignorance? Litasse could easily believe that of Ridianne.

What of the rest of Lescar now that the year had turned? She had no way of knowing what was afoot, not until Karn reappeared. She'd had no letters from her mother since Solstice. Who knew what that betokened?

Had Tormalin's legions crossed the River Asilor? Their muster had been the talk of the festival. Could Emperor Tadriol rout this murderous rabble who had overrun Parnilesse? How quickly would word travel west? A courier dove could cover such a distance inside two days but a man on a horse would be lucky to do so inside six at this time of the year, even if he could ride unhindered from Solland through lands held by their foes.

How much longer before any secret dispatches brought to Ferdain became the stuff of gossip among the servants, which Litasse worked assiduously to overhear? If only Pelletria was still with her.

'Your Grace?' The maid plucked at her elbow.

Litasse ignored her. Iruvain's appeals to the Caladhrian parliament couldn't have prospered, otherwise Marlier Castle would have made ready for war. Unless such preparations took place wherever Marlier's mercenaries were quartered under the Vixen's eye. Uncertainty tormented her.

'Your Grace?' the girl repeated, insistent.

'What?' Litasse burned to vent her frustrations by slapping the moppet. But she dared not alienate the Marlier servants while she was trapped here, so friendless and alone.

'You don't have a riding dress, Your Grace,' the maid quavered.

Litasse glared but that truth couldn't be denied. 'There must be some lady in this ant heap of a castle with much the same stature as me. You have until noon to find one who is willing to lend me a riding dress.'

'Your Grace.' The maid bobbed another curtsey.

Her wretched expression tried Litasse's patience near to breaking. 'Then go and do so!'

The girl offered a fearful protest. 'I should be attending Your Grace.'

Litasse clenched a fist, hidden in the folds of her skirt. 'I hardly need an escort to my sitting room. I shall spend the morning with my needlework.'

The maid's face lightened. 'Very good, Your Grace.'

'Don't forget to tell His Grace's Vixen,' Litasse said acidly.

The maid had the sense not to say a word, ducking her head as she scuttled away.

'Don't forget to find me some boots!' Litasse shouted after her.

Now she was truly alone in the sunlit corridor. She sighed. Would Ridianne frustrate her hopes simply by forbidding the maid to find her the necessary clothing?

What did the grizzled whore think she would do? Suppose she managed to persuade this horsemaster to ride beyond Marlier Castle's encircling walls. Suppose she gave him the slip on whatever pensioned-off mare he considered a safe ride for a lady.

Litasse's skirts thrashed angrily as she strode back to her detested sitting room.

Where could she possibly go in Marlier? She had no friends to shelter her. She had no money to travel unescorted. She would risk rape and robbery if half the maids' whispers about plundering brigands were to be believed.

If she fled back to Adrulle? There was nothing for her there. There was no point in fleeing to Ferl in hopes of finding Iruvain. He could be anywhere on the roads in between.

To Triolle? She had no hope of any welcome there, thanks to Iruvain's cowardly flight. To Sharlac? Her mother was as much a prisoner as she was, however much this so-called Duke Rousharn claimed to be her protector.

Litasse hugged her anger close as she stalked through the castle's endless corridors. Anger was better than the despair that so often threatened to overwhelm her.

She reached her gracious apartment in one of the inner courtyards. Overlooking a peaceful garden, it would indeed be a pleasant place for quiet needlework and contemplation. She walked to the work table in the bay window and contemplated the chemise she had been hemming. Snatching it up, she ripped the fine linen from neck to hem.

The door behind her closed. Litasse whirled around to berate whoever disturbed her. But there was no one there. Instead, a compactly muscular man stood beside the fireplace.

'You!'

It was the wizard who'd killed Master Hamare.

'Your Grace.' The blond intruder bowed though his eyes didn't leave her own.

'You have come to kill me?' Litasse recoiled, as if in fear.

As her body shielded her hand, she reached through the slit in her skirt, through her petticoats to the dagger sheathed on her thigh.

'Why would I do that?' the blond man asked, curious.

'To see Duke Ferdain accused of such infamy, in hopes of turning his people against him?' Litasse challenged. 'To see him and my husband kill each other in some trial by combat?'

'I don't see Iruvain risking his neck for your sake.' The Mountain Man smiled. 'But he's as big a fool as he is a coward, not to value you as you deserve.'

'Do not mock me,' snapped Litasse.

'My lady, I wouldn't dream of it.' As the blond man bowed again, his sapphire eyes momentarily softened. 'Unless you're being a silly pullet.'

'How dare you!' Litasse was torn between affront and mystification.

Unbidden recollection of that terrifying night in Adel Castle confused her. This Mountain mage's wizardry had saved her, when that vile traitor Minelas had sought his escape by throwing her into sorcerous fire. She couldn't deny the blond wizard had also saved her from that hard-eyed magewoman who would have delivered her to the Archmage's wrath.

Litasse still didn't understand why. Disgracing her could only have furthered the exiles' cause. Besides, she was undoubtedly guilty. If Litasse could see one thing undone in her life, it would be her utter folly in suborning that monster Minelas in hopes of saving Triolle with his magecraft.

But that was done and the wizard was here and he had killed Master Hamare.

Litasse took a step towards the door. 'Leave before I call every guard in this castle!'

'Scream and you'll just look foolish.'

Litasse heard the soft click of the door's lock. A lock to which she had no key, she recalled with fresh anger. Duke Ferdain had the gall to call her an honoured guest?

'I'll be long gone before any halfwit with a halberd can break in,' the intruder pointed out.

Just as he and his infuriating associate had vanished from their first encounter in Triolle. The guard right outside Master Hamare's door had been too slow to see them, to save her from suspicion of murdering her lover.

Litasse grasped her hidden dagger's hilt. 'What do you want?'

If she could draw him into conversation, perhaps she could get close enough to kill him. Then Hamare would be avenged. Whatever this mage had done since, nothing could make amends for that murder.

'I came to tell you what's transpired in Parnilesse,' the blond wizard said briskly. 'Duke Ferdain won't hear for some days and I don't imagine he'll share such news with you.'

Litasse rallied quickly. 'What news?'

The Mountain Man didn't move from the fireplace. 'We've rid Parnilesse of those traitors to our cause who murdered Duke Orlin and his family. The men responsible are dead, though death in battle is more honour than they deserved. Emperor Tadriol is content to call that justice and to acknowledge that the rule of law was upheld by Lescari hands. Tormalin legions won't cross the River Asilor this spring to prompt Caladhria's barons to muster their households.'

He smiled coldly this time. 'Now we will rid Lescar of these brigands that your husband and Duke Ferdain have been using to goad Caladhria's riverside lords. A bold stratagem, Your Grace, but futile.'

'I don't know what you're talking about.' Litasse moved to sit on a chair between the window and the fire. She wasn't within striking distance yet but she was closer.

'Only lie when there's some chance you'll be believed,' he chided. 'I'll wager Master Hamare taught you that.'

'Don't mention his name!' Litasse sprang to her feet.

The Mountain mage looked at her for a long moment. 'Forgive me.'

His apparent sincerity reminded her of his first apology, moments after he had murdered Hamare. When he had persuaded his fellow assassin not to kill her then and there.

In their last nightmarish encounter, he had acknowledged that death as a debt between them. He had offered Minelas's death as some recompense, and his forceful arguments in her defence to save her from her stupidity in suborning sorcery.

Litasse sat slowly down, tormented by her bewilderment.

'Scholars and priests and guildsmen are drafting an equitable settlement for Carluse,' the blond wizard continued calmly. 'As For-Spring advances, we will propose the same accords to Parnilesse, Draximal, Sharlac and Triolle. Then we'll invite the folk of Marlier to choose between sharing such peace and freedom or staying crushed beneath Duke Ferdain's boot.' He smiled briefly. 'Which do you think they will choose?'

'Do you expect me to tell him this?' Litasse lifted her chin, defiant. 'How should I explain I came by such knowledge? He'll think I've run mad!'

The blond mage smiled. 'Ferdain has capable friends, not least Ridianne the Vixen. He's stowed away a fortune in gold with Relshazri moneychangers over these past decades. Whatever happens, he'll fare well enough.' He gazed at her. 'You'll need a friend, though. I'll be at your service whenever you might need my help.'

'How dare you?' Her incredulity turned to rage. 'It's your fault I have no one. You killed Hamare. You killed Pelletria!'

'I had no hand in Pelletria's death.' He took a step away from the fireside. 'That was an accident, truly. She fell down those stairs.'

'Only lie when you might be believed!' Even as her voice cracked with distress, Litasse measured the distance between them.

'I won't ever lie to you.' He took another step forward. 'I killed Hamare, but he took his chances in his war of secrets and spies.

You've made no such choice. Haven't you had your fill of death and deceit?'

Litasse just pressed her lips together and glared.

He shook his head. 'Do you want to live in exile with Iruvain? A man you so justly despise, who cares more for his dogs and horses? You're brave and intelligent and you've fought for Triolle as best you can. Iruvain has just thrown up his hands and whined for someone else to come and save him. However misguided your actions, Master Hamare would have been proud.'

'I told you not to say his name.' She gripped her hidden knife. The wizard's own knife. The blade that had killed the man she loved. 'You'll pay for that crime some day. You should look over your shoulder morning, noon and night.'

'For fear of your man Karn catching up with me?' He pursed his lips. 'Are you going to waste your life for the sake of revenge? I can believe it of Karn. Now the dukes are thrown down vengeance is all he has left. All he's ever known is pain so he feels nothing for the pain he inflicts. He has no hope for the future so he never looks beyond the task in hand.' He shook his head. 'When that brings him to the point of my blade, don't expect me to regret ending such a wretched existence.'

He smiled, more charming than ever. 'But you know hope and love and relish for the pleasures of life. So I'll hope some day you'll forgive me and let me be a friend to you.'

'You—?' Litasse broke off and looked anew at the Mountain Man's pristine linen, his neatly combed hair and the excellent tailoring of his cobalt doublet, silver buttons polished. Realisation took her breath away. 'You think to woo me? You fancy yourself duke of Sharlac by marriage?'

Unable to contain her fury, she spat full in his face.

To her outraged astonishment, he laughed. 'You are a silly pullet. Didn't you listen to a word I said? There will be no more dukes. This war is done, even if Ferdain and the Vixen don't yet see it. Your lineage will mean nothing.' He shrugged. 'Your birth, your marriage, never has meant anything to me.'

Taking a kerchief from a pocket, he shook out its folds. As he lifted the linen to wipe away her spittle, Litasse ripped the knife free of her skirt and thrust it straight at his heart.

He stepped sideways and struck her wrist hard enough to numb her fingers. Then his hand closed around her own and he twisted the blade to point upwards between them.

She could feel his breath on her face, spiced with costly toothpowder. Litasse glared defiantly and waited for the steel to bite her throat. She wouldn't beg or weep or protest.

'I won't ever hurt you,' he said softly. 'I value you too highly, for your courage and your wits and your beauty. I will cherish you as you deserve, if you ever grant me that blessing. Regardless, I will be your friend, whether or not you wish it. I will watch over you, whether or not you know it.'

Litasse opened her mouth but yelped instead as he twisted her hand in an instant of agony. As the knife dropped from her nerveless fingers, he deftly caught its hilt.

'But however much I adore you, I won't let you stab me.' He tossed the long thin blade onto the ruin of the shift. 'Though I am glad to know you're so ready to defend yourself.'

To her outrage, he pressed a swift kiss on her cheek.

'How dare—?'

He was gone in a shock of azure lightning.

Litasse stood frozen, thoughts and questions chasing each other inside her head. When an urgent hand knocked on the door she had no notion how much time had passed.

The knock came again. The maidservant?

'One moment!'

Litasse stared at the door. It was locked and she had no key.

But the door opened unhindered, to reveal Karn. 'Your Grace?' His shadowed eyes searched the room, finding the torn shift on the table, the knife gleaming upon it. 'What happened?'

'I'm sick of stitching.' Litasse did her best to cover her confusion. 'What brings you back here at long last?'

He closed the door. 'Your Grace, I have news.'

'I—' But how could she explain knowing what had transpired in Parnilesse? Besides, the thought of Karn knowing she had spoken to the Mountain wizard scared Litasse somehow. 'Where's Iruvain?'

'In Adrulle, where the Caladhrians only offer him sympathies, no matter how many bandits we send to harry them.' Karn's gaunt face hardened. 'Let's see if the barons stay so indifferent when corsairs sail up the Rel to burn their crops and steal their children.'

'Corsairs?' Litasse was shocked. The ship-borne raiders who lurked in the northernmost Archipelago islands had an evil reputation. Worse, she knew they had indulged Minelas's appetites in return for his renegade wizardry helping them rob and murder innocents. But Karn had kept that from her, as he seemed to keep so much.

'We agreed to do whatever it took,' he reminded her.

'Corsairs don't sail in Lescari waters,' objected Litasse. The long black ships only raided western Caladhria and the coasts of the Gulf of Peorle.

Karn was untroubled. 'Men in Relshaz buy their plunder and sell whatever they cannot make or steal for themselves. I've had them lure a boatload or two with the prospect of loot hereabouts.'

Litasse frowned. 'The Relshazri secure the Rel with chains and floating bridges.'

Karn smiled callously. 'The corsairs will sail up the River Dyal and carry their boats overland to the headwaters of the River Oisin. That will carry them to the Rel.'

'That's ten or twelve leagues across Marlier land,' Litasse protested.

'They've done as much before,' Karn assured her. 'They'll steal horses and carts and we can blame every theft and death on these rebels. That should stir up Ferdain and his Vixen,' he said with sudden venom. 'With this fresh uproar, the Caladhrian Spring Parliament will vote for a muster, I promise you.'

'I see.' Litasse tried to hide her unease.

Karn noticed nothing amiss. 'The corsairs should make the lower reaches of the Dyal about twenty days into For-Spring. There's more we can do in the meantime. Do you recall that rebel hero who defied us at Adel Castle, with those Mountain assassins who killed Pelletria and Minelas?'

'What of him?' Litasse asked slowly.

'Now I know his name, Your Grace.' Karn's smile turned cruel. 'Carluse's tavern-warriors are delighted to claim him for their own. He's called Tathrin Sayron, and he's the man who secured the rebels' victories at Ashgil and Wyril.'

'What of it?' Litasse's apprehension grew.

'Now he's coming to lead Carluse's militias against the brigands we've brought up from Relshaz.' Karn grinned like a death's-head. 'Kill him and the rebels will have no one to command their army. The Vixen will fight on those terms, and we will have Master Hamare avenged.'

If Litasse's thoughts were in disarray before, her turmoil was redoubled now.

Chapter Twenty-Eight

Tathrin

The Lily Pond Inn, Abray,
Caladhria,
5th of For-Spring

'You may rest assured that peace is returning to Parnilesse.' He realised he was speaking more forcefully than was courteous so softened his words with a smile. 'Triolle, Draximal and Sharlac have enjoyed calm since before the Winter Festival, as I'm sure you will have heard, Master Cardel.'

The two men sitting across the polished table didn't look impressed.

'What of these bandits plaguing travellers?' demanded the stout man whom Tathrin addressed. 'What peace can honest merchants expect?'

'There are few reports of banditry along the Great West Road,' Tathrin pointed out politely. 'We have held Sharlac Town and Losand for half a year now and their militiamen patrol the highway.'

'Taking whatever tolls they fancy.' The stout man's lip curled. 'Our profits this past winter can be reckoned in copper cut-pieces!'

Tathrin would have liked to deny that but several towns further along the road into Sharlac and Draximal lands were indeed levying their own charges. That was merely one of the growing list of concerns that Aremil and Kerith had laid before him, when he had paused at the castle on his way to spend this past handful of days chasing brigands out of thickets.

He turned his attention to the white haired older man. 'Baron Dacren, we will bring that peace to Carluse before the season turns again.'

'But what of Marlier?' Shrewd eyes belied the baron's deeply wrinkled face. 'Every market day brings families fleeing across the bridges into Caladhria with their tales of woe.' He gestured towards the tavern parlour's window with an age-spotted hand. 'For-Spring offers us precious little to feed the hungry.'

'Mercenaries.' Master Cardel scowled. 'Plundering Marlier and Carluse ever since you cut them loose after recruiting them in the first place. I thought you people claimed to be putting an end to hired swords riding roughshod over Lescar. All I see is yet another spring heralding a summer of war.'

'All the mercenaries who fought with Captain-General Evord have long since departed, sworn not to raise arms against Lescar again,' Tathrin told the russet-clad merchant firmly. 'These bandits are mere freebooters. I have militia companies from Losand, Dromin and Carluse Town hunting them down as we speak. Successfully, I might add. Would you like to see the full tally of those we've already pilloried and flogged? There will be no more war in Lescar, not this year or in any to come.'

Master Cardel snorted but Baron Dacren raised a commanding hand before the merchant could speak again.

'What does lie ahead for your countrymen? You say the day of the dukes is done, but who will govern the folk of Lescar in future?'

'We have scholars, priests and guildsmen discussing those very concerns in Carluse Castle,' Tathrin assured him. 'Several notable lords have returned from exile to lend their voices to the debates.'

Aremil had told him so, only that morning. Tathrin welcomed the news though he'd been more pleased to see how his friend was steadily regaining his strength.

Master Cardel snorted a second time. 'Now their lordships have outstayed their welcome here.'

Tathrin forbore to comment though Aremil had said as much. On the other side of the scales, Kerith reported that at least as many nobles who had abandoned Carluse and Triolle were heading south for Relshaz or west towards Ensaimin instead of returning home. A lot of the Parnilesse lords who'd escaped Reniack's slaughter by fleeing into Tormalin showed no signs of shifting and a goodly number from Sharlac and Draximal were joining them.

Baron Dacren raised his hand once again. 'When do you think your scholars and priests will come to some conclusions?'

'We will set our proposals before all the Guilds on the twelfth of For-Spring in Carluse Castle's great hall. We are confident our settlement will be accepted.'

That's what Aremil had said. Tathrin only hoped that he was right.

He was too tired to judge for himself. These opportunist scum drifting up from Relshaz might not put up much of a fight but they were still cursed hard to find.

'The sooner we see Lescar committed to peace the better.' Baron Dacren reached for his silver-headed cane. 'The same goes for clearing these brigands off the highways.' He grasped one arm of his chair and got stiffly to his feet. 'Once the Spring Equinox is past, interruption to Caladhria's trade with Tormalin will become a pressing concern.'

Master Cardel didn't move, still looking sternly at Tathrin. 'The barons voted against intervention at Winter Solstice but the tally was close. You may be certain the question will arise again at our Spring Parliament.'

Tathrin nodded and rose courteously to his feet. 'The barons convene in Duryea, I believe?'

'Quite so.' Unwilling, Cardel stood up. 'Where I'm sure those towns and fiefdoms of Ensaimin who share our interests in the roads heading west will be pressing us to act.'

Kerith had already warned Tathrin that the patience of merchants as far away as Vanam was wearing thin.

'I have every hope the Spring Festival will see a new beginning for Lescar; a prospect that all men and women of goodwill shall find wholly acceptable.'

That's what Aremil and Branca believed. Tathrin hurried to open the door in case these visitors mistook his exhaustion for doubt. Amiable chatter from the hostelry's dining room drifted into the parlour.

Baron Dacren smiled as he walked out into the hall. 'Good day to you, Captain Tathrin.'

'We will call again tomorrow.' Master Cardel's parting words held more threat than promise.

Tathrin bowed low. 'You will be most welcome.'

Closing the door, he went to slump in a chair by the fireside. Tiredness weighed him down like a physical burden. A yawn inadvertently closed his eyes and he contemplated just going to sleep. But he needed to read those reports from the Carluse company that had ventured towards Hengere. Reher was increasingly certain that these bandits were selling their captives to Relshazri slavers. That could not be allowed to stand.

'Sweetheart?' The door creaked.

Tathrin forced his unwilling eyes open to be rewarded with a cheering sight. 'That's a pretty dress.'

'Isn't it just?' Gren agreed, following Failla into the parlour.

'Kerith had more of my things stored than I realised.' Failla turned this way and that, apricot silk rustling.

Coming to Abray had been worth it, Tathrin reflected, for more than being able to bathe and shave and enjoy clean shirts and bed sheets for the first time in an age.

Failla's smile turned rueful. 'I may as well enjoy silks and lace while I can. We must see everything sold before we leave, to make some gesture towards meeting Master Gruit's obligations.'

'How are you being received?' Tathrin would rather she wasn't playing the penitent on the old rogue's behalf but Aremil and Kerith were adamant that persistent ill will in Abray could only cause problems to come. 'Do they still think you're Gruit's niece?'

'No.' Failla smiled pertly. 'They know I'm Master Ernout's niece, and that's worth more than I realised.'

'A fair few have had dealings with the Woodsmen,' observed Gren.

'None of the merchants whom Gruit fleeced seem to be overly popular.' Failla came to sit on Tathrin's lap. 'If we can offer something towards his debts, most of his creditors will let bygones be bygones, now that the full story is known.'

Gren chuckled. 'With your charming smile and those beautiful eyes, how could any man with blood in his veins doubt your sincerity?'

Failla settled herself comfortably and laced her hands around Tathrin's neck. 'Abray folk with Lescari blood welcome the prospect of peace across the border, however many generations it's been since their forebears fled.'

Tathrin slid his arms around her waist. 'Where's Sorgrad?'

He still wanted to know exactly where Master Gruit had got to. Now they were beyond Lescari borders, he wanted to ask the Mountain mage to scry for the old merchant, and Jilseth's edict forbidding magic be cursed.

'He'll be here soon.' Gren sauntered across the parlour to look out of the window. 'How did you fare smoothing ruffled feathers this morning?'

Tathrin grimaced. 'I don't think Master Cardel likes me.'

'Master Cardel was eager to woo me,' Failla observed, her eyes bright with mischief, 'when I was Master Gruit's wealthy and widowed niece.'

'But now you're Master Ernout's niece with my betrothal ring on your finger.' Tathrin grinned. 'Would you like to be a Spring Festival bride?'

Her eyes widened with hope. 'Will we truly have peace by then?'

He held her close. 'If we don't, it won't be for lack of trying.'

'We better had,' Gren growled. 'Aft-Spring's the real start of the fighting season.'

Tathrin felt the weight of his weariness once more. 'You expect Ridianne to march? Doesn't she have her hands full hunting down these vermin raiding Marlier?'

Gren shrugged. 'Even if she stays close to home, there'll be other troublemakers thinking they can still turn a coin with their swords.'

'And exiled lords willing to hire them?' Failla looked perturbed.

Tathrin nodded grimly. 'Baron Dacren told me that Garnot's elder daughters are soliciting funds from Caladhria's barons in hopes of reclaiming their birthright.'

'We need a settlement agreed across Lescar,' Failla said firmly, 'to show everyone that there's nothing to be gained by more fighting.'

'How long till Aremil and his ink-stained friends have something we can nail up on the shrine doors?' demanded Gren.

'They'll have their proposals ready for the twelfth of For-Spring,' Tathrin reminded the Mountain Man.

The Greater Moon would be full, with the Lesser at its half, so as long as the weather held fair, interested parties could travel from far and wide to hear what Aremil had to say.

'How can we put forward a settlement for all of Lescar when Marlier's duke still holds on to his domains?' Failla said, frustrated.

'We will march on Marlier Castle while Aremil's envoys take the settlement offered in Carluse to all the other towns. Ferdain can go into exile like Secaris or make a fight of it.'

Tathrin didn't relish that prospect, heartily sick of blood and battlefields.

'The Vixen will make a fight of it,' predicted Gren. 'With her back against the river and nowhere else to go.'

'She won't prevail against our army,' Failla said with conviction.

'Just as long as all the fighting's done with by Equinox.' That would bring the year full circle, since he and Aremil and Gruit had first discussed ending Lescar's unceasing strife.

Tathrin was already looking forward to spending Aft-Spring sleeping till noon, rising to freshly cooked meals and not setting a foot in a stirrup iron. Even if he had to put every bandit in Carluse and Marlier to the sword first.

Gren grinned. 'A few of Ferdain's treasure chests would settle Gruit's debts with gold to spare.'

'One thing at a time.' Sorgrad came into the parlour. 'To begin with, we're making fine progress against these brigands.' He handed a sheaf of letters to Tathrin. 'Your regiments' reports, Captain-General.'

'Do you think we'll be rid of them by Equinox?' demanded Failla.

Awkwardly, with her still on his lap, Tathrin sorted through the terse and blotted documents. His erstwhile mercenary lieutenants would win no praise for penmanship or lyrical prose but they told him what he needed to know. 'It's looking promising.'

One letter was still folded and sealed. He didn't recognise the sloping, educated handwriting. It was addressed to *Tathrin Sayron, Scholar*, and that was an oddity these days. The frequent pleas for coin, for news of loved ones and the rambling litanies of insults and accusations were mostly sent to *Captain Tathrin*.

He waved it at Sorgrad. 'Where's this from?'

'Losand.' The Mountain Man looked up from his own correspondence. 'It was sent to the Merchants' Exchange with a request that it be forwarded to you. When the clerk heard you were here they sent it on with the latest reports from the high road.'

Turning the letter over, Tathrin saw its wax seal bore the double-bladed axe of Misaen set within a horseshoe. He frowned. That wasn't a Mountain blazon. The smith-god was honoured all along the Great West Road, where farriers worked their hearths night and day to keep merchants' wagons rolling and passing horsemen mounted.

Gren was pursuing their earlier conversation with Sorgrad. 'Will bringing the Vixen to battle prompt the Caladhrian parliament to vote for war?'

Tathrin contemplated the letter. The closest shrine to his family's home was dedicated to Misaen. His sister's husband shod horses for visitors to his father's inn.

Sorgrad answered his brother. 'The barons might well consider that the rune that tips the hand, so we need to break Marlier at the first opportunity. It must be a hard and fast campaign.'

Tathrin ignored them. The paper was of a quality his father might use; neither the finest nor the cheapest. Jerich Sayron had the coin to buy what suited his needs and no desire to waste money on ostentation.

What might a letter from home have to say? His father had condemned him for a fool when Tathrin had taken a horse after the fall of Losand, riding at breakneck pace to be sure his family was safe.

He had tried to explain himself, but his father accused him of ingratitude, stupidity and worse for abandoning his apprenticeship in Vanam. He wouldn't listen to a word. Mercenaries never brought peace to Lescar. What manner of fool was Tathrin? Or was he looking to fill his own pockets with plunder instead of working hard like an honest man?

For the first and only time in his life, Tathrin had felt an urge to raise his fist to his father.

But he couldn't do that to his mother. She was hysterical with weeping. She had been so proud, she sobbed, to know he was a scholar wearing Vanam's silver ring. That had been her one comfort after sending him so far away. But now he had squandered his future to risk his life on this folly. Tathrin had ridden off, heartsick, with her laments ringing in his ears.

'Will a hard and fast campaign be more hazardous?' Failla asked apprehensively.

Gren shrugged. 'That's usually how it goes.'

Tathrin snapped the seal and unfolded the paper. Looking for the signature, disappointment compounded his fatigue. This letter wasn't from his father. Why had he imagined it might be?

Why would Master Granal Camador write to him? Swift unease banished any thought of tiredness.

'Sweetheart—'

As Failla took the hint and stood up, he rose and carried the letter to the window, the better to decipher the noble-born priest's paradoxically illegible handwriting.

'My parents' inn has been ransacked by raiders.'

It wasn't till he heard his own words that Tathrin realised he'd spoken aloud.

'What?' Failla rushed to his side, searching his face before peering at the letter.

Tathrin let her take it. 'The Ring of Birches is three days' ride from here.'

'Four at this season,' Gren objected.

'Three!' Tathrin took a blind step towards the door.

Gren shrugged. 'You promised Aremil you'd be back in Carluse inside five days.'

'Aremil will understand.' Tathrin glared at him. 'I need a horse and a remount—'

'No you don't.' Sorgrad plucked the letter from Failla's hand without apology. 'I'll have you there inside five paces.'

Tathrin watched Sorgrad narrow his eyes, reading swiftly.

'Or do you want to go to see this priest?' The Mountain mage looked up. 'This is dated the thirty-ninth of Aft-Winter—'

'Darkest night of the season,' Gren observed. 'A good night for a raid.'

Sorgrad silenced him with a warning look. 'The priest says he doesn't know what's become of your family, but he might well have had news since he wrote this.'

Tathrin couldn't think. Either prospect held unknown horrors. Would it be better to find his parents, his sisters, already ashes in their funeral urns, safe in Master Granal's care? Or was it his duty to retrieve their bodies from the ruins of their home?

'Whoever did it, we'll find them and kill them.' Gren wasn't boasting or threatening, merely stating a certainty.

For once, Tathrin shared his dispassionate bloodlust. 'We'll go to the inn. We'll pick up some scent there, of my family or of the villains responsible—'

Responsible for their murders? The words stuck in his throat.

'You need travelling clothes.' Failla took a step towards the door. 'And your armour and swords. You'll need to take some food, and you should eat before you leave—'

'No!' Too late. Tathrin was stung by the shock on her face at his refusal. 'Forgive me, sweetheart.' He drew her into his arms. 'If I eat before Sorgrad takes us there, I'll be as sick as a dog when we arrive.'

'He's not wrong.' Gren's irrepressible chuckle did little to lighten the atmosphere.

'Aremil said he would speak to me tomorrow.' Tathrin held Failla close. 'If his Artifice touches you in the meantime, or Branca's, let them know what's happened.'

Sorgrad folded the letter and handed it to Failla. 'Keep this under lock and key, my girl, along with all our militia captains' reports. Tell Abray's Guild clerks and any nosy chambermaids that the three of us have ridden for—'

'Dromin,' Failla suggested.

Sorgrad nodded. 'I've travelled that road. I can take us close enough, after—' He glanced at Tathrin. 'Whenever suits.'

Tathrin blinked. 'But you'll be using magic inside Lescar.' He wondered why he was saying this. He wanted to find out what had happened as fast as he could, didn't he?

'Madam Jilseth can go ride a fiddlestick,' Sorgrad said curtly. 'There's no time to waste so close to success in all that we have worked for. We need to find out if your family were merely unfortunate or if someone is looking for revenge on you. If they cannot stop us, there will still be some who'll take pleasure in staining your victory with blood.'

Tathrin wouldn't have thought it possible to feel any more hollow with dread. He should have known better, knowing Sorgrad.

Chapter Twenty-Nine
Tathrin

The Ring of Birches Inn,
near Losand, Lescar,
5th of For-Spring

'WE SHOULD STEAL some horses.' Gren jogged along the road.

'And lose what's left of the daylight?' Sorgrad loped by his side.

Tathrin wasn't having this quarrel. 'If bandits have passed through, any beast not locked in a stable is gone.'

Gren wasn't to be denied. 'Let's borrow some farmer's wagon?'

'Next time you see one, you ask nicely,' suggested Sorgrad.

In the half-chime they'd been on the highway, they hadn't seen a vehicle, a rider or anyone walking.

'Haven't you ever passed my father's inn?' demanded Tathrin. 'Couldn't you have brought us closer?'

'Do you want to arrive in the yard with a flash of magelight?' Sorgrad slowed to a walk, forcing the others to do the same.

Tathrin wished he hadn't. Perversely, while they were running he could ignore his fatigue. 'You don't imagine the bastards will still be there?'

'There could be more than carrion crows picking over the place.' Gren drew his sword. 'I'd rather see them before they see me.'

'With any luck your father will be sweeping up broken glass while your mother dumps smashed crocks in the midden,' said Sorgrad. 'But don't you think they've already had enough shocks to last the season?'

Tathrin couldn't allow himself to hope he would see his family. Nor could he face the prospect that one or more of them might be dead. So he concentrated on stoking his wrath with silent, angry questions.

Who was responsible? While Sorgrad and Gren had gathered their gear, he searched through all the reports from Lescari company captains hunting down brigands. He found no mention of trouble so close to Losand.

Whose fault was that? Which lieutenant had been so lax, so unobservant, that these ruffians had crept through the undergrowth to rob an innocent family of their home and livelihood? To murder them in their beds?

Gritting his teeth, Tathrin broke into a run again. Sorgrad and Gren ran silently beside him.

As the road curved, he saw the birches first, where this shallow ridge thrust a finger of higher ground southwards. The stand of silver-barked trees opposite the inn overlooked the fields below. The first birches had been planted generations ago. Folk hereabouts tended the trees and the saplings that had renewed the grove ever since. Master Granal speculated the circle might have been sacred to the long-vanished plains-people, whom tavern tales called cousin to the Eldritch Kin.

There was no point in debating the trees' origins now. They were gone as surely as whoever had planted them. The birches were blackened skeletons, their leafless branches scratching the sky.

Tathrin ran faster. They rounded the bend.

'Slowly, long lad.' Sorgrad stopped him with an unyielding hand.

Tathrin looked at the ruin of his home. Both wings of the tavern, set at right angles to each other, were burned ruins. The stables across the yard, the barn beyond and his brother-by-marriage's smithy by the roadway, all were utterly destroyed. Stone walls cracked beneath charred beams and tangles of laths that still bore fragments of shattered tiles.

He could not to go on. Nor could he retreat. What lay beneath that wreckage?

'Careful,' warned Gren.

Tathrin turned his helpless fury on the Mountain Man. 'In case I damage something?'

Gren shrugged. 'I imagine Failla would rather a falling rafter didn't split your skull.'

'Keep watch.' Sorgrad walked across the road towards the birch trees. He ran a finger down one charred bole, sniffing at the soot.

Tathrin followed; the lesser of his evil choices. 'Is this magecraft?' He struggled to credit the possibility but Triolle's duchess had suborned a renegade mage.

Sorgrad rubbed his forefinger and thumb together. A faint flame flared and vanished. 'Pitch and sulphur,' he called out to Gren who was walking into the debris-choked yard.

'Always effective,' the younger Mountain Man approved.

Sorgrad crossed back over the road to the inn and turned to look at Tathrin, still hesitating on the verge.

'Come on, long lad. When will you next sleep, if you don't know?'

Reluctant yet desperate, Tathrin gazed at the fallen roof of the kitchen wing. His bedchamber had been up there. Childhood treasures that he'd left safe, his possessions sent back from Vanam when he abandoned Master Wyess's counting house; everything was gone.

Gren poked his sword at burned planks still held together by long iron hinges. 'I reckon this door was open, when the fire took hold.'

'Someone got out?' Tathrin tried not to hope. Forcing himself to go to the smoke-stained taproom entrance, he found any way in was blocked by charred floorboards fallen from the bedrooms above.

'This door was open too.' Sorgrad looked thoughtfully over his shoulder. 'I reckon someone came out to see those trees burning.'

'That would empty the taproom.'

Tathrin could picture the scene all too easily. The tavern would have been quiet, given the season and these uncertain times. Only local farmers and perhaps some labourers from the hamlet on track to the forest would have come in search of ale and conversation.

The weather had been clear, and as Gren had said, it would have been a nearly moonless night. Only the last sliver of the Lesser Moon would have risen, and late at that. They would all have rushed out, agog, when the light from the blazing grove burst through the unshuttered windows.

It was the last thing his father did each night: bolting the oak shutters, dousing the lamps that offered travellers welcome. Had it been the last thing he ever did?

Tathrin studied the blackened windows with their glass all smashed. The shutters hung from hinges twisted by the flames. But they were hanging open and the bolts were drawn back. 'This happened before my family went to bed.'

'I don't see any bodies.' Gren had gone into the kitchen through the gaping void where the fireplace in the end wall had collapsed. He shoved rubble aside with his boot.

'They'd hardly have been left for the crows.' Tathrin had to force the words out.

He looked around, helpless. They should have gone to the shrine. Master Granal would surely tell them more than this silent devastation.

But could the priest tell him who had died here? Or had he conducted Poldrion's rites for charred bodies so horribly disfigured that no one knew them for Tathrin's family or anyone else?

He closed his eyes on vile memories of the dead of Wyril. Tathrin hadn't shirked his share of the duty of retrieving those ghastly, contorted corpses from the drifts of ash.

A still more sickening thought wrung his heart. Had someone come to wreak their revenge on his family, for the sake of those who'd died at his order?

'I don't see any sign of rain,' Gren called out from the kitchen, 'but a lot of this is sodden. I reckon folk threw water on this blaze.'

'Or damped down the embers,' Tathrin countered bleakly, 'when they came to retrieve the dead.'

'No horses died in here.' Now Sorgrad was picking a careful path through the ruined stables.

'Someone got the beasts out alive?' Tathrin drew a shivering breath.

'Look out!' Gren sprang onto the ash-choked kitchen range.

Tathrin was already turning when the arrow struck him. The bodkin point split his hauberk's steel rings apart to bite deep into the back of his shoulder.

Even as he staggered from the brutal impact, he realised he'd been lucky. If he hadn't been moving, it would have gone right through his chest. Better yet, that was his off-side. He could still use his sword arm. Though the numbness of shock was yielding to sickening pain, he turned, ripping his blade free of its scabbard.

Appearing from the slope beyond the birches, a double handful of men ran across the highway. All wore chain mail, some wielded two blades, others favoured shields with a single sword.

They had been watching for just such an opportunity, Tathrin realised angrily, waiting till the three of them were so awkwardly divided.

He retreated as best he could, hampered by the wreckage underfoot. Gren was running forward from the kitchen, shouting ripely offensive insults. Sorgrad sprang onto the soot-blackened wall of the barn, only to retreat. There was no safe landing if he jumped down into the yard just there.

Three men advanced on Tathrin. He could retreat no further. If he tripped, he'd be dead. At least the ruination meant they couldn't get behind him. But could he still fight?

He swept his blade around and gasped at the agony in his wounded shoulder. But it was worth it to see the advancing men hesitate. He had the reach on them all; none were close to his own height.

The first tried to close on his wounded side. His swarthy skin indicated Archipelagan blood while his shield and round helmet looked Relshazri.

Tathrin thrust hard before cutting across to parry a crop-headed youth's questing blade. He wore an unlaced mail coif and a bold red kerchief round his neck.

As their blades met, with a shock of pain that made Tathrin bellow, the red-kerchiefed youth recoiled. Tathrin couldn't follow up that advantage, needing instead to smash aside a downward stroke from the bald and burly third man who was cursing him in clotted Caladhrian.

The Relshazri cut again. Tathrin parried. The red-kerchiefed youth and the bald Caladhrian both attacked but hampered each other's strokes. Tathrin took a sidestep closer to the taproom wall.

Better protected, but now cornered, the best he could do was turn their vicious blades aside. His shoulder was excruciating. He felt terrifyingly cold, far more than the chill day should warrant, yet sweat was sticking his shirt to his back. Tathrin was just grateful he couldn't feel blood running down his arm. The arrowhead must be plugging the wound.

A man died with a bubbling shriek. As the red-kerchiefed youth and the Relshazri's eyes flickered across to the far side of the yard, Tathrin reached for the long dagger sheathed on his belt. Two blades would be better than one—

It was nearly a fatal mistake. Hot agony blurred his vision. As he gasped, every breath prompted fresh anguish. Worse, his wounded arm now hung limp and useless. All he could do was swing his sword in a reckless arc.

That was enough. Taken unawares, all three attackers recoiled.

Tathrin summoned all his resolve and arched his back, desperately twisting his shoulders. That lifted his helpless arm just far enough to hook his thumb onto his sword-belt. The agony receded to the fragile edge of endurable pain.

The Relshazri drove the hammered boss of his shield straight at Tathrin's face. He drove it back with a hacking stroke. The red-kerchiefed youth stabbed at his thigh, the blade scraping against Tathrin's long hauberk.

Stumbling, he saw the Relshazri's sword come down towards his injured shoulder. Tathrin met the descending blade with a stroke born of sheer instinct. Pain froze the breath in his chest.

In that same instant, the Caladhrian's blade sliced through his leather breeches, just above his knee. The cut burned. Tathrin wrenched his sword around and had the brief satisfaction of ripping the point across the Caladhrian's throat.

Clapping a hand to his neck the man sneered. 'A cat-scratch.'

Then blood flooded through his fingers and he sank to his knees, slumping dead on the sooty cobbles.

Tathrin parried a murderous blow from the Relshazri. The red-kerchiefed youth redoubled his assaults. Tathrin knew he was weakening fast. A thrust by the Relshazri scraped the mail protecting his ribs. Misjudging a stroke from the red-kerchiefed youth cost him a bruising smash across the knuckles. He could feel blood from the wound in his thigh pooling inside his boot.

'No you don't, you son of your grandfather!'

Sorgrad leaped the wreckage. His blades were swift and deadly and the Relshazri retreated from the storm of blows.

The red-kerchiefed youth's attack faltered. Tathrin threw all his fading strength into driving his sword into the youth's face. The thrust went clean though his skull, the emerging blade dragging his unlaced coif backwards.

But Tathrin couldn't pull free. His sword was caught in bone and steel. The dying youth toppled backwards. Tathrin tried to let go but his bruised fingers were too slow.

The best he could do was drop to his knees rather than sprawl headlong. The jolt sent fresh agony through his shoulder. Bile surged into his mouth. He grabbed desperately for the fallen Caladhrian's sword. It lay just out of reach.

The Relshazri shouted, startled. Tathrin saw Sorgrad had punched a dagger right through the leather and wood of his shield. The Mountain Man ripped it out of the startled Relshazri's hand to fling it away.

The Relshazri swung at Sorgrad's unarmoured head. Sorgrad blocked the stroke with his sword. As he did so, his free hand seized the Relshazri's sword-arm. Pulling the startled man towards him, the Mountain Man smashed the studded hilt of his own blade hard into his enemy's face.

The Relshazri staggered, spitting blood and teeth. Sorgrad kicked him viciously in the side of the knee. The man screamed at the crack of bone and sinew and fell hard, landing flat on his back.

His shoulders barely touched the ground before Sorgrad's sword-point pricked his throat.

'Where are they? The folk from the inn?'

All sound of fighting had given way to a few dying whimpers. Tathrin ignored them, his attention fixed on the fallen man.

'Where are the family who lived here?' Sorgrad asked again with growing menace.

The Relshazri hissed something in an unknown tongue. Tathrin saw Sorgrad's face harden. The very tip of the Mountain mage's sword pierced the man's windpipe and Tathrin heard the Relshazri's breath whistling through the wound.

Forcing the man's chin up with his blade, Sorgrad leaned down and pressed a finger to seal the hole. 'Tell me, or I cut the rest of your throat.'

The man tried to spit in his face, blood from his broken teeth sliding down his cheeks.

'Your choice.' Sorgrad sliced through his neck as efficiently as any slaughterman. The man thrashed for a moment and lay limp.

Sorgrad glanced at Tathrin. 'Find something that belonged to your family. I'll see what I can scry.' His eyes were as cold as winter in the Mountains. 'If Jilseth turns up to ream out my arse for unsanctioned magic, she can make herself useful and find out where this bastard has been.'

Before Tathrin could speak, Gren stormed across the courtyard, yelling at Sorgrad in their Mountain tongue, his wrath beyond all reason.

Despite the agonies in his shoulder and thigh, Tathrin stayed still and silent. Draw Gren's attention and just at this moment he honestly feared the Mountain Man would kill him, before he knew what he was doing.

Now Sorgrad was shouting back, just as spirited.

Gren slashed the empty air with his sword, roaring with incandescent rage.

Sorgrad was still shouting him down.

Finally the younger Mountain Man stormed away, to hack at the charred beams of the barn, heedless of damage to his blade.

Tathrin struggled to speak through his pain. 'What was that all about?'

Sorgrad pursed his lips before deciding to answer. 'One of the men who attacked me was Karn.'

'Duchess Litasse's man?' Tathrin tried to look around the yard but the slightest movement was torture. 'Did you kill him?'

Sorgrad shook his head. 'That's why Gren's so cross.'

'Didn't he try to kill you?' Tathrin fought to make sense of this.

When they had last met, both brothers had promised the Triolle spy a violent death. The man Karn had responded in kind.

Sorgrad looked at him, contemplative. 'I think they wanted you dead. That's why I had to let the bastard run.' He kicked the dead Caladhrian's boot. 'To stop these heroes gutting you.'

'Thank you,' Tathrin said through clenched teeth.

Gren came back still speaking in the Mountain tongue. Sorgrad curtly replied.

'What now?' Tathrin demanded.

Once again, Sorgrad paused before responding. 'Gren thinks I should have used wizardry to bring him down.' He cut off his brother's retort with an angry gesture. 'Do you think she'd ever forgive me?'

But now Gren was looking up the highway. 'Here we go again.' Tossing aside the sword he'd just ruined, he stooped to pick up the fallen Caladhrian's blade.

'Who the curses are they?' Sorgrad glowered at the men rounding the bend in the road.

'It's Ersegan.' Forgetting himself, Tathrin tried to stand, only to find both his feet had been numbed by kneeling. With the wound by his knee, he would have fallen if Sorgrad hadn't darted forward.

That might have been preferable. Tathrin screamed as the Mountain Man's arm slid around his ribs and jarred his ruined shoulder.

'Murdering scum!' A thickset man gripping a sledgehammer broke into a run. A phalanx armed with scythes and flails followed.

Gren whooped with feral glee.

'No!' Tathrin yelled.

Sorgrad shouted something in the Mountain tongue and to Tathrin's inexpressible relief, Gren lowered his sword.

'Ersegan!' Tathrin gasped. 'Are they—?'

'All safe.' His sister's husband halted ten paces away, regarding Gren and Sorgrad with suspicion.

'Thank Saedrin.' Tathrin sagged against Sorgrad. 'And these men are friends, truly.'

'Do you want to give us a hand?' the Mountain Man invited Ersegan.

'You need a surgeon, Tath.' The farrier stepped forward, brow still creased. 'Your ma won't like this.'

Tathrin nodded. At least he could breathe easier with Ersegan's strong arms supporting his unwounded side. 'Where are they?'

'In Viscot, with my own family.' The farrier smelled strongly of stale sweat and unwashed linen.

Tathrin saw the other Carluse men were as filthy and dishevelled. He was relieved to recognise most of them.

The newcomers were gawping at the dead men in the yard.

Gren was looking at them with mistrust. 'How do you just happen to be on this stretch of road precisely when we find ourselves attacked?'

'We were hunting those scum,' retorted Ersegan. 'They torched the trees and the tavern six days ago but we managed to drive them off.' He glanced at Tathrin with a wry grin. 'Jerich had called a meeting of the Woodsmen, to discuss what we could offer the needy, what with it being the eve of For-Spring.'

'Saedrin save us,' Tathrin muttered.

Ersegan looked grim. 'He did, all but Agest, Rabold and Short Deffa. They're ashes now, poor fellows.'

Tathrin closed his eyes. 'I'm sorry.'

'You did well to drive off this gang,' Gren remarked, more friendly.

'You did better.' Ersegan glared at the dead men. 'We've been beating the bushes for these curs every day since.'

'They've been waiting for news of this burning to bring us here, one keeping watch while the others laid low.' Sorgrad sheathed his sword. 'Where have you been resting up between hunts? Not all the way over in Viscot?'

'In Geryl Brake,' Ersegan explained.

'That's a hamlet on the forest road,' Tathrin explained blearily.

'Let's get him there and we can send word to Carluse. Can your men make a litter?' asked Sorgrad. 'Now, long lad . . .'

'What?' Tathrin watched with misgiving as the Mountain mage unsheathed a dagger.

Sorgrad looked steadily at him. 'We'll leave the arrowhead for Master Welgren but I have to cut that shaft. If it gets knocked as we carry you, it'll make that wound a cursed sight worse and it looks bad enough already.'

Tathrin couldn't speak. All he could do was nod.

Even with Ersegan's massive hands holding the arrow shaft as still as he could, there were no words for how much it hurt. Every infinitesimal tremor felt like hot knives gouging Tathrin's flesh.

He could only hope that Master Welgren would dose him to insensibility before he did anything else. He desperately focused his thoughts on what lay beyond the apothecary's probes and lotions and wadding to keep a wound from festering.

Once Welgren had done his work, how long would it take his shoulder to heal, at least sufficiently to hunt down this man Karn? Because this war would not be over till Tathrin had had his revenge, whatever settlement Aremil might fashion for the rest of Lescar.

He lapsed into insensibility on that silent oath.

Chapter Thirty
Aremil

Carluse Castle,
Lescar,
12th of For-Spring

He negotiated the doorway to the grey-panelled room. 'How are you feeling this morning?'

Tathrin winced as Master Welgren adjusted his sling. 'I never realised how irritating you must find it, to have people always asking you that.'

'Since you mention it, yes, I do.' Resting on his crutches, Aremil grinned.

On the other side of the scales, seeing his friend arrive unconscious on a horse-litter three days before had given him a better understanding of the anguish that his own illnesses must cause others, his latest most of all.

'I can take some good from being wounded.' Tathrin supported his injured arm with his free hand. 'Even from losing my home, though by all that's holy, don't tell my father. But it'll be easier to face those who've suffered now I feel something of their pain.'

'Indeed.' Aremil wished he could say the same.

Master Welgren secured the knot behind Tathrin's neck. 'Do not be tempted to try using that arm,' he warned sternly.

'You said the wound is healing cleanly?' Concerned, Aremil searched Tathrin's face for any sign of fever.

'The wound's less of a concern than the damage that arrow did in striking his shoulder so hard,' explained the apothecary.

Tathrin looked at Aremil, about to shrug before he clearly thought better of it.

'Three thick sinews join the collarbone to the shoulder blade.' Welgren pointed to his own shoulder. 'A fall, or in this case a blow, can snap them.'

Aremil winced at that notion.

'Did you know that before you came to Lescar?' Tathrin asked sourly. 'Or from your battlefield anatomising?'

'Tathrin!' Aremil was surprised at his ingratitude.

They owed Master Welgren for more than his medical expertise. The apothecary had sought knowledge denied him by Vanam's physicians for some summers now, paying his way across Lescar by tending the ailments, real and imagined, of noble lords, their ladies and children. Inevitably, his path had crossed Charoleia's and they both benefited from that acquaintance.

Welgren didn't seem perturbed. 'No, the particular structure of the shoulder is something Col's medical scholars have seen fit to share with their humbler shopfront brethren. Since those of us soiling our hands with commerce don't share your university rivalries, we soon saw diagrams of those dissections in Vanam.'

'I see.' Tathrin said shamefaced. 'I'm sorry.'

The apothecary continued as if he hadn't spoken. 'I believe you suffered rupture of all three sinews. An incautious move and you'll be all the longer in healing.'

'I understand.' Tathrin's tone suggested this wasn't the first time Master Welgren had warned him.

'Perhaps you should stay here and rest,' ventured Aremil.

Tathrin very nearly shook his head. 'I promised I'd be at your side today. Why else endure that cursed journey and Master Welgren digging out that arrowhead with his pincers?' he said vehemently.

'You won't be fit to ride for at least another twenty days.'

As Welgren spoke, Aremil saw the annoyance in Tathrin's eyes. Annoyance and defiance.

'Where are you planning on riding?' he asked quickly. 'Aren't you staying here until we have this settlement agreed?'

'Once we have Carluse's agreement, we need to take these proposals to the other provinces.' But Tathrin wouldn't look him in the eye, gazing out of the window as he spoke.

'Indeed,' Aremil observed cautiously. 'But we have to secure Carluse's agreement first, so we should make our way to the great hall, if you're sure you're fit to come.'

'I am.' Tathrin got to his feet with an incautious speed that made him blench.

'Go carefully and good luck.' Welgren turned to tidy his marble table.

Tathrin closed the door behind them with his free hand. 'Let's not keep them waiting.'

'You'll hardly be rushing anywhere if you're walking with me.' Aremil made his way cautiously through the salon still crowded with pallets.

He could have been relieved to see how few patients remained if he hadn't known those worst wounded in that last battle for Parnilesse were being tended in Brynock.

'I honestly thought that was my last fight,' Tathrin said unexpectedly.

'Against Reniack?' Aremil concentrated on skirting an awkwardly placed chair.

Tathrin nodded. 'I was all set to do as Captain-General Evord said after that.' He raised his hand to shield his injured shoulder as they went through the door to the staircase. 'To stay out of harm's way and delegate fighting with the brigands to my best lieutenants.'

Aremil was relieved to see a little smile tug at Tathrin's mouth.

It vanished. 'Until I heard about my parents' inn. Even Evord couldn't expect me to set that aside.'

Had Tathrin's mother and father visited him this morning? Aremil desperately wanted to ask but didn't dare. Failla had told him they'd arrived in Carluse Town late last night after the farrier

Ersegan had rushed back to Viscot with his news. Bad news but not nearly so ill as it could have been.

Aremil couldn't decide who had the best or the worst of this particular spread of runes.

His parents were no better than strangers, now fled to some Tormalin haven surely beyond recall. Search his innermost heart as he might, all Aremil could feel was relief that one fewer intransigent duke remained to complicate their efforts to bring this upheaval to an end. A conclusion that would validate all that they had done, heralding a peace to balance the scales against lives lost and suffering endured.

Was the price of that to be Tathrin left so bereft? Once a beloved son now so reviled, his honourable motives entirely misunderstood?

They reached the bottom of the wide stone staircase.

Tathrin studied Aremil as he descended the final step. 'You look tired.'

Since Aremil could shrug, he did. 'Hammering out this settlement has cost a lot of lamp oil.'

That and he'd lain awake long after all the candles were snuffed last night buffeted by Tathrin's dreams. He had been imploring his father not to blame him for the loss of the inn. But Master Sayron had simply continued picking through the ruins of his livelihood, unable even to hear his son.

After Aremil had finally slept he had woken with the stink of burning in his nostrils and indignation acid in his stomach. How could Tathrin's parents fail to see their son's heroism? Or were those Failla's thoughts, rather than his own?

Once this settlement was agreed, Aremil decided, he must work still harder with Branca to learn how to shield his innermost self.

The keep's main door opened and Tathrin shied away to protect his wounded side.

Aremil made what passed for a bow on his crutches. 'Mistress Serafia.'

'Master Aremil.' She smiled at Tathrin. 'My Aunt Derou sent word. You're to dine with your parents and my Uncle Ernout at her table tonight. She won't accept excuses,' she warned.

'Very well,' Tathrin said tightly. He glanced at Aremil. 'They're staying with Master Ernout. He and my father are acquainted through the Woodsmen.'

'Oh, I see.' As Aremil spoke, he caught an echo of Tathrin's indignation.

His father had striven to frustrate the dukes since before his children were born. How could he blame Tathrin for succeeding where the Woodsmen's stealthy campaign had failed? Or was that the true root of his resentment?

Aremil blinked. 'If you'll excuse us, Serafia. We must get to the hall.'

'Of course.' She held the door for them both.

Aremil took a breath of air, refreshing after sickroom staleness and Tathrin's bad-tempered thoughts. Outside, the path had been swept clear of a late flurry of snow.

'Don't slip.' Tathrin forced a grin. 'I can't catch you.'

'I'll be careful,' Aremil assured him.

They proceeded slowly along, Tathrin matching Aremil's pace.

'How do you think your proposals will be received?' Tathrin was looking ahead to the castle's great hall.

'We've weighted the runes as far as we can.' Aremil couldn't restrain a little cynicism. 'Every fifth man or woman will be one of Ernout's allies primed with arguments in our favour.'

Tathrin nodded. 'Assuming it's all agreed, Kerith takes to the road for Sharlac before going on to Abray?'

'While Branca leaves for Draximal, once she's sent word of the outcome to Charoleia in Parnilesse, while Failla heads for Triolle. A fine pair of heroes we are,' Aremil observed with a grimace, 'asking the ladies to run our errands while we nurse our infirmities.'

Tathrin had other concerns. 'That just leaves Marlier to be settled.'

Aremil saw his friend gazing far beyond Carluse Castle's walls. How desperately he wished Sorgrad or Gren had managed to kill that villain Karn.

'What do you suppose Lady Derenna and Lord Rousharn will make of our proposals,' he asked, 'and Duchess Aphanie?'

'What they think doesn't matter if the populace agree,' replied Tathrin with a glint in his eye. 'Any more than Ferdain or Hidarin of Marlier's opinions.'

Aremil saw there was no turning his friend's thoughts anywhere else. 'Kerith will take our proposals to Marlier Castle,' he said firmly, 'after securing Baron Dacren's opinion that Caladhria's barons won't interfere in Lescari affairs. Ferdain of Marlier will have no choice but to capitulate.'

Once again, Tathrin visibly curbed an impulse to shrug. 'We shall see what we shall see.'

Aremil suspected that statement meant more than it seemed. But there was no time to pursue such concerns. The great castle bell tolled the five chimes of noon.

'Want a hand?' Sorgrad was waiting as they reached the outer stair to the great hall.

'I'll manage.' Aremil had been practising this climb daily with Branca's assistance, just as he had rehearsed this speech time and again, pacing his breathing to avoid stumbling over the words.

As they reached the top step, Gren opened the door to Sorgrad's knock.

An urgent murmur enveloped them. Only for an instant. As they entered, hush swept through the vast hall to leave an echoing silence.

Aremil's crutches scuffed the floorboards as they made their way to the dais. Two chairs waited in front of the empty high table.

Tathrin turned to the throng. 'Please be seated.'

The scrape of benches barely concealed the flurry of speculative whispers. Priests from any shrine within five days' ride had been invited to record everything said and agreed here today, along with those both devout and efficient who administered the shrine fraternities' charities for the poor. Guildmasters, town council members and Watch constables had been summoned and they all seemed to have come.

Aremil was pleased to see plenty of women in the gathering, from youthful matrons married into their husbands' responsibilities to grey-haired widows well used to managing their own affairs. Failla had insisted that every Carlusian must hear what he had to say.

So he was also relieved to see a coterie of Carluse's remaining nobles; some who had risked opposing Duke Garnot; others who had prudently, or cravenly, held aloof from the ducal circle. There were even a few whom gossip was still inclined to condemn as profiting from Garnot's rule or merely failing in their duty to their tenants. Were they intent on making a fresh start?

The silence became expectant. Taking his chair, Aremil glanced at the door where Branca and Failla sat together, hands folded demurely in their laps. Both women were already dressed for travelling. Gren lounged on a bench, boots outstretched. Sorgrad sat beside him, his countenance unreadable. He met Aremil's gaze with a slow wink.

Aremil looked back to the gathering. For the first time in his life, he was grateful for his weak eyesight. He couldn't see any faces beyond the first few rows, which made this so much easier. He began speaking without preamble.

'There's not one of us here unaffected by the battles of this past year. If we haven't been wounded ourselves, we know those who have been bereaved, dispossessed or suffered the loss of everyone and everything they hold dear. The same is true for men, women and children from Sharlac to Triolle, from Marlier to Draximal and Parnilesse. Like you, they are asking themselves if this frail spring promise of peace can possibly endure.'

As he took a longer breath, Aremil felt rather than heard the responses barely restrained by his audience. They wanted to ask a good deal more than that. He spoke on before anyone seized the chance.

'The answer is no, because this is not peace,' he said bluntly. 'Absence of warfare is not peace. Lescari know that better than any other folk. For generations past, any respite in fighting has only meant the dukes are biding their time, to hoard coin wrung from their tenants and vassals before they squander it on fresh violence.'

He shook his head. 'Don't blame us for bringing warfare to Lescar. We have done what we must to halt this endless, fruitless round of aggression and retaliation, all in pursuit of an empty crown. Because there can be no more dukes if Lescar is ever to truly know peace.'

Now he could feel them united; in relief at having someone to blame – in the case of Carluse's duke, someone who was safely dead. Let them enjoy that for a moment, Aremil thought grimly.

'But if there are no more dukes, what becomes of us? Who is to ensure that the common folk prosper, tilling their land and tending their trades? Who should honest peasants trust? Their liege lords, when so many have gathered up their moneybags and fled to Caladhria or Tormalin?'

He raised a hand to quell barely suppressed indignation somewhere in the middle of the hall.

'Such cowards have done a grave disservice to those honourable men and women who have borne every duty laid on them by their noble birth. Such nobles have endured their own losses without complaint, still dealing with their tenants as fairly as they could. Are they to be rewarded with disgrace for the crimes of others?'

He challenged the uncertain stillness with a fresh question.

'Are we to trust merchants and guildsmen? True, many have risked their lives, across all of Lescar, to see innocents and the unjustly accused taken secretly away to safety. They have spent their own coin to help those beggared by excessive levies. Believe me, the Woodsmen are no tavern tale.'

He let that murmur of surprise swell before cutting it short.

'But should we trust those merchants who have callously sold whatever pitiful harvests our farmers have won from some respite in their suffering? What of those guildsmen who pay their journeymen and prentices a pittance, knowing they're too desperate to feed their families to risk being cast out from their trade? Then there are those who aided and abetted the dukes in the interests of their own profits first and last. You know who they are.'

A dark murmur acknowledged that truth.

'We all know shrewd and honest men and women, however humble their birth. Every festival-tide, they give a share of what little they have to those even less fortunate. Why should they bend their necks to those who can claim no such virtue to go with their greater wealth?'

The hall was silent. Aremil shook his head.

'If noble birth is no guarantee of a noble spirit, humble origins offer no more assurance of virtue. The anarchy in Parnilesse proved that. Reniack was as intent on brutal retaliation as the most bloodthirsty duke. His allies were as arrogant in condemning those who did not agree with their philosophies as any noble who ever flogged a man for no better reason than his base birth.'

He fought to keep his voice strong. 'Yes, our endeavours to see Lescar free offered Reniack and his kind their chance for their vile revenge. We acknowledge our guilt and we will answer for it whenever we stand before Saedrin.'

He jabbed a feeble hand at the assemblage.

'But before you stand in judgement upon us, search your own consciences. Have you never acted with the best of intentions only to see disaster follow? Before you condemn those whose actions have added to Lescar's misery, even if only by a pennyweight, ask yourselves, truly, have you ever acted out of fear, out of wilful ignorance, to save yourselves and your loved ones, even at a cost to someone else? No, we are none of us innocent, just as there are none so guilty that we can load all the blame onto their shoulders to relieve our own.

'So what are we to do?' He shrugged, ungainly, not caring how that looked. 'Shall we sit and wring our hands and protest we're better than some and not as bad as most? What difference will that make to the price of bread?'

He folded his hands in his lap. 'Looking back has been Lescar's curse. Our dukes and their forebears harked back to the very days of the Chaos in search of their claims to a throne that never even existed. But they are not alone. Every town, every family has cherished its grudges, nurturing fresh hatred in every new generation. What good has that ever done? What difference will that make to the price of bread?'

That stirred a puzzled murmur. Aremil smiled.

'You've seen the price of grain for bread and beer rising through the winter seasons. You know merchants beyond our borders are calculating precisely what our markets will bear through the spring so they can take as much of our coin as they can. You know they will play Draximal off against Parnilesse, to pay the lowest prices for timber, leather and linen. They'll ship their booty down the Asilor and the Rel. Dastennin forfend such merchants should use

Triolle's rivers and pay a fair price towards the upkeep of Lescar's bridges.

'Give them half a chance and travelling merchants will set Carlusians against Sharlac's Guilds in order to pay the lowest tolls to travel the Great West Road. They'll grow all the richer selling Caladhrian goods in Tormalin and Tormalin goods in Caladhria. There's no point in visiting Lescar's markets. We'll have no coin to spare given the rising price of bread.'

Now the murmur was agreeing with him.

'Who will curb such abuses? Tormalin lords who would happily subject Lescar to their Emperor's rule? They could replace our dukes with provincial governors, as in the Old Empire. Their legions would guarantee no more warfare as Tormalin's great princes profited from our disarray.'

He shrugged again. 'Unless Caladhria's barons march to see our dukes reinstated, to curb those brigands looking for richer pickings across the Rel once they've stripped us of anything worth stealing. Could you blame them? Those beyond our borders are convinced we're too stupid to rule ourselves.'

He raised his voice above the affront stirring the gathering.

'We need more than an absence of fighting to prove those naysayers wrong. We need to establish justice for all regardless of rank. We need safe trade on fair terms so that none can be exploited. We need to levy even-handed dues to maintain our highways and town gates, to fund the soldiery who will guarantee this peace won at such a cost.'

That wasn't too popular. Aremil pressed on, regardless.

'We need to build for the future. Every family from lowest to highest deserves legal title to their farm, their workshop, their demesne. No one should lose home and livelihood on some duke's whim or the malice of some mob. Those who have been dispossessed must be reinstated or recompensed. Unjust debts must be written off. With goodwill on all sides this can be done.'

As Branca had predicted, these ideas won guarded welcome. Aremil hid a smile, leaning back in his chair.

'Who's to decide what is equitable? Who should benefit and to what degree? Which debts must be honoured and which discarded?'

He shook his head. 'Not me. Not us. We came to overthrow tyranny, not to impose our own. It's for you to decide on a new order for Lescar. We recommend you act swiftly,' he added, 'before the Caladhrians or Tormalin's Emperor decides to save you from yourselves.'

He nodded thoughtfully.

'There are different philosophies to consider. Follow the Caladhrians and hand over your future to those born with title to land, whatever their flaws or merits. They can talk and talk and never get anything done. That should at least be peaceful.'

It wasn't much of a joke but Aremil was relieved to hear a few nervous laughs.

'Merchants rule the Relshazri and Ensaimin's city states,' he mused. 'Do elected magistrates govern in the best interests of their citizens or of their own purses? Does amassing the coin to buy votes prove fitness to rule?'

No one was laughing now. He acknowledged the silence by leaning forwards.

'No single faction can be trusted with unchallenged authority. Even the Tormalin understand that. For all their loyalty to their princely houses, they know their Emperor holds any would-be tyrant in check. Even the humblest Tormalin can appeal to the Imperial Throne. In turn the Emperor's powers are balanced by the Convocation of Princes. Without their consent, he cannot rule.'

He looked at the uncertain faces in the rows closest to him.

'I believe we Lescari can improve on all those philosophies. All those neighbours, who so despise us, will envy this opportunity. Let us forge our new future linked by common purpose, with every voice an equal!'

Now those closest faces looked cautiously expectant.

'We don't wish to rule but we would make a suggestion. Let this coming Spring Festival see a Conclave of the Lescari Estates drawn from every dukedom.' He gestured at the lofty elegance of the hall. 'You have these fine castles at your disposal, built with the coin wrung from your labours.'

That prompted muted agreement.

'Let every town send their guildmasters. Let all those who hold land choose respected men and women from among their number to equal those chosen guildsmen. Let those who have neither land nor trade gather at the shrines and put forward those whom they know to be sincere and wise, in equal number to the guildsmen and to the landowners.

'Let such representatives meet at Solstice and Equinox in each dukedom by turn. This conclave can decide Lescar's laws and hold assizes, assess levies and debate how such coin should be spent in the interests of all. The Conclave can speak with one voice for all Lescari, to Caladhria and Tormalin, to Relshaz and Ensaimin's cities. If any would challenge Lescari fitness to govern, the Conclave can arm our soldiers.'

He reached for his crutches and hauled himself to his feet. Tathrin rose beside him.

'We recommend you hold your first conclave here at this Spring Festival. Meantime, we are laying out the same truths and choices to the people of Sharlac and Draximal, Triolle, Parnilesse and Marlier. You should let them know what you decide. Good day to you all.'

With that, Aremil began making his way to the door. He had covered nearly half the distance before the stunned silence in the hall erupted into consternation.

Sorgrad and Gren were already there to deter anyone from waylaying him. Failla and Branca opened the door. Aremil hurried through it as fast as he could.

Tathrin took the lead down the steps. 'This way.' He headed to the range of buildings that had once housed Duchess Tadira's retinue.

Sorgrad laid a hand on Aremil's shoulder. 'Just this once.'

Before he could answer, the Mountain Man lifted him off feet and crutches and carried him swiftly down the stone stair.

Aremil would have objected if he hadn't seen a gaggle of Carlusians emerging from the other end of the hall, searching for him in the castle's inner courtyard.

'Have they seen us?' Branca wondered.

'Yes, but they can't decide what to do.' Gren chuckled.

Aremil simply allowed Sorgrad to carry him to the doorway where Tathrin and Failla waited.

'In here.' Branca crossed the hallway to open a modest sitting room, once the refuge of the duchess's waiting-women. 'When the courtyards are cleared, you can go back to the inner keep.'

Failla embraced Tathrin, mindful of his injured shoulder. 'Kerith has already gone to the stable yard. Vrist has already told us twice that Horsemaster Corrad has our coaches ready and he won't want the horses standing in this chill.'

'Off you go.' He dismissed her with a last snatched kiss.

Branca hugged Aremil. 'We must make the best of the daylight.'

'Of course.' His lips lingered on her cheek before he forced himself to withdraw.

Failla halted on the threshold. 'Nail a cut-piece to the shrine door for us.'

As Branca shut the door behind them, Aremil fell back onto an upholstered settle. 'So all we can do now is wait.'

'Do you really think so?' Tathrin sat down carefully on an upright chair. 'Wouldn't you like a chance to play the hero for once?'

Aremil looked apprehensively at him. More worryingly, Sorgrad and Gren were smiling with ill-concealed anticipation.

Chapter Thirty-One
Litasse

Marlier Castle,
Lescar,
15th of For-Spring

HER HEART FLUTTERED like a trapped bird's wings beating against her ribcage. Wiping sweating hands on her blue velvet skirt, she was grateful for the knife beneath her petticoats.

'Your Grace!' Today's sneaking maidservant caught up. When she realised where Litasse stood, she clapped a horrified hand to her mouth.

Litasse contemplated the uncommunicative oak. 'Run away if you don't want to be whipped.'

As she knocked, the maid fled. Muffled voices paused then resumed their conversation. Knocking again, Litasse didn't wait for a response. She went in.

'Your Grace?' Duke Ferdain sat in a high-backed chair by the fire. It was a long moment before he hastily rose to bow.

Iruvain stood by the withdrawing room's window overlooking the duke's private garden. 'What do you want?' Seeing Ferdain's frown, he forced a smile. 'My lady wife.'

'My lord husband.' Litasse acknowledged him coolly before curtseying to Ferdain. 'Your Grace.'

'The honour is mine.' Marlier's duke sat back down in his chair. Feather-filled cushions notwithstanding, he looked horribly uncomfortable.

As well he might. Litasse didn't doubt that the castle's spies had told Ridianne, who then told Ferdain, that Iruvain of Triolle hadn't visited his duchess's bedchamber since his return. How he spent his nights drinking himself into oblivion.

The grizzled captain of mercenaries was sitting in a corner, her black breeches and high boots splashed with mud from the road.

Litasse didn't acknowledge her. Though she wondered if Ridianne had told Ferdain that Iruvain was also availing himself of any maidservant willing to spread her thighs. This past handful of days, Litasse had learned that much from servants' scandalised whispers.

Ferdain cleared his throat. 'How may we serve Your Grace?'

'I come to be of service to you.' She spared her husband a belated nod. 'To all Lescar's surviving dukes.'

'You?' Iruvain couldn't restrain his scorn. 'How?'

Litasse addressed herself to Ferdain. 'You recall Master Hamare, Triolle's chief intelligencer since the days of His late Grace Duke Gerone?'

'I do,' Ferdain acknowledged in strangled tones.

What did he think she was going to do? Burden him with every detail of her adultery with her cuckolded husband in the room?

The notion of humiliating Iruvain, of admitting her transgressions while laying bare all his guilt in the joint failure of their marriage was certainly tempting. But no, or at least, not yet.

Litasse reached into her pocket for a folded scrap of parchment. 'Master Hamare gathered news and rumour from far and wide. His skills were second to none when it came to separating the wheat from the chaff. I have continued to glean what I can from his informants since his untimely death.'

She allowed herself a reproachful glance at Iruvain. Let Ferdain make what he chose of that, and Ridianne too.

'My manservant Karn, one of Master Hamare's most trusted enquiry agents, continues to serve me faithfully. He has sent a most startling letter.'

'He serves Triolle,' snapped Iruvain, 'at my command.'

Iruvain stepping forward to take credit for whatever she had discovered was hardly a surprise. Rather than argue, Litasse used the parchment to gesture towards Ridianne, so fresh from the road.

'I imagine Captain Ridianne has told you of these outrageous proposals the misbegotten rebels have made in Carluse?'

'Indeed.' Ferdain folded his arms. 'We still have friends thereabouts.'

Litasse recalled Hamare telling her how a man's mood could be read in his stance. This news from Carluse had Ferdain on the defensive.

She raised her finely plucked brows. 'Has she told you their envoys are even now travelling to Sharlac and Draximal, to Parnilesse and to Triolle?'

Ferdain looked sharply at Ridianne.

The Vixen shrugged. 'I haven't had word but it's only to be expected.'

'Do you know they are sending an envoy to Hengere?' Litasse challenged the grey-haired woman before returning her gaze to Ferdain. 'Your Grace, you have done your people a great service by so wisely refusing to be drawn into this warfare, but I fear the ignorant mob may not have fully understood your purpose. The commonalty have been sorely oppressed by those fleeing from Carluse and Triolle in these hungriest of seasons. They've been harried by these brigands broken loose from those faithless mercenary companies.'

'Marlier's mercenaries are loyal,' Ridianne interjected harshly.

Iruvain couldn't help himself. 'So I saw before the very gates of Triolle Castle.'

Litasse took a step forward to reclaim Ferdain's attention. 'These rebels have spread their scurrilous writings so widely among your people that if they rally sufficient fools and malcontents to Hengere, if they offer venal guildsmen and priests this delusion of a voice in Lescar's rule—' She broke off with a shake of her head.

Iruvain rounded on Ridianne. 'This is where your cowardice has left us.'

'Has your eloquence secured a Caladhrian army?' she retorted.

Litasse spoke up before Iruvain could retaliate. 'I fear no Caladhrian baron will vote for a venture across the border now. Karn tells me some rebel envoy to Abray already flatters the lords and merchants there by saying Lescar's parliament will be patterned on their own.'

Ferdain snapped his fingers at Ridianne. 'Is this truly what they are planning?'

'I cannot say for certain.' She shot Litasse a penetrating glance before shaking her head. 'It makes no odds. We still hold Marlier.'

'For how long?' sneered Iruvain.

'Enough!' Ferdain's shout startled them all. He grasped the arms of his chair, his amiable face anxious. 'We must decide what to do.'

'Your Grace?' Litasse spoke up while Iruvain and Ridianne glowered at each other. 'I have taken the liberty—'

'Of doing what?' Iruvain took a pace towards her, clenching his fists.

'If you please, Your Grace.' Now Ridianne was on her feet. 'Mind your manners to your lady wife.'

Litasse shrank away from her husband to sit on a footstool conveniently close to Ferdain's chair.

'Master Hamare got wind of these rebels in Vanam, though alas not soon enough to save Sharlac and my father and brother.' She ducked her head as her voice faltered. 'He learned all that he could about them and since then Karn has learned more.'

'At my instruction,' Iruvain interrupted.

Ridianne squared her shoulders. 'His Grace learns everything he needs to know from my enquiries.'

Litasse laid a hesitant hand on the arm of Ferdain's chair. 'Karn discovered who commands the rebellion's army. A man called Tathrin Sayron.'

'Just so,' Ridianne agreed. 'He—'

'Karn has killed him,' Litasse said quietly.

'*What?*'

Iruvain and Ridianne spoke as one, astounded.

Litasse looked up at Ferdain. 'Karn discovered that bandits had burned this man's family's home, so he went there to lie in wait.' She shook her head in apparent disbelief. 'These people don't believe they have any more battles to fight. This Sayron, their captain, went in search of his family. Karn felled him with an arrow,' she said simply.

'Let me see that.'

Iruvain strode forward to snatch the parchment from her trembling hand. Ridianne would have moved to his shoulder to read it but he warned her off with a glare.

'What does this mean for us?' Ferdain demanded of his captain of mercenaries.

Ridianne was watching Iruvain with narrowed eyes as she ran a hand through her ragged hair. 'They still have mercenaries and militiamen under arms. We have more, so if it comes to a battle we'll have the upper hand. If their captain is dead it depends how able his lieutenants might be. There are two Mountain Men, experienced—'

'If?' Iruvain was appalled. 'You're still too craven to fight?'

'Call me craven, Your Grace?' Ridianne hissed his title like an insult. 'I didn't flee the battlefield at Pannal nor Castle Triolle before that.'

Iruvain's face reddened with anger and humiliation. 'If you were a man I would run you through for such insolence.'

'If you were a man you might stand some chance of success,' Ridianne riposted.

'Enough!' Ferdain bellowed.

But Litasse heard the infinitesimal break in his voice; of uncertainty and fear.

'Your Grace.' She looked up, beseeching. 'Perhaps no one need fight?'

'You be quiet,' Iruvain spat.

'Your Grace!' Ferdain sat up straight to rebuke the younger man. 'Extend your lady wife some courtesy in my presence!'

Iruvain stood motionless before retreating with a stiff-necked bow. 'Forgive me, Your Grace.'

Litasse noted he didn't apologise to her. That look in Iruvain's eye also boded ill for the next time they were alone. Looking penitently down, she focused on the stiff line of the dagger beneath her skirts.

'Thank you.' Ferdain composed himself. 'My dear, you wished to speak?'

She looked up to see hope and apprehension battling in his dark eyes. 'Your Grace, Master Hamare discovered two prime movers in this rebellion from its very first days in Vanam. One was this Tathrin Sayron whom Karn has now killed. The other was a scholar known as Master Aremil—'

Ridianne cut in quickly. 'In truth the firstborn son of Duke Secaris.'

'A cripple,' scoffed Iruvain, 'laid low by his weakness for days at a time.'

Litasse held Ferdain's gaze. 'This Master Aremil is coming to Hengere. These rebels know they cannot send anyone less when Marlier has remained so stalwart. He may be a cripple, Your Grace, but by all accounts he is eloquent and erudite. If anyone can persuade your people to doubt you – forgive me – Karn says he is the man to do it.'

'Then we kill him,' Iruvain crushed the parchment in his hand, 'if he's such a wise fool to venture into Marlier territory.'

'Or we capture him,' Ridianne said thoughtfully. 'All the better to force whoever claims authority in Carluse to come to terms with us.'

'I believe that would win the Tormalin Emperor's approval,' Litasse ventured.

Ferdain nodded unhappily. 'Since he is sheltering Duke Secaris, murdering Draximal's heir would hardly be politic.'

Iruvain threw the letter to the floor, contemptuous. 'What has Tadriol the Provident to do with our affairs? His legions have dithered beyond the Asilor since the turn of the year.'

Ferdain looked at Ridianne. 'Will Tadriol intervene?'

The mercenary woman stooped to retrieve the parchment. Her whole stance challenged Iruvain to try to take it back as she smoothed it out and read.

'Tadriol has no interest in Tormalin rule over Lescar,' she said eventually. 'He wants to extend his dominion over these new lands across the eastern ocean. But he won't allow Lescari chaos to damage Tormalin interests. He's watched and waited all through the winter. As the weather improves?' She shrugged. 'If there's anarchy in Parnilesse and Draximal the legions will march.'

She cut off Iruvain's incoherent protest with a curt hand. 'But as long as someone can convince him that they can secure peace, he will watch and wait. I'll bet a sack of gold crowns against the same weight of goat shit that these rebels have sent an envoy to Toremal along with whoever pleads their case in Sharlac, Draximal and Triolle.'

Ridianne flicked the parchment with her hand. The noise was startlingly loud.

'If we let this folly of a Conclave proceed – and that will flatter Tormalin sensibilities, my lord, just as much as it will seduce the Caladhrians – this war is as good as over. So we must act, and quickly, before the Spring Festival. If we capture this cripple, we can draw out negotiations for his ransom.' She smiled viciously. 'Our first condition for his safe return, as opposed to his richly deserved execution, will be dismissal of this Conclave nonsense.'

'And then?' Ferdain wondered.

'Then there will be no summer of fighting to provoke His Imperial Majesty. But there will still be no rule of law, no guarantee of safety for the honest and the innocent.' Ridianne shook her head. 'While we tie up these rebels in offer and counter-offer for their cripple's return, we must convince Tadriol to lend us his legions to re-establish Lescar's remaining dukes.'

She glanced at Iruvain. 'Since his aid will be best secured by offering the most generous terms on tolls along the Great West Road, I suggest you take yourself off to the Caladhrian Spring Parliament. Convince the barons how sorely they will lose out unless they lend their shoulder to our wheel.'

Litasse thought Iruvain would argue but to her surprise, he just scowled. 'Indeed.'

Satisfied, Ridianne continued, 'With allies on both flanks, we offer these rebels the choice of fighting or retreating into the Dalasor grasslands and wherever they may care to run after that.'

'We'll offer them a noose or a headsman's axe!' cried Iruvain.

Ridianne shook her head. 'Corner the smallest rat and it'll take on a dog that outweighs it a hundredfold. We don't want them to fight and draw Emperor Tadriol's legions across the River Anock.'

Ferdain looked at Iruvain. 'You don't want to find Triolle encumbered with whatever settlement best suits Tormalin.'

Litasse saw hope winning out over the apprehension in the Marlier duke's eyes.

'Karn says the cripple's heading for Hengere. If he gave this speech in Carluse three days ago—' Ridianne paused for a moment. 'Your man must have killed a horse or two to get word to you. Where is he now?'

'Already gone,' apologised Litasse. 'He said he would find the scholar's carriage on the road to Hengere and try to kill him himself.'

Ridianne clicked her tongue, exasperated. 'Carluse to Hengere is seventy leagues. On those roads, at this season, that's four days' travel—'

'At best,' objected Iruvain. 'For a cripple whining at every jolt?'

Ridianne ignored him, addressing Ferdain. 'I will need to ride fast and light, my lord. I'll be gone before noon with a small troop of chosen men. But I will catch this rabbit, never fear, before Karn can have his throat out.' Clearly relishing that challenge, she thrust the parchment at Litasse. 'Write on the reverse of this to prove it comes from your hand. Insist that he yield to me.'

'Karn will do as I tell him.' Iruvain was adamant. 'So I will accompany you.'

'If you insist.' Ferdain looked a trifle anxiously at Ridianne.

Litasse was amused to see the mercenary captain's feral smile. 'I will be honoured by Your Grace's company.'

Now Iruvain looked a little uncertain.

Litasse spoke up quickly. 'Then there can be no misunderstanding. These rebels will see from the outset that we are united. Just as Triolle will have a hand in this villain's capture, so we will play our part in every negotiation and settlement that follows.'

'Quite so.' For the first time, Iruvain favoured her with cold approval.

Litasse avoided his gaze, her eyes modestly downcast. She was still thinking how best to avoid him until he rode north with Ridianne.

Her next task would be all the easier. As soon as Ridianne's troop had departed, Litasse would throw herself on Duke Ferdain's mercy. She would plead and weep till he agreed to support her claim to Sharlac in her own right.

She had all her arguments marshalled. Her mother had no right to install some upstart. No wonder the Sharlac Guilds were ignoring the man. To put an end to this Conclave idiocy, Sharlac needed a ruling duchess of Duke Moncan's blood. Indeed, that would win them all the more support from Caladhria's barons and Toremal's princes; a clear demonstration of the rights of birth and rank.

Ferdain had seen for himself how Iruvain showed her such scant respect; as his wife, as his duchess. He didn't even respect Marlier's hospitality; debauching Ferdain's servants and nightly swinishly drunk on His Grace's finest wine.

Litasse was almost sorry Iruvain hadn't been provoked into striking her earlier. No matter. She would tell Ferdain he had been beating her since the very day of their wedding. There were no servants here from Triolle Castle who could give the lie to whatever she claimed.

After all this was done, she never wanted to see her husband again.

Chapter Thirty-Two
Aremil

The Hengere Road,
in the Dukedom of Marlier,
17th of For-Spring

'BRANCA SHOULD REACH Wyril sometime today.' Tathrin looked through their carriage window, squinting upwards to assess the weather.

'Halfway to Draximal,' Aremil agreed. He winced as a wheel hit a frozen rut. These cloudless days came at the cost of icy temperatures.

Tathrin settled himself back carefully on the padded seat. 'What news from Kerith?'

Aremil grinned. 'He tells me Lord Rousharn has decreed his vassal lords must send out their tenants to make good any damage to the Great West Road from the winter's snows.'

'That's customary duty at the start of For-Spring unless you want to pay an extra Equinox levy.' Tathrin cautiously rubbed his shoulder. 'Are the Sharlacs doing so?'

Aremil chuckled. 'The villagers turned up with their mattocks and spades and barrows of stones and gravel but wouldn't start work until their liege lords agreed to pay them. They won't take a coin with any duke's head on it either. It's Caladhrian or Tormalin marks or the potholes can break wheels and axles from now to next year.'

'Every merchant from Ashery to Vanam scorns the dukes' coinage now.' Tathrin looked more serious. 'We must give some serious thought to minting new Lescari currency.'

Aremil nodded. 'Though I don't know how until we have a reliable source of bullion.'

Tathrin grinned. 'Let's ask Sorgrad.'

Aremil looked quizzically at him. 'I don't doubt he and Gren can tell us which lords are sitting on the most Tormalin coin. Do you propose some levy or simple robbery?'

Tathrin began a shake of his head before stopping with a wince. 'I meant there might be some elemental means of drawing the silver out of the lead that our noble dukes stamped their heads on.'

Aremil hadn't thought of that. 'Would Planir the Black allow it?'

'It's hardly using magic for warfare,' Tathrin pointed out.

'As long as we've secured the peace first.' Another thought struck Aremil. 'If such a thing can be done, Triolle's silver mines would be worth a cursed sight more.'

'Tell Failla to drop a few hints to the Triollese guildsmen.' Tathrin looked at him, expectant.

Given half a chance he'd have Aremil sending his endearments across the aether night and day. Aremil sympathised but he would rather not be privy to all those glimpses of the passion Tathrin and Failla shared.

'I cannot work any Artifice while I'm being jostled like this,' he apologised.

As he spoke, the coach swayed violently round a bend. Aremil used his crutches to avoid sliding to the floor. With his back to the horses, Tathrin held his injured arm close, bracing himself with his feet.

'Failla said she was cordially received in Triolle,' Aremil reminded his friend once they were back on an even keel. 'Charoleia has enlisted Parnilesse's most influential men to our cause.'

A wry smile tugged at Tathrin's mouth. 'What disgraceful secrets do you suppose she's selling back in return for such cooperation?'

'No, I really think she's persuading them this is Lescar's best way forward.'

Aremil had no doubt that Charoleia was second to none at deception and dissembling face to face. But she wasn't quite so practised at hiding her thoughts from an adept of Artifice. He had been assailed by echoes of countless conversations and glimpses of faces; guildsmen, priests, merchants and tapsters, along with their wives and housekeepers and maidservants.

'Parnilesse folk seem more eager than any other—'

He broke off as the carriage lurched to a halt. A shadow fell across the window as a rider approached.

Tathrin rubbed his injured shoulder before throwing open the door.

The rider calmed her affronted horse. 'That's far enough.'

'Master Aremil, may I make known Ridianne the Vixen, Marlier's Captain of Mercenaries,' Tathrin announced with mock formality. 'Captain Ridianne, I have the honour to present you to Master Aremil, scholar of Vanam.'

'No scholar without the university's ring.'

Aremil saw the woman's sharp eyes had taken in every detail of his narrow shoulders and withered legs, his trembling, ungloved hands.

He noted her casual ease in the saddle, easily controlling the spirited horse, along with the sword sheathed by her muscular thigh.

'You're looking well for a man who's supposed to be dead.' Ridianne smiled at Tathrin, friendly enough. 'Do I have your oath that you'll behave as long as you're in my custody?'

'In your custody?' Tathrin queried.

'You two are hardly going to make a fight of it.' Ridianne snapped her leather-gloved fingers and whistled.

Shifting closer to the carriage window, Aremil saw their mounted outriders were being escorted back down the road. Ridianne's men, mercenaries wearing Marlier's red shield with its three silver swords surmounted by a fox's mask, outnumbered their own soldiers two to one.

'We're not here to fight,' he said. 'We merely offer the folk of Marlier the prospect of lasting peace.'

Ridianne shook her head, sunlight catching the jay's feather in the band of her low-crowned hat. 'Not at the cost of His Grace's rule.'

'Not at any price?' Aremil enquired. 'Not for clear title to your manor and demesne free of any fealty? Not for freehold property for your sons, for them to bequeath without hindrance to their own blood? Instead of whatever scraps Duke Ferdain and his noble-born heirs might throw whenever they need to whistle up their hounds?'

'You're wise enough to know when not to fight,' Tathrin urged her. 'I saw that at Triolle Castle.'

'You've seen me fight when I must,' retorted Ridianne.

Tathrin nodded. 'Your men didn't falter at Pannal.'

Aremil saw a flash of emotion in the woman's eyes as she answered.

'Because they fought for Marlier above all else, so Orlin of Parnilesse didn't crush your Soluran and trample all of Lescar underfoot as he snatched the High King's crown. Do you think I will break faith with those fallen, one in six of my own, by letting you ride in to overthrow Duke Ferdain?'

'How?' Tathrin scoffed. 'We have one sound arm between us and only this escort to dissuade bandits.'

'If Duke Ferdain is so beloved by his people they'll reject our proposals out of hand.' added Aremil.

'Do you honestly think you can hold Marlier's borders against such ideas,' Tathrin persisted, 'once Triolle men and Carlusians are managing their own affairs? When Sharlac and Draximal and Parnilesse all share the benefits of trade with Tormalin and their lands beyond the ocean, along the Great West Road and all down the Asilor?'

'Enough,' Ridianne said briskly. 'No war's over till the last battle's done. I'm still ready to fight on my own terms. Now, if you'll give me your oath, you need not be chained until we reach Hengere.'

Aremil sighed. 'You may have my word for what it's worth. I can hardly make a run for it.' He gestured with his crutches.

'You have mine,' Tathrin said, more grudging.

Ridianne smiled. 'I'll have your sword too.'

'If you must.' Tathrin retrieved the blade from the rack above Aremil's seat, scabbard, belt and all.

'Thank you.' Ridianne leaned forward to take it through the carriage doorway. 'Secure that latch,' she advised. 'We'll be on our way.'

Tathrin closed the door and sat back on his seat. He looked at Aremil. 'Did you really think she would throw in her runes with us?'

Aremil shrugged. 'It was worth a try.'

'Where do you suppose—?'

The carriage swayed as the horses leaned into their harness. It didn't move. Shouts rang out. Furious responses all around were punctuated by the stamp of hooves and clashes of steel. After a few cries of surprise and pain, silence fell.

'Shall we?' Tathrin gestured towards the door.

'Why not?' Aremil gathered up his crutches.

Tathrin opened the door, kicked the folding step down and got carefully out of the carriage.

'Can I offer you a hand?' A grinning youth with a cream and gold armband waited on the road.

'Thank you.' Aremil allowed the man to take his arm, leaning on him as he stumbled down the step.

The sun outside was painfully bright. Once he was secure on his crutches, he raised one hand to shield his eyes.

Ridianne still sat on her horse though her reins were now held by a burly man wearing a cream and gold kerchief. He had her sword in his other hand.

'I believe this is yours, Captain-General?' A scar-faced sergeant offered Tathrin back his own weapon. The man's badge showed the Lescari standard's halberd blade atop his old company's knotted stave.

'Thank you.' Tathrin carefully raised his sling to allow the sergeant to buckle the belt around him.

The disarmed Marlier troop was now surrounded by thrice their number wearing Lescar's colours.

'So this was your plan all along?' Ridianne shook her head, more amused than angry.

'We wanted to give you the chance to yield first,' Tathrin said sincerely. 'But once you took my sword? That was a clear sign you weren't ready to accept our terms.'

'A sign to the curs dogging our footsteps and inside my own boundaries too. I should have been more careful.' Ridianne looked severely at her discomforted cohort. 'I lost my best lieutenants at Pannal, or you'd never have caught me out.'

'I don't doubt it.' Tathrin bowed.

'What now?' she demanded. 'Ransom?'

'I'm afraid not,' apologised Aremil. 'If Duke Ferdain is still willing to fight, Marlier has no hope of success without you at the head of his army. You will be escorted to Carluse Castle and held until Marlier's surrender is settled.'

'If you'll give us your oath that you won't try to run,' Tathrin added, 'you need not be chained.'

Ridianne looked at him, a glint in her eye. 'Why don't you give me back my sword and we can settle this in single combat, captain to captain? I'll strap one arm to my side.'

Aremil recalled the tales of her challenging rival mercenaries to games of white raven, and not only when her own forces were outnumbered. Ridianne had won the day so often that men soon preferred to endure her mockery rather than face that trial.

'Thank you but no.' Tathrin bowed before gesturing to his shoulder. 'My surgeon would skin me alive if I undid all his handiwork.'

All the men laughed; both the Lescari and Marlier contingents. As their amusement died away, Aremil saw a brief commotion among those waiting further down the road.

'Look what I found!' Gren shouted cheerfully.

The Lescari soldiers parted to let the Mountain Man through and Aremil saw a gagged man slung across his horse's shoulders. Gren shoved and the man fell to the frozen ground with a painful thud. His hands were bound behind his back and roped to the leather belt lashing his ankles.

The captive writhed in his bonds. Tall and well muscled, his handsome face was bruised and his expensive clothes were muddied. He looked otherwise uninjured.

'I have the honour to make known His Grace Duke Iruvain of Triolle,' Gren proclaimed.

Ridianne laughed out loud.

'Care to share the joke, Captain?' Gren invited.

'Why not?' she said obligingly. 'When I got word that you were on the road, we left him tucked up warm in Hengere, snoring like the drunkard he is.' The Vixen bowed, mocking. 'I did you a disservice, Your Grace. How did you capture him, runt? How did you know who he was?'

Gren smiled, taking no offence at Ridianne's casual insult.

'There are some good likenesses hung in Triolle Castle. So when I recognised him, it was too good a chance to pass up. I rode ahead and stretched a cord across the road. He was riding like a man chasing some thief, so it snatched him right off his horse.' He shrugged. 'Then I just took his sword and knocked him senseless.'

As if that had been no challenge, Aremil thought; fighting a man at least a head taller and a practised swordsman to boot.

Ridianne turned to Tathrin. 'This is a whole new cast of the runes.'

Aremil took a cautious step forward. 'Madam Captain, you said you were ready to fight for Marlier. I take it Iruvain of Triolle is your ally?'

'For what little he's worth.' Ridianne didn't hide her contempt.

'You're aware of these brigands who've been plaguing Carluse and Marlier?' Aremil continued. 'Even venturing into Caladhria?'

'I am,' Ridianne replied with slow suspicion.

'Did you know they've done so on Iruvain's orders?' Aremil asked, guileless.

'I knew you weren't to be trusted.' The Vixen glared at the fallen duke.

Aremil nodded. 'Do you know they're selling their captives to Relshazri slavers?'

'That's where his gold comes from?' Ridianne's hand went for her absent sword.

'I think he wants to say something,' Gren observed.

Aremil turned to see Iruvain thrashing wildly on the ground.

'By all means.' Tathrin nodded and the scar-faced sergeant knelt to tug the gag free of the erstwhile duke's mouth.

Scarlet-faced and breathing hard, dead leaves tangled in his hair, Iruvain spat out a mouthful of phlegm. 'Scum!'

'Brave words for a man tied up and flat on his back.' Gren dismounted. 'Want to try that after I kick in your teeth?' He drew back his booted foot, smiling cheerily.

'Let him speak,' Tathrin reproved. 'First,' he added, menacing.

Iruvain stiffened, still defiant. 'I don't answer to swine like you.'

Aremil glanced at Ridianne. 'Like every duke, he thinks he's above any law, thanks to nothing more than the accident of birth. This is the tyranny we will lift from Lescar.'

Ridianne's face twisted with distaste. 'He thought the raids would provoke the Caladhrians into fighting and see him restored to his domain?'

'When that didn't work, he decided to raise the stakes.'

The Lescari cohort parted once again to let a second horseman through.

'Sorgrad?' Aremil had been wondering where he was.

'Corsairs, Captain.' Sorgrad looked at Ridianne. 'They'll be sailing up the Dyal any day now before cutting themselves a path overland. The Oisin's headwaters will be running red before they're finished. Then they'll be sailing on down to the Rel, heading north and south to slave and plunder as they go.'

'His doing too?' Ridianne looked ready to murder Iruvain with her bare hands.

'His man Karn's.' Sorgrad nodded. 'He knows all manner of vermin in Relshaz.' He looked more thoughtful. 'I'm guessing black ships will loot and murder right up to Triolle Town. So much for this hero's duty to his vassals and their tenants.'

Aremil glanced at Tathrin. 'I'll warn Failla,' he promised at once.

And of course, their duke's fresh treachery would help her persuade any faltering Triollese. Kerith, Charoleia and Branca could add this news to their own arguments. He restrained a grimly satisfied smile.

Then he saw that this news was no great surprise to Tathrin. He had known already and more surprising still, he'd concealed it all from Aremil. That was curious.

'It's a filthy lie!' Iruvain struggled uselessly against his bonds.

Gren kicked him hard in the thigh. 'Didn't your mother teach you to tell the truth?'

As Iruvain gasped with pain, Tathrin shrugged. 'We'll know when the black ships appear.'

Ridianne shifted in her saddle, flexing her empty sword hand. 'We must make ready to fight them off.'

Gren raised a questioning hand. 'Can we cut off his head?'

Sorgrad looked at Tathrin. 'That's a fitting penalty for such treachery.'

'I am not answerable for crimes done in my name, without my approval!' Iruvain rolled over, as far from Gren's boots as he could.

Ridianne's eyes narrowed. 'Let's see what Karn has to say about that.'

Iruvain fought to sit up. 'You cannot convict me on the word of one man so far below my rank, even if you find him.'

He finally succeeded in sitting upright and Aremil saw frantic hope in Iruvain's white-rimmed eyes. He swallowed his own disquiet. That villain Karn had proved horribly elusive thus far.

Sorgrad rode a pace closer. 'I think your own duchess's letters and testimony will convict you in any assize that we care to summon.'

'Litasse?' Ridianne was shocked.

'She's a traitorous whore and a lying bitch—'

Iruvain's hate-filled outburst was cut short by Gren's ruthless boot driving into his other thigh.

'Keep a civil tongue in your head,' the Mountain Man warned genially, 'or I'll cut it out.'

Iruvain tried to wriggle away, still protesting through gritted teeth. 'Karn was always her man from the first to last. Whatever he's done, it's her order—'

'Liar!' Ridianne shouted him down. 'You claimed all his successes as your own not a handful of days ago!'

Aremil saw the assembled Lescari soldiery exchanging eloquent glances with the Marlier mercenaries. Iruvain of Triolle was truly friendless here.

He looked at Tathrin. 'What do we do now?'

Ridianne wrenched her reins free of the man restraining her horse. 'Captain, you took me fairly and I'll ransom myself without argument. Name your price and I'll pay it. I have gold of my own and my companies will raise the rest.'

The Vixen's voice hardened with desperation. 'If you take me to Carluse, there's no one to lead Marlier's swords against these raiders. How can you claim to defend the innocent and weak if you leave them to be slaughtered by corsairs? You have to let us go to warn the villages in danger, to raise the coastal defences in Capast!'

Aremil could see the Marlier swordsmen who had been apparently resigned to the earlier turn of events were now readying themselves to fight unarmed against blades if needs be.

Tathrin raised a hand. 'Your men can go to raise the alarm if you come to Marlier Castle with us.'

'Why?' Ridianne looked at him, alert for some new possibility.

'To convince Ferdain that he must yield. That Marlier must be free to send its people to the Lescari Conclave at festival.' Tathrin looked at her, resolute. 'That's your ransom, Madam Captain, the price of your freedom to fight these corsairs.'

Ridianne barely hesitated. 'Done. Will you shake to seal the deal?' She stripped off a glove to offer her hand.

'Gladly.' Tathrin walked over to do just that.

'You cannot—' Iruvain choked on his outrage.

'Gag him,' Tathrin ordered the scar-faced sergeant. 'He can go back to Carluse loaded with all the chains you can find. While we're in Marlier Castle we will retrieve Duchess Litasse from Duke Ferdain's hospitality. Let's see what she can tell us of this man Karn and his dealings.'

'And of Iruvain's other heroics,' mused Sorgrad, 'from Tyrle onwards.'

Aremil saw a shadow of fear cross Iruvain's face. Something about that prospect frightened the duke even more than Gren standing a few paces away, dagger in hand. But Triolle's duke was gagged again, unable to speak.

Before Aremil could pursue that thought, another chased hard on its heels. How did Sorgrad know about these corsairs coming to sail up the Dyal?

Surely it couldn't be a bluff? Ridianne would strangle him with his own entrails if that proved to be the case. And Sorgrad was promising that Duchess Litasse could offer proof of all the accusations he had made. How did he know that?

'Come on.' Tathrin urged him back towards the carriage. 'Let's make for Marlier and see an end to this once and for all.'

Chapter Thirty-Three
Litasse

Marlier Castle,
Lescar,
20th of For-Spring

As the gatehouse's shadow engulfed her, she shivered.

'Your Grace?' Horsemaster Hamber laid a kindly hand on her arm. 'You're too cold.'

'Not at all.' Litasse favoured him with a smile as dazzling as the frost on the roof tiles. 'Some Eldritch Kin stepped on my shadow, nothing more.'

They rode through the arch into the next of Marlier Castle's courtyards.

Litasse would have sworn that tales of the Eldritch Kin were old wives' yarns spun to school foolish children. But now she had seen wizardly magic and he had hinted at more eerie sorceries. She shuddered again.

'Your Grace.' As the horsemaster pulled up his mount, Litasse's mare halted with its stablemate. 'Perhaps we should reconsider. The ground will be brutally hard on the beasts.'

Litasse got a grip on herself. 'Not where the sun has lingered, on the south side beyond the orchards.'

She had to be outside, to see them arrive. He had sworn they would be here before noon.

'Very well, Your Grace.' Fatherly and tolerant, Hamber chirruped and both horses obediently walked on.

He had sworn she would be safe. Going over and over his words in her mind, Litasse had finally decided to trust him. She recalled he had said he would watch over her. She had still felt an utter fool, writing in letters as tall as her hand on a single sheet of paper.

Help me.

So close to the fire that she could throw the notes into the flames before any interloper saw them. Her pen had still shaken so dreadfully that she had blotted each individual letter.

Whatever his secret, he had come and she had told him all she knew. He had told her his name was Sorgrad and that the other blond killer was his brother, Sorgren by name. Gren for short, he explained, amused, since lowlanders so inexplicably persisted in confusing the two names.

Before he vanished he had promised to return. This morning as she washed her face, his shimmering message had come and gone in the bottom of her washstand basin. He would come for her today.

Litasse had decided to trust him. She still found him deeply unnerving.

'Horsemaster.' The guard at the gate in the next low wall bowed low.

Before Hamber replied, Litasse heard carriage wheels rumble. Across the gravelled yard, Ridianne rode her horse alongside the coach's driver. A taller man sat up beside him.

Litasse recognised the Carlusian she'd seen at Adel Castle, his broad shoulders stiff beneath borrowed Marlier livery. Then she saw the outriders close behind and felt weak with relief. Sorgrad and his brother wore purloined uniforms with their striking blond hair concealed under close-fitting helms. Cheek guards further obscured Sorgrad's face but Litasse saw him wink at her.

That was all very well but what was Ridianne doing with them? Who was inside the coach?

Litasse turned swiftly to Horsemaster Hamber. 'Forgive me, I'm being selfish. You know what's best for your horses. We should take them back to the stables.'

'If you're sure, Your Grace.' He didn't hide his relief.

The guard was already opening the gate to admit the carriage, so Litasse allowed her mare to fret until the rattling equipage passed through.

'Good day, Your Grace,' Ridianne greeted her breezily.

Litasse tensed. Could the mercenary woman still raise some alarm? Would Marlier's guards race out of all the doorways like ants defending their nest?

'Your Grace?' Master Hamber was waiting.

Litasse shook off her fears. 'Alas, Madam Captain, I fear it is rather too chill for a pleasure ride.'

She submitted to Hamber's firm hand on her horse's bridle and they followed the carriage back to the stable yard, through the archway that housed the castle's shrine to Trimon.

Where were they going now? Fear froze the breath in Litasse's throat as the gates swung closed behind them. They were trapped if Ridianne turned against them. The mercenary woman still had her sword.

Though of course, there would have been questions if she hadn't. Litasse rode over to the mounting block and prepared her skirts to descend.

'Your Grace.' Already on foot, Sorgrad hurried to hold her horse's head. Once she had dismounted, he offered his hand as she descended the steps. 'Good girl,' he approved in low tones. 'You're no longer on your own.'

Litasse looked sideways through her lashes. 'I am not your girl.'

'Not yet.' His smile came and went as fast as that message in her basin.

Ridianne summoned a stable-boy with a piercing whistle. 'Take this to His Grace, as quick as you can.'

Was some warning message concealed in those few scrawled words? Litasse settled her skirts. She would stay close to Sorgrad. If all this went horribly awry, she could only trust in his promise to protect her.

The Carlusian opened the carriage door. Litasse wondered if anyone else had noticed that he was only using one arm. Why was that?

Then Ridianne reached inside and removed a pair of crutches. That prompted muted speculation around the coach yard.

Litasse tidied her hair as Ridianne helped an ill-grown man out of the carriage. This must be the scholar from Vanam. As she studied his face, Litasse thought she could see some trace of Duke Secaris's blood.

Ridianne looked around at the gawping servants, a lazy smile curling her lip. 'Haven't you lackwits got better things to do?' That warning sent them all hurrying away.

'Your Grace.' Master Hamber came to take charge of Litasse's mare.

Litasse smiled sweetly. 'Forgive me for wasting your time.'

'Let's hope for a thaw tomorrow, Your Grace.' He was already leading both horses back to their stable.

'Your Grace?' Ridianne approached. 'Please join us. We're to pay a visit to Duke Ferdain.'

'As quickly as we can.' Sorgrad was looking warily around the stable yard.

'Naturally.' A wry smile momentarily lightened the Vanam scholar's drawn features.

Litasse found the man's ungainly, wasted limbs and his hesitant, Vanam-accented speech disconcerting. It was so demonstrably at odds with the quick intelligence in his eyes.

'This way.' She opened a door before being stricken with doubt. Was this the most direct route to Ferdain's withdrawing room? She still didn't know all the intricacies of this castle. Should she let Ridianne lead?

But the scholar was already hurrying clumsily along the corridor on his crutches, flanked by Ridianne and Tathrin.

'Your Grace?' Sorgrad bowed low with a sweep of his hand to indicate she should go ahead of himself and Gren and the scar-faced man who had driven the coach.

Litasse walked after Ridianne, Tathrin and Aremil, her poise impeccable, her heart racing. Wouldn't someone wonder why a coachman and outriders had followed Ridianne into the castle? Wouldn't someone realise that none of these men had been in the hand-picked troop that had departed a bare handful of days before?

'Do you know where Karn is?' Sorgrad quietly asked.

Litasse shook her head. 'I've not seen or heard from him since he left to kill your friend.'

She looked apprehensively at the Carlusian's back. Of course, that explained his arm. Would there be a reckoning for his wound?

They made their way through the labyrinthine twists and stairs, ignoring the few passing servants and encountering no inconveniently courteous nobles. Litasse couldn't imagine how she might introduce the Vanam rebels' crippled leader.

Though surely no one would dare stop them? Not Marlier's famed captain of mercenaries striding ahead of Triolle's duchess, the rightful heir to Sharlac. But what was Ridianne doing here? Sorgrad had said she would be taken in chains to Carluse. And where was Iruvain?

After what felt like half a season, Litasse's curiosity growing with every step, they turned into the hallway to Ferdain's private apartments.

Ridianne knocked and entered without waiting for an answer.

Litasse felt Sorgrad's urgent hand at her elbow. 'Quickly.'

Gren and the other man pressed so close that someone trod on the hem of her cloak.

'Ridianne?' Ferdain sat by his fireside, her note in his hand. The duke's smile widened and he rose to bow with stately condescension. 'Lord Aremil of Draximal?'

'Master Aremil, if you please,' the cripple replied, composed, 'of Vanam.'

Ferdain's smile faltered as he resumed his seat. Then he saw Litasse and simply looked confused. 'My dear, that's to say, Ridianne, where is His Grace of Triolle?'

'Quite safe,' replied Ridianne. 'Just listen, Ferdain.'

'We're here to talk terms.' Master Aremil lowered himself awkwardly onto a settle. 'Lescar doesn't deserve another year of war.'

The duke clasped his hands on his velvet-covered paunch. 'I am very pleased that you have seen sense. The first thing you will do is write to your envoys and repudiate this Conclave nonsense.'

'You misunderstand me,' apologised Aremil. 'We're here to agree the terms of your abdication.'

'To make fair settlement for your children and your duchess,' added Tathrin, 'provided they quit all claims to dominion over Marlier.'

Ferdain gaped at Ridianne. 'What is this?'

'This war's over, Ferdain.' She walked to the window and contemplated the garden. 'Make the best deal you can.'

'You betrayed me?' His voice broke on his anguish. 'You have betrayed Marlier?'

Ridianne didn't turn. 'I hope not.'

Ferdain stared at her uncommunicative back before forcing a smile for Litasse.

'Never fear, my dear. Your husband—'

'Is on his way to Carluse, securely shackled.' Once again, Aremil apologised.

Litasse couldn't help herself. She shot Sorgrad a sparkling smile of delight.

Ferdain gripped the arms of his chair. 'Guards!'

No one moved.

The duke sprang up to snatch at the bell pull by the fire. He yanked it so hard that the tapestry strip tore.

'That won't work,' Sorgrad said calmly. 'You can shout as loud as you like. No one will hear you, Your Grace.'

'What?' Now Ferdain gaped at him.

'I'm a wizard, Your Grace.' Sorgrad waved an airy hand. 'No sound, nor anything else, will leave this room without my say-so.'

Gren obligingly stepped away from the door as Ferdain hurried over to haul on the handle. The door stayed unshakeably shut.

The duke looked wide-eyed at Sorgrad. 'Wizardry is forbidden in Lescar.'

'The Archmage forbids the use of magic in Lescar's *wars*.' Sorgrad removed his helmet. 'Assuming we come to terms, the last battle was fought some time ago.'

'You'll escape his wrath by quibbling like a lawyer? Imprisoning me with your sorcery until I abdicate? Very well!' Dramatic, Ferdain flung up his hands, stalking back to his chair. 'I will sign whatever you want. As soon as I have my liberty, I will tell everyone from the Archmage down how my signature was forced from me. What will you gain from that?'

Gren took off his own helmet. 'You can't say anything if we kill you once the ink's dry.'

Ridianne turned swiftly from the window. 'Try it and see how far you get.'

'Enough!' Tathrin barked. 'We're here to put an end to bloodshed.'

'All that magic will do today is ensure we're not interrupted.' Aremil reached inside the deep pocket of his cloak. 'Your Grace, I think you'll see abdication is preferable when the alternative is disgrace. Duke Iruvain soon agreed.' He offered Ferdain a parchment.

'What is this?' The duke took the document and reluctantly read. 'He signed this of his own volition without a sword at his throat?'

'He did,' Ridianne assured him.

Ferdain thrust the parchment at Litasse, his hand shaking. 'Your Grace?'

She gave it a cursory glance. 'That is my husband's writing.' She had no interest in the details.

'But why?' Ferdain beseeched Ridianne.

'Corsairs.' She was staring out of the window again. 'Iruvain of Triolle has offered up Marlier to the black ships in hopes of blaming their raids on the rebels, in hopes of forcing us to fight.'

'Corsairs?' Ferdain subsided into his chair.

'Your Grace?' Ridianne's sharp gaze pierced Litasse.

'It's true.' She looked down at the sumptuous carpet.

'I can fight them off,' Ridianne assured Ferdain, 'as long as I'm free to do so.' She shrugged. 'Bringing them here was the price of my freedom.'

'That's not Iruvain's only crime against your dukedom,' Aremil observed. 'His man Karn has been recruiting these brigands to stir up trouble in order to bring the Caladhrians to battle.'

'Filling his pockets with Relshazri slavers' gold,' growled Ridianne.

'Am I to be punished for his villainy?' Ferdain reddened with outrage. 'Why should I give up my domains when I have done nothing wrong?'

'What have you done right?' Aremil challenged him. 'What have you done to salve your people's hurts when mercenaries have abused them, when vassal lords have beggared them to keep themselves in luxuries and to buy your favours with their gold? What have you ever done to bring peace, to offer prosperity to all Lescari?'

Ferdain stared at him, uncomprehending. 'What are you talking about? No!' He folded his hands tight beneath his armpits. 'I will sign no document you put before me.'

Aremil shrugged. 'Then we will hold you securely and in comfort while Marlier sends honest men and women to the Conclave along with the rest of Lescar's provinces.'

'You will hold me here?' scoffed Ferdain. 'Or do you think you can escape my guards, even with her treachery?' He shot Ridianne a wounded look. 'You'll be cut down before you reach the outer courtyards!'

'Your Grace?' Sorgrad smiled. 'I can take you leagues from here without anyone being the wiser.'

Litasse caught her breath as he kindled azure magelight around one upraised hand.

'You'll let them do this?' Ferdain appealed desperately to Ridianne.

'I'll be busy fighting off corsairs.' She was still looking out at the garden.

'You'll hold me lifelong?' Ferdain's voice trembled with fear and anger. 'With no one the wiser?'

'Once the Conclave is established you'll be released,' Tathrin said coldly. 'By which time you will be disgraced. Everyone will believe that you share in Duke Iruvain's guilt for these brigands plundering Carluse, Caladhria and Marlier, for summoning these corsairs.'

Litasse was startled by the Carlusian's harsh words. He seemed such a mild-tempered man. Then she recalled how effectively he had waged this merciless war.

Ferdain shook his head stubbornly. 'No one will believe it of me.'

How long were these men going to talk themselves round and round in circles? Litasse couldn't stand it any longer. 'They will when I bear witness.'

'You would perjure yourself?' Ferdain was genuinely wounded. 'When I have given you my protection and my hospitality?'

Litasse hardened her heart. 'I would do that and more, Your Grace. Iruvain has greater crimes than this to answer for and I will swear you share his guilt.'

'Like what?' Ferdain demanded, as petulant as a schoolboy.

'His complicity in Duke Garnot's murder during the siege of Tyrle.' Litasse knotted her cold hands together behind her back to stop anyone seeing them shaking. 'His man Karn killed Garnot and Iruvain has sheltered him ever since, in full knowledge of that crime.'

Ferdain was appalled. 'I cannot believe it.'

'If you don't believe Her Grace, I'll wager the Archmage can find the truth,' Sorgrad mused. 'A handful of Duke Garnot's ashes and Planir's necromancer can reveal his last moments.'

'Is that possible?' Ferdain looked unnerved.

'It is, and the Archmage has already sanctioned necromancy,' Tathrin said thoughtfully, 'to uncover the truth of Duke Orlin and Duchess Sherista's murders.'

Gren glowered. 'We made sure of justice there.'

'Emperor Tadriol will bear witness to that,' Aremil assured Ferdain. 'You may write to His Imperial Majesty or send an envoy.'

The duke could only gawk, astounded.

'That's not the worst of it, Your Grace.' Sorgrad snapped his fingers and the magelight disappeared. 'There was a renegade wizard in Adel Castle ready to use his magic to aid Triolle and Parnilesse during the Battle of Pannal. He tortured our envoys, even killed one.'

Ridianne spun around. 'Iruvain suborned sorcery?'

'I can bear witness to that,' Tathrin said icily, 'as can the women who were abused.'

'Is this true?' Ferdain whispered, horrified, to no one in particular.

'I killed the bastard,' Gren assured him grimly.

Litasse couldn't speak or move. She had been such a fool. The Mountain mage had only brought her here to betray her.

Sorgrad shrugged. 'Duke Iruvain and Lord Geferin were both in Adel Castle. Who's to say whose idea it was? Though we do know this renegade mage had ties to these corsairs.'

'Is that so?' Ridianne's eyes promised murder if she ever came within striking range of Iruvain.

Still frozen with fear, Litasse saw Aremil and Tathrin exchange an opaque glance.

Aremil searched the pocket of his cloak for some further document. 'Duchess Litasse did all she could to save our envoys.'

Tathrin nodded. 'Once she discovered what appalling deeds were being done in Triolle's name.'

'My dear, is this true?' Ferdain asked in strangled tones.

Litasse could only nod, tears filling her eyes.

'Once this is known?' Aremil pushed a second leaf of parchment into Ferdain's unresisting hands. 'Do you think anyone will trust you again, whether or not they believe you agreed with Iruvain's plans?'

Litasse found she could breathe more easily. Was she forgiven for her vile folly?

'Make the best of it, Ferdain,' advised Ridianne. 'Take your gold and you can be safe in some comfortable exile before anyone even knows that you're gone.'

'Or you can wait to be driven out with brickbats and horsewhips,' Gren offered with an unexpectedly genial grin.

'Hidarin will be furious,' Ferdain said slowly. Abruptly, he looked straight at Litasse. 'Why?'

Amid all the half-truths in the room, the pain in his eyes compelled her honest answer.

'What are we fighting for? To impose our will on vassals and peasants who resent us? To pursue old quarrels bequeathed by sires and grandsires? To see innocent blood shed for enmities we never sought or deserved?'

The loss of her brothers twisted in her heart like a knife.

'To live surrounded by the debased loyalties of swords for hire? To marry for imagined advantage and live miserable for want of true affection? To condemn our children to the same wretchedness, shuffled around like birds on a white raven board?'

Tears spilled down her cheeks. She wiped them away with trembling hands.

'Why, Ferdain? Because I want to be free of it all.'

The duke did not answer. Aremil silently handed him a third parchment. Ferdain slowly read it through and then, still without a word, he rose and crossed to a writing desk. The inkwell clinked and a pen scratched.

Sorgrad moved to Litasse's side and offered a pristine handkerchief. She dried her face, biting the inside of her lip to stem any more tears.

Ferdain flung all the parchments at Aremil. 'And now?'

Aremil waited for the scar-faced man to retrieve the documents from the floor for him. He blew on the duke's signature to dry the ink before carefully rolling the instrument of abdication. 'Now you may make your arrangements to depart while we return to Hengere and secure Marlier's participation in the Conclave.'

'With Ridianne at your side,' Tathrin added, 'in case you think of going back on your word.'

The mercenary woman shot him a warning look. 'Only till I'm needed to kill those corsairs.'

'Bear in mind that copies of that abdication will be with Emperor Tadriol and the Archmage by nightfall.' Sorgrad smiled.

Aremil nodded. 'And nailed to shrine doors across Lescar on the first day of the Spring Festival.'

'And sent to the Caladhrian parliament,' Tathrin concluded.

'Thank you, Lord Ferdain, and we'll bid you good day. My lady?' Sorgrad opened the door.

Litasse saw Gren and his falsely liveried companion help Aremil onto his crutches. Tathrin went to offer his hand to Ridianne, who was gazing through the window. Ferdain stayed slumped in his chair, staring at the floor.

Litasse hesitated on the threshold. 'It's all over?'

'It is for you,' Karn hissed in her ear as he dragged her bodily into the hallway.

He flung her hard into the wooden panelling. As she slid down to the floor, breath knocked out of her, she saw the door opposite stood open. He must have got wind of their presence in the castle and lain in wait.

'I told you there'd be a reckoning.' Sword and dagger ready, Karn stood between her and Sorgrad.

The Mountain mage drew his single sword. Gren and the falsely liveried mercenary flanked him, naked blades in hand. Tathrin guarded Ferdain's doorway.

'Once I've gutted your sunny-haired friends, I'll finish you and your limping pal,' Karn promised him.

'Karn!' As Litasse protested, pain lanced through her. She pressed a hand to her bruised ribs.

'I won't betray Master Hamare, Your Grace,' he hissed.

Litasse managed to draw a shallow breath. 'Hamare would understand.'

It was true. She knew Hamare would see there was no longer any victory to be won here. They could have run away together to a new life in Col, letting Iruvain find his own path to Poldrion.

Litasse closed her eyes on the pain of her lover's loss. She could have been back in that tower room with the scent of his blood turning her stomach, its stickiness beneath her fingers.

She looked at her hand. It was red. Karn had stabbed her. She looked wonderingly at a stubby dagger fallen onto the carpeted floor. The scabbarded blade beneath her skirts mocked her.

Would she find Hamare waiting for her at Saedrin's door?

''Grad!' Gren's harsh voice cut through her confusion.

Sorgrad rasped something in the Mountain tongue before advancing on Karn. 'You shouldn't have done that, friend.'

Karn launched a sword blow to his head. Sorgrad blocked it with a downward-pointing blade. Karn took a sidestep to thrust his dagger at the Mountain Man's midriff.

Sorgrad caught that blade with the hilt of a knife drawn from some concealment. With a deft move, he stepped beyond the gaunt man's dagger's reach. As he did so, a twist freed his sword to slice at Karn's neck.

Karn leaped backwards out of danger. Sorgrad pursued him, sword still swinging towards Karn's head. The gaunt man parried the blade with his dagger as his sword hacked down and around towards Sorgrad's knee.

The Mountain Man brought his sword down to ward off the blow. That freed Karn's dagger. He ripped it across Sorgrad's forearm. Blood sprayed across the panelling. Sorgrad barely avoided Karn's sword spilling his entrails across the carpet.

Karn thrust again. Sorgrad foiled the sword with his knife and swung his blade hard at Karn's head yet again. Karn caught the blow with his own dagger. They stood braced, unable to break free without offering the other a killing blow.

Litasse saw Sorgrad smile. Quick as lightning, he pulled his sword free and drove the tip deep into her faithful servant's thigh.

As blood gushed from the wound, Karn cursed. Litasse saw his hand let the dagger fall. Only he caught the hilt, his grip reversed. Karn threw himself forwards to plunge the dagger into Sorgrad's chest and they fell tangled together.

Litasse tried to cry out but she couldn't breathe. Everyone else was shouting. Tathrin and the liveried man dragged Karn's body away. Now Ridianne guarded the doorway with her unsullied sword. Gren embraced his brother, blood turning his red livery to maroon.

Sorgrad threw him off and crawled towards Litasse. As Karn's dagger slid from his wound, swift darkness spread across his scarlet Marlier livery.

'Forgive me, dear heart,' he said tightly.

Litasse had no breath to answer as he reached for her hand. Unutterable pain tore through her, to release her from all her torments.

Chapter Thirty-Four
Tathrin

Carluse Castle,
Lescar,
Spring Equinox Festival, Fifth Day, Evening

THE OUTER COURTYARD was full of people coming and going. He walked more swiftly, refusing to let anyone catch his eye. Let them think he was about some urgent business.

Where to go to find peace and quiet? The castle's inner ward would be just as crowded, the same endless, unanswerable questions flung at him.

Tathrin was exhausted. As each day of this festival had ended his head was aching fit to split. It was all he could do to beg some relief from Master Welgren and fall into bed beside Failla. He was lucky to stay awake long enough to find her hand among the quilts, before waking to take up the same burdens again.

What if he left the castle? Could he pass through the gates without some sentry delaying him until an importuning crowd gathered? Where would he go in the town if he did? It was full to bursting with all those gathered for this cursed Conclave. Even men and women with no formal involvement had travelled to Carluse out of sheer curiosity. He wanted Failla but she had hurried away after their hastily snatched breakfast and he hadn't seen her since.

'Tathrin!'

He could almost have sworn his exasperated thought had summoned her.

'Come on.' She laced her fingers through his, drawing him towards the great hall.

'Where are we going?' He couldn't face another flurry of introductions swiftly followed by competing demands.

Failla stopped and smiled. 'No guildsmen, no priests, no nobles, no questions.'

Tathrin felt his weary spirits lift a little. 'That sounds promising.'

'Master Sayron!' A sturdy matron bustled towards them.

'Forgive me, Mistress Hesdin.' Failla bobbed a curtailed curtsey. 'We're needed elsewhere.'

Tathrin managed to smile apologetically as Failla pulled him away. 'Where are we going?'

'Through the little gate behind the inner keep.' Failla was almost running to match his pace as they passed through the great hall. 'No, don't slow down.'

Tathrin cut across the inner ward's once sacrosanct lawn. Halcarion, goddess of love and luck, combed her hair in the midst of the fountain, newly freed from its winter shrouding. Crystal water glistened on her white marble curves.

Tathrin sighed. Precious little else in Lescar was untouched by all this past year's upheavals.

'My love?' Failla squeezed his hand.

He halted. 'I don't know if it's all been worth it.'

'You're tired.' Her eyes were warm with love and sympathy.

True enough but he still felt a flare of irritation. 'It's not only that.'

But he didn't know what it was that left him so dispirited.

'Come on,' she urged.

Too weary to argue, Tathrin let her lead him to the small door in the castle's far wall. Failla knocked three times on the weathered wood.

A key turned and the door opened. 'Password?'

Failla set her hands on her hips. 'Ferl River white?'

'Good enough.' Gren stepped back.

As soon as they were through, he relocked the door.

'How long have you been hiding here?' Tathrin didn't know whether to be pleased or angry.

'Barely long enough to open a bottle of wine,' retorted Aremil.

'Ferl River white or Angovese red?' Kerith stood by a small table holding bottles and mismatched goblets.

'The Angovese, please.' Tathrin looked around. He'd never had occasion to visit this private garden. Some dead duchess's folly, it had been laid out between the castle's curtain wall and the deadly cliff face. The crag plunged sheer into the gathering dusk far below.

'We decided we deserved something of a celebration.' Branca sat on a bank of cushions on a carpet plundered from the castle.

Aremil lay propped beside her, looking more at ease than Tathrin could ever recall.

'Serafia.' Tathrin accepted the wine that Kerith offered and raised the glass to acknowledge her.

'Fair festival.' As she smiled, Tathrin saw how truly pretty she was.

It would be churlish to say this had been the most tediously unrewarding festival he had ever spent, so Tathrin nodded. 'Fair festival.'

But he recalled what Failla had confided a few nights ago. She was pleased that Kerith had brought her bereaved cousin some comfort but she couldn't help pitying Milar. The tavern keeper had loved Serafia so long and so hopelessly. Every time she looked at his ruined hand, though, she recalled her beloved Elpin's death in that same battle.

It seemed to sum up so much for Tathrin. No success was without its blemish.

'Why so glum?' Sorgrad sat cross-legged on another rug.

Tathrin shrugged. 'Just tired. How are you?'

'Tired of Master Welgren asking,' Sorgrad said lightly, 'but as neatly mended as a thrifty housewife's apron.'

As it turned out, Karn's dying blow had gouged along Sorgrad's ribs rather than penetrating his vitals beneath.

Tathrin forced a smile as he raised his glass. 'Your— Lady Litasse.' That was all the title she would answer to. 'How are you?'

'Master Tathrin.' She inclined her dark head, her expression as impenetrable as ever.

Karn had so nearly killed her, his blade penetrating her lung. Without Master Welgren's skills she'd be dead.

'I am very well, thank you.' Litasse shared Sorgrad's rug, her skirts neatly tucked around her slender ankles. Was there some yielding in her reserve as the Mountain mage poured wine into her goblet? Tathrin knew Gren was taking anyone's wager that his brother's persistence would outlast her resistance.

Tathrin wasn't about to bet against him, not after seeing Sorgrad vanish from Marlier Castle in a snap of azure magelight. Even so, he had barely been in time for Master Welgren to save Litasse.

He wondered if Litasse had any idea of the bond between the brothers. Gren would have charged straight for Marlier's stables when his brother disappeared, killing anyone standing between him and a horse to gallop all the way to . . . where?

Thankfully Aremil had tripped Gren with a crutch between his shins and Ridianne had wrestled him to the ground. Then Branca's urgent call through the aether had told Aremil where Sorgrad had gone. Naturally she had seen all that had transpired through her beloved's eyes.

'I wonder how much of Lescar you can see from here.' Charoleia stood on the unfenced precipice, silhouetted against the evening sun.

Tathrin had a good head for heights but he wouldn't have gone so close.

Charoleia stepped down to safer ground. 'Are you heartily sick of this Conclave? Of the pettiness and squabbles and rivalries and factions?'

'Sullying this honourable peace that we secured with so many deaths and threats and lies?' Suddenly reckless, Tathrin drained his glass. 'Have you been learning Artifice to read my thoughts?'

'No, but I've seen so many golden hopes descend to tarnished reality. You should polish up your triumphs afresh,' Charoleia teased him. 'Is anyone actually fighting? Isn't that an improvement on what's gone before?'

'A couple of guildsmen came close to trading punches this afternoon.' Gren sprawled on the dewy grass.

'The Conclave has made considerable progress,' said Aremil firmly. 'We have comprehensive agreements on all tolls and levies.'

'And laws.' Kerith nodded. 'Quarterly assizes will be held in each province to try those who fall foul of each district's watchmen. In the meantime, there's an amnesty for those who honestly served their dukes in the recent battles and an edict against private revenge. Accusations of any misdeeds over this past year will be tested by a panel of judges drawn by lot from all the estates of the Conclave.'

'We have agreed how claims may be made by the dispossessed, and tested,' Aremil added, 'in the case of exiles returning in hopes of their thrice-great-grandsire's inheritance.'

'Who's to manage all that?' Tathrin winced at the prospect of shouting crowds waving tattered documents and affidavits at him.

'Each dukedom had its reeves and clerks and notaries,' Aremil assured him. 'They're as happy, if not happier, to use their skills to serve the Conclave and the cause of peace in Lescar.'

Kerith continued. 'Those without home or livelihood can apply to the Conclave to take a vacant land-holding or a workshop in hand for a year to prove their fitness to full title.'

Tathrin wondered how his erstwhile mercenaries would feel about such protracted legalities, more used to taking what they wanted at the point of their swords.

Aremil was still speaking. 'Thanks to Lady Litasse, we have also made remarkable progress with those still thinking they have some claim to a dukedom. Most now accept the lands that they hold are as much kingdom as they're likely to see.'

'Given the choice between that and the bleakest of futures, dispossessed and disinherited.' Litasse's smile was as inscrutable as ever.

'But can this truly work?' Tathrin stared into his empty glass. 'All the Caladhrian barons do is talk and talk and they make a worthwhile decision as rarely as there's a moonless night.'

'Caladhria's barons know there'll still be food on the table if they wear out the timepieces with their debates,' Charoleia said tartly. 'Lescar's Conclave has no such luxury and that's a powerful incentive to avoid wasting time so that merchants can get back to their wagons and farmers can till their fields.'

'Everyone wants to rebuild,' Aremil assured him. 'They have to cooperate to do that.'

'And stand shoulder to shoulder to deter Caladhrian and Tormalin interference,' added Charoleia, 'or another Reniack.'

'That fear should keep the most resentful nobles honest,' Litasse observed.

'Even Lord Rousharn of Nolsedge sees the wisdom of our arguments,' Sorgrad pointed out. 'He is returning to his alchemical and philosophical studies.'

'Lady Derenna will educate Garnot's younger daughters,' Failla told Tathrin quietly, 'until they're of an age to inherit their manors granted from their mother's dowry.'

'And if they inherit their mother's resentments?' He still couldn't put his worries aside.

'Can you think of a better solution, long lad?' Gren demanded. 'No, and nor have any of these scholars and priests who've been sweating over these questions. Can you think of any worse answer? Of course you can and so can we all. So let's settle for the least worst plan and drink with our friends while we still have the chance. Tomorrow's soon enough to deal with tomorrow's problems.'

Aremil laughed. 'You can congratulate me on my own challenges ahead. The Conclave has granted me seizin of Fordetal. That's a modest estate to the west of Chinel.'

'Congratulations.' Tathrin wondered how much he had already had to drink.

Sorgrad saluted Litasse with his goblet. 'My lady is chatelaine of Abrewold, a day's ride north of Sharlac.'

'It was the manor traditionally granted to Sharlac's heir. With my brother Jaras dead, I deprive no one of their rights.' She was looking down into her wine. 'I shall care for my mother's dowry manors till my sisters are of age to leave her and return to Lescar.'

Tathrin recalled hearing that Duchess Aphanie was still beseeching Tormalin princes for their aid in restoring her, but the sieurs of the great houses took their lead from Emperor Tadriol.

He had proclaimed his support for the Lescari Conclave while granting a pension to the erstwhile Duke of Draximal. In return, Secaris had lodged the decree of his own abdication with the Imperial Courts in Toremal, to join those signed by Ferdain and Iruvain.

According to Charoleia, Ferdain and his family had established themselves in Relshaz, more than comfortably provided for. Iruvain by contrast was steadily drinking his way through the coin realised from the sale of his family's heirloom jewellery, which had been dispatched from Triolle.

Tathrin set his glass down. He couldn't stay here with everyone so content while he was so unaccountably ill at ease.

'Wait.' Failla opened her reticule and produced two letters and a document with a freshly stamped lead seal dangling from a ribbon. 'This is the title to Inderast Manor.'

'No.' Tathrin was adamant.

He had made his refusal plain when Aremil first raised this question. Tathrin had never looked to his own advantage when he had set this rebellion in motion. Now he couldn't bear to think that he might profit from all those countless deaths.

It was different for Aremil. His infirmity limited his ability to make his own way in the world. Tathrin would earn a living digging roads if needs be.

'It's not for you.' Failla looked sternly at him. 'It's where Anilt was born. I think she deserves that much.'

Tathrin opened his mouth but could find no words. Now he felt even worse.

'Will you make your home with us?' Failla challenged him. 'Will you look after her interests till she's old enough to manage the manor herself? Shall we build a future with whatever children of our own may follow her?'

Tathrin felt an utter fool.

'I recommend you agree,' remarked Sorgrad. 'Before Gren and I throw you off that cliff for discourtesy to the lady.'

Tathrin drew a deep breath of the cool evening air, as if some great weight had been lifted from his shoulders.

He looked ruefully at Failla. 'I asked you to be a Spring Festival bride but we've missed our chance. Shall we settle for the summer instead?'

'Why not?' She smiled. 'I'll have a better choice of flowers.'

He would have embraced her but she held up the letters. 'These are from your father and mother.'

'We advised Ersegan on how your family may claim restitution from the Conclave,' Aremil called out, 'to rebuild the Ring of Birches.'

'The first thing you must do is replant those trees,' insisted Gren.

Failla tucked herself under Tathrin's arm. 'Your mother wrote to me as well. She invites us all to visit them in Viscot as soon as this Conclave is concluded.'

'More wine?' Kerith offered Tathrin back his glass, refilled with ruby liquid.

'Thank you.' He accepted it with a sheepish smile.

Branca cleared her throat. 'If you're to wed at midsummer, perhaps we could celebrate together.'

'You're to marry?' Tathrin's exclamation was lost beneath everyone else's congratulations.

'Come here.' Aremil beckoned to him. 'I can't get up.'

Tathrin went over with Failla still close in the circle of his arm. They sat down on the cushions together.

'Fordetal Manor is where I was raised, before I was sent to Vanam. It was Lyrlen's home.' Aremil glanced at Branca, who had risen to return Charoleia's embrace. 'We're going to Vanam, to fetch her.' He hesitated. 'And to share everything with Mentor Tonin – all that we've learned of Artifice, good and bad, through all our trials and errors. I don't imagine we'll be back before Summer Solstice.'

'Do you want me to come with you?' Tathrin wondered briefly whether Sorgrad intended to present himself to the Archmage. They had neither seen nor heard from the magewoman Jilseth since Charoleia had left her in Tormalin.

Aremil shook his head. 'You have nothing to answer for. It's Branca, Kerith and I who must explain ourselves.' His gaze slid to Serafia. 'She's coming too, her and Kip. I don't think they'll be coming back after everything they've endured here.'

'I think I understand.' Some part of Tathrin envied them. There were all too many memories that he wouldn't mind leaving behind.

A smile twisted Aremil's face. 'After that, provided Mentor Tonin hasn't banished me to the Wildlands beyond Solura, I will present myself to the University mentors. They can record my parentage however they wish as long as they grant me their ring and seal. Scholar is the only title I seek.'

'You'll secure their approval ten times over.' A shadow still dimmed Tathrin's tentative tranquillity. 'Though I thought we were done with all this travelling.'

'Why should you think that?' Charoleia smiled down. 'You'll need to meet at every festival to keep watch on each Conclave.' Her sweeping glance encompassed them all. 'I can already tell you who I've noted pleading rather too urgently for particular Guilds and towns.'

'We have shared much of Master Hamare's wisdom.'

Litasse's nod startled Tathrin. Didn't she know Charoleia had ordered the master intelligencer's death? He would have thought the erstwhile duchess would sooner have cut her throat as cooperated with her.

But Litasse continued, composed. 'I shall offer a sympathetic ear to those nobles who might fall prey to discontent.'

Sorgrad smiled fondly at her. 'While Gren and I will keep you all apprised of swordsmen getting too nostalgic for the old days.'

Tathrin looked at Aremil. 'Did you know about this?'

Aremil shrugged. 'No, but it makes sense. This new settlement is still so fragile and Lescar cannot thrive if we're caught unawares by some new Reniack.'

'Though the fear of some new Reniack might have its uses,' mused Charoleia. 'The longer the people's need to cooperate persists, the more ingrained the habit becomes. Then it'll be all the harder for anyone to upset the balance of the Conclave.'

Tathrin looked at Failla. 'So we're still not done with spies and conspiracies.'

'I'd rather talk of necessary vigilance,' Aremil reproved, 'to maintain this balance of rights and responsibilities that we have devised.'

All at once, Tathrin felt absurdly happy. Now he realised what had cast this black cloud over him in recent days. It had been the thought of everyone going their separate ways after they had shared so much. Knowing they would continue to meet united in common purpose? The prospect warmed him like the wine in his belly. He blinked, belatedly realising how strong that wine was on his very empty stomach.

He lay back on the cushions by Aremil. Kerith was discussing the different routes back to Vanam with Branca. Serafia was talking to Litasse while Gren was chuckling at some jest of his brother's.

'Sorgrad,' Tathrin called out. 'Where is Master Gruit? Don't tell me you don't know.'

'He's in Vithrancel,' the Mountain Man replied.

'Truly?' Tathrin marvelled at the thought of the bold old man braving the ocean crossing to Tormalin's newfound, unexplored lands. 'Well, I don't suppose his creditors will chase him all that way.'

'We have friends over there,' Gren commented. 'They'll lend him a hand if needs be.'

'Good.' Tathrin was pleased. After all, they owed the canny merchant debts that went so far beyond coin.

Failla was content to hold him close in companionable silence. Looking up, Tathrin saw the first stars appearing as the sun sank far away in the west. He yawned sleepily.

There was a great deal still to do but there were a great many people to do it, he realised with profound relief. It wasn't all his responsibility.

He wasn't some great man of history. He had simply been one of this valiant circle of men and women who had found themselves in the right place, at the right time. Who had fought to be there just often enough through this past year.

They had succeeded, and all they had done, all they had achieved, all they had endured, had forged ties between them that would never be broken.

He felt Failla slipping into sleep beside him and let himself drift into a dreamless reverie.

When he woke they would see a new dawn, a new day, a new life in a peaceful Lescar.

Dukedoms of Lescar

EXILES AND REBELS

Tathrin: Originally from the Lescari dukedom of Carluse, apprenticed to Master Wyess, a fur trader in Vanam.

Aremil: A nobleman crippled from birth living a scholarly life in Vanam.
Lyrlen: His loyal nurse.

Reniack: A rabble rouser and pamphleteer, born to a whore in the mercenary enclave of Carif. Leader of the mob that murdered Parnilesse's ducal family, thus breaking his ties with the Vanam exiles and rebels.
Jettin: An Aetheric adept of Lescari blood born in Vanam. Now wholly committed to Reniack's independent cause.

Lady Derenna: A noblewoman exiled from Sharlac when her husband fell foul of the duke
Lord Rousharn of Nolsedge: Her husband and would-be Duke of Sharlac.

Master Gruit: A Vanam wine merchant originally from Marlier.

Failla: Previously mistress to Duke Garnot of Carluse.
Anilt: Her daughter.
Lathi: Failla's cousin and Anilt's foster-mother
Serafia: Failla's cousin and mother to the orphaned Kip.
Derou: Their aunt and Ernout's sister.

Ernout: Priest of Saedrin at the shrine in Carluse town and Failla's uncle.
Master Settan and Master Findrin: Guildmasters of Carluse town, conspiring with Ernout to relieve local people's suffering.
Master Odlan: Their ally in Ashgil
Jerich Sayron: Innkeeper at the Ring of Birches. An ally of the Guildmasters and Tathrin's father.
Ersegan: His son by marriage, a farrier by trade.
Granal Camador: Priest of Misaen's shrine on the Losand Road. Ally of Master Ernout and the Woodsmen.

Reher: A mageborn blacksmith now commanding the Carluse Militia.
Milar: A Carluse innkeeper, ally of Ernout and the Guildmasters, Reher's lieutenant.
Vrist: Castle groom, Failla's cousin, now marching with the Carluse Militia.

Branca: A student at Vanam's University, born of Lescari blood. Adept at using the ancient enchantments called Artifice.
Kerith: Scholar and Aetheric adept, Vanam born of Lescari blood.
Mentor Tonin: A Vanam scholar unravelling the secrets of Artifice.

Charoleia: An intelligent and beautiful information broker.
Her aliases include Lady Alaric, Mistress Larch, Lady Rochiel, Mistress Halisoun, Mistress Lanagyre, the Relict Den Sarascol.
Trissa: Her maid, murdered by the renegade mage, Minelas.

Welgren: Travelling apothecary now in charge of tending all those wounded in the course of the rebellion's battles.

Sorgrad and Gren: Mountain-born brothers. Mercenaries long involved in shady dealings the length and breadth of Einarinn.

Evord Fal Breven: Captain General of the Exiles' Army.
Dagaran Esk Breven: His principle lieutenant, also from the ancient Kingdom of Solura, to the far west of the Great Forest.

Sia Kersain: Dalasorian Clan Lord and commander of the northern grassland lancers.
Rega Taszar: A Dalasorian clan lord.
Pata Mezian: A Dalasorian clan lord.

Mercenary companies hired by Captain General Evord include:

The Wyvern Hunters, commanded by Captain Arest
The Gallowsfruit, commanded by The Hanged Man.
Juxon's Raiders
The Tallymen
Longshanks
Vendist's Spearmen
Nyer's Watch
The Shearlings
The Sundowners
The Wheelwrights

Lescari Militiamen:

Dinant: Sergeant at Arms, Losand
Brimel, Halarey, Akaver and Quenel. Journeymen, Triolle.

THE DUKES OF LESCAR

CARLUSE

Insignia: a black boar's head on a white ground.
Colours: black and white

Duke Garnot: Slain in the fighting for Tyrle.
Duchess Tadira: Born sister to the Duke of Parnilesse, slain in the Carluse Garrison uprising.
Lord Ricart: Heir to the dukedom, slain in the Carluse Garrison uprising.
Veblen: Duke Garnot's bastard son, killed in battle two years ago.

Corrad: Carluse Castle's horse master.
Lord Zervan: a nobleman in exile in Caladhria.

TRIOLLE

Insignia: a green grebe on a pale yellow ground.
Colours: green and yellow

Duke Iruvain: Succeeded his father Duke Gerone barely a year ago.
Litasse: His duchess, born daughter of the Duke of Sharlac.
Pelletria: Her attendant and confidante. Also an enquiry agent. Previously confidante of the late Duchess Casatia. Killed in a fall down stairs.
Karn: An enquiry agent. Born in Marlier and orphaned as a child.

Lord Roreth: Duke Iruvain's brother and heir, slain in the Battle of Pannal
Hamare: Litasse's lover, Triolle's spymaster and erstwhile scholar of Col's university. Now dead.

Minelas of Grynth: A renegade wizard, treacherous and depraved, deservedly dead.

SHARLAC

Insignia: a russet stag on a green ground.
Colours: brown and green

Duke Moncan: Slain in the battle for Sharlac Castle.
Lord Kerlin: Second son and heir, slain in the battle for Sharlac Castle.
Lord Jaras: Heir to Sharlac previously killed in battle by Veblen of Carluse.

Duchess Aphanie: Mother of Litasse of Triolle, now widowed.
Lord Leysen: Still loyal to the old regime and a conduit for Duchess Aphanie's letters.
Lord Cullough of Satheron Manor: Acting as intermediary between Duchess Aphanie and the exiles and rebels in the interests of peace for all.

DRAXIMAL

Insignia: a golden brazier on a blue ground.
Colours: red and gold

Duke Secaris and Duchess Nisina: Aremil's parents.
Lord Cassat: Draximal's heir, slain in the fighting for Tyrle.
Lord Matrim: The dukedom's surviving male heir.

MARLIER

Insignia: three silver swords on a scarlet ground.
Colours: silver-grey and red

Duke Ferdain.
Ridianne the Vixen: His mistress and captain of his mercenaries.
Duchess Hidarin: His wife, living independently in her demesne of Saltebre.
Lord Jainen: One of Duke Ferdain's numerous, obsequious retinue.
Hamber: Horse master in Marlier Castle.

PARNILESSE

Insignia: a green wreath overlaying black sword and halberd crossed on a blue ground.
Colours: green and black

Duke Orlin and Duchess Sherista: Murdered by Reniack's mob along with all their children.
Lord Geferin: Duke Orlin's brother and commander of his army. Died in the Battle of Pannal.
Lord Brehard: Last of Duke Orlin's brothers. Murdered by Reniack's mob like every other relative by blood or by marriage.

Mercenary companies serving the dukes of Lescar include:

Wynald's Warband (defeated and disbanded after the battle for Losand)
The Moonrakers
The Red Hounds
The Slippery Eels
The Locksmiths
The Tunnellers' Sons
The Quicksilver Men
Steelhands
Alsar's Eaglets
The Flintstrikers
The Brassnecks.

Ducal mercenary companies turned renegade:

The Bonebreakers
The Swallowtails
Reskin's Prowlers
The Boot Snakes
The Triple Knot

OTHER INTERESTED PARTIES

INDEPENDENT MERCENARIES

The Pine Martens: Based in the Carifate and commanded by Ekarre Amber-Eyes and his formidable female lieutenant Verista
The Shady Moths: Based in the Carifate.
The Knotted Staves: Based in the Carifate
The Firebrands: Based in Relshaz and commanded by Captain Shanish.

TOREMAL

Tadriol the Provident: Emperor of Tormalin, Third of that Name.
Yadres, Esquire Den Dalderin: Equerry to Tadriol, representing his uncle, the Prince of that House.

Eofin, Sieur Den Daldern: The emperor's trusted advisor and intelligencer.
The Sieur Den Breche: An influential prince and ally of Ferdain of Marlier.
The Sieur D'Orsetis: An influential prince and ally of Iruvain of Triolle.

THE WIZARD CITY OF HADRUMAL

Planir the Black: Archmage.
Jilseth Disimonea: Magewoman and enquiry agent.

RELSHAZ

Mellitha Esterlin: Magewoman and tax-collector.
Egil the Toad: Information broker.
Downy Scardin: Introductions agent, now inconveniently dead.

CALADHRIA

Baron Dacren: An elderly nobleman with interests along the river Rel, highly respected in the Caladhrian Parliament.
Master Cardel: A senior guildsman of Abray.

SOLURA

King Solquen IV

Juliet E McKenna has been interested in fantasy stories since childhood, from *Winnie the Pooh* to *The Iliad*. An abiding fascination with other worlds and their peoples played its part in her subsequently reading Classics at St. Hilda's College, Oxford. After combining bookselling and motherhood for a couple of years, she now fits in her writing around her family and vice versa. She lives with her husband and children in West Oxfordshire, England.

CHRONICLES OF THE LESCARI REVOLUTION

IRONS IN THE FIRE

"Juliet McKenna is a master of the complex political and emotional landscapes of epic fantasy, and Irons In The Fire *shines."* –

JULIET E MCKENNA

UK ISBN: 978 1 844164 68 4 • US ISBN: 978 1 844164 68 4 • £7.99/$7.99

The country of Lescar was born out of civil war. Carved out of the collapse of the Old Tourmalin Empire, the land has long been laid waste by its rival dukes, while bordering nations look on with indifference or exploit its misery. But a mismatched band of rebels is agreed that the time has come for a change, and they begin to put a scheme together for revolution.

WWW.SOLARISBOOKS.COM

Follow us on Twitter! www.twitter.com/solarisbooks

CHRONICLES OF THE LESCARI REVOLUTION

BLOOD IN THE WATER

JULIET E MCKENNA

UK ISBN: 978 1 844165 31 5 • US ISBN: 978 1 844165 31 5 • £7.99/$7.99

The exiles and rebels determined to bring peace to Lescar discover the true cost of war. Courage and friendships are tested to breaking point. Who will pay such heartbreaking penalties for their boldness? Who will pay the ultimate price? The dukes of Lescar aren't about to give up their wealth and power without a fight; nor will they pass up a chance to advance their own interests, if one of their rivals suffers in all the upheaval. And the duchesses have their own part to play, subtler but no less deadly.

WWW.SOLARISBOOKS.COM

Follow us on Twitter! www.twitter.com/solarisbooks